THE LEGACY OF ELIZABETH PRINGLE

THE LEGACY OF ELIZABETH PRINGLE

KIRSTY WARK

ISIS
LARGE PRINT
Oxford

First published in Great Britain 2014
by
Two Roads,
an imprint of Hodder & Stoughton

Published in Large Print 2014 by ISIS Publishing Ltd.,
7 Centremead, Osney Mead, Oxford OX2 0ES
by arrangement with
Hodder & Stoughton,
an Hachette UK Company

CIP data is available for this title from the British Library

ISBN 978–1–4450–9916–3 (hb)
ISBN 978–1–4450–9917–0 (pb)

Printed and bound in Great Britain by
T. J. International Ltd., Padstow, Cornwall

To my father

Isle of Arran

LOCHRANZA

FIRTH OF CLYDE

KILBRANNAN SOUND

Pirnmill

Beinn Tarsuinn

Beinn Nuis

GOATFELL

Glen Rosa

Brodick Castle

Ferry to Ardrossan (train to Glasgow)

Brodick

The String

Machrie

Standing Stones

Shiskine

Blackwaterfoot

Lamlash

Holy Isle

Whiting Bay

Glenashdale Falls

0   5
miles

There you stood at the edge of your feather,
Expecting to fly.
While I laughed
I wondered whether
I could wave goodbye,
Knowing that you'd gone.

Neil Young, *Expecting to Fly*

ELIZABETH

Holmlea
20, Shore Road
Lamlash
Isle of Arran

1 January 2006

Dear Mrs Morrison,
   A long time ago, almost thirty-four years past, you wrote to me requesting that I contact you should I ever wish to leave my home. I knew then that I would never live anywhere else, and so there was no point in my replying to you. I have lived in this house since I was eight years old but I am what people these days describe as "ancient" and somewhat frail, and though I have managed perfectly well on my own until now, I know I am not long for this world. I have told my doctor I will move to a small nursing home as I realise it will be less trouble for him, and I have finally locked up the house.

1

My family such as it was, is long dead. There is no one alive but me.

I recall very clearly the summer that you put the letter through my door. I was sewing in the cool shade of the dining room when I heard the letter box clatter. I was so startled I put my needle into my finger and dropped a spot of blood onto my canvas.

I saw you almost every day, pushing your carriage pram along Shore Road, your long hair flying, and your bright skirt billowing about your ankles. You looked very young. The sound of your voice carried up my garden as you sang to your daughter, or perhaps it was just the lilt of your voice as you talked to her, and she made a soft mewling sound back. I remember that on one occasion you waved to me, and I think I tilted my head towards you. Perhaps you did not see. There have been times when that scene has come to me vividly, and I have wondered what has become of you both. My life has been spent here on this island.

I am instructing my solicitor to write to you at the address on your letter. Holmlea is yours if you still wish it. If he does not hear from you within three months, or if you write to say you no longer have any interest in living here, he will follow alternative instructions.

This may of course now seem a fanciful idea to you, but if you do still think my house is "the

loveliest in Lamlash", and you come to live here,
I ask only that you keep my garden well. It has
been a source of peace and joy to me.

Yours sincerely,
Elizabeth Pringle

MARTHA

Martha put her hand on the calloused iron gate and, as she pushed it back, it replied with its familiar whine of resistance. The other Victorian villas in The Oval seemed to crowd around, watching her, alert to her upturned collar, her mouth set firm, the worry in her eyes. The tall trees on each side of the path stood out against the grey of the Glasgow March sky, their spidery branches intertwined in a crooked canopy. As she walked towards the familiar red front door, the gravel beneath her feet was unforgiving. It had been barely a month since Martha last visited, but the foreboding that had settled in her chest like a piece of granite, was now joined by a sharp pain of loss. It threatened to crush the breath from her.

Anna Morrison was no longer at home. There was no excited greeting.

Martha stepped into the hall, a carpet of scattered mail obscuring the wooden floor, and was shocked by the echoing silence. Doors stood open to rooms, as if begging for company. She breathed in the stale air, suffused with an acrid scent like the smell of a charity shop filled with its jumble of cardigans and winter coats

4

and once cherished china teacups, remnants of past lives hastily discarded.

She sat down heavily at the old pine kitchen table, indelibly scored and scarred with family life: a much scrubbed coffee ring, the indentation of a line of writing, and stared at the painting of the two of them on the opposite wall. Martha, a little girl on Anna's knee, in a white blouse embroidered with roses and a pink dirndl skirt, her long legs splayed and her feet bare, and her mother holding her close, her eyes cast downwards. It always reminded Martha of a painting by Mary Cassatt. Perhaps that's what the artist intended, but as Susie loved to point out, if it was, it was a very pale imitation.

People said Martha had grown up to look just like Anna, the big brown eyes and high forehead and the same slender frame; but most of all, friends said they had the same beautiful smile. The compliments embarrassed and delighted Martha. But as she looked around her favourite room she caught sight of herself in the old mottled mirror, saw her auburn hair flat against her head, faint worry lines between her strong arched eyebrows. Today she was looking all of her thirty-five years.

Martha was wearing her favourite grey cashmere cardigan with her jeans, the one she had bought to celebrate her first by-line in *The Caledonian*. She still loved the feel of it, but in the watery light it seemed to drain any colour from her face and she realised how wan and dejected she must look to the outside world.

5

Hanging from the corner of the mirror were some amber beads threaded and knotted on brown twine. Anna Morrison could never quite shake off the hippy in her, even as her sixtieth birthday approached. Martha, once so mortified by her mother's abiding passion for long skirts and floppy hats, now longed for her standard greeting, "Hey, how are you babe?" and the enveloping, sometimes too urgent embrace that followed, redolent with Rive Gauche and roll ups.

Martha closed her eyes and pulled together fragments of an old late-night conversation, the two of them sitting at the pine table in the flickering candlelight.

"But did you *never* feel you lost out by having us so young?"

"How did I lose out? You were both a gift to us," Anna had replied serenely.

"But you'd hardly started your career, and god knows you tell us often enough that the world is just waiting for us!"

"I loved your dad, and I wanted his babies." Martha remembered that she had faltered, brushing her long bejewelled fingers along her arm before she went on softly, "And it was just as well that we got to it, wasn't it?"

Now Martha turned her head towards the window, where a collage of once brightly coloured tissue paper was stuck on a square of greaseproof paper taped to the glass. In sunshine the light danced through the faded orange and purple and blue, throwing motes of colour into the room, but today the hues looked flat and solid.

At the edge of the picture were written the words, "Susie, aged six, after Matisse." Attached by a paperclip, there was a curling photograph of a little girl holding the collage with a young man crouching beside her, smiling proudly; their father John Morrison. They had been there, attached to the glass, for as long as Martha could remember. Neither she, nor Anna, and especially not Susie, would ever take the photo down.

Martha went over to the high mantelpiece above the wood-burning stove and touched each familiar thing: the chipped Wemyss pottery candlesticks decorated with blowsy pink roses that she had given Anna for Christmas two years before, the Edwardian carriage clock with the chequered inlay that they'd found on one of their foraging expeditions around junk shops. Its once comforting beat was now silent.

Martha felt for the little key beneath it and, turning the clock around, prised off a brass disc and wound up the spring until it was tight and the clock came back to life. She adjusted the hands and stepped back a little to admire it, listening as the kitchen filled with its tick, tick, tick.

Her hand passed over the empty bottle of Krug they had downed to celebrate Martha's English degree, her name and the date scrawled on the label. She lifted the jar that stood beside it, of sea glass and pieces of patterned china, precious treasure collected on rainy briny beaches, and rolled it around between her hands, watching the shapes tumble over

7

each other, coming together and separating in random arrangements.

As she was about to return the jar to the shelf, she noticed it had been sitting on top of a letter. The envelope, addressed to a Mrs A Morrison and marked "Urgent", had been torn open and roughly resealed. The anxiety that had recently become Martha's constant companion suffused her chest as she pulled out the single sheet of cream notepaper. The letter, from a Glasgow firm of solicitors, Hardie and Lynch, was short and formal, requesting that Mrs Anna Morrison contact Fergus Hardie at her earliest possible convenience.

Martha stood still. The clock sounded louder and harsher and the distant traffic roared closer. She sank down again at the table and laid her forehead on her arms, wondering if her mother had done something untoward.

Instinctively she sought out the photograph in the tarnished silver frame on the bookcase. Anna wearing a long, embroidered cheesecloth dress, a circle of flowers in her hair, the glint of her dangling Indian earrings. Her father, his arms encircling Anna tightly, grinning, a cheroot clamped in his teeth beneath his droopy Zapata moustache, his cowboy boots adding to his tall, already gaunt frame. Anna's stories of 1969 were of a golden year. They had danced to Dylan's "Lay Lady Lay" after the wedding ceremony. Then, when Martha was little and Susie after her, John Morrison had held them and sung the song over and over as he shushed them to sleep.

8

Martha stared at the picture of her father, trying to summon him up, wishing him here now. She remembered that day in the hospital, watching his raggedy cackly breath finally ease away to a sigh. Anna had laid her head on his chest, Susie whimpering, terrified, beside her. Martha's sixteenth birthday.

The offices of Hardie and Lynch were on the top floor of a handsome, pale sandstone building in the heart of the city. Martha had decided to walk in from the West End in the morning sunshine, hoping to gather strength from the solid straight streets of Glasgow's Victorian grandeur. Every so often she glanced up to catch the sparkle of a curved window, its emerald and blue stained-glass pictures speaking of past seafaring glories. She glimpsed the outline of an angelic face framed by red sandstone curls, blowing a current to hurry merchant ships eastwards to China, or perhaps west to New York.

Reaching Gordon Street, she passed between the statues of Britannia flanking the entrance and pushed back the heavy mahogany doors. A brass plate announced that Hardie and Lynch were on the top floor and she started up, her footsteps echoing on the stone stairs as she climbed past walls of ornate tiles. She heard the lift thrum down past her, and then crank its way up again, the voices within murmuring softly.

The young receptionist behind her desk at Hardie and Lynch wore a mask of orange makeup and a sullen expression, her tight white shirt open to reveal the frill of her Day-Glo pink bra. Martha could practically hear her mother's favourite rant, "What do you think Martha? Was feminism just a hallucination? It must have been those magic mushrooms." Martha looked at the girl. She might not give a toss for feminism, she thought, but she would be able for anyone in a fight.

"Hi. I'm here for an appointment with Mr Hardie."

The receptionist merely inclined her head and lifted the phone, announcing Martha's arrival in the same bored voice that she recognised from her call to the office. Then, barely looking at her, she directed her down the corridor.

Martha arrived at a door on which the name "Fergus Hardie" was written in gold lettering, just as it opened from within. A tall, distinguished looking man in a well cut tweed suit appeared and shook her hand. "Please, Miss Morrison, do come in," he said, with a warm smile.

The vast corner room was lined with heavy glass-fronted book-cases, crammed with legal books. A Persian rug was spread over a threadbare carpet, and on Fergus Hardie's desk, piles of dog-eared files tied with pink and red cords threatened to engulf him.

"Do have a seat. Thank you for coming so promptly. You indicated on the phone to Fiona that you have power of attorney, and the reason for it. That's good."

"Has something terrible happened? Has my mother done something?"

"Nothing bad, I can assure you, but this might all be a bit bewildering, so perhaps I should just give you these to read straightaway and then we can talk."

10

Fergus Hardie stood in front of her, a weather-beaten man, she thought in his early seventies, whose clear grey eyes rested on her kindly. He had two letters in his hand and he motioned her towards a leather armchair beside his desk.

As she took the first letter, he handed her a whisky. "A small Ardbeg might be just the thing for this."

Martha looked down at the first sheet of paper and was startled to see Anna's beautiful copperplate writing. She took a deep sip from her glass, welcoming the soft burn as the malt whisky hit her throat.

July 1972

Dear Miss Pringle,

I hope you don't mind my writing out of the blue. You don't know me but most days for the past month I have walked along Shore Road pushing my daughter, Martha, in her big blue pram, and sometimes you've been working in your beautiful garden. I've waved and I think perhaps you have seen me in the distance. My husband and I are staying for the summer in a back house, on Hamilton Terrace.

Well, I hope you don't think me rude or presumptuous, but I've been coming to the island for years, and of all the villages on Arran, Lamlash is the prettiest and your home, the loveliest. If you ever decide to sell, would you mind letting me know? If I were you I would never leave! How wonderful to open your curtains every morning and see Holy Isle across the water. But just in case, I enclose a stamped addressed envelope.

Yours sincerely,
Anna Morrison

Martha felt as if something was pressing hard on her throat, stopping her breath. Oblivious to the room and Fergus Hardie sitting opposite her, she suddenly saw her mother's face as it was then. It smiled out from one of a collection of photographs in a frame in Anna's bedroom. Anna was leaning over Martha in the pram, her long hair blowing in the breeze.

Martha, her eyes swimming a little, refocused. Reddening, she looked quizzically at Fergus Hardie. He smiled and proferred the other letter. "Your mother's wish has finally come true."

Martha studied the frail but educated hand and, as she took in the offer contained in Elizabeth Pringle's letter, looked at the lawyer uncomprehendingly. "What does it mean?" she blurted out, "that the house is Mum's?"

Fergus Hardie nodded. "Let's take this slowly, shall we," he said gently, pressing the tips of his fingers together in front of him.

"But it's going to be too late for my mother. She might not even understand."

The lawyer held up his hand. "There may be a solution. It depends on you. First things first. I'll just tell you how all this happened." He raised the crystal tumbler to his lips and took a long drink of the golden whisky. "It is one of the few remaining joys of this profession that sometimes, and it's not very often, you are asked to do something intriguing.

"Elizabeth Pringle describes me as her solicitor but in fact I never met her. I think she may have been a client of my father but I have searched, very thoroughly I might add, and I can't find any old files." He took another sip. "Two months ago she sent me the letters you have just read, along with a series of instructions. A week later I was informed by her GP that she had died, and then a copy of the death certificate duly arrived."

"It seems so incredible . . . after all these years."

"It may *seem* incredible, I agree, but actually it is quite straightforward."

"Really? Do you mean that Mum could have this house if she wanted it?"

"Well, you have power of attorney, so you can make that decision for her." Fergus Hardie leaned forward on his desk. "Miss Morrison, the house and its contents are yours, should you choose to accept Elizabeth Pringle's offer. I have checked everything. She was, it seems, of perfectly sound mind. She was ninety-five when she died, and as she said, she has no relatives. As far as I can ascertain there are no competing claims. And I am at liberty to tell you that, apart from some small bequests to local organisations, this is the sum total of her estate."

Martha's mind was racing. "But I have a younger sister. What do I do about her?"

"That's entirely up to you. You have the power to make the decision, not her. Of course, whether you discuss it with her is your business."

Martha looked away for a moment. Susie. She had chosen to remain in Copenhagen, even though Anna was deteriorating. An image of their mother three years earlier came into her head. Laughing, a little tipsy, she and Martha sat on the beach with a picnic, their backs to Shore Road, on a weekend trip to Arran. And yet she had never mentioned the house nearby, or even the letter. Martha's chest tightened. Of course, even back then, Anna was starting to forget.

She became aware of Fergus Hardie's reassuring voice. "Miss Morrison, this must all seem somewhat surreal. You don't have to make a decision right this second."

Martha straightened up and drained her glass, then looked directly at him. "I'm sorry, it is so odd, and yet in some strange way, it fits. I can imagine Mum writing that letter. It's just the kind of thing she would do. It reminds me what she was like, before . . . It's a good feeling, actually."

She paused, and then she experienced a sudden thrill. "There was a time when Mum was impulsive, and people say I'm like her."

Fergus Hardie shrugged his shoulders and held out his hands as if to say, *what do you have to lose.* Martha saw that he was holding two keys. "Look, there's nothing orthodox about this. Why don't you take the keys and have a look? After all, it's just a hop across the Firth of Clyde."

14

He hesitated. "Will you take your mother with you?"

Martha shook her head and Fergus Hardie said quickly, "Forgive me, that is really none of my business."

"No, it's fine. They want to keep her in a secure unit in the hospital while they assess her." Martha felt tears prick her eyes. "And anyway, it might all be too confusing for her."

Fergus Hardie smiled the smile of man who had witnessed all manner of family trauma within the confines of his office. He stood up and came round from his desk to give her the keys. "I see. Well, I'm sure you are best placed to gauge what to do. *Bonne aventure*, Miss Morrison."

Martha walked out into the warm spring sunshine and, turning her face up to the rays, closed her eyes and replayed the conversation with Fergus Hardie. She could not quite believe what had just occurred, and yet it was all so matter of fact. All the angst and upset, the panic-stricken moments of the last few weeks receded, and Martha felt a bubbling sensation in her gut. Excitement. This was a chance to escape. Selfish yes, even reckless, but what was undeniable, she reasoned, was that it was Anna who had given her this opportunity, the Anna who had once been young, and dazzling and headstrong. So who was Martha to deny her mother's dream, even if Anna's memory of it had disappeared, like dandelion heads blown away on a soft breeze.

Her decision made, Martha quickly made a checklist in her head and walked straight to a nearby internet cafe. The first email she wrote was to Sister Adabayo at Kingswood Hospital.

Dear Sister Adabayo,
   I received the consultant's report, so I realise Mum will have to stay in Kingswood for more tests. I am so grateful for all you are doing for her. I was planning to come in tomorrow as we discussed but most likely it will be the day after. I wonder if it will make any difference to her? The fact that she is not distressed is a great comfort to me.

Best wishes,
Martha

Martha looked at the last sentence. Was it true that Anna was not distressed?

Martha's first encounter with Kingswood Hospital had taken place almost a month earlier. It was a cruel joke, she thought, that the old TB hospital had the appearance of a mock baronial fortress built not to repel invaders, but to keep the sick inside. It was surrounded by tall oaks, standing like sage and sympathetic guards, who'd seen the afflicted and the frightened twice, in different eras. The first were struck down with that terrible disease that sucked the breath out of people, the second were cursed with a different kind of illness, one that, sometimes quickly, sometimes slowly, steals people's story of themselves.

Clumps of white narcissus patterned the grass, but against the optimism of an early spring day, the soot-stained hospital had appeared worn out, as if exhausted from trying to hold together lives that persisted in distorting and disappearing.

"It's not very lovely, is it? But I promise, it's not as grim as it looks." That first dreadful day, Sister Adabayo had tried to reassure her. "It's important that you know your mum hasn't been anxious."

Martha had followed the nurse along the long bare corridor to the locked ward. "Your mother — can I call her Anna?—" Martha nodded distractedly, "—is comfortable, and she knows she is safe here." Sister Adabayo paused at the dull metal door to punch in the security code. "But I'm afraid we've found a marked deterioration since her last MRI scan."

Martha had started back, as if recoiling from a sharp slap. "What do you mean? What MRI scan?" The kindly face of the nurse swam in front of her.

Sister Adabayo steadied her with both arms. "I'm so sorry. I thought you knew." Martha felt as if she might faint. "According to her notes she had an early warning." Sister Adabayo went on softly, "She didn't want to alarm you. I'm sure that was it."

Martha studied the deep dark brown eyes that determinedly held her gaze, unsure as to whose side the nurse was on, and shot back, "You don't agree with that, do you? Surely she should have told me?" Martha fought back tears. "Oh god, I don't want to be angry with her when I see her, but this is a nightmare." Her voice rose. "We share everything. Why the fuck didn't she tell me?"

"Perhaps if I tell you a little more before you go in, it will feel more bearable."

Martha gave Sister Adabayo what felt like her most wan smile. "OK, Sister, please do. I'm sorry. That was rude of me."

She was aware of the nurse taking a deep breath.

"The scan was four years ago."

"What?" A fresh mixture of alarm and hurt ricocheted around Martha's head. "So she knew then it was dementia? *That* long ago? Really?"

"Yes, but no two people are the same. It's not easy to predict how quickly someone will deteriorate."

Martha leaned against the wall. "No, but she could have prepared me for it. And Susie, too. We made decisions . . ."

"Maybe she wanted you both to be free to make those decisions."

Martha snorted. "But look what happens. She's done some pretty bizarre things in her time, but never anything like this."

"Please, Martha." Sister Adabayo's voice was firmer now. "Be gentle with her, for both your sakes."

As they walked along the corridor Martha tried to avoid looking into the rooms, filtering out the different sounds: a lone radio's chatter, humming, words repeated over and over, and sometimes the glimpse of a silent figure slumped in a chair. Eventually the nurse

18

stopped at a half open door and made way for Martha to enter.

Anna was sitting with her back to the doorframe, on the edge of the bed, looking out of the window. Her favourite cashmere cardigan was draped around her hunched shoulders, her hair was askew, held up with a clasp. Martha felt so overwhelmed she had to breathe slowly. "Mum," she said quietly, trying to keep her voice steady.

Anna whirled round and rushed towards her daughter and they stood clinging to one another, each trying to banish the fear that was as acute as a sharp pain.

"Oh Mum, it's so great to see you."

"Martha, something bad happened. I was so scared."

"I know." Martha guided Anna back to the side of the bed and noticed the nurse withdrawing from the room. "We can talk about it. It's OK."

"When did I come here?"

"You've been here for two days. I got here as soon as I could. I was in New York doing an interview for the paper."

Anna looked at her blankly, then her eyes blazed and she clutched her daughter's hand, her voice rising in panic. "I've no idea where I am. What is this place?"

"You're safe, I promise." Martha put her arms around her, noting a new sharpness in her bones. "You're in Kingswood Hospital. You know, near the house. You're only ten minutes from home."

"Why, though . . . what happened?" Anna said in a small trembling voice.

Martha could hardly bear it, her mother's once confident engaging tone, reduced to a pathetic whisper. She pulled her closer. "The cleaning staff arriving at Kelvingrove Art Gallery found you on the steps in your nightclothes . . . and the doctor thinks you had been there since the early hours of the morning." Martha's voice faltered. "Mum, you had hypothermia. You could have frozen to death."

Martha watched as a memory flickered past Anna's eyes like a piece of old newsreel. Her mother looked down at her hands and twisted her thin gold wedding band. "I am so sorry, Martha. Why would I do that?" Her voice was barely audible. "I'm so embarrassed."

Tears welled up in Martha's eyes and quickly she turned her head to brush them away. "I don't know. Perhaps you were thinking about a painting. You know the Collection so well." That idea hung in the air for a moment until, trying to sound calm and matter of fact, she ventured, "Mum, why didn't you tell me you had an MRI scan a while ago?"

"Did I? Why would I have had that?"

"You know what it is?"

"Of course I do." Suddenly Anna sounded irritated. "I need to get home. I have a hair appointment and Susie will be back for dinner."

"Susie's in Denmark, Mum, and you and I were at the salon last month. Remember? You and George were talking nineteen to the dozen about something or other. I swear he talks faster than he cuts."

A heavy silence fell on the two women. Martha had contradicted Anna, something that, recently, had been

20

happening with increasing frequency. It had triggered arguments, once so alien to both of them.

Tears trickled slowly down Anna's face. Anna, whose zest for life was always a marvel to her friends, was slipping out of her own control. She seemed to hear her daughter as if from the other side of a high wall.

"Mum, I want to get you home, but you can't be there by yourself. You do see that, don't you? I need to sort something out so you won't be alone."

Martha shivered, remembering how despondent she had been, how much she had wished that she and Susie could deal with the repercussions together.

Looking up from her email she noticed two Muslim girls across from her giggling in front of their screen, heads together, their bright headscarves creating a splash of colour. All around, others, perhaps students, from Latvia, or Boston or Belfast, were intent on the screens in front of them. She thought about their lives, their parents, their secrets, how little people knew about each other, each one connecting with their own world.

One of the Muslim girls caught her eye and smiled. Martha smiled back, wondering if her face had betrayed her thoughts.

She typed in her editor's address at *The Caledonian*.

Hello Tom, thank you so much for sanctioning my compassionate leave. I really appreciate the time out. It was such a scare but Mum is in good hands, which is a great relief. I'm going to sort out a few things, one of which has come as a bizarre surprise! And I might go for that redundancy deal after all. I'll keep you posted. Martha. x

Tom McMillan had been an unfailing support and a wise counsel to Martha, his old head belied by his younger shoulders. He was a bookish forty-five-year-old who missed nothing, certainly not the beery bleary sideways glances of reporters and sub-editors (the few that remained), many of them good journalists worn down by the proprietors' demands of more for less. Nourished by his advocate wife and gaggle of children, he accepted blows from both sides, all the while trying to encourage the younger ones, like Martha. Their futures, he knew, would probably not be in his hands for long.

Martha logged onto the Caledonian MacBrayne Ferries website and booked herself onto the early evening boat to Arran. Two hours later she was embarked on the short drive to the Ayrshire coast in Anna's Volkswagen Beetle, muffled against the cold bright day in her fur-lined parka, her sunglasses on and with the roof open to the skies.

Once through the little town of Dalry, she thought she could taste the salt air on her lips. A long ago mantra came to her, one her mother repeated every time at this exact point on the road, her excitement infectious. "Girls, girls, can you smell the sea? That means we're almost at the ferry."

As she reached a long sweeping bend, Martha caught sight of a new marker on the journey, a forest of silver windmills rising from the moor, glinting in the late afternoon sunshine. She slowed the car to listen to the sombre whirr of the blades as they swooped through the air and marvelled at their elegance, the way their tall strong stalks grew out of the earth. As the road rose towards them they sank gracefully into the bracken until almost out of sight, only to rise triumphantly as she passed them, a great battalion of whirligigs, waving her on to the coast.

Martha was aware that she was bolting, but she felt the rush of almost forgotten sensations: anticipation, elation, the fizz of reckless excitement in her stomach. She punched "Hallelujah" on the CD player on the dashboard and the soaring sound of Rufus Wainwright carried her down to the port of Ardrossan.

ELIZABETH

My earliest memory is of being in a rowing boat with my mother and father. My father had a big moustache and a shock of brown hair. I remember him sitting in front of me, dressed in dark clothes. He wore a gold fob watch on his woollen waistcoat that dazzled me as the boat dipped and danced in the waves. He always wore that watch, on its heavy chain, even when he was out in the fields. As a treat he would let me wind it up and hold it to my ear. It was smooth and heavy, like a stone polished by the constant ebb and flow of the tide, and I would turn it over in my hands and feel the pattern of the engraving on the back. I was too young to read and when I traced my fingers along the lines, I would ask him about the letters. He would reply, "It's a secret message from your mother."

When he splashed his oars into the water I squealed as the salty spray hit my face, and my mother wiped it with her prickly white handkerchief, and called out for him to stop. She laughed as she held me tightly to her. Even now when I smell the sweet heavy scent of lavender, it reminds me of her.

Perhaps my father was rowing to Holy Isle. He was fit enough; it can be a taxing crossing. I think I must have been there a thousand times or more, but most times with the ferryman.

Sometimes, when I close my eyes and concentrate, I can summon up the echo of my father's firm footfall and my mother's gentler step as we climbed up, round and round the stairs in the dank coolness of the lighthouse at the South End of Holy Isle. I loved to stand at the top in front of the big mirrors. From an early age I knew that the light meant the difference between life and death for seafarers. For all my life it has stood there, and for more than thirty years before that, strong and constant. I often sit in the dark by the window, when sleep refuses to come, still comforted by its rhythmic winking. Sometimes I count out an hour passing. When I was little my father would often tell me it was the lighthouse that drew him to my mother. There would come a time when I wondered if it was a siren call.

There was a small sampler that hung in a mahogany frame in the parlour at the farm. It was stitched very simply with their names and the date of their wedding, and the words, "Love is not love which alters, when alteration finds." When I pestered Mother for the story of their romance she would stiffen, and my stomach would feel as if a hand were squeezing it tightly; but I persisted, my heart thumping, my nails digging into my palms. She would push her hair back from her forehead the way she always did as she gathered her thoughts.

"How many times do I have to tell you, Elizabeth? Goodness, you'll soon know it off by heart." She would sigh, then start. "His people were from across the Irish Sea, from Ballycastle. He captained his father's boat back and forth from Islandmagee to Lamlash, carrying limestone to Arran for the fields. And when the weather was rough he would anchor the boat in the lee of Holy Isle and row ashore for eggs and bread. Your grandfather used to graze sheep on the island, and one day, when I went with him to look them over, your father was sitting on the grass by the pier, for all the world as if he was waiting for me."

Each time she repeated the story she would finish the same way: "for all the world as if he was waiting for me." I would always hope for a little more, something of him, something of her, and, depending on her mood, there might be an extra precious detail. "His hands were strong and his eyes were the deepest blue you would ever see." Was there more to their story? Yes, there was much much more, but it was too hard for Isabel Pringle to tell her daughter about the man whom she entrusted with her life, even though I was their only child, and even once there were just the two of us.

I was born in April 1911, in the middle of the lambing. Mother said it was "an Arran day", the lemony primulas scattered in the fields and soft billowy clouds scudding across the sky. She said that no sooner had she taken off her coat to warm her back in the sun, than she felt the rain on her shoulders. That is how it is on the island. She was high on the hill behind the farmhouse, tending a sickly lamb, when I let her know in that insistent way of mine that I was about to arrive. "I thought you were trying to knock the breath out of me with your hard little fists and feet. I'm surprised you weren't shouting out loud as well."

My father sent one of the farm boys on his bike for the doctor and I was born at midday in the big bed in my parents' bedroom. I have always loved that high brass bed with its smooth brass globes at each corner. I used to put my face up close and laugh at how strange I looked. I liked to burrow down in the thick eiderdown, like a tiny field mouse, peering out at the flickering light of the paraffin lamp, safe between them both when the wind howled up the Ross Road and rattled the windows. My mother worried it would wrench the roots of the little monkey puzzle tree that she had planted for my second birthday out of the ground.

So Lamb was the pet name they gave me, but it was a childish sort of endearment that lasted no more than a dozen years. Beyond that, the affection my mother showed me was of a practical sort. She taught me cures for coughs, how to embroider, plant vegetables and identify the flowers that did best on an island warmed by the Gulf Stream — most of all her beloved rhododendrons — and how to cook, and bake and make preserves. But by then we two were on our own, often with just each other for company. She was showing me how to be a good wife, or making sure I had the tools I would need to survive on my own, just in case. And here I am, alone in the end, in my ninety-fifth year, pulling memories out of the crevices and cupboards and old boxes of my life, where they have remained unexamined for decades, some of them, and it is taking me all my strength.

Benkiln Farm was left to my mother by her father. Her two brothers had died of diphtheria before either was five, and so when she and my father married, she educated him in the ways of farming: the prevailing winds, the character of the dark loamy soil and the foibles of each of the sheepdogs. He was happiest out of doors. He loved every beast, every blade of grass, even when he had to walk through driving nail-hard sleet to feed the sheep.

Once I had learned to walk he often took me over the farm in the early evening light, pointing out the peewits' nests in the deep grasses, and the holes where the rabbits dived at the shudder of our footsteps, and the rowan for luck, high on the Ross hill behind the barn.

I am surprising myself. Suddenly my recollection of those days is as clear as a rock pool, as if the long years have blown away like cotton on the wind. As I sit at my work, by the window, I am not so much tired by the exercise of writing as the intensity of remembering. Is there so much to recall? What do I truly remember? I have promised Saul that I will "give expression to my life" as he puts it, on these pages, for it was his queer idea that I commit my story to paper.

There certainly is no peace in the passing of years, though only Saul would sense it. My hands are red-veined and chafed now, the skin as papery as the layer of an onion and speckled brown, my mother's wedding ring loose on my right hand.

When I was four I had cropped brown hair without much of a wave, and when Mother pinned it to the side with a tortoise-shell clasp you could see my cow's lick. I know this because there is a photograph of me with my father, taken the day "The Ulsterman", as he was called, earned his membership of the tight farming community into which he'd come. That was an unusual occurrence in itself.

It was the day of my fourth birthday. My father entered the island's annual ploughing match, a test like no other for a young farmer. He harnessed our two great Clydesdales to the green painted gig and we drove over the moor to Springbank Farm in Brodick, where there were crowds and noise to match, more people than I'd seen in my short life. Bunting blew amongst the trees and tables, and makeshift stalls were laid out with barley sugar sticks and tablet, and a man with a big moustache and a red waistcoat walked amongst them playing an accordion. In a big field beyond the gathering, hundreds of furrowed rows stretched as if to the ends of the earth, as farmers coaxed their teams to plough deep and straight.

My father took his turn with a borrowed plough. He had decorated the horses with primroses on their halters to celebrate my birthday, and there was great excitement when he won a prize. I remember my mother smiling shyly when John Stewart from Sandbay Farm at the other end of Lamlash from us, doffed his

29

cap and put his big weather-beaten hand in my father's and offered his congratulations.

I knew nothing of the turmoil in the world that overshadowed that day. I was too young to sense the undercurrent of anxiety or to catch furrowed brows and murmured conversations, but the war had come to Arran. It wasn't until much later, a good six years hence, when I was in school, that I heard the story of the *Atalanta* and her cargo, which had brought the island unwarranted derision and scorn in an infamous article in a Glasgow evening paper. A single-funnelled steamer had arrived at Brodick pier unannounced on 9 August 1914, shocking those who saw her as it was the Sabbath, not a working day. The boat was quickly loaded with horses for the Front. It was reported sneeringly in the Glasgow paper that all Arran had managed to muster for the war effort was eighty horses and one man. By the end of that terrible war the island had lost at least its fair share of young men and many families were left broken-hearted, my own small one included.

On a warm summer's day the next year, 1916, my father left Lamlash pier for the war. Eventually he was chosen for the Machine Gun Corps. That day, the bay was teeming with boats, just as it had been almost seven hundred years earlier when the Viking king, Haakon, gathered his fleet before the Battle of Largs. There were fishing boats, skiffs, motor launches, a few grand yachts, and steamers. The fastest of them all, the *Duchess of Argyll*, with its two big red and black-topped funnels belching coal smoke, was ready and waiting to take my father away.

There was a great throng of people crowding round him: the two farm boys; two of his elderly aunts over from Ballycastle in their long black serge wool dresses, with long faces to match; the minister, the Reverend Craig, and the whole village besides. I remember I was bewildered by it all, the sea of looming faces, and I wanted them all to go away and leave us be.

My father lifted me up and I buried my head in his shoulder as he held me tightly. I tried not to cry, as Mother had warned me well, but soon tears were streaming down my cheeks, making them itchy and hot. I looked across at her, silently imploring her to make him stay. She did not cry, and the image of her closed face stays with me still. But her eyes, two deep dark pools, betrayed her sadness. I was frightened by her stiffness, and as she stood apart in her Sunday clothes, it seemed she hardly spoke to him, though he said her name several times over, very softly.

He started up the gangway, then turned around and called me to him. He knelt down, put his smooth heavy fob watch into my small hands and closed them around it. "Keep safe, my dearest darling Elizabeth, and look after your mother." That I would look after her seemed a queer thing to say, but I nodded solemnly through my tears.

As the steamer sailed away its horn sounded a long mournful blast, and everyone remained where they stood, not wanting to leave, fluttering their handkerchiefs and Union flags. I wonder now if they were trying to make up for Mother's strange stillness, perplexed by her seeming indifference to the going of a man they had so recently welcomed, and whom they feared would never come home.

We stood on the pier until I could no longer make out my father waving, and finally, as the *Duchess of Argyll*'s smoky trail drifted into the sky like an offering, the steamer disappeared round Clauchlands Point and Mother took my hand firmly, cajoling me home with the promise of a story.

MARTHA

The light was fading as the *Lord of the Isles* cut through the inky blue of the Firth of Clyde, the frothing wake white for a moment before it rolled over and down into the depths. Martha leaned on the railings of the top deck. She watched cormorants dive like black arrows into the water while the gulls screeched and birled overhead, ready to swoop on the detritus from the galley below. The ship ploughed through the water and Martha, turning her face up to the wind, closed her eyes. Slowly the cacophony of sounds — the engine room's hum, the call of the birds, the barked orders from anxious parents to children careering along the decks — all receded, and she recalled Anna saying laughingly to her friends, "*You* know Martha! Headstrong, to a fault. Typical teenager!"

Was anything really so very different now? The behaviour that Anna had presented all those years ago as charming impetuousness, when stripped bare, might be simple selfishness. If Anna had any idea what she was up to, would she dismiss this dash to Arran so airily? Martha gripped the rail a little more tightly. Did

33

she really have any right, beyond a piece of paper granting her power of attorney, to take possession of a house on behalf of her mother when Anna might never remember how much she loved it, or that she loved it at all?

Martha tried to calm her restless thoughts but there was no avoiding the fact that she was making a break for freedom, not only from Anna's illness but also from her own steadily intensifying feelings of unfulfillment. And strange as it was, Elizabeth Pringle had come to her rescue.

As the ferry sailed into Brodick Bay she could just make out the smoke rising like a pall from the houses dotted over the hillside and down on the shoreline. There was the outline of the tower of Brodick Castle and behind it Goatfell, the highest peak on the island, rearing out of the gloaming.

She was startled from her thoughts by the high-pitched ping pong sound of the electric bell that heralded the purser's announcement. "Would all drivers please return to their vehicles. We are about to arrive at Brodick." The words were always the same, but they sounded much too mundane for the journey Martha was making. She smiled to herself. I must be the person on this boat with the most bizarre reason for being here, she thought, and as she gripped the two keys in her pocket it suddenly struck her that apart from Fergus Hardie, nobody knew where she was.

It was already dark as she joined the procession of twinkling lights of the ferry traffic travelling the three miles over the hill to Lamlash. When she reached the highest point of the road, Holy Isle hove into view, a great dense black cone illuminated by the bright white moon, the lighthouse on the southern tip of the island blinking across the bay. It was just as the painter Craigie Aitchison had rendered it.

One of his many paintings of Holy Isle hung in her flat in Edinburgh. Unlike her other pictures that she had long ceased to notice, Martha always registered the searing intensity of the Aitchison. "Isn't it dramatic?" Anna had said as Martha unwrapped it on her twenty-first birthday. "Your first piece of serious art my darling girl." Anna's presents had always been more than simple gifts; they were pieces of herself handed to her daughters. Recently, as she became more forgetful, the gifts had become all the more precious, more heartbreaking. Martha's sense that Anna was desperately trying to preserve her identity through the things she gave her daughters, grew more intense.

As Martha arrived in Lamlash she was overcome with weariness and, in an unusual act of restraint, she decided to wait until morning to search out Elizabeth Pringle's house. She parked on the seafront outside the Glenburn Hotel, and carrying the bag she had packed in Edinburgh anticipating a few days' stay at home in Glasgow, dumped it down heavily in front of the reception desk. She pressed the little brass bell on the counter. A tall handsome woman, flame-coloured hair tumbling down her shoulders and dressed in a floral shirt and Levis, appeared from the room beyond. She looked at Martha with a wary, quizzical expression, as if the idea of someone actually coming to stay in the hotel was faintly preposterous.

"Welcome to the Glenburn. Can I help you?"

Martha smiled. "I hope so. Would you have a room for one night?" She hesitated and then her words came tumbling out. "Or maybe two . . ." She blinked anxiously. "Sorry, I just don't know yet."

Catriona Anderson waved her hand across the board behind her. All eight room keys were in place. "You're in luck!" she laughed. "You can have your pick of the place. I imagine you'll want a room that looks out to the bay?" She rushed on without waiting for Martha to answer, "And there's no extra charge for the view. It's just thirty pounds for bed and breakfast. Is that OK?"

"Great. Really great," said Martha, nodding, just stopping herself from saying, "God, that's cheap as chips."

Martha was conscious of Catriona looking at her intently as she signed the register and suddenly her oversized expensive parka, her diamond studs and cashmere scarf felt overdone, like she had the wrong uniform on.

"Would you like me to show you up to your room?"

Martha got the feeling she was keen to prolong the conversation but in her current mood she didn't have it in her to oblige. "It's OK, thanks. If I put one foot in front of the other I'll just about find my way." Then she instantly checked herself. "Sorry, that sounded rude. How awful of me. I'm just a bit bushed." She smiled wanly, and taking the key to "Pladda" turned to go. "Goodnight." Her voice trailed away and she felt

Catriona watch her as she trod heavily up the tartan stair carpet to her sea view room.

Martha switched on the bedside light and lay down on the soft enveloping bed, closing her eyelids in an effort to catch all the thoughts ricocheting around her brain. Sometime in the night she woke to distant reedy droning high overhead. She listened as the single-engine plane came closer, until it sounded as if it were hovering for a moment above the roof, searching her out, and then just as quickly, it faded into the distance. She thought about the pilot, surveying the solid ground from his flimsy little metal machine, buffeted by the wind across the vast space of the night sky. Perhaps he was on his way to an emergency on the Mull of Kintyre, or listening to the comforting chatter of air traffic control, perhaps carrying a passenger further west to Ireland, someone who had to be there before morning broke. Martha had always thought the engine's tremulous whirring was the loneliest of sounds in the night sky. She remembered that once, when she was little and they were holidaying on the island, when the thrum finally trailed away and, no matter how she strained she could hear nothing except the rushing inside her head, she had run to her parents' bedside to ask her father if the aeroplane had fallen off the edge of the world.

She pushed herself up onto her elbows and surveyed her room, the floral wallpaper and matching faded chintz curtains, the heavy oak furniture and the bookcase full of tattered paperbacks that were destined to be abandoned in small Scottish seaside hotels: Nevil

Shute, Nigel Tranter, Lillian Beckwith, Ian Fleming, with the odd dog-eared Jackie Collins muscling in.

She noticed the hotel notepaper on the writing desk and it occurred to her that there was a letter she was ready to write. She shivered at the thought of putting the words "Dear" and "Andrew" side by side, but before she could make a move to find a pen, she drifted back to sleep, lulled by the soft sound of the water lapping back and forth over the stones on the shore, and the slow comforting blink of the lighthouse.

Catriona arrived with a plate in one hand and a cafetière of coffee in the other, just moments after Martha sat down at the table.

"Good morning," she said brightly as she laid both down on the orange and pink linen tablecloth, a pot of purple primroses in the centre. Before Martha could reply she went on, "I thought you might not have had dinner last night so I decided to make you the works, bacon, eggs, mushrooms, black pudding, scones and homemade jam. You're my only guest so I might as well spoil you." She lifted the jug. "Is coffee OK?"

Martha nodded her head as Catriona poured the steaming dark liquid into her cup. "It all looks and smells lovely," she enthused, rousing herself. "Thank you." She had thought to have some muesli and yoghurt but there had been no opportunity to say so, and certainly not now. As she took her first mouthful, she realised Catriona had simply moved back a little from the table as if waiting for a verdict on her cooking.

Martha buttered her scone. "Can I ask you something? Did you know Elizabeth Pringle? She lived here, along Shore Road."

Catriona put her hands on the back of the chair opposite Martha. "Yes, of course," she replied, "but only in the way most people did. I mean, she was very solitary but she always said hello and sometimes she commented on the hotel garden. She liked my roses." Catriona hesitated before enquiring lightly, "Did *you* know her? Are you a relative?"

"No, I didn't," Martha replied quickly, and then more emphatically, "and I'm not a relation." She paused, weighing up how much to say. "I'm just here on business related to her."

Catriona looked expectantly at her guest but, as no more information was forthcoming, she smiled broadly and extended her arms out to the room. "Well, you're welcome to stay as long as you want. The hotel isn't exactly packed to the gunnels at this time of year." She pulled her hair up on top of her head, securing it with a pencil from her apron pocket. "And if you do decide to stay, will you be wanting dinner?"

Martha took a final sip of coffee and smiled. "That would be great."

"Well, I'll bank on you staying then."

As they met each other's eye, a flicker of interest passed between them, warmth even. In her head Martha was already confiding in the striking redhead standing in front of her, hands on her hips, her wrists festooned with silver bangles.

★ ★ ★

Ten minutes later, Martha walked along the grass verge onto a deserted Shore Road, imagining unknown narrowed eyes following her progress. From the little she now knew about Elizabeth Pringle, she realised that the moment she unlocked Holmlea's front door she would be fair game for the gossips. A long lost relative? A new owner? "Would you credit it?" they would say, suspicion in every syllable, "a house in a prime position, on the best road on the island, and never even on the market."

She had no real measure of Arran now, but memories of childhood holidays surfaced as she walked. She had travelled along this road many times, safely in her child's seat on her mother's bicycle, her father transporting Susie the same way, pedalling alongside. Susie would squeal with delight and pummel her father's back as he zigzagged one way, then the other, throwing her from side to side. Martha, the more grown up, would sit still but reach her arms forward and tangle her fingers through her mother's long thick hair.

Except for that weekend three years earlier, it had been almost a decade since she and Anna had spent time on the island together. For years, Martha had found the lure of Paris, Venice and San Francisco stronger than the promise of fleeting sunshine and the certainty of smirring rain. And yet, although she had only a tenuous connection to the island and precious little history except for two letters separated by more than thirty years, she suddenly had a powerful feeling of knowing the ground beneath her.

She looked up from her daydream and saw the red sandstone house on her left, across from the shore. It was set on its own, far back from the road. The bay windows on either side of the front door were framed by half-shut dark curtains, and there were two dormer windows on the first storey with another tiny one set into the centre of the roof, above the door lintel. Her heart hammered against her ribs as she surveyed the elegant old house. She felt a strange sensation that it was watching and waiting for her. Long ago the woodwork had been painted a rich dark green, but now the villa looked forlorn, the flaking storm doors shut against the weather and the outside world.

But the garden was different. It was well loved, just as Elizabeth had wished. The long lawn that sloped down to the stone wall abutting the road had had its first cut of spring, and beautiful icing-pink flowers on the rhododendron bushes that flanked the path to the house were being coaxed open by the warm Gulf Stream. Two half whisky barrels filled with tall strong daffodils flanked the front door.

Martha turned the bigger, heavier of the two old keys in the lock and pushed back the storm doors to reveal a hallway with a beautiful patterned floor of terracotta and bright blue encaustic tiles, on which was lying a single postcard, face down, the picture a profusion of flowers. She picked it up and turned it over.

Dear Elizabeth,
    This is turning out to be much more than a field trip. The Himalayas are fantastic and I have

seen amazing giganteum. The pink centres are more vivid than ours — more like the colour of bubblegum (not that I imagine you have ever seen bubblegum!). I will bring some seeds home, though Arran is hardly short of rhoddies. I feel like the young George Bowen. In fact I have met the descendants of the family who looked after George Forrest when he was collecting, and they have given me some photographs for my dissertation. Looking forward to seeing you very soon, yours aye Niall.

Not always a solitary soul after all, Martha mused, and put the postcard in her pocket. She opened the etched glass inner door with the other key and tiny motes of dust danced around her in the sunlight as if excited by her arrival. Ahead of her was a curved wooden staircase, carpeted with a threadbare red blue and yellow runner. To the left, against the wall beside an open door to the dining room, was a fine rosewood Georgian side table, on which lay a walnut tray inlaid with mother-of-pearl flowers. Beside it stood two Japanese porcelain dishes. To her right the door was closed.

Martha stopped in her tracks, suddenly unsure. She had no business being in Elizabeth Pringle's house, prying, walking where she once walked, unconsciously imitating the footsteps of a woman she never knew. She held on to the banister for a moment, suddenly nervous at the idea of pushing open the door. If there was something upsetting behind it, that would be no more than she deserved.

She contemplated retreat but then forced herself to breathe deeply, straightening up as she slowly approached the door, listening for the slightest sound beyond the thudding of her heart. She turned the smooth wooden knob, and when she adjusted her eyes to the gloom, the walls seemed to come alive. She began to make out tapestries and samplers, each one worked with an array of delicate flowers and faeries that flitted through branches or sat on petals, their legs dangling. The wooden frames hung so closely together that the faded flowers of the wallpaper were hardly discernible, gloriously upstaged.

Martha stepped gingerly to the window and pulled the curtains back as far as they would go. The room burst into a kaleidoscope of colour. She noticed that at the lower right-hand corner of each picture were sewn the initials EAP. The largest frame, of pale carved oak, hung over the fireplace and the woodland scene it contained was stitched in turquoise, purple and red shimmering silk thread. It was breathtakingly beautiful.

As Martha stood by the hearth marvelling at Elizabeth Pringle's industry, she saw that the fire was set with newspapers prepared in perfect origami folds and kindling on top, and the brass scuttle beside the hearth was brimful of glittery black coal. Beside it, logs were stacked neatly in a shallow basket.

She returned to the hall. When she opened the door to the cupboard beneath the staircase a clutter of household objects were stood to attention. Here was an ancient Hoover with a bulbous nose and a houndstooth fabric dust bag, a similarly decrepit Bex Bissell carpet sweeper, a selection of long-handled feather dusters up on end, like characters from a Dr Seuss story, and beside them a battered leather golf bag, with an assortment of clubs. She felt calmer now she was amongst the paraphernalia of everyday life, and she stood for a moment inhaling the quiet peaceful atmosphere, as the house introduced itself to Martha, and she to it.

The kitchen was no more than an old Belfast sink and, where a range had presumably once nestled in the chimney space, a precarious looking cooker and a Calor gas bottle. A well scrubbed wooden table sat in the centre of the room, surrounded by spindle back chairs, and an old oak dresser displayed a selection of Indian Tree crockery. Overhead, dish-towels and kitchen cloths hung neatly on a wooden pulley. A small round Timex clock on the window ledge had stopped at ten past two. Martha wondered how long it had been since the final tick, then the moment of anticipation of the next tock, before it fell silent. She made a mental note to replace the battery, then, looking around, imagined what the room could be like if she set to work on it, sketching a wide open light-filled space, experiencing a thrill that momentarily obliterated all doubt and complication.

She started up the narrow stairs, past the little bathroom on the half landing, to the upstairs hall, which was lit from above by an old skylight. There were open doors to two bedrooms, each with a sloping ceiling. Entering the first one, Martha ran her hand over the old wallpaper, which was decorated with children in pretty smocks and bibbed shorts playing together. She took in the high wooden bed, its striped mattress bare except for an old paisley-patterned quilt folded neatly and placed at the end. Beside it was a tall white painted press. It held no fear for Martha, who was now beginning to enjoy herself, safe in the house's embrace. When she turned the little key that sat snugly in the lock of the cupboard, the scent of lavender spilled out from shelves that were lined with brown paper and laden with crisp white sheets and pillowcases, all freshly laundered. On the ledge beneath lay plump pillows covered in black and white ticking, and woollen blankets edged with satin.

She crossed the landing to the other room where a big brass bed, similarly bare, almost filled the space. A dressing table was laid with a silver-backed brush and mirror set, and in the wardrobe hung two coats, one a lamb skin, the other an old fox-fur jacket.

It was when she stepped back to close the wardrobe doors that her eye was caught by a small, black ink and watercolour sketch above the fireplace. A woman sat framed against a window, a densely patterned curtain at her shoulder and a delicate teacup and saucer and an open fan on a table beside her. The sitter had strong sharp features and short hair that accentuated her jawline.

Martha couldn't quite believe what she was seeing. She was sure she recognised the artist, and could this be Elizabeth Pringle? She moved to examine the picture more closely and saw the unmistakable signature, the initials FCB separated by dots, and then the surname, Cadell. She sat down on the bed, a little stunned. "The house and all its contents," had been Fergus Hardie's words, but a Cadell, too, albeit a sketch rather than one of his oils, which were now worth a fortune?

Martha hurried downstairs and retrieved her mobile phone from her bag but when she tried to call the solicitor she couldn't get a signal. "Damn these hills," she shouted out loud to the echoing house and, locking both doors behind her, she headed for the telephone box further along the still deserted road. She fed her change into the slot and, wedging her foot in the door to try to dispel the dank, sour smell of urine, she lifted the grubby receiver and dialled.

"Hello, Miss Morrison, lovely to hear from you. Are you in Lamlash?"

"Yes, I am. But Mr Hardie, there's one thing about the house I need to tell you straightaway."

"Has it come with a ghost?" Fergus Hardie replied, chuckling at his own joke.

Ignoring him, Martha went on. "Elizabeth Pringle has a Cadell sketch. I'm sure it's Cadell. It's of a woman sitting by a window."

"How marvellous."

"But what should I do?"

"Well, first things first. What do you think of the house? Have you made a decision?"

Martha took a deep breath. "I've hardly looked around, but, yes. I like to think of Mum being here." She stopped. "Sometime, anyway . . ."

"That's good news, very good news," the lawyer broke in. "We'll get the papers signed as soon as possible, then."

"But what about the painting?"

"I'd say it's astonishingly good fortune. Not only do you have a house on Shore Road on Arran, you have a Cadell to go with it."

"Then it's really OK?"

"Miss Morrison, Elizabeth Pringle was obviously sharp as a tack. If she left the sketch in the house it's because she wanted it to remain there. Don't worry about it. And I look forward to more news, if it's as exciting as this instalment."

Martha pushed the door of the phone box and stepped out into the fresh air. As she walked back along the road she became conscious of the phut phut sound coming from a little boat in the distance, cutting through the water as it crossed from Holy Isle to Lamlash. A tall man in what looked like a long loose robe stood at the tiller looking directly at her. After a while he waved, and without really thinking, Martha waved back.

ELIZABETH

Our farm was my playground, my domain. I knew every corner, every hiding place, the stone step outside the stable for mounting the pony and the red painted door to the hayloft, set high in the whitewashed barn wall. If I close my eyes I can still see the house, so handsome, brilliant white against the hill. I see its grey slate roof, the sheltering circle of trees and the steadings to the left, gable end to the sea. It seemed so solid and safe to me.

I had my menagerie for company, rabbits, newts and snails, which I kept in a little shed. Mother tacked some old dress material at the window for curtains, and I would arrange my blue and white dolls' china tea set on a little wooden table. I can see the Japanese figures on the saucers still, standing beside a pagoda, or on a little fretwork bridge. I used to fill the tiny milk jug and sugar bowl, and serve Mother tea from the teapot with the broken lid mended with two metal staples.

I have a photograph of me sitting on the doorstep of the shed wearing a blue and green checked dress with smocking and a white Peter Pan collar. I found the dress in Mother's dressing-table drawer after she died. I never imagined she would have kept such a thing, but perhaps it reminded her of the time, during the years my father was at war, that she and I were closest. She had little to do with the running of the farm, then. My father had asked one of the neighbouring farmers, John McInnes, to look after Benkiln while he was at the Front. Mr McInnes was a dour sort and he had a smell as sour as his old leathery face, so I kept well out of his way. He used to complain about having to work both farms but I am sure Mother paid him well enough, and eventually he would come to be well and truly rewarded.

During those years Mother spent her time knitting blankets and socks for the war effort, and nursing soldiers at the Public Hall. The Hall had been renamed the Arran Red Cross Auxiliary Hospital and the women of the island, as many as could, bandaged and fed and soothed the wounded. They were brought from Glasgow on the requisitioned steamers, slow processions of stretchers and wheelchairs and crutches, men damaged on the inside and on the out. I would meet her after school at the door of the hospital to walk home and I was always eager for stories about the men she tended. Once she told me about a letter she had written for a soldier to his mother in Aberdeen, and how happy she would be, knowing that he was out of the fighting.

"Even with his leg missing?" I asked.

"Oh, yes, Elizabeth," she replied gently and without reproach, "for such a wound means she will have him home safe."

There was a softness in her voice when she talked about the soldiers she looked after. I can hear it now, in the way she visualised the island for one of them, a lad no more than eighteen. His sight had been badly damaged by the mustard gas that the Germans (or as she called them, in the language of the soldiers, the Boche) sent in acrid waves into the trenches. She described the majestic Sleeping Warrior, lying on his back, the succession of crags that formed his forehead, nose and mouth visible from the mainland on a clear day. She told him about the oyster catchers skittering over the water onto the beach and the ringed plover with its black and white collar sounding the alarm as you approached up Glen Rosa. She told him of the red stags standing alert, their antlers jagged magnificent crowns, calling for mates, their roars echoing around the hills and carrying for many miles on the September wind. He said he would like to go there, before he was sent home to the soot of Glasgow, because it sounded like such a wild and beautiful place, and so Mother arranged it. She collected him on the farm cart with Willie, our old dairyman, and when they reached Glen Rosa he walked, held safe between them, over the springy heather a little way up towards Coire a'Bhradain, before sitting down for a picnic. She said the boy lay on his back, the sun on his face, and sang "The Skye Boat Song" in a voice that would break your heart. She was capable of such kindnesses all her life.

Sometimes I would see soldiers on crutches, smoking and joshing outside the hospital, or sitting reading on the grass across the road by the shore. Other times I would peak in at the long rows of narrow khaki camp beds. I was not allowed to venture inside, but Mother never told me why. For a long time I thought it was perhaps because my father was among the wounded, with injuries so terrible that she didn't want me to see him. When I finally asked her if it was so, the slap to my legs was a shock I never forgot, nor, I think, ever truly forgave. I can feel the sensation of that single stinging hit still, and with it the confusion and sense of injustice. I had no idea why what I said had angered her so much. "Where did you get such nonsense?" was her only response, but she had never raised her hand to me before, nor did she ever do so again.

We sent Daddy boxes filled with homemade fruit cake, socks and cigarettes, and sweet tablet wrapped in greaseproof paper. I drew pictures of the farm, and the lighthouse, and my kitten. Letters back from France were a special occasion. Mother would read passages to me. "Please tell my lamb how much I am looking forward to taking her in the skiff over to Holy Isle. We will climb to the top of Mullach Beag and shout and sing and dance with joy, and scatter the sheep with our caterwauling."

I don't suppose, at that age, I had any real sense of time passing. Every morning in class we prayed for the safe return of our fathers and uncles and brothers and cousins. It was the same for many of the children in the school, the only difference was that others had more than one member of their family at the Front. I do not know if that was better, or worse for them.

For my seventh birthday Daddy sent me a package of three lace hankies embroidered with my initials and a paper parasol painted with red poppies. Enclosed was a postcard from the village in France where he was billeted, resting from being up in the line. It was a picture of a row of lattice windowed cottages with baskets of flowers set outside the low doors. It was only after Mother's death that I found it again, tied with a small bundle of his letters, letters that would help me understand my mother's closed silence the day he left from Lamlash pier.

But I am getting ahead of myself in my rush to set all this down. I have seen my other self walking ahead of me, my gait slower and unsteady, my approaching death, and I know that I must keep the pen on the paper, even though my hand is stiff and my eyes sore with the strain.

It was while my mother was volunteering in the makeshift hospital that she met a kindred spirit. She was born Mary Louise Douglas Hamilton, and was by marriage Duchess of Montrose, and the two women, similar in age but of very different social standing, became lifelong friends. Much later, Mary was another mother to me when it was she, and she alone, who was my confidante.

The war changed things. Although the duchess lived in a grand new Edwardian house in Lamlash, set in grounds laid out with rose beds and exotic ferns, and had what Mother called a wheen of servants and a big shiny green car I loved to sit in, there was less distance between them than there would have been in earlier peaceful times. But in any case, I suppose people rubbed shoulders more on Arran than in a big city like Glasgow. I liked to watch the two of them laughing together, observing my mother relaxed and gay, the way she threw her head back, her eyes sparkling. They shared a passion for gardening and many other things besides, not least the furtive cigarettes secreted in the pockets of the long serge skirts they wore when nursing. They smoked together at the Whitehouse, sitting on the wrought-iron seat by the duchess's ornamental pond while I skittered around the wooden floor of the big echoing hall in my socks. When Mother glimpsed me through the open door she called out to check me but Mary just winked at me and said, "Izzy don't be so stuffy, Elizabeth is helping the housekeeper with the polishing. Just look at these floors, they're far too much for one person."

Each was clever, and though educated very differently, they shared a love of books. I often listened to them discussing characters as if they were real people. Was Mr Rochester right to bring his wife back from the West Indies? Could Jane Eyre have helped her had she known? Was Mrs Rochester trying to kill herself in the fire, or was it an accident? I loved their easy intimate conversation, and as I recollect it now, I remember that it was the kind of friendship that I always hoped I myself might enjoy.

It was Mary who raced to Benkiln that fateful September of 1918 clutching a newspaper with news from France. I have read the cutting so often I know it by heart. "Arran gunner in brave attack on the Hun. Sergeant James Allan Pringle showed conspicuous gallantry and devotion to duty during an attack north of Bray-sur-Somme on 22 August. The fighting was fierce, but British forces pushed on to the border with Belgium."

That day I watched my mother's face as Mary read aloud from the newspaper and exclaimed, "Izzy, what bravery. Thank God he wasn't wounded. It's wonderful news. Please Izzy," she implored, looking swiftly from my mother to me, "smile, please, and be happy. They say it's almost over."

We sat together on the doorstep, Mary between us. "He'll be home soon. I'm sure of it," she said, squeezing our hands in hers.

I looked at Mother who smiled faintly and, looking straight ahead, replied, "God willing."

Mary would be Mother's comforter before long. Two months later came the Armistice.

MARTHA

The silence that greeted Martha's return to the Glenburn Hotel was broken only by the handsome grandfather clock solemnly marking time in the hall, the dull cracked patina of its face consigning the painted Highlanders to the mist.

As she approached the desk she made out the faint notes of a Chopin piano concerto crackling on a radio. She shook the little brass bell in front of her and flushed a little, embarrassed at having executed such a peremptory summons.

"I'm sorry for ringing," Martha said quickly, as soon as Catriona appeared from behind her, dressed in blue overalls with her hair piled up on her head, a smudge of dust across her cheek. "I didn't know where you were."

"No need to apologise. That's what the bell's for. I was just grappling with an ancient mattress that seems to have a life of its own." She laughed as she removed her rubber gloves. "Ha! Actually that's probably true. Mice are a bit of a hazard around here." She looked at Martha's horrified face. "It's OK, they're country mice. I've laid some friendly traps but don't worry. They

55

don't seem to make it up the stairs." She paused for a split second. "You are staying? Aren't you?"

Martha nodded. "I'll go back to Glasgow tomorrow."

Catriona smiled. "Well, it's dinner at eight then." She paused. "And I was thinking, as you're my only guest, we could eat together if you like, at the kitchen table."

"That would be lovely," said Martha, yearning for company after the revelations of the day. "And now I'm going to soak in that big old tub in my bathroom."

"Go right ahead, I've put some candles on the shelf."

When Martha walked into the kitchen and exclaimed how lovely it all looked, Catriona blushed with pleasure. "I feel like I might be getting the hang of this hotel keeping thing," she laughed. "I know I should have started by renovating the bedrooms, but I love to cook, so . . ."

She gestured at the huge bright orange French cooker with a mosaic of old Moroccan tiles behind, and her collection of copper saucepans on the whitewashed walls. Bunches of sage and rosemary hung on a rack by the stove and pots of marjoram and lemon thyme provided bookends for a library of cookery books that stretched along a wooden shelf under the window. The old polished flagstone floor shone in the light from four tall hurricane lanterns on the console table.

"It's absolutely wonderful. And this smells delicious," said Martha, whose appetite was rising at the sight of grilled langoustines and what looked like homemade mayonnaise and bread.

So began a conversation that lasted three courses and two bottles of wine, and zigzagged about as the two women got the measure of each other. Tentatively, they laid the foundations of a friendship that neither had expected.

Martha, her tongue loosened by wine and the warmth of the beautiful kitchen, sketched out her strange story, to Catriona's widening eyes.

"It was as if Elizabeth Pringle had prepared for Mum's arrival, the sheets and pillowcases freshly laundered, and the fire set in the grate, wood by the hearth." She took a long sip of wine and folded her arms on the table. "I don't think of myself as at all spiritual, it doesn't really fit with journalism, but I felt very peaceful once I'd walked through the rooms. I know this sounds weird, but I felt as if there was a presence. Although I suppose that's hardly surprising with everything there, just as she left it."

Martha drained her glass and Catriona opened the second bottle of wine.

"Does anyone else know about the house, do you think?"

Martha shrugged. "I don't know. I wonder about that all the time. What will people think . . ."

"I wonder if Niall knows."

"Niall? There was a postcard from him behind the door. Who's he?"

"He's my brother. He's just back from giving a lecture in Malaysia."

57

Martha, her face flushed a little, thrilling at the information, leaned in towards Catriona. "And he sends postcards to Elizabeth Pringle?"

"He was away when she died. They were friends . . . good friends, actually." Catriona laughed. "They bonded over rhododendrons."

Martha concentrated now, trying to counter the effect of the wine, as Catriona told her how her brother had arrived on Arran four years earlier to take up the position of head horticulturalist at Brodick Castle. It was there that he met Elizabeth Pringle. They had shared a grand passion for plants. "Niall said he learned more from Elizabeth than he had in all his training at Kew. He must have been almost sixty years younger than her but it didn't seem to matter. Recently, when she became frailer and the garden got to be too much, he helped her with the lawn and all the pruning."

"That explains why it's still so lovely. He must be looking after it, even though she's dead." Martha looked at Catriona quizzically. "Sorry, but, isn't that a bit strange?"

"Not if you knew Niall. Maybe it's his way of staying close to her. Maybe it's his way of grieving." Catriona looked directly at Martha. "You should meet him when you get back from visiting your mum."

"I should go to Elizabeth Pringle's grave," Martha said suddenly, "to pay my respects . . . when I get back from the mainland."

Catriona smiled. "You're only going for the day, there's plenty of time for everything. I'm sure you've got a lot to figure out but there's no rush." She hesitated. "And you know, I'm very happy to help."

Martha put her face to the wind in an attempt to blow away her hangover and allowed the damp spray to cool her face as the ferry ploughed its way to the mainland. Her dull thumping headache was a price worth paying for Catriona's company, this spirited vivacious woman whose warmth and openness had come as a lovely surprise. But as her head cleared, the nagging guilt crept back and burrowed down in her chest. Anna's illness was her passport to this adventure, Martha knew. And she wrestled with an even more difficult truth. There was no one but her to cope with Anna, not really. Certainly not Susie, who phoned her for "updates" much as she might check on the weather. And not her mother's well meaning friends, who rang the ward bell at Kingswood armed with their love and kindness, bringing familiar pictures and music to coax a memory to the surface, but who could not stand sentry over a woman who might walk silently out of the house into the freezing February darkness.

"Your mum has been very agitated over the past couple of days. We've given her a mild sedative and she's a little calmer this afternoon."
Sister Adabayo enclosed Martha's hand between her two warm strong ones as she came to greet her in the visitors' room. "I'm afraid you're going to have to get used to this." As if reading Martha's mind, she went on, "I don't think it would have been any different if you'd

been here. Today she told one of the nurses that your father had locked her up in here. He has passed on hasn't he, a number of years ago?" Martha nodded. Sister Adabayo hesitated a moment. "And your sister, Susie. She phoned last night, but I'm afraid your mum didn't know her, so your sister became upset. I tried to reassure her that Anna was in good hands. I'm sure it's hard for her, being far away, I mean."

Martha closed her eyes, trying to stop the rush of irritation, imagining Susie's angry unfinished sentences, her hysterical defensive tone.

Sitting by her mother's bed and looking at her peaceful face, Martha realised that never before had she watched Anna sleeping. Did she dream the same way as she did before? Or was there the same confusion, the mismatch of people and places, the random fractured memories of events real or imagined, that now filled her waking life? Was there any respite in sleep?

Martha put her hand gently on Anna's brow. "Mum. Mum," she said softly.

Anna opened heavy misty eyes. "Martha, I've missed you so much."

Martha began the conversation she'd rehearsed over and over as she drove back from the ferry.

"I've been to Arran, Mum. I went to see a house in Lamlash that you've always loved. Do you remember it? It's called Holmlea, on Shore Road."

Anna looked at her blankly, her eyes unblinking.

Martha pulled out her mobile phone. "I took some pictures on my new phone. If you see the house, it might help you to remember."

Anna looked away.

"Please, Mum, just look at it for a minute."

Anna's eyes flickered towards the photo of the house taken from the gate, and then, suddenly distracted, she screwed up her face. "Where's my tea? I want a cup of tea."

"It'll come soon, Mum. Please, don't harass the nurses," Martha said imploringly, "they're so busy."

"They hide my tea from me," Anna's voice rose, "*and* they give me nothing to eat."

"That's not true, Mum, *sshh*, please don't say that." Martha tried another tack. "I found a letter on the mantelpiece, from a solicitor asking you to get in touch. You must have put it there a while ago."

"I don't know what you're talking about." Anna started fiddling with her wedding ring.

Martha persisted, mistaking the moment for a battle of wills. "All right, Mum, have it your way." Her voice rose a little. "I wanted to tell you about a house that you loved and now *you* own, but it doesn't matter, not at all. We can talk about it another time."

Anna didn't seem to notice Martha's change of tone or be able to understand the words she was saying; she just smiled beatifically at her older daughter.

Martha, now defeated, slumped forward to kiss her. "I'll take you there one day. Maybe you'll remember it when you see it." She knew this was the limit of what she could promise. She could not tell Anna that she would be home soon. If her mother *were* to return to The Oval, Martha would have to find someone to watch over her, now and always.

As she left the room a friendly nurse auxiliary bustled in with tea and toast. Martha hesitated beyond the door for fear that Anna might berate the smiling woman.

"What a lovely visit. That's your older daughter Martha, isn't it?"

"What on earth are you talking about?" Martha winced at her mother's tone. "I haven't seen my daughter for months."

The words hit Martha like a hail of stones.

As she retreated to the car she tried to concentrate on summoning up the Anna she remembered, the strong selfless mother who had suppressed her own anguish day after day to spare her teenage daughters the worst of their father's advancing cancer. Martha would never forget the early morning click of the bathroom door that presaged the agonised racking coughing which went on and on, until she imagined her father's insides were red raw and he had used up every gasp of breath. No matter how tightly she had pulled the pillow over her head Martha heard the dreadful sound echoing around the house, mixed in with Susie's pleading to her mother to make Daddy stop.

That last year, when Martha was fifteen, Anna made sure that the girls had the best of him, that he spent every ounce of his remaining energy on them, not her, accompanying his excited daughters on a school trip, or taking them to the latest Bond film, or just waiting for them at school on rainy days, detouring to a book store or a record shop on the way home, while Anna kept on working full time. She had tried so hard to create a treasure trove of memories for her girls, and now Martha desperately wanted to keep that Anna alive in her own mind.

ELIZABETH

I have not written anything for two days now because the wet weather has brought the pains to my hands and stiffness to my arms. Saul offered to help me but I do not think I could speak my thoughts out loud, and besides my mind has been jumping from this spot to that, like a child playing hopscotch. But now I have settled down to it again at my table looking towards the garden. I went out for a little while this morning, just to feel the salt air on my skin. I walked up to the cemetery in the damp and sat on my coat on the Faerie Hill in front of the old wall. The lichen makes such a beautiful pattern on the stones, and the faerie foxgloves hang on for dear life in the crevices, making little splashes of purple.

Is that what I am doing? Hanging on for dear life until I can tell my story, the whole story? I felt my other self beside me again, a whisper on the wind, and I know I have not long with this ground beneath my feet. Perhaps while it is in my mind I should write about Saul. I know it will upset my chronicle, but after all, when it is read I will be dead, and some things are best told out of sequence. I have been thinking about the way he came unbidden and unlooked for into my life, just as Niall did not so long before him, my two pillars, tall and strong on either side of me. I could never have imagined it.

When the Buddhists first came to Holy Isle more than a decade ago I followed all the indignant correspondence of people who make it their business to judge others. Goodness knows, Arran has its fair share. There were hysterical articles and badly composed letters in the *Arran Banner* full of over-blown sentiment. Buddhism, they declared, outraged, would corrupt Arran life, and even the local presbytery voted against sending emissaries to the monks' first interfaith service. It probably did not help that the monks were such a ragtag lot, all ages and accents, with knobbly shaven heads — men and women alike — and their strange uniform of purple and orange robes that billowed in the wind. They were as exotic as the white flowers of the snowbell tree at the Castle, which make a carpet of snow in the summertime. I suppose I was only worried that after more than eighty years I would no longer be free to walk around the shoreline to the lighthouse, or stand looking over to my home from the little jetty at the north end of Holy Isle.

But gradually the monks won us all over. Perhaps I had fewer anxieties because my beliefs, which I keep to myself, have followed a different path. Some would say a queer one, but as I am a curiosity to some anyway, I have always kept my own counsel. And after all, long before the monks arrived, Vikings, worshippers of the Norse gods, carved runes in the cave on the island, a eulogy to a long dead king. Holy Isle has always been a place of otherness.

I first met Saul when I was returning one afternoon from Brodick Castle after my weekly voluntary duties. If people thought that at the age of ninety-three I was too old for the task, they never said, at least not to me. I stepped off the bus and stumbled over the verge, sending the fir cones that I had collected for kindling, rolling all over the road like a swarm of giant insects. I was flustered and, I must say, embarrassed. I had always been so surefooted. I became conscious of someone at my elbow and then a hand on my arm and the sound of laughter, which riled me a little at first, but when I looked up I realised the man, Saul, was laughing at the sight of the cascading cones. He was wearing yellow robes — I had yet to discover the term is "saffron" — and had very short grey hair and brilliant blue eyes. When he spoke I realised he was an American and I was momentarily taken aback, his voice an echo from the past. An intense memory, long buried, flooded my senses.

"Let me help you, ma'am," he said, raising me to my feet. I remember, to my shame, that I was a little abrupt. I think I said, "I can manage very well, thank you," but I was a little dizzy and held onto his arm, firm beneath the cotton robe.

"It is not a sign of weakness to accept a little help," he said, smiling at me. "You know, we Buddhists are pledged to commit random acts of kindness. You would be denying me!"

I felt churlish and ungrateful and I thanked him. I watched as he picked up all the scattered fir cones and then we walked slowly together along the road, Saul, I noted, protectively on the outside.

He stopped and turned to me. "I should introduce myself. Saul Braunstein."

"Elizabeth Pringle," I said, as we shook hands.

"I've seen you reading by the lighthouse, haven't I?"

"It's quite possible." I bristled a little at the thought I had been watched. "It's a favourite place of mine. It always has been since I was a little girl." And then I carried on. I do not know why I said what I did; perhaps I was already at ease. "When I was young, I imagined it was a magical tower and I was Rapunzel, trapped there."

He laughed. "I love it, too. To me it's a symbol of adventure and danger, but safety, too. Near to where I grew up there's a famous lighthouse. Have you heard of Cape May?"

I confessed I had not.

"It marks the State of New Jersey's southernmost point. I guess it's kept ships from all over the world from smashing on the rocks."

His casual expectation of continuing acquaintance unnerved me into conversation. "I like symbols of strength. Have you been to Brodick Castle?" I rushed on without waiting for his reply. "These cones are from the magnificent Douglas firs which were planted there more than a century ago. I collect them every year for the fire."

"I guess they do the job pretty well." He smiled and I noticed the deep lines around his eyes.

"They do indeed, and they fill the room with a wonderful perfume. I always think of the Douglas fir as life affirming, tall and strong and safe, the antidote to the yew that neighbours it. Did you know that the yew is the tree of death?"

Saul laughed. "Buddhists don't think of death like that."

We neared home. "You have a fine garden," he said.

I was never one for compliments but his words pleased me. He had a quiet confidence belied by the humility of his calling. Then he asked me for advice. The Buddhists wanted to plant thirty thousand trees on Holy Isle, but he was interested in just one, a special tree, the ancient rock whitebeam. There was only one remaining, and he wondered if I could help him coax it back to health. I was flattered, I confess. I was not used to such a rush of intimate conversation. I think I have always been what is called, "stand-offish," and although I know of a great many people on Arran, their families and their history and sometimes their feuds and foibles, I have never really sought company. Even when I did, once, in the middle of my life, it brought me only fleeting happiness.

But now, late in my time on earth, improbably, I had made two friends, each of whom I came to rely on in different ways and both of whom I care about very much.

I have unlocked Mother's little oak box. It is inlaid with petals of mother-of-pearl that shimmer when the sun streams through the window and has sat on her walnut desk unopened for more than sixty years, but I know its contents so intimately I could almost recite the words it contains. Saul called it a Pandora's box of sorrows. In his quiet way, on one of our beach walks, he took my arm to help me over a rivulet and urged me to open it and let the grief out into the wind to join the cries of the peewits and oystercatchers.

"You will breathe more easily, Elizabeth," he promised.

The letters it contains seem more fragile than life itself, just flimsy cheap lined paper, and yet they bear the weight of a man's heart. Here in faded pencil, is the last letter my father wrote.

16 November 1918
My dearest beautiful girls,
   I scarcely know how to express my feelings at the wonderful news. What has always seemed an impossibility to me has at last come to be a reality. We have been through some wonderful scenes these past few weeks when we released the largest town in France from the enemy's hands. What happy days you will be spending together knowing that the war is over. This will be our last Christmas apart, and I will content myself with the glorious thought of the meeting that is to be. I am as happy as a lark. The only thing I worry about is that the flu might get over the sea to Arran.

Warmest love from your loving husband and adoring father.

My father is buried in the village cemetery at Ascq, near Lille. He lies there with other British soldiers, comrades in arms, but men he never knew. I still have a curled photograph of the new headstones standing in rows, a sheltering of dense dark trees behind. In the black and white picture they appear to be almost luminescent, as if in the glow of a full moon. James Allan Pringle did not have a last Christmas in France. Two weeks after he sent his joyous letter he was dead, killed by the Spanish flu he was so terrified would claim his wife and daughter hundreds of miles away.

More people came to our door in the days that followed the news of his death than at any time before. I watched their sombre procession until they arrived to stand, grave and shy, on our step. The men wore their dark three-piece suits, their caps folded tightly in their hands; the women carried a pot of jam or perhaps a cake covered in muslin. Mother, in her black wool ankle-length skirt and taffeta high-collared shirt to match, greeted each one and put them at their ease with a faint smile or a soft word. She offered tea, or, to the men, a dram. They sat a while, not too long, sometimes mentioning some help my father had offered, or a piece of advice sought from him and willingly given.

In those days Christmas was a day like any other, especially on a farm, but there was always church. That first Christmas, so soon after the news of my father's death, we walked to the kirk through an icy wind. I remember Mother carried a basket in which was a posy of Christmas roses, which she grew in a sheltered suntrap by the garden wall. She set them in a glass vase on the pulpit, in front of our pew. The Reverend Craig, a tall, stooped, bony man with a hooked nose and a shock of white hair, delivered the sermon. When he spoke my name I was both startled and embarrassed and gripped my mother's gloved hand. Then I realised he was saying a special prayer for our family, for Mother and me. I looked at her face beneath her heavy-brimmed black hat, searching for clues, desperate to know how to feel. She squeezed my hand and then pushed a little strand of hair from my face, and putting her mouth so close to my ear I could feel the breath of her words she whispered, "It will always be just the two of us."

Is that what really happened? I am so tired with the effort of remembering, but down through the years that image of Mother in church, straight backed and proud, has returned to me, recently, more clearly than ever before.

In the weeks and months that followed, at church, or at the Post Office, or at the ferry, Mother would always greet the returning soldiers and their families, relieving them of the awkward moment. She took their stumbling hesitant words from them and wove them into a gentle conversation about their plans, or their gardens, or news of jobs at the creamery. That supreme effort was made all the harder by the small cold stone pressing on her chest and the weight of the decision that she would soon have to make.

At first our daily lives had continued their rhythm, but that spring I saw Mother and John McInnes outside the stables, the angle of their bodies hostile, and I knew by the timbre of her voice that she was uneasy and angry. Far too soon after news of my father's death, John McInnes had come to Mother angling to buy the farm to merge it with his own. She had given him short shrift, but now he was back, pestering her for more money for his efforts, knowing full well the farm had no more to yield.

"I cannot pay you any more. The farm won't bear it."

"In that case it seems to me, Mistress Pringle, that you have two choices. You can find someone else to work Benkiln, or you can sell it to me."

"Or to someone else," Mother said sharply.

"Aye, lass. Who else? I have done well by you over the past two years, and I'll give you a fair price."

Mother stiffened at his forthright familiar tone, but this time she did not see him off.

Of course as a child, I knew nothing about the economics of the land, but I believe that had she truly wanted to remain on the farm, she would have found a way. Goodness knows, after the war there was plenty of willing labour. Perhaps without my father she had no heart for it, but as I grew into adulthood I resented her bitterly, for she had sold my birthright, my dowry if you like. It would never be my land to walk on, and that loss set the course for my future.

By the summer everything had been packed up. My memories of the day we moved are not of sadness but of excitement and bustle. The procession of horsedrawn carts, tarpaulins drawn tight over our possessions so that each one looked as if it was carrying a huge green parcel, made its way clattering and clip clopping down the hill, over the little bridge, past the cottages at the hamlet of Cordon and into the village. All in all a scant two miles. I was allowed to sit with the drayman in the front cart and when we reached Shore Road he gave me the reins for a little while, before retrieving them to make the turn into the house where I sit now. And then as now, Holy Isle fills the window before me, a scene that alters almost imperceptibly with every new day. Above Mullach Beag, the vapour trails of transatlantic aeroplanes create soft-edged patterns like messages threaded through the sky. (This sort of poetic vocabulary is Saul's doing, I might say. I have been listening to him now for three years and something of his way of describing the world around him has rubbed off on me.)

Our farmhouse was more than one hundred years old, built by a long ago relative, with low lintels and thick panes of glass that slightly distorted the world outside. But we were the first inhabitants of our new home, which I found thrilling in itself. It had been built just twenty years earlier by a coal merchant from Ayr, but it was said that his wife never liked the house and it had lain empty since the last slate was tacked on the roof.

I was allowed to take my kitten, the rabbit and my newts, perhaps to make the short journey easier for me, but the kitten kept returning to Benkiln until I was forced to leave her there for good, a parting more real and traumatic to me than the death of my father.

Mother and Mary set to work on plans for decorating Holmlea and Mary lent us a gardener from the Whitehouse to work the bare ground into the beginnings of a garden. He brought brown paper bags full of seeds and old boxes stamped with "Burma", which he used to transport seedlings he'd cultivated for the Duchess's beloved garden.

This was my first true education. Mary brought a beautiful leather-bound atlas from the Whitehouse and pointed out where George Forrest, the plant collector and explorer, discovered so many species of the rose tree, including rhododendron sinogrande, with its clusters of delicate creamy bells and long delicate leaves. For more than half a century I have noted the day, each spring, when the first bloom unfurls at my garden gate like a wonderful yearly gift.

Mary told thrilling stories of George Forrest's derring-do, how he had braved sickness, bandits and uprisings in pursuit of his passion. He had sailed to Rangoon and trekked across the Burma-Yunnan border to Tengyueh in China. It was the first time I had imagined a world beyond the island, and it never occurred to me then that such an adventure would have cost a fortune. As a child I did not think of Mary as the wealthy landowner she was, nor did I understand that she, along with the Rothschilds and other grand families, had bought into many of Forrest's expeditions in return for precious seeds. Looking back, the passion for gardening that Mother and Mary kindled in me was their way of guiding me into their world, and giving me my place in it.

In those first weeks in the new house even Mother's black mourning clothes could not camouflage her excitement over the possibilities of our new home. My room was the first to be decorated and Mother sent to Wylie and Lochead in Glasgow for sheaves of wallpaper samples. I can still remember the name of the one we picked: "Oranges and Lemons Say the Bells of St Clements." A chain of brightly dressed girls and boys held onto each other's smocks and patterned dresses and danced around a pair of entwined orange and lemon trees. I do not believe that any other child in Lamlash Primary School had a room specially decorated for her. I would lie in bed and, in the dancing light of my little oil lamp, trace my hand across the smooth wall, repeating the names I had given them: Annie, David, Jeannie, Walter and Jessie, and imagine they were my faerie friends.

MARTHA

"I haven't seen my daughter for months."

Try as she might to banish them, Anna's final gut-wrenching words played in a loop in Martha's head as she drove away from the hospital and headed for the ferry. She thought she had steeled herself for just such a moment but her defences were still too puny. It suddenly seemed unfair that she was the only one there to take the blows. But then, Martha knew she was incapable of a settled view of her sister. When Susie had taken the job in Denmark two years earlier, she had been nothing but encouraging. Anna was forgetful, yes, but that was no reason for Susie to turn down an opportunity to work in a prestigious design studio. Distance had not lent perspective for either sister, in fact the opposite. Susie persisted in her belief that Martha exaggerated Anna's condition. "Typical journalist," Susie had mocked, and Martha in turn was convinced that Susie's denial was a deliberate provocation.

As she guided the car onto the boat, a memory came to Martha of her mother sitting in their garden, engrossed in a book. Martha and Susie were on a tartan rug on the grass playing games with their Sindy dolls, piles of tiny clothes all around, dressing and undressing them, bickering over accessories. Her father appeared from the house in his jaunty straw hat and Che Guevara tee shirt, with a jug of juice for them and a glass of wine for Anna. She pulled him to her and kissed his cheek. "Isn't he the most handsome waiter in the world?" she said girlishly.

When Anna started to have episodes of confusion Susie had railed at Martha, "Dad should be here to deal with this."

"For God's sake Susie, grow up," Martha had sighed. "This is not Dad's fault. You're being ridiculous."

"Oh, really? No one made him smoke. He did it all on his own. And it's not like he started before there were warnings. He *knew* he could get cancer."

"What's the point of all this, Susie?" Martha said fiercely. "Do you really think it helps either of us?"

Martha was still deep in thought as she arrived back at the Glenburn.

"A penny for them." Catriona smiled sympathetically. "Was it tough?"

Martha nodded and sighed. "I just want to get her home but I need to get a carer, and that's a pretty big ask, isn't it, for someone who might open the front door and walk out into the night?"

"It's certainly not a job for the fainthearted. God, sorry, that sounded awful."

"It's OK. You're right." Martha smiled reassuringly.

Catriona frowned for a moment, a thought slowly forming. "It's not a big ask for the right person, though, and there *are* people who have infinite patience . . ." She stopped mid-sentence, ruminating.

Martha laughed. " Conjure one up, then, please."

"That might not be as far-fetched as it sounds," went on Catriona slowly. "I have an idea, but leave it with me for a couple of days."

Martha curbed her natural inclination to press further, intrigued that she was unusually relaxed about letting someone else take charge. Then Catriona took her by surprise. "I hope you don't mind, but I've asked Niall to come by. I thought we could walk to the Falls. It's a beautiful hike, and there's something special for you to see there."

"Something about Elizabeth Pringle? Are you sure he's happy to do this?"

"Why shouldn't he be?" Catriona shrugged and laughed. "If he wasn't, he'd soon tell me, and you too, probably."

But Martha noticed her new friend's almost imperceptible uncertainty. She remembered their late-night conversation over dinner. Catriona had told her about her relationship with Niall — they were as close as siblings could be, she said — but still she found his emotional life a mystery. "Sometimes, I feel it's as if he has built an invisible shield to protect himself, but from what I'm not sure. There was one romance, ages ago, but he seemed more stoic than bereft when it ended. Our parents, perhaps . . ."

Catriona's voice had trailed off. Martha had looked at her, willing her to go on. "Ever since Niall and I were children they'd owned a hotel near Rothiemurchus in the Highlands. They died in a car crash. It was a foggy night and they were travelling home from a trip to Perth on a lethal stretch of the road north. A head-on collision, they must have been blinded by the headlights coming straight at them the wrong way."

"How awful, Catriona, for you both . . . What a terrible shock."

Catriona nodded. She was eighteen at the time, she explained, and so her brother left his training at Kew and headed for Edinburgh's Botanical Gardens, determined to shepherd her safely through her archaeology degree. "He was adamant he wanted to be in the same city, to keep me on an even keel. He did it, too, but then I couldn't settle. I've done everything from selling insurance to managing a pub. The nearest I've come to a career in archaeology was a stint volunteering on a dig," she told Martha, "but he has never reproached me, not once."

When Niall was offered the position of chief horticulturist for the National Trust at Brodick Castle, Catriona visited more and more, watching her brother grow into his life there, a natural leader, brimful of ideas, displaying a patience that she knew did not always come easily. Increasingly she felt the pull of the island, so when the Glenburn came up for sale, she knew immediately she wanted to take it on. Niall offered to pool his inheritance with hers, and so they bought what was little more than a forlorn seaside boarding house and Catriona set about transforming it into a bright welcoming hotel.

"And is Arran home now . . . I mean, for you both?" Martha had asked.

"I feel as rooted here as the Standing Stones round the coast at Machrie, and I know Niall feels that, too," Catriona said, shaking her head, "but you have to accept that even if you had arrived in Lamlash Bay with the Vikings you would still be an incomer."

Martha had laughed. "Well then, I've got absolutely no chance!"

She heard a car door bang, which snapped her out of her recollection of last night. She followed Catriona's eyes to the window. "Here he is. The handsome woodcutter, as the people at the Castle have nicknamed him."

Martha watched Niall walk towards them. He was tall and athletic, with a shock of short red hair and fair Celtic skin. His khaki shirt was rolled up at the sleeves and his hands were thrust into the pockets of a pair of battered dark brown corduroy trousers. He was unmistakably Catriona's brother. When he came into the kitchen Martha felt oddly disconcerted by his presence, as if she were trying to hold her ground against the undertow of a fast moving current. His handshake was firm and cool and he looked at her for just a moment too long. His gray eyes, flickering, signalled a wary interest, or more like, Martha thought, a judgement.

When she spoke, her friendly tone was forced. "I'm glad to meet you. I know you were a friend of Miss

Pringle's. You must have been very sad . . . I mean, I am sure you still are." He shot her a cold look and she trailed off, her colour, and her temper, rising.

It took Catriona to break the silence. "Come on, before it clouds over." She grabbed her jacket. "Martha, you jump in the front."

Martha looked at her, horrified. "No, honestly, I'll sit in the back," she pleaded, desperate not to have to sit alongside Niall on the bench seat.

"I insist," laughed Catriona, "the back's a tip. Look at it. Niall, I swear this fertiliser's mutating it's been here so long. It's about to burst out of the bag."

Martha's heart sank as she climbed awkwardly into the front.

Niall threw the old Land Rover into gear and coaxed it up the steep hill to Whiting Bay. "You need to see to the facade of the hotel soon; the guttering looks pretty bad," he said gruffly.

"I know, I know but there's only so much I can do, Niall," Catriona replied wearily.

Martha listened as they talked about the hotel, discussing replanting the adjoining garden, replacing water butts, advertising the revamp, everything, it seemed to her, but Elizabeth Pringle and, unless she imagined it, Niall was determinedly not talking to her at all.

The timbre of his voice, his physical proximity, unnerved her. She stared hard out of the open window at the pale opal sea, the horizon barely perceptible beneath the overcast sky, trying to work out why she cared that he was keeping himself at a distance.

They parked beside the narrow track across from the sea wall. At first they walked in single file, hemmed in between tall hawthorn bushes and a row of sycamores, Niall leading and Martha behind him, in the middle. She watched his broad shoulders, squared against her it seemed, as he strode ahead. Was he so taciturn because he was irritated by her presence? Or perhaps it was nothing to do with her. Perhaps it was grief. Whichever it was, they were going to have to speak sometime. She addressed his back. "Miss Pringle's garden is beautiful. But it would have been a lot for her. You must have helped her so much."

He spoke without turning round to her. "Only when she let me."

Martha kept on. "Was she very independent?" As soon as she had spoken, she flushed, mortified by the lame question to which they all already knew the answer.

"She was very stoic, if that's what you mean. She worked in the garden in weather that would have kept people half her age indoors. Sometimes she would cut the grass in a howling gale, and then I really did have to prise the mower from her."

"C'mon, Niall, she enjoyed it when you worked alongside her, and I got the sense that she quite liked you bullying her a little," piped up Catriona from the back.

"Maybe she did. I certainly liked her company, not that we were always talking. Often we worked together in silence. She wasn't one for inane chatter."

Martha took his words as a rebuke and stung by his sharp tone, she fell back a little, but Catriona, sensing her dismay, chivvied her on and the path slowly widened until there was no option but to walk alongside Niall.

"Tell Martha how you met."

"You don't have to," Martha jumped in quickly.

Niall ignored her. "She volunteered at the castle. In fact she never missed a day in all the years she worked there. She took the bus at least once a week, often more. Not long after I started, in 2002, I was cutting back rhododendrons down by the lower wall, when I heard a quiet voice behind me. I'll never forget it. 'Young man,' she said, 'that is not what I call pruning. If I am not mistaken, you are hacking that poor rose to death.' She must have been almost ninety-two but she was ramrod straight and quite tall. She wore little round hornrimmed glasses and a brown tweed checked coat. I think she wore that coat almost every day."

Niall turned to them with a faint look of surprise, as if the fact of her unchanging appearance had just dawned on him for the first time. He looked evenly at Martha for a moment, and slowly, starting to enjoy remembering, he went on. "After that day we became friends, and she was a wonderful, generous teacher. She could identify every flower at the castle at a hundred paces, and sometimes she could even recall when it had been planted.

"I remember one day she appeared at my shoulder when I was clearing some rotting leaves beside a patch of snowdrops, down by the Bavarian summerhouse, and she talked about her mother. It was the only time she mentioned her to me. She said, 'I always thought it was a shame to cut these little flowers out of the ground, but that is what my mother and I would do every year for Snowdrop Day.' And then, looking beyond me, she carried on talking as if I wasn't there. 'We were at our best together when we were working, tying bunches of snowdrops, saying not a word.'

Niall stopped, looking pensive. "She had a very formal way of speaking. I remember thinking it was a strange thing for her to say. It was as if her mother had been on her mind, and she was talking almost unconsciously."

They walked on, up towards the Falls, past strong slender ash trees resplendent in their new foliage and tall graceful alders, stamping along a well worn path that was veined with the sinewy gnarled roots of the woodland, its edges marked with bright yellow primroses. Pungent wild garlic infused the crisp air and Martha drew the heady scent of it all into her lungs, luxuriating in the atmosphere of the forest. A shrew darted across the path in front of them, as if responding to a dare, and dived for cover in the undergrowth.

"Come over here. There's something I want to show you." Catriona took Martha's arm firmly and guided her, Niall at her back, undergrowth pricking her skin, through a thicket to a tall oak, its trunk almost hidden by the smaller trees around it. On it were two names chiselled deeply into the bark, "Angelica and Medoro," the words bound together with a delicately carved rope.

Martha traced the names, her fingers deep in the grooves. A little way around the trunk was the outline of an open book, and across the pages scrolled, "Abelard and Heloise," in an even more exquisite copperplate hand.

"This is unbelievably beautiful!" Martha exclaimed.

"There's more!" said Catriona, pointing towards the back of the tree.

Martha stepped carefully past some bluebells and saw that, low down, where the trunk was at its thickest, was an intricately decorated banner containing the words, "Tristan and Isolde."

"Now look higher," instructed Catriona.

Martha raised her eyes. Carved above her head were the names "Elizabeth" and "Robert", linked by a rose and surrounded by a perfect love knot. She turned to Catriona, avoiding looking at Niall. "Is this Elizabeth Pringle?"

"I bet it is," replied Catriona, "but ask Niall."

Reluctantly she turned to Niall, noticing his jaw set firm, and asked, "What do you think?"

"How should I know?" he said, shrugging.

"He didn't ask," said Catriona, in mock irritation. "He didn't think it was his business."

"Exactly. It wasn't."

"Maybe this was her true love," said Catriona clutching at her heart dramatically, "and she never knew that Niall had found it."

A shadow passed across her brother's face and he turned away and walked towards the Falls, the tumbling water crashing down over the stones.

Martha watched him stride off, his hands thrust deep into his pockets again, his head down.

"That was probably a bit insensitive of me," said Catriona, grimacing. "He was very upset not to be here when she died. It hit him very hard."

"Well, my being here won't help, I'm sure," said Martha, suddenly irritated at Catriona for bringing her without warning her about Niall's grief. She felt clumsy and brash.

"He hasn't said what he thinks. He's not one for snap judgements." Catriona looked at Martha's doubting face. "But there's one thing I know for certain — the house isn't an issue. He wouldn't have wanted it for himself, if that's what you're thinking, and he wouldn't have wanted anything in it, except perhaps for some gardening books."

Martha thought about the rows of books, all ages and sizes, fiction, poetry, plant journals. "He can have anything he wants, anything at all. It's not as if any of it belongs to me."

She tentatively broached the subject of the painting. "There's a lovely ink and watercolour portrait in one of the bedrooms. I'm sure it's by Cadell, but I don't know if it's Elizabeth or not. If it is, Niall would be welcome to it."

Catriona looked at her in surprise. "That's amazing. Cadell *was* here in the thirties. He was commissioned by Caledonian MacBrayne to make a series of paintings of their steamers. I saw them at an exhibition in Brodick last year."

"The painting is of quite a young woman. Do you think you might recognise her?"

"I might not but Niall would, I'm sure. And Saul, too, I bet."

"Who's Saul?"

"Oh, I'm sure you'll see him around," Catriona said airily. "He's an American who came to Holy Isle a few years ago to help build the Buddhist community. You can't really miss him, craggy, handsome, weather-beaten, short iron-grey hair, hip, cultured . . . All that and, oh, an object of lust the island over," she added casually.

Martha remembered the tall figure on the boat. "So he knew Elizabeth Pringle, too?"

"Yes. He befriended her, spent a lot of time with her, particularly during the last months when Niall was away."

"Another younger man. Impressive." Martha smiled. "Did she collect them?"

"Just two, as far as I know," laughed Catriona, "but both quite good catches. I'd say, anyway."

They walked towards the crashing water, the noise filling the air and reverberating through the woods. Niall stood at the rail overlooking the Falls, studying the two women as they approached.

Martha's colour rose as she felt his cool grey eyes trained on her. She swallowed and then said quickly, "Catriona said you might like to go through Elizabeth's gardening books, but please take them. All of them." She smiled uncertainly.

His face was impassive. "I will then. Thank you very much."

Although she could not be certain, she thought she detected a faintly mocking tone.

The next day Martha sat on the wooden seat under the dining room window in the garden of Holmlea waiting for Catriona to arrive, and surveyed the ground that ran down to the road. She knew very little about gardening, that had been Anna's preserve, but in the long border she recognised hellebores of all different varieties, still in glorious bloom. Strong stems of green-centred white flowers waved gently alongside smaller purple stalks topped with lilac petals. Beside them, yet more black flowers gathered together, their bells shimmering in the soft breeze of the Gulf Stream. She had a sudden pang of longing for that Anna, and the trips they had made together that brought her mother so much pleasure, to Hampton Court and to Sissinghurst, and one wonderful summer to Giverny where they had both felt overwhelmed by the glory of Monet's garden. That was in the days when Anna had meticulously planned their annual week away together, handing Martha a sheaf of cuttings before they set off, delighting almost as much in the careful preparations as the holiday itself.

But she wouldn't bring her here yet, not until the house was fixed up and made safe for her, and not until she could try to help her make some sense of it all. And she would have to wait until she herself was on firmer ground, her own emotions more even.

She thought about the day she had found Anna in the hall at home, standing stock still, unable to find her way to the kitchen door. Martha had simply taken her arm and guided her to the kitchen. A moment later the old Anna was back, as if she had never been away. "Be a darling and hand me down Nigel Slater's file," she had said. "I want to make that great pork stew from last Sunday's *Observer*."

Then Martha shuddered, remembering the time Anna had slipped from her side and attached herself to a group of noisy boys, as if she was as longstanding a member of the gang as any of them. In their casual cruel adolescent way they had laughed at her, mocking her childlike attempts to insinuate herself, copying their patois, even spitting on the ground. Anna had started to cry and Martha, rushing to her rescue, felt the adrenaline rush of pure hate, her desire to do physical injury to the boys' slack idiot faces almost overwhelming. But instead she had just glared contemptuously at the jeering grinning group and led her mother away, calculating that if she made any attempt to explain Anna's illness to them, her mother might understand what had happened and suffer a further heartbreaking humiliation.

Now Martha looked up, startled by the sound of Catriona dropping her bike against the wall with a clatter, and pulling herself back to the moment, waved at her as she walked up the garden.

"It looks lovely. Niall's done a good job, hasn't he?" Catriona called out. "Perhaps he'd keep helping if you asked him."

Martha smiled. "I think you might have got that a bit wrong."

She didn't wait for an answer but pushed on with a bigger question, which had been gnawing at her since they'd returned from the Falls. She stood back to let Catriona into the hall. "I need to ask you again, just to be certain, for the avoidance of doubt, so there's no problem."

"What is it?"

"Are you absolutely sure that Niall wouldn't have expected to be left this house?"

"Yes. I know for sure Niall wouldn't have wanted it."

"Did he actually tell you that?" pressed Martha. "I mean, you and I don't know each other very well yet, so this might seem a bit out of order," she took a deep breath, "but I'm not getting a very warm vibe from Niall, and—"

"He didn't need to tell me," Catriona broke in, "and don't be concerned about his mood. Sometimes he's just a bit abrupt. It doesn't mean anything, believe me."

Martha looked dubious.

"Look, Martha, he has an amazing house of his own. You should see it. He designed it himself."

"Here in Lamlash?"

Catriona nodded. "You wouldn't really notice it from the road; it's so high above the village. Imagine a long wooden box with one end looking back into the woods on the hill and the other hanging over a stream, looking out to sea. It's his homage to Frank Lloyd Wright and Mies van der Rohe rolled into one."

Well, we've got *that* interest in common at least, thought Martha. "Does he live on his own?" she asked, as carelessly as she could, but Catriona burst out laughing.

"Do you mean — 'does he have a girlfriend?' "

Martha blushed. "I'm curious, that's all. I assure you I'm not scoping him out."

"Not now. There was someone a while ago, a girl he worked with at the castle, but she went back to New Zealand. She was apparently prepared to miss him a lot more than she was willing to miss her home. Wellington, I think it was. Green, wet, not that different to here, really." Catriona paused. "And that was before he built his house, or, as I call it, his eyrie."

"His eyrie?"

"Yes, he can sit up there, virtually out of sight, and watch the world below him. I overheard one of the locals saying it looked like a giant ship's container with both ends blasted out. Niall was really quite pleased about that."

"I thought it was practically impossible to buy land on Arran. Isn't there some feudal throwback or other?"

"Yes. Normally, for mere mortals anyway. But Niall being Niall, managed to find a way." Catriona laughed. "He's surprisingly good with the boss class."

She stopped at the open door of the sitting room, surveying the pictures covering the walls. "Wow, these are amazing, they're works of art."

She peered at tiny fairies entwined with dark green ivy, their hair, strands of pale silk, and each one carrying a harp with strings of gold thread. Along the top and bottom of the frame there were brilliant blue flowers with white centres. "Baby blue eyes," said Catriona, "or to give them their proper name, nemophilias."

"I'm impressed," laughed Martha.

"Niall isn't the only one in the family who knows his flora and fauna." Then, leaning in to the corner of the canvas, she gestured to Martha to examine it. "Look, she's embroidered the word 'May' into the stem. Perhaps that's the time of year when she finished it, or it's the flowers of that month. So this is how Elizabeth Pringle wiled away the years. I would never have guessed she was one for elves and fairies. Too Presbyterian, I would have thought."

"Do you know of any reason that I should feel . . . you know, uneasy here. Scared, even?" Martha caught Catriona's disbelieving expression but went on quickly, "I mean, I know it's ridiculous, but should I?"

"*Have* you felt scared here?"

Martha shook her head. "No, not scared, just, I don't know, thoughtful, I suppose. Like I'm conscious of something but I don't know what it is."

"Well, there you go. Dead people stay dead, Martha," Catriona said emphatically, "and if you believe in karma, it feels like a good atmosphere to me." She smiled reassuringly. "Now come and show me the painting."

As Martha led the way up the wooden stairs, Catriona looked around admiringly. "This really is a lovely house. I'd be very happy to help you make it even lovelier."

"I'd like that, a lot," said Martha. She stopped on the landing and turned to Catriona, breaking into a smile. "Maybe I do need to take some proper time off from work. I love the writing and, you know, the chase of the story, but it's consumed me for a long time. Too long. Standing here I can feel my centre of gravity shifting . . . I can feel the pull of this house. It's hard to explain."

Catriona ran her hand over the rich wood of the banister and said softly. "Well, perhaps that is Elizabeth Pringle's real gift."

"So the sketch is over here." The two women stood in front of the ink and watercolour portrait. "What do you think?" asked Martha. "Isn't she elegant?"

"She's beautiful." Catriona looked closely at the wistful face, trying to recollect the features of the woman she only ever saw fleetingly. "Sorry," she said, shaking her head. "I think you'll have to try Niall. I don't recognise her as Elizabeth Pringle."

Suddenly there was a gentle click from the floor below as the letter box shut, followed by the soft fluttering sound of a note falling onto the mat.

Catriona looked out of the window. "I wondered how long it would take for Saul to show up," she said, a scintilla of sarcasm in her voice. They watched the tall figure returning to the road, his saffron robes billowing around him.

Downstairs, Martha pulled the page from the cheap buff envelope and read aloud, "Hello, I think your name is Martha. I live on Holy Isle and I was a friend of Elizabeth Pringle. I would be happy to meet and

93

perhaps tell you a little about her, if you'd like. Just leave this note under the stone by the front gate adding a time that suits you, Saul."

She passed the note to Catriona. "Intriguing."

Catriona snorted. "I notice he doesn't really expect you to turn down his offer. Why am I not surprised? That's Saul."

"Well," replied Martha, "I don't suppose there's any harm in meeting him. I want to know as much as there is to know."

"No, of course not," replied Catriona casually, but Martha noticed her shoulders stiffen a little.

ELIZABETH

Before Niall came to the island, for years my conversations with men were limited to the odd enquiry after my health, or an occasional meeting with my bank manager in Brodick, or some exchange of information at the castle, or, if I could not escape quickly enough, a sanctimonious greeting from the Minister the odd time I ventured to the kirk. And to most young people I am probably somewhat forbidding. But I was not always so old.

I was seventeen when I met Robert Stewart and he was almost twenty, the youngest of three brothers from Balnacraivie Farm by Shiskine.

There had been a lot of talk about encouraging young people to take part in drama. Mother was active in the Women's Rural Institute, "The Rural", as it was usually known, and it was under its auspices that the first Isle of Arran Festival came about. I was in my last year at school and there was a great deal of excitement that seven teams were to perform — from Brodick, Shiskine, Kilmorie, Lochranza, Pirnmill, Corrie and Lamlash. Mother helped with the stage preparations and I carried props from the house for a play titled,

"Telling The Tale". I have the programme still. Mary "Her Grace, the Duchess of Hamilton", as it was written, was the chair of the Festival. Mother even chose me a dress from the Pettigrew and Stephens catalogue for the opening night, a beautiful midnight blue barathea dress with a velvet collar to match.

The hall was packed and full of excited chatter. The men congregated at the back to let the women have the seats. I turned my head to marvel at how many had come, and that is when I first caught sight of Robert. He was a full head taller than the men beside him, and his dark wavy hair fell over one eye. He was smiling at something the man standing alongside him had said, and his whole face was lit up in delight. His skin was sallow, almost olive, and his eyes were framed by long lashes. He stood with his arms folded across his chest, so handsome in his Sunday suit. In the months to come I would love the feeling of that rough tweed brushing against my own skin when we walked out on a Saturday afternoon.

I watched him for as long as I dared, my heart thudding and my hands squeezing my linen handkerchief into a thousand creases.

Suddenly there was a commotion when Mrs Paton along the row was asked to remove her hat by the tutting women behind her. I quickly looked away, the moment over. I could hardly concentrate on the performance, and at the end I rushed to help serve the tea and lemonade.

Did I court him? If wanting him to notice me was courting, then yes, I did. When he stood in front of me, waiting for me to pour his tea, I looked directly at him and said, "Did you enjoy the play?"

"It was funny all right," he replied, "but I was a long time standing. You were sitting near the front." He looked at me shyly and I think I blushed, for a smile played on his lips. "I know who you are. You're Elizabeth Pringle. Your family used to farm Benkiln."

I remember that it was his turn to redden then, and although he had to move on to let others be served, he returned to help me clear away. At that moment an invisible thread had spun itself between us and I had no doubt that he would come back, even though it was awkward, with Mother beside me.

"Good evening, Mrs Pringle," he said very courteously. "I'm Robert Stewart from Balnacraivie. My father still speaks of your husband, and what a fine man he was."

I could sense Mother stiffening beside me but as I glanced at her I noticed the smallest flicker of a smile, a softening, and Robert bravely pressed on. "Your daughter is very like you. She's very bonny."

Mother laughed then, and looked at him intently for a moment while telling me to collect our coats and the lantern. Robert smiled at me and then he offered to walk us both home. "Thank you, but we can manage fine," Mother said, not unkindly, and he shook our hands, almost as if a pact had been made. We all knew it was a beginning.

He came to the house the following week and asked Mother if he could take me out. Over the next months we would meet in the village on a Saturday when

Robert was free from the farm, and cycle for miles; or sometimes he read to me as I lay on the grass on my back, sideways to him, my head on his chest and my face to the sun. He would trace his finger across my forehead and tell me I was beautiful. He made me think it was true, although I had never even thought myself pretty. He would take my hand to his mouth and kiss my palm and then bury his head in my hair and tell me he loved its scent. That summer we lay on the hill on the Ross Road, in the lea of our old farm, and told each other how happy we made the other.

Robert should have stayed on at school. He loved history, and enthralled me with stories about the American Civil War and his hero, Abraham Lincoln. He should have tried for a scholarship for university, because the farm was never going to be his. But his father needed him. Mr Stewart was confined to the house with crippling arthritis and Robert had to help his oldest brother Angus with the farm, and tend to his next brother Andrew, who had polio. There was no welfare state in those days, and little money for doctors. But if Robert was resentful, he kept it to himself. He loved them and he would do anything for them. Even now when I look back down the great distance of the years, I cannot see what signs there were, that I missed, that he was searching for so much more.

That autumn I began as a "pupil teacher", training in the infant class in Lamlash. I had never been so happy; my days were filled with the children and feeling for the first time since I was their age, that I was cherished.

If Mother was jealous of the time I spent with Robert, she never spoke of it. My course was set without any fanfare. I didn't need to measure Robert against anyone else; I had only ever been used to the company of women.

It was Mary, not Mother, who would put her arm around my shoulder and ask me questions that made me blush. "Does he make you prickly all over?" she would tease, or more seriously, bid me close my eyes and ask me if I could imagine us, old and gnarly, together. "I want you to be sure, Elizabeth. You have your whole life ahead of you. Is Robert the man you will love in sickness and in health, for richer or poorer?" I never knew if her questions were at Mother's behest, but I answered as if Mother were listening.

I remember on one occasion that first spring, he collected me from school with the pony and cart and the children gathered round, giggling, as he helped me up — his hands around my waist, not that I could not manage myself. "Isn't your teacher bonny?" he called to them mischievously, and they all shouted back, "Aye she is, mister." I was embarrassed beyond words. As we were about to set off, he put a fine new paisley shawl that he'd bought for me around my shoulders, and took my arm and put it firmly through his. The children clapped, whooping and jumping about, and ran after the cart.

We rode over to Brodick to collect a parcel for Mother and stopped outside a new cottage. He told me that he and his brother Angus had helped build it in a day and a night. It was the home of a man well known on the island, a sheriff officer who had been given short notice to quit the house he was renting and had persuaded local people to help build his new home.

Robert looked at me. "Perhaps I'll build a new farmhouse one day."

"Where would you like it to be?" I asked eagerly, thinking it would be over by his people at Shiskine.

"Oh, I don't know," he laughed, "perhaps I will just spin the globe and see where my finger lands."

We took the cart over to Balnacraivie and I helped him with the lambing and then ate my evening meal with the family. I remember that his brothers teased him gently about our romance until his father tapped his finger on the table. "That's enough now," he said, lifting his eyebrows. "Haud yer wheesht, and leave the poor boy alone."

By the time Robert brought me back home the light had faded and the moon, hanging high in the sky, illuminated the road in front of us with a bright white light. That night, in the midst of all the teasing and merriment, or perhaps because of it, I think I realised that this was the man I wanted to marry, and although it was as yet unspoken, he wanted to marry me. I walked up the garden, as if on air, and saw Mother's silhouette bent over the flickering light of the oil lamp in the parlour, her sewing in her hand, and my heart leapt at the sight of her, so stoic, and strong. When I entered the room she barely raised her head. "Well, Elizabeth," she said quietly, "you'd better pray there isn't another war."

100

At that moment I wanted to take her pale, blue-veined hands in mine and comfort her, and ask her about my father. Had she felt the same joy in meeting him that I felt in my heart for Robert? Did she too have that certainty? But I lacked the courage to ask, to push aside the barrier she had placed in front of me. Instead I closed the heavy storm doors, heated the kettle on the range to fill the stone pig for her bed, and wrapped her long embroidered flannel nightdress around it. But that night I buried my face in the pillow and cried for her.

Twice a year, on a Saturday, Mother would make the journey to Glasgow to visit a childhood friend who had married and left the island. She always laid out her clothes the night before: her finest silk blouse, on which she pinned her oval gold-edged intaglio brooch, with its fine inverted carving of a woman's head; her dark Donegal tweed skirt and new undergarments, "in case," she said, "the trams are too fast for me and I am flattened. I would want to look my best, after all."

I never liked to hear her worry about her safety and I always made sure I was there to meet her off the last boat, so I could accompany her home on the local bus. By the end of these travelling days she looked so tired and a little grey, but I looked forward to her expeditions nonetheless, because I so rarely had the house to myself.

I was always a dutiful daughter but I had come to resent the way Mother rebuffed me when I asked a question about my father, or a cloud passed over her face at the mention of his name. After all, I was no longer a child and I thought it unfair that she shut me out. There was no one else I could or would talk to because, although Mary was like an aunt to me, a sister to my Mother, I could not speak about my anger to her. It would have been disloyal to Mother, and if she had ever found out, a hurt that I would not have been able to heal. But I felt I was entitled to know more about my father. Although he was her husband, I was their child, and he was my flesh and blood.

Mother's old box, inlaid with mother-of-pearl, was the only thing in the house that was locked. After I waved her off on the bus to Glasgow one Saturday, I returned to the house and stood in front of it, resolved to discover what was so secret that it had to be kept from me. I was sure the little key in the drawer in Mother's bureau would fit the lock. As I tried it I felt faint with terror at the thought of my treachery. It turned easily, and inside, lying on the blue silk lining, was a bundle of flimsy pages tied with a black ribbon. As Saul said, it was a Pandora's box of sorrows.

The letters, from France, written to "My dearest wife, and darling Elizabeth," were written in pencil, in a clear educated hand. He described everything he saw around him, the privations of the French people and his involvement in the heavy fighting, though each letter was written only after his company was pulled back from the line. But as the letters progressed and the weeks turned into months, my father's tone became more urgent. He wrote movingly about the friends he had lost, more than once as they crouched beside him, and about the terrible carnage in the trenches and in the fields that stretched to the horizon, though, he said, he could not write about the worst of it. He had not the words, nor did he want to upset us, and perhaps he was mindful of the censor. On page after page I sensed the powerful need to bear witness, the urgency borne of the knowledge that he could die at any moment, and the realisation that war had altered the soul of every single soldier.

Then I read the letter that explained, finally, Mother's bitter anguish, the information that helped me to an understanding of their own conflict, which had all but destroyed her. My father did not have to go to war. As a farmer, he was deemed as valuable at home as he would be at the Front.

> Izzy, my precious wife, can you ever find it in
> your heart to forgive me for leaving you both? It
> preys on me more and more each day I am
> spared. I long to be at home with you and
> Elizabeth, and to try to make up to you for my
> stupid pride. I thought it was shaming to stay on
> the farm when men all around the island were
> enlisting, especially when we were taunted in the
> newspaper for sending horses to the Front from
> Arran and not men. Can you understand that?
> But as this hellish business grinds towards its
> end, we are losing men to not one but two evils,
> the Boche and Spanish flu. And now I hear
> Arran is in the grip of it, so close to my precious
> girls. I pray to God to keep you safe. I am in
> terror that you or Elizabeth will become ill and I

will not be there with you. I live in hope that I will be back at Benkiln before Christmas and I promise you, Izzy, that I will never leave you again.

Your loving husband James.

At the bottom of the bundle there remained a small brown envelope. On it was written, in my mother's spidery hand, just two words — The End — and inside, the short story of my father's death.

Dear Mrs Pringle,

I am filled with deep sorrow for the loss of your brave husband, Sgt J A Pringle. The matron will have written to you telling of his illness. I watched him daily and he was brave in the last fight and gave himself every chance of recovery, but the skill and good nursing did not avail and he passed away on 29 November. Yesterday I conducted his funeral, with sad heart.

I had hoped that my prayers would be answered but God took him to the life beyond. The mystery is great but God is love. Permit me to commend you to his grace and may you find calm in this sorrow, so great, a fountain that brings comfort.

Yours sincerely,

Cpt Fraser Campbell C.7 Company chaplain

My father, James Allan Pringle, had died a victim of the terrible epidemic he feared would strike us, from a virus that claimed more lives than the conflict itself.

The chaplain's letter was dated 2 December 1918, five days before he was due to embark for England, and home. I remember that I sat, the letters on my lap, my face drenched with tears, understanding more about my father than many children would know in a lifetime. I was devastated. It was unbearable to think of him lying alone, in a canvas field hospital, or the echoing classroom of a requisitioned school, so far away, without us. In his delirium did he call for us, or clutch at a nurse, mistaking her for his wife, and ask for her forgiveness, my father who manned the guns week after week month after month, with death his constant companion? And had she known how hellish it was for him, beyond his description, would my mother have forgiven him? I would never know. As I held the letters in my hand I imagined taking his side in an argument with my mother, but I knew that, in reality, I could never cause her that much pain.

I had not foreseen how much I was to be affected by the knowledge of their estrangement; and that I had found out the truth only by prying, made it impossible to talk to her directly. Instead, in the weeks that followed, I tried to be by her side as much as I could, silently willing her to talk to me about the past. I suggested a walk to Benkiln. "Shall we see how the oak is doing that Daddy planted on my first birthday?" I asked gently.

"You go if you want to, Elizabeth. I am content it will be growing just fine."

"But Benkiln was where we were all together, once," I ventured in a wheedling voice that made me wince inwardly. As I thought, its only effect was to irritate.

"No, Elizabeth. I have no interest in going back," she said flatly. "Please, do not ask me again."

MARTHA

Once Saul had disappeared along the road the two women sat in the sunshine on an old patchwork quilt Martha had found in a cupboard.

"I'm going to Edinburgh to pack up the flat and rent it out for a while. It'll feel good," Martha said emphatically.

Catriona squinted at her. "So you live on your own?"

Martha nodded. "Thank god. Less to disentangle," she laughed weakly. Catriona raised a questioning eyebrow. "There was someone, but it was just a three-act tragedy: swept off my feet, a bumpy ride, then crashed to earth in a lucky escape."

"Heart broken?"

"No, just a mixture of bruised and relieved, really. He was another journalist. Always a bad idea."

They sat in silence for a moment, each woman aware that they were at the point early in adult acquaintance when there is an expectation of a back story, a divulgence of crucial details which will either propel a friendship forward, or kill it stone dead. Martha certainly didn't want to give the impression she had ever been needy and pathetic or, most of all, a poor judge of character.

Catriona looked at her in anticipation.

"He started well. He was smart, witty, we both loved going to the same films, he appreciated art and he was hugely attentive. Ticked lots of boxes. I was flattered . . . And he was a bit madcap."

"How madcap?"

"Well . . . like this. Soon after we started seeing each other he told me he was taking me to the beach. I assumed it would be to Gullane or somewhere else nearby, but he arrived at the flat in an ancient open-top sports car he'd hired, handed me an old pair of goggles, and the next thing I know we're racing through Glencoe and all the way to Morar."

"Sounds pretty exciting to me," laughed Catriona.

"I suppose it was," said Martha, "the Harvey Nichols hamper, the champagne, the tent on the beach. But after a while it dawned on me that he was only happy when he was in total control."

She fell into silence, stroking the Missoni scarf round her neck that Anna had given her for her thirtieth birthday, hoping that this thumbnail sketch would satisfy Catriona, at least for now.

"Well," she responded, alert to Martha's reticence, "I have news. I might have found someone to look after your mum."

"What? Really?" Martha straightened up, fully back in the present.

"Her name is Beatrycze Starecki, but she goes by Bea," Catriona went on. "She came here from Poland with her son and daughter-in-law and their two children. He's a carpenter, plasterer, everything, really.

They love it here, but she finds it too quiet. She helps me in the hotel sometimes, but I thought of her because she's a trained nurse—"

Martha broke in, "Have you mentioned Mum to her?"

Catriona flushed a little. "I'm sorry, I might have overstepped the mark," she breathed in nervously, "but yes, I have."

"It's fine, it's more than fine," said Martha eagerly, her mind skipping ahead. "What did she say?"

Catriona relaxed. "She's very interested."

Martha sat back on her heels. "I can't quite believe it. You are amazing. I've known you for five minutes and . . . you're my good fairy."

Warmed by the compliment, Catriona threw her hands out and lifted her shoulders. "But it would be good for Bea, too."

Martha laughed. "OK, so you're *her* good fairy as well!"

Catriona asked more tentatively if Martha could be sure her mother would accept a stranger in her home, but Martha was now in no mood for doubts. She shook her head. "Look, she might not even know *me* in the future. It's worth trying it, just to get her out of that locked ward and back home with her own life round about her."

Barely an hour later Bea Starecki knocked gently on the door at Holmlea, a hazy still figure behind the etched glass. Even as Martha welcomed her in she had her marked down as her saviour, and minutes later she was certain of it.

Bea was a slight woman with short grey wavy hair, an open friendly face and soft laughter lines around her eyes.

"Thank you for coming straight away," Martha said warmly as they shook hands.

"I'd like to be a help if I can," Bea replied, her English accented with a Scottish burr, "and I think you already know from Catriona, you would be helping me, too."

They sat together in the garden, sipping tea from pretty cups patterned with forget-me-nots. Bea explained that she had been a nurse at one of the hospitals of the Medical University of Lodz for many years, and it had been a wrench to leave her job, and the city. She smoothed her hands down over her skirt and then looked at Martha. "Of course, I wanted to be near my grandchildren. What grandmother doesn't? But they are so happy and settled here, and so busy. They don't need me all the time, and I . . . Well, I need something more." Bea paused. "Perhaps that sounds a little selfish, no?"

"Not at all, "Martha said quickly. "You're just being honest."

Encouraged, Bea went on. "I mean, I think I still have some life yet to live. I'm fit and I am interested in the world."

"But wouldn't you feel as trapped with my mother as you feel on Arran? She can be just like a child. I mean, she can be irrational and unpredictable."

Bea shrugged. "Aren't we all sometimes?" She took a sip of her tea. "No, we would have a bargain. That's

110

how I see it. I would keep your mother safe, and she could show me Glasgow."

"Are you sure?" Martha looked at Bea gratefully.

"We can only try, no?" Bea stretched over and put her hand on Martha's. "It is a hard thing for a daughter, to see her mother vanishing before her eyes."

Martha thought about Susie, who was not witness to the small daily disappearances of Anna's old self. "I'll need to let my sister, Susie, who's in Copenhagen, know that you're coming to stay. But this is my decision," she added emphatically.

"It sounds as if you are, how do you say it? Carrying the weight on your shoulders."

"It's not Susie's fault," she said momentarily defensive. "Copenhagen's the best place for her to be just now."

Bea studied Martha's face and smiled a little, her eyes soft. "Ah, well then, it's the way it has to be."

The two women had made the pretence of a simple transaction but both knew it was freighted with much more, a guarantee of Martha's freedom as much as Anna's safekeeping.

After Bea left to tell her family her news, Martha sat down at the walnut bureau. On the wall above it was a print of a work by William Blake, a macabre ink drawing of a woman stooping under a willow tree to lift a baby from the ground. Martha shivered. Blake, she thought, was an acquired taste. Underneath the drawing the artist had written, "I found him beneath a Tree," and below that, "Published in May 1793 by W. Blake."

111

She opened the desk top and rested it on the supports that glided out easily from each side of the bureau. The compartments were crammed with cuttings from gardening magazines. She picked up one and felt a frisson of excitement as she recognised Niall's scribbled handwriting at the edge of the frayed page. "Look at this. I was on that very mountainside." An arrow pointed to a story about botanists in Edinburgh who were attempting to save a rare rhododendron tuhanensis, which grew on just one site on the slopes of Mount Kinabalu in Malaysia. Martha looked through empty seed packets bunched together with a rubber band, each marked with the years they were planted. On some Elizabeth Pringle had written, "successful", "too short a flowering season", or "colour not as intense as I expected."

In another compartment was a small tray of assorted silver thimbles of various sizes, some dented, and one so worn there was a hole in the top. There were postcards of paintings by Ingres and Titian, and one by Mark Rothko, intense dark brown blocks of colour that bled into a magenta background. On the back was a message. "Dear Elizabeth, this is the Rothko I mentioned. Good for the soul. See you Thursday, Saul."

Martha studied the card. She felt irrationally excluded from the closeness that had existed between the Buddhist and Elizabeth Pringle. She returned the postcard to the compartment and picked up a little cardboard book on which was attached a colourful series of Player's Number Six cigarette cards depicting garden flowers, slotted into their allotted spaces. The book had obscured a little drawer in the centre of the desk. Martha opened it and found two keys, one larger and cruder than the other, a rose gold wedding band and a diamond ring, all threaded together on a velvet ribbon and lying on an old brown envelope.

Martha examined the ring. There were three diamonds in a traditional yellow gold setting, and as she moved it between her fingers the stones glittered brightly, released from their dark resting place. She looked closely at the engraving on the inside of the band. The lettering was fresh and clear, "RS and EMP 27 March 1932". Just for a moment she considered untying the ring and putting it on her finger but suddenly, imagining Niall's appalled, penetrating gaze, she thought better of it and put the ring and keys to one side. Instead, she opened the envelope and took out a ticket for passage by boat from Greenock to Fremantle, Western Australia, on 1 October 1933. It had never been stamped.

ELIZABETH

I do not know whether Saul will read these pages when I am dead. They may be of little interest to anyone but me, and certainly not to anyone at Balnacraivie. So it will be, as Saul says, a way of clearing my path ahead, and that will be enough. I think now that we have been on a journey, he and I, one I doubt I would ever have undertaken by myself. From the beginning our conversations were unlike any I'd ever had. Not long after he helped me collect my scattered pine cones that first day, when I next crossed to Holy Isle to walk to the lighthouse, I left an old book on the rock whitebeam at the Buddhist Centre in an envelope marked for him, though I only knew his first name. The rock beam is a strange native species, surviving with extraordinary determination in rocky inaccessible places, often quite alone. I liked to watch it dancing in the wind, as if it was showing off to the clouds, believing itself unobserved, its lithe sinewy branches waving to and fro to reveal the soft white underside of its leaves.

"How can it live in isolation?" asked Saul, when he came to meet me returning along the path.

114

"Because," I said, "it is apomictic. It can produce a viable seed without the need for sexual exchange."

Saul laughed. "Well then, that gives me hope of a next generation! It seems only right that a Buddhist should take heart from a plant that doesn't rely on sex."

It was too intimate a conversation, but perhaps it was on account of my years, and Saul's directness, that I found it exhilarating. Gradually we talked more and more about ourselves. No one had ever asked me about my life before, and truthfully, had they, I would have thought it an unwanted intrusion. This was altogether unlike my conversations with Niall, who was a different soul, and who, in many ways, reminded me of Robert. But Saul had a curiosity that could not be described as prying or prurient, and I began to look forward to our outings. With Saul I did not feel a dry old stick.

I imagine that people on the island had all sorts of ideas about me, if indeed they gave me more than a passing thought. We must have made an odd sight — companions separated by almost fifty years, an elderly spinster in a tweed skirt and stout shoes and a tall weather-beaten Buddhist in his colourful garments, on occasion carrying a tall shepherd's crook with a fluttering multi-coloured pennant. If we wanted to draw attention to ourselves the flag certainly helped no end, but I thought it would have been impertinent, and even hurtful of me, to ask him to leave it behind.

He told me stories of his old life in New York, the cacophony of sounds, all day and all night, the tide of people from everywhere, washing in and out, and about where he lived, in an area between the skyscrapers and the towers of Mammon, as he described them. He called it the Village, though of course I realised it was nothing like Lamlash. He read me the poetry of Robert Frost and Elizabeth Bishop, and in turn I recited Christina Rossetti.

Fast asleep. Singing birds in their leafy cover
Cannot wake her, nor shake her the gusty blast.
Under the purple thyme and the purple clover
Sleeping at last.

I had the impression that his old life was as chaotic and eventful as mine was ordered and simple, and I like to think that perhaps I helped him towards the calm he was seeking.

One summer's day I took him to the bridge over the Benlester Burn and we stood on the bank where, as a little girl, I would gaze at the old wooden bridge now long gone, replaced by a stronger ugly structure to take the weight of the motorised vehicles. But I described it as it was then, how the water below had made a mirror of the scene, the lines of the wooden railings, the trees blacker than above, and when I threw a stone in the burn it all but disappeared like shattered glass, only to come back into life exactly as before, after a few seconds. I told Saul that as a child I played a game at this spot, in which I had magical powers to change the scene when the water settled, and that, if only for a few minutes, I could bring my father back to stand over me. Saul listened and then thanked me for my story. I found myself telling him that it had been many years since I had shared anything of my inner life. "After all," I reasoned, "what use are my memories except to me."

"No," he replied, "you are wrong, Elizabeth. They can be a gift to someone if they are set free, and something distant and faded can be painted in bright colours again."

"But," I said, "I have memories that can never be set free."

Saul said nothing, but I think that was the moment I knew that somehow he could help me, and in doing so, I would at long last find peace.

Robert and I roamed the island, on foot and by bicycle. We climbed Goatfell and took the well worn path along the ribcage of the Sleeping Warrior, up his chin, along his gnarly nose and over his brow; but there was one place we claimed as our own.

Robert asked me to marry him on Easter Sunday. I was twenty-one, he two years older. We had cycled with a picnic to Whiting Bay to walk to the Falls. I remember there had been days and days of rain, and the burn was in full spate. But that day, the soft wet smirr of the evening before had finally given way to the bright warming sunshine of spring, and amongst the trees the moisture from the ground rose into a faint mist. The sycamores and alders were all in bud, ready to burst out to meet the sun, and the air was a profusion of bees and blue tits. By the path, the dazzling green and lemony moss made a beautiful patterned carpet of the ground. The scent of wild garlic was everywhere, so fresh and alive. Robert sang as we strolled, and now and then, when we could see no other walkers, he would pull me to him by my waist and run his finger down the outline of my neck before inclining his head to kiss my throat in the little indentation where it met my collarbone. He said it was the sweetest spot in the world. I had never felt so exhilarated, so free.

When we came to the soft pink sandstone slabs that crossed the burn on the way up to the Falls, the rushing water roared above us as it foamed and danced, spraying at the edges before it cascaded down the rocks towards us. Our game was to stand, one on each bank of the burn, and shout across, trying to guess what the other was saying. Robert crossed the wet shining stones, which sparkled like black marble amidst the bubbling water, and when he was safely on the other side, he threw his cap into the air. I saw a beautiful shy smile light up his face as he went down on one knee, as if in slow motion, and I watched the shape of his mouth as he spoke the words I could not hear. "Elizabeth, will you marry me?" It was as if he was speaking inside my head and I shouted back as loudly as I could, "Yes! Yes! Yes! I will marry you Robert Stewart."

He ran straight towards me, missing some of the stepping stones in his haste, the water splashing and soaking his clothes, to grab me and kiss my face all over. We held each other so tightly, I thought I would not be able to breathe. I could hardly believe that someone loved me so intensely, so utterly, so overwhelmingly. I cleaved to him as one half of a whole being, as if I had become who I was meant to be. The love I felt for him was so powerful I sobbed with the joy of it, and I have relived that day over and over again, in

118

the deep of the night, feeling him encircle me, when my heart hammers still, and sleep stubbornly refuses to claim me.

"I will ask your mother for your hand," he said, as we lay on the velvety moss, our arms entwined, watching the scudding clouds decorate the blue canopy above us.

As I thought of all the things Mother might say, I felt a dreadful wave of anxiety for both of them. "Of course you must, Robert, but you know she can sometimes be, well, restrained." I did not add, "And I am all she has got, and though she made it her duty to prepare me for marriage, I have no way of knowing what it would do to her to be alone."

He raised himself on one elbow and looked at me gravely as if he had read my mind. "Do you think it will be hard for her to say yes?"

"I don't know, and that is the truth," I said, and a small knot of sadness entered my heart. Had I known the awful tribulations that were to flow from that day, would I have said yes to Robert's marriage proposal? It is something I cannot ever know, even though he is the only man I ever truly loved.

The following Saturday Robert called at the house, freshly shaved and dressed in his Sunday suit, his waistcoat hung with his grandfather's gold fob watch, his brogues polished and his shirt starched. Mother was sewing by the dining room window, and kept to her work as I went to answer the door. Robert asked me if he could speak to her alone and my hand was shaking as I turned the knob on the door and conveyed the request. Her face betrayed no emotion, she simply

119

nodded a little and returned to her needlework. Once he was inside the dining room, she asked Robert to close the door.

I took myself off to the garden, out of sight. I was feeling so faint, I had to lean on the wall of the house for a moment before I busied myself weeding and riddling the rose bed, but no sooner had I scooped earth into the round mesh tray than Robert was at my shoulder, squeezing it gently. "Elizabeth, we have her blessing. We are to be married."

I hardly even looked at him before I ran to the house and found Mother in her bedroom, sitting on the edge of the brass bed, her eyes gazing downwards at her hands, which were clasped tightly on her lap. She looked up at me through a film of tears and I fell down in front of her, grasping her hands.

"Well, Elizabeth, you are to be a wife and, I pray, one day, a mother too." She stroked my hair and I could feel her hand trembling as she moved it rhythmically over my head, as though she were intent on making a permanent mark, a memory for us both.

"There will be much to do," she said in a quiet steady voice. "We'll ask Mary to help us, shall we?"

She set me back, went over to her wardrobe, and opened the bottom drawer. She took out a prettily patterned cardboard box that I had never seen before, and handed it to me. "I would like you to wear this," she said softly. I opened the box carefully and fingered the delicate oyster-coloured lace. On it was embroidered tiny flowers, and the border was worked in entwined ivy. It was her wedding veil. I put my arms around her and felt all her frailty and bitterness and unfulfilled dreams. It was as if she might collapse in on herself at any moment, and I was suddenly terrified that I might lose her.

"Mother, it is so beautiful, and I am so honoured." It came to me suddenly. "And you will be by my side when I walk down the aisle wearing it."

She put her hand on my arm, at first gently, and then when I saw a dark shadow cross her face she became agitated. "Elizabeth, I know it has sometimes been hard, with just the two of us."

"No," I interrupted, fearing what she might say. "You are everything to me. You have made me strong."

"It was all I could do for you." She faltered. "It was all I was capable of." She put her hand on mine. "But now you deserve to be happy."

MARTHA

Martha arrived at the shiny black door of her tenement in the Grassmarket. She had always thought herself lucky to live there. The New Town was elegant and ordered, with its airy, expansive Georgian streets and tall, small-paned sash windows, but the buildings of the Old Town, the vennels and the wynds, reeked of history, tumult and secrets. It thrilled her that she might be walking in the steps of Daniel Defoe, who frequented the capital in the months before the Union, and was rumoured to be a spy for the Crown, sniffing out Jacobite dissent. Her favourite Sunday walk took her down the Royal Mile, past the kirk of the Canongate to the elegant proportions of the magnificent Renaissance Palace of Holyrood, and facing it, the new Parliament. But now she felt as if she was in Edinburgh by stealth, eager to pack up and be gone from the city she once loved, before she encountered any of the curious and concerned friends to whom she'd given only scant details of her flight to Arran. She was aware she was relying on the deposits she had made in what they all laughingly called over the years, the Bank of Friendship. As she wound her way up the three flights of turnpike stairs, sixty stone steps that had often been a late at night challenge to Martha and her friends, she thought of the long sessions of wine and music and over-wrought emotions, and she realised that she was escaping that, too. Nor did she want to risk bumping into Andrew, so before she started packing, she texted Tom McMillan. "Hello Tom. I am at the flat. Are you free to meet for a chat? The coffee is on and I would rather not come to the office. Martha x"

"Well, hello stranger," said Tom warmly, as Martha opened the door an hour later. "How is your mum doing?"

"She's OK. I'm going to get her home from hospital soon. I just need to sort a few things out."

Martha looked at Tom's expectant face as she handed him a cup of steaming hot espresso. She had missed his supportive friendly presence in her life, and she was dismayed at how careworn he looked. What she was about to say was certainly not going to make his life any easier.

She sat down across from him and, tightening her hand on her cup, she made her announcement. "If it's still on offer, I'd like to take the redundancy after all."

After a moment of awkward silence, Tom cleared his throat. "I'm sure you're thinking of your mum but . . . Listen, I'm speaking solely as a friend, and please take this as it is intended but, has this got anything to do with Andrew?"

Martha coloured, flustered in spite of herself. "No, actually, it's really not about that. But the fact that he

123

will be completely out of my life is certainly an added bonus."

Tom leaned in to play his ace. "So the fact that he's moving south to the *Daily Sketch* won't change your mind?"

"Really? That's great news, Tom, but . . ." She shook her head. "But hey, the paper will be a happier place."

"I gave him a glowing reference."

"He's a pretty good journalist underneath it all, but, really, not even a health warning?"

Tom shook his head slowly. "Not a chance. The editor's an adulterous bastard who used to be married to my sister. He deserves what's coming to him, or I should say, who's coming to him."

Martha laughed. "I'm going to miss you, Tom. You are a lovely, lovely man."

Now it was Tom's turn to blush. "Ha! Tell that to the trees! Well, I'll be coming to you for features once your redundancy deal plays out. I still want to see your name in the paper. And I bet you won't lose your thirst for it altogether."

They talked for a while. Martha sketched out Elizabeth Pringle's strange bequest and Tom told her about his wife's elevation to the Bench, warm pride in his voice. Then, when he could no longer ignore the insistent ping of his phone alerting him to emails, he reluctantly said goodbye. "I hope you'll write about it all one day."

"Maybe." Martha smiled.

"Oh, and let me know when you're ready for the McMillan clan to descend on you."

124

"Definitely," she laughed.

Once Tom had left, Martha filled two suitcases, took her laptop, a selection of CDs, her Craigie Aitchison print, her two paintings by Dorothy Johnstone, some comfort reading and consigned the rest of her possessions to a locked cupboard. She would collect the rest when the rental agency found her a tenant.

Her glance fell on the pots of long dead herbs on the windowsill, and she thought of Niall's unnerving gaze. She realised that she found his reserve both alluring and irritating. She hated people to think ill of her and had an almost pathological need to please, but she could tell that she liked this man. It wasn't just that she needed him to like her. Martha felt dread, as well as excitement. What if she made a fool of herself. Again? The emotional damage wouldn't be so easy to repair a second time.

Being back in her flat, it was impossible not to remember Andrew. Her thoughts returned to the night of her birthday, six months before. Their relationship was creaking and cranky, not least because of Andrew's betrayal of a source on an investigative story, which put a prostitute's life in danger; but he'd offered to make her a special dinner. She'd declined in favour of a visit home to see Anna but, on the last train back to Edinburgh, feeling remorse at her lack of grace, she dialled his flat in Cumberland Street.

As soon as he answered, she knew something was wrong.

"I wasn't expecting you to call so late," he said, abruptly.

"I know, but you're a night owl, and I thought I might come over," Martha whispered.

She heard the sharp intake of breath. "Actually, I'm really tired and you must be too. I'll see you tomorrow, we can have lunch. OK? Goodnight, Martha."

The line went dead, and in that instant Martha knew that he wasn't alone.

She felt a wave of nausea and all at once her abhorrence of his journalistic methods, her disdain for his arrogance and her belief that she deserved better, dissolved into a pathological fear of rejection. She could analyse it in an instant but she was engulfed by irrationality. She texted her friend Ruth. "You still up, can I call? Mx"

Immediately her mobile rang. "What's up? And Happy Birthday, by the way. Are you just back from Glasgow?"

Martha burst into tears. "I'm a fucking idiot. Andrew's shagging someone. I just called him and she's there."

"Bastard, bastard, but Martha, fucksake are you surprised?" Ruth listened for a response but none was forthcoming. "Sorry, that was a bit harsh."

"You're right. You were all right about him," she sobbed.

"Martha. I know you. You'd better not be thinking of going to his flat. Promise me."

It took all Ruth's powers of persuasion to convince Martha that a showdown at Cumberland Street in the middle of the night would do nothing but demean her, but as Martha lay on her bed fully clothed, watching the little luminous clock count out the slow empty hours, her anger got the better of her. As soon as it was light, she pulled on her boots, gulped a cup of strong coffee and headed for Andrew's flat. She was surprised how many people were on the streets already but she paid them no heed and marched on, driven by a frenzy of outrage and rejection, looking neither left nor right, her hands balled into hard fists in her pockets.

She kept her finger pressed hard on the bell for what seemed to her an age before the door finally opened. Andrew was at first dishevelled and bleary but then, when he focused his half-shut eyes on Martha, his body appeared to succumb to a sudden jolt of electricity.

"Why didn't you buzz me in?" Martha hissed, but before Andrew, rather reeking of alcohol, could say anything, she carried on, her voice rising. "Of course you're not going to buzz me in, are you?"

"Martha, please, we don't have to have a scene."

"Don't patronise me, not on top of everything else. I just wanted to see your face to know what a lying bastard you are, and yes . . . It couldn't be more obvious."

She managed to deliver her short speech without her voice cracking, but as soon as she turned on her heel, tears of rage and humiliation ran down her cheeks. As soon as she was out of sight of Andrew's flat, she stopped and sank down on some cold stone steps, exhausted with the drama of it all. But as she finally composed herself, she managed a weak smile. Perhaps

127

such a tawdry end to a malignant sort of affair was fitting.

Bouquets of red roses kept coming, and with them endless apologies and the explanation of an ex-girlfriend unexpectedly in town for the night. Martha ignored it all, and slowly and finally, the hurt turned into a kind of weary relief.

She sighed as she looked round the flat that she loved. The Georgian table she had painstakingly restored; the verdigris art deco mirror, the last lot in an auction when the dealers had long gone; the Orkney wicker chair she'd found in a skip. They would be fine without her.

As she struggled down to the car with her suitcases and boxes, she thought about all the people who had worn down the stone in the deep stairwell; more than two centuries of sad leave-takings, drunken tumblings and the skipping steps of children. She listened to her own echoing footfall as she added her swift steps to the tread of all the others who had moved on.

It was early evening before she arrived back at Holmlea. Her heart lurched when she saw Niall in the garden, his back to her, oblivious to her arrival as he pushed the lawnmower up the slope, the grinding clatter of its motor drowning out the car engine and her shouted "hello". She touched his sleeve and he whirled round, startled, and yanked the mower to a halt. They stood in the cavernous space of the sudden silence, and Niall's annoyance at being caught unawares oscillated around them both.

"I didn't expect to see you here," she said quickly, disconcerted by his closeness, the rise and fall of his chest and the gleam of sweat on his forearms.

"It's spring," he replied, as if no other explanation were needed, before adding, redundantly, "the grass has started growing again."

She just stopped herself from saying, "Do I look stupid?" as she caught the shift from irritation to a faint embarrassment.

"I appreciate you doing this, Niall." She paused as she heard herself enunciate his name. She liked the sound of it, and it suited his singularity, its difference from the more usual "Neil". She looked up at him, shading her eyes from the evening sun with her hand, and said earnestly, "I really will try to get to grips with the garden."

He laughed now at her ridiculous solemnity. "It's fine, honestly. I'm happy to help out, and anyway, from what Catriona's told me, you have a lot on your plate. So if it's all right with you, I'll deal with the garden until you get the house in shape." A shadow crossed his face. "Besides, I like being here, so you'd be doing me a favour."

He stood still, both of them suddenly awkward after the unexpected rush of words, and then Martha seized the moment. "Please, come in for a beer," and she started towards the house before he had a chance to answer. As he followed her, she knew he was studying her as she walked, perhaps watching how her hair revealed the back of her slender neck, or the way her shoulder was exposed when her loose striped tee shirt fell to one side.

"It still has the scent of Miss Pringle, lily of the valley. She always wore it," he said, as he surveyed the hall. "It's strange how it lingers."

"I like it," said Martha, "and anyway it's still her house, and it always will be, at least to me." She retrieved two beers from the old fridge and handed one to Niall. He smiled and put his bottle to hers, clinking them gently. "To Miss Pringle." He gestured towards the living room. "May I?"

"Of course, please. You don't need to ask."

He looked around the room and then turned to Martha. "You haven't changed anything at all," he said, surprise in his voice.

"I'm not sure where to begin, and I feel as if I am just starting to get to know her. I mean, obviously I'll never know her, but everything in here helps a little . . ." Martha stopped mid sentence. "Does that make any sense?"

"What would you like to know about her?"

Niall looked at her directly and Martha suddenly felt the sensation of emotional vertigo. She feverishly tried to calculate the right tone, her anxiousness not to upset or offend him compounded by the fact that it was dawning on her that she definitely found him utterly overwhelmingly attractive.

"OK. You must have known her well. I mean, you didn't always call her 'Miss Pringle' did you?"

Niall narrowed his eyes, seemingly wondering where this was leading.

"Your postcard was behind the door when I opened the house up. You know, bubblegum-coloured rhododendrons."

"Always the journalist, then, reading other people's mail," he said, teasing her gently, but then he inhaled deeply and his tone became wistful. "Here in the house, with her absent, it seems a bit disrespectful but yes, I did call her Elizabeth, eventually. Though I'm sure Saul called her by her first name right from the moment he met her," he added, his voice hardening a little.

Martha tried to give the impression that she hadn't noticed the barb. "Another beer? Or would you like tea? I mean because you're driving."

Niall smiled. "I think I can work out my limit all on my own, but thanks, tea would be good."

They wandered into the kitchen. "I'm sure I can find some Earl Grey or something."

"Actually, Elizabeth always drank Lapsang Souchong. She said she used to drink it with the Duchess of Hamilton. There's probably still some here." He pulled down an old tea caddy from the shelf and opened it. "It's full," he said, surprised, and bending his nose towards it he exclaimed, "and fresh! We should have some."

He looked over to the elderly gas cooker on which Martha had put an even more ancient kettle. "I don't really think Elizabeth would expect you to hang on to everything. Certainly not that cooker," he grimaced.

131

Martha grinned at him. "If you think that's bad, take a look at the Calor gas bottle. It's almost an antique."

"I'll disconnect it for you. You don't want to blow up the house as soon as you've found it."

Finally, their mundane exchange had calmed the static that had crackled around them since Martha had opened the front door.

Niall sat down at the table and Martha poured the fragrant tea.

"We always sat in here," he said, as he clasped his long strong fingers around the bone china cup. "I used to think of it as her classroom. Elizabeth was an amazing teacher." He absent-mindedly ran his hand across the wooden table, before his eyes came to rest on Saul's note.

Martha picked it up and offered it to him. "Read it if you like. He wants to meet."

Niall put his hands up in protest. "It's none of my business. Saul's a bit of an operator, that's all. For a while I wondered if he had plans of his own for the house."

He registered the shock on her face. "Sorry, I've no right to say that, and I've got no evidence either. Saul *was* good to Elizabeth, and I was glad he was around when I was away. Just before I left I noticed she was getting much frailer, though she tried to hide it." He shook his head. "I even caught her chopping wood out the back, the day before I left."

"And she must have carried coal in before she died," added Martha, "because the fire has been set."

Niall drained his cup. "She knew somebody would come. Anyway, you should see Saul. He'll have a story or two for you, I'm sure. He gets about, notices everything."

Martha detected his faintly sarcastic tone. "Oh, I'm sure. And what about you?" she parried. "What do you look at from your big glass window?"

Niall's grey eyes drilled into her and he said without smiling, "Curiosity killed the cat."

Martha flushed. It was one thing for Niall and Catriona to discuss her, but quite another for her to have been caught gleaning information about him from his sister.

"Come over and see for yourself sometime," he said evenly, as he scraped back his chair.

"I'd like that," Martha replied, and the air became strangely still. She stood up to face him, awkwardly, as if an interview had just ended, and abruptly she swept her arm round the room. "If I can renovate in here, and get the structural work done, and the heating installed, I can move in. Then I can get to know Elizabeth Pringle better."

They walked around downstairs as she sketched out her ideas, her pulse slowly settling. "If I knock down the wall to the dining room here, and put a range cooker here, and make this side window a glass door, I'll flood the place with light."

He took her pad from her, their fingers touching momentarily as she handed him her pencil, and began to draw a different plan, a better one, opening up the back of the house, too. His brows were furrowed in concentration as he deftly produced a three-dimensional blueprint, almost to scale, marking the new apertures.

She watched him shade different areas, wielding the pencil like a draughtsman, until the image of Holmlea was complete. "Something like this," he said casually, handing her the drawing. Martha laughed. "*Exactly* like this. Maybe you should have been an architect."

"Actually, I like what I do," he said, folding his arms.

"I'm sorry," said Martha, thrusting her hands into her jeans pockets, a perplexed look on her face, "I only meant it as a compliment."

They stood looking at each other for a moment, trying to calibrate the conversation. Niall was first to speak, his tone friendlier now. "I thought about it for a while. In fact, I applied to the Mac in Glasgow and got in, but horticulture is endlessly fascinating. And I'm better outdoors and in all weathers, sometimes the worse the weather, the more exhilarating I find it. Anyway, architecture requires a patience I don't think I have."

"But you helped Catriona with the plans for the hotel."

Niall's face tightened and he looked away. "No, that was someone else."

Martha automatically opened her mouth to ask who, but sensing danger, she quickly changed tack. "Look in here."

She opened the dining room door, Niall at her back. The mahogany table and ornate sideboard were covered in a pall of dust and the windows were framed by heavy brocade curtains, once a rich green but now faded and tired, as if worn out by years of holding the world at bay.

"I've never been in here before. I can't really imagine Elizabeth in this room, it's all too gloomy," Niall exclaimed.

Martha nodded. "I don't want any of this stuff. It's so ugly and oppressive. I want it white and light."

Niall murmured in agreement and bent down in front of a small bookcase filled with children's books, their titles etched in dark ink: *The Adventures of Tom Sawyer*, *The Secret Garden*, *Robinson Crusoe*, *Little Women*. Martha looked over his shoulder. "It's a perfect selection, isn't it?"

Niall pulled out a little book, and as he opened it two cards fell out on the floor. "*The Tale of Samuel Whiskers*. Amazing. It's a first edition," he said, flicking through the pages.

Martha picked up one of the cards. It was a sepia photograph of an older woman dressed in black, wearing a large hat and framed in a doorway under a wooden fretwork lintel. "Miss Beatrix Potter" read the caption.

She turned the card over and read aloud, "Dear Miss Pringle, how lovely of you to write to tell me about the joy my characters are giving your pupils. Please accept this copy of *Samuel Whiskers* in gratitude, Yours Beatrix Potter, August 1936."

But Niall's attention was focused on the other card. "How strange is this? I have never seen any photographs of Elizabeth but I'm sure this is her."

Martha looked at the technicolour photograph and saw a tanned woman, perhaps in her early forties, her dark wavy hair held back from her face with a broad red Alice band. She was wearing a floral dress, its full skirt cinched at the waist, and she was leaning back on a stone wall, smiling at the camera. Each arm was round a child sitting perched on top of the wall and they were all squinting into the sun, the girl in a yellow ruched swimsuit, her short hair held to the side with a clasp, and the boy, almost as tall but younger, in an open-necked Aertex shirt and striped shorts.

Martha turned the picture over. The inscription was in a fine hand: "Brodick, July 1955, with Esme and Peter." She felt a sudden panic. "The lawyer insisted there was no family, no one else. Maybe he made a mistake after all?"

Niall assured her he'd never heard Elizabeth mention either name. "Maybe they were friends' children. She must have known all sorts of people over the years."

"I suppose so." Martha knew she didn't sound convinced.

"Look," said Niall, an idea slowly forming, "maybe there's someone who could reassure you. The volunteer organiser at the Castle is getting on a bit. Why don't I ask if the names mean anything to him?"

Martha looked at him doubtfully. "Are you really sure you want to get involved?"

"Involved in what?" he said, a little sharply, "it's hardly investigative journalism."

Martha smarted for a moment and then rallied. "Well, talking of that, there's something I want you to see."

She ran upstairs and unhooked the frame from the wall and as she came back down, she was aware that Niall had moved to the foot of the stairs and was watching her intently. She handed him the picture. "Isn't she a handsome woman?"

Niall held the painting in front of him at arm's length and nodded. "Very. Do you know who she is?"

"I thought you might recognise her."

He shook his head slowly. "It's not Elizabeth. The features are too sharp and there's a hardness about her gaze that I don't recognise."

"So who could it be?"

"Sometimes things have to stay unexplained; maybe she'll just be an enigma." He laughed sardonically. "Could you cope with that?"

Martha stared at the painting. "Probably not. I suppose I just want it all to fall into place, and quickly. But then, impatience is one of my many failings."

"Some people might find that endearing," he said, his eyes fixed on the portrait.

Damn it, thought Martha, there he goes again, but before she could work out whether he was making fun of her, he was gone.

Martha sat on the stairs spooling back through the previous hour, summoning up Niall's expressions, the way he inclined his head towards her, and the creases at the side of his mouth when he broke into a smile. Her emotional compass had proved faulty in the past, but there was no mistaking the force field surrounding them both in the garden, at the table, when their heads almost touched as they bent over her sketches. She could have reached out and touched it.

It was almost dark when she retrieved Saul's note from the kitchen table and set it under the stone by the gate, before walking back in the twilight to the Glenburn.

ELIZABETH

Robert gave me his grandmother's diamond ring, freshly engraved. Knowing it had been hers made it all the more special, not to say unusual, for back in his grandparents' day not every bride-to-be received an engagement ring. When school returned after Easter, I set off on the walk to Brodick, turning my hand now and then to catch the glint of the beautiful stones. Soon everyone would know we were to be married.

I caught Currie's Albion bus outside Brodick Post Office as usual, and at the next stop, Patricia Anderson, who taught Latin to the older children, waved her greeting and sat down beside me. Before we had even turned onto the String Road she exclaimed loudly, "Elizabeth Pringle, look at your hand!" as if the presence of the glittering ring would come as much of a surprise to me as it obviously did to her.

Patricia Anderson was a clever woman. She had been on the suffragette marches in Glasgow, and in her middle years appeared to be content to remain unwed. By all accounts she was an excellent teacher, and on many weary journeys home she would complain bitterly that her salary was less than that of Mr Picken, who taught navigation. Mother said that Patricia Anderson had nothing to worry about because her late father was a doctor and she had a wheen of money.

"The children will miss you," she said, startling me, and in a tone that implied I was letting them down. It had not occurred to me that I would have to give up the classroom, but of course it would be expected of me by Mother, and Robert, too. "I expect you'll get Mrs Croft at Shedock to make your dress. Her twins Donald and Bella are my best pupils, not yet twelve and they can recite Virgil. You can walk up from the school at lunchtime for your fittings."

"No, Mrs Croft won't be making my dress. Mother says she will send a note to Copelands with my measurements, and they will send me dresses to try."

"This'll be the duchess's doing, I suppose?"

I was too taken up with happiness to rise to her poisonous bait. I simply smiled at her, which I suppose maddened her all the more, and squinted out of the window at the steep tawny hillside in search of a roe deer grazing on the new heather or a hawk rising on the thermals into the sky.

The bus often travelled too quickly for me to take in all that I could see, but then sometimes I felt the same when I travelled by bicycle. I kept an inventory of the island in my head: the day the linden tree at the foot of Glen Rosa unfurled its first leaf in the spring sunshine; the perfect squared-off edges of the high copper beech hedge at the Castle, when the gardeners trimmed it on the last Friday in the month; the moment the sun sat high enough in the evening to cast a halo around Holy Isle.

Shiskine School was quite modern, a little over thirty years old, a solid red sandstone building with tall windows and polished wooden floors; and in 1932, it was packed to the gunnels. After the war two of the big farms, Balnacoole and Shedock had been turned into smallholdings for the returning men, and the villages of Shiskine and Blackwaterfoot became almost as busy as Brodick.

I can still see the two classrooms, the little wooden desks perfectly regimented so every child knew his place. I never cared to put the brightest at the back and the slowest at the front. I devised my own alphabetical system, and although I never commented upon it, I am certain that children knew we were being subversive, and kept it to themselves.

It was the time of the school year when the classroom walls were festooned with papier mâché Easter bonnets decorated with brightly coloured tissue paper. A basket of eggs we had dipped in dye and then painted, sat on my desk. That day when I set aside the basket and opened the lid to retrieve the register, I heard some of the girls whispering and giggling. "Wheesht, children, there will be time for talk in a moment."

I used my firm voice. I doubt I ever sounded very stern, but I never had any need of the long heavy tawse, its leather as rough as a cow's thick tongue, which lay beside the register in the dark of my desk. And unlike the other teachers, who looked at me in dismay and

141

irritation when I told them, I encouraged my children to speak up with their news at the start of the day.

I had forty children in my class. The youngest, Jessie Lyons, was a bonnie wee thing, just five years old, who came to school in her sister's hand-me-down black lacing boots which she skliffed and stamped along the wooden floor to keep from walking out of them. The oldest, John Murchie, a sturdy handsome boy, was eight.

John's hand shot up first. "Miss Pringle, the Dasher's arriving with a special cargo of pipes today and I have to help my father load potatoes for the return. Can I leave an hour before the bell?"

The instant I nodded my head, Jane McNicol from Balnacoole ventured shyly, "Don't you have news yourself, Miss?"

"I have," I replied. "The daffodils are out in our garden this morning. They are a beautiful sight and as Mr Wordsworth said, they flutter and dance in the breeze."

The children looked puzzled, and then there was laughter.

"Yes, Jane, I am to be married, but not until autumn next year so I will be your teacher for a while yet."

The older children started off the clapping and then Jessie put her hand up. "Do you think someone will give me a ring like that when I'm grown up?"

"I think someone might, Jessie."

"I hope so, Miss. I've never seen a ring as fancy as that before."

Happy as I was to be betrothed, I dreaded an inquisition by the other staff as much as I delighted in Jessie's innocent questions. When I shooed the children outside to eat their pieces and drink their milk, I walked along the road to a copse of trees and unpacked the lunch that Mother prepared for me every morning and parcelled up in a brown paper bag. She loved to make Irish soda bread and often buttered two slices together, with a hardboiled egg and perhaps a biscuit in a greaseproof wrapper, or if it was the season, an apple or a pear; and always, a flask of tea. She never forgot to put a freshly laundered napkin embroidered with my initials in the bottom of the bag.

In the afternoons I practised arithmetical tables with the children, and whilst the youngest recited their two and three times tables in one group, the older ones I put to the other side of the classroom to tackle the bigger numbers. Forty children repeating their numbers in their lilting Highland accents was a bewildering sound, more akin to a religious chanting than a mathematical exercise, especially when each group tried to outdo the other. The children were always very attentive and still at story time, and that day I remember I chose one of Aesop's stories, "The Dog and the Shadow". It was one I liked especially. A dog was carrying a piece of meat in his mouth and as he jumped onto a plank that spanned the river he looked down into the water and saw another dog with a bigger piece of meat. So he dropped his piece of meat in order to bite the other, and in so doing, he lost his dinner, teaching us that when we are blessed with good things

143

we should be content, rather than greedy for more. I liked to watch their faces as I told the story, and wait for their questions.

"Miss, why didn't the dog recognise itself in the reflection?" asked Betty.

"Now, I wonder," I would say, making great play of searching my brain for an answer. "Dogs do not have the same power of understanding that we humans have."

"But, Miss, Whisky our sheepdog knows the old ewe who's lame," said Malcolm emphatically, "and he runs to my granny when she comes, to get a sweetie. So they do know who's who."

I thrilled at that sort of conversation, when the children cross-examined me. "The dog," I said, "does not understand the idea of a mirror." I explained that it was the moral of the story that was important — to be happy with your lot — but I didn't tell the children that I did not always believe it.

Malcolm said he was going to go home and conduct an experiment with Whisky and the hand mirror his mother kept in her room, and in the morning he would tell us what happened.

Saul says I have to remember myself as I was at that time, and not the more measured person I seem to have become. I do not think that I was ever given to skittishness but, in the weeks that followed our engagement, I ricocheted between elation and anxiety.

I recall a visit I made to Mary that November. I remember we were served tea by her new maid, Lorna

Murray, a girl with whom I had unhappily shared a double desk for a year before she left at the age of fourteen. She thought I was a snob and I wrongly accused her of stealing my favourite marble. When I found it in a crevice inside my desk I apologised, but the damage was done. As she put down the tray on the low inlaid table in front of the roaring fire, she steadfastly ignored me.

When she left the room, Mary leant over and squeezed my hand. "You have a glow about you, Elizabeth, but your eyes tell another story. So tell me, what's wrong?"

Robert and I were to move to Kildonan after our marriage. Had Robert's brother been able to share the farm with him, he would have done so gladly, but there was not enough yield from the land to keep two families and provide care for Ian besides. Instead Robert was to take over Auchindrain, a small dairy farm round at Kildonan, after a promise had been made to his father by an elderly bachelor cousin. But it was a good nine miles from Lamlash.

My worries spilled out in a rush. "What if being a new wife and the farm work leave me no time to visit Mother? It's more than an hour's cycle ride, and almost as long on the bus. And what if she will not travel to see me? I have been with her every single day of my life."

"My dear, it's not so far, and if you think of it you could have been with Robert's people away over at Shiskine, had the circumstances been different." She looked at me closely. "Elizabeth, I have known you since you were smaller than the gatepost, there's

145

something else. I know you are worried about Izzy, but that's not what this is about, is it?"

It was true. From the moment that I had allowed myself to think that Robert and I might have a future together, long before our engagement, bitter thoughts had crept into my heart. I nursed them and felt sickened by them in turn, but I could not banish them, and now I said what I had come to say.

"If Mother had not sold the farm, if she had kept it going for my sake, Robert and I would have lived there. It would have been mine, and he could have worked it just like Daddy did when he married Mother. We would have stayed here in Lamlash, and Mother with us." These were spiked words, laced with anger and hurt.

Mary sat quietly as I tried to compose myself. Even when I had talked to Robert about the farm my great-grandfather began, and the solid handsome farmhouse and steadings he built, I was careful not to blame Mother but rather to excuse her. He knew how torn I was, but he also knew I would never be disrespectful towards her. "It was hard for her, Elizabeth," he said reasonably. "She would have had to employ someone for the rest of her days, and how was she to know you would become a farmer's wife?"

But Mary knew something more.

"Please tell me why Mother won't talk about Benkiln. She won't even walk by it, though I've begged her time after time."

Mary sighed and looked at me imploringly. "Perhaps her memories have always been too upsetting. Perhaps

146

she was afraid that if she confronted them, she wouldn't be able to parcel them up again."

She paused and, deep in thought, put her hand gently over her mouth, before returning it to clasp the other in her lap. "She told me she would never speak ill of your father to you, Elizabeth, but when he went to war, when he could have stayed on the farm and there would have been no shame in it, she felt abandoned."

"But he was so brave! He did the harder thing and went to fight for his country . . . and died for it." My voice quavered.

"Yes, he *was* so brave, but Izzy was bereft." Mary hesitated for a moment. I had put her in the invidious position of having to decide whether to tell me everything, or to keep her friend's confidences. "Your father, for his own good reasons, ignored your mother's pleading, but then something else happened. He left his regiment to enlist in the new machine-gun corps, and she was devastated all over again."

"But why?"

"Because the Germans turned all the firepower they could muster towards the machine-gunners."

"But that's not what killed him."

"No," she said, looking at me carefully, "it wasn't. He survived the onslaught for all that time, only to have the cruellest death, but your mother believed he was careless of you both, putting himself further in harm's way."

"Did they ever speak about it?"

"Not after he left. How could they? He was so far from home, and he was never granted leave."

I began to sob quietly. I could not help it, as I imagined the father I hardly knew in the hell of the fighting, thinking of us at home, and without the comfort of my mother's blessing. I put my face in my hands and remained there, pressing my forehead hard with my fingers, until Mary leaned over and gently pulled them away.

"Elizabeth, please do not think ill of your mother," she said firmly, "because the longer you keep this knot of anger in your heart, the harder it will be to untie it, and that will be a terrible sadness for you both, and for your life ahead with Robert. Perhaps your mother did not *want* to stay on at Benkiln, did you think of that, my dear?"

In the weeks that followed I tried so very hard to do as Mary said, but the knot only tightened again when Mother's decision to sell Benkiln came back to haunt me.

MARTHA

The next morning Martha woke early and lay for a while, luxuriating, replaying her encounter with Niall, embellishing it a little, giving herself wittier lines, imagining his admiring glances, until she was overcome with the feeling that she had been ridiculous, embarrassingly coquettish even, and that his attention had been simple uncomplicated courtesy.

Suddenly her head was filled with the screeching argument between the gulls and the oystercatchers on the beach below as they engaged in their daily territorial battle. She had an overwhelming desire for the sanctuary of Holmlea and she jumped out of bed and doused herself in the bath for a moment before grabbing the first clothes that came to hand, an old tee shirt and a pair of dark tight jeans and canvas Converse shoes. She left a note for the still sleeping Catriona, picked a banana from the fruit bowl and cycled fast towards Shore Road, breathing in the salty breeze, hoping upon hope that Niall wasn't at that very moment, standing gazing out of his wall of glass.

The first thing Martha did when she arrived at the house was to throw open all the windows, a surprisingly

149

easy task for such old sash and casement frames. She smiled to herself. Elizabeth Pringle had thought of everything. She found a pair of old wooden stepladders in the cupboard under the stairs and, balancing precariously on the top step, she unhooked the heavy brocade curtains in the dining room and dropped them to the floor, one by one, each time sending up a puff of dust. As light flooded into the room, Martha felt elated. She had begun.

Manoeuvring the stepladders out of the dining room into the hall, she knocked the hall table where Niall had left the photograph of Elizabeth and the framed watercolour portrait, sending one fluttering and the other crashing to the floor. They landed side by side, the glass frame miraculously intact, and as she bent down to pick them up it suddenly dawned on her. How could she have missed it before? They were so clearly mother and daughter. Elizabeth had a wide generous smile and high cheekbones, while her mother's mouth was more set, her jaw more determined. But they both had the same poise, the same direct gaze, the same long tilt of the head, these two women who had lived together under this roof.

She looked in the mirror above the table and once again searched her face for the imprint of her own mother, evidence of the genetic thread that linked her with Anna and Susie, and her father. She realised she had never thought of the similarities between herself and her sister, only their differences. But when she looked hard, the likeness was there, the same high forehead, the strong arched eyebrows. Then there were the mannerisms, the way they both pushed their hair out of their eyes and screwed up their noses when they concentrated.

Had she thought more about what connected her to her sister rather than all the traits that divided them, had she been more generous towards Susie, would their relationship have been less brittle, less fraught? Susie believed that Anna had given Martha the lion's share of her attention, an accusation Martha had repeatedly dismissed, often with a sigh of frustration, but perhaps Susie had been right?

Martha straightened her shoulders and pursed her lips in the mirror. She would call her soon. She had put off telling her about Holmlea for too long, and now there was the presence of Bea Starecki to explain, too. If she were honest, in neither decision had she considered her mother's other daughter.

She was startled by the tinny sound of the old bell pull. She opened the front door to find a tall figure backlit by the soft glow of the morning sun. "Hello, are you Saul?" she said, blinking against the light.

"Unless you know any other Buddhists on Arran, then yes . . . I guess I'm your man."

Martha smiled and waved him into the house. As he passed her she noticed that the long robes enclosed a tall wiry frame. She was startled by his almost turquoise blue eyes, their luminescence dazzling against his lived in face.

He inclined his head very slightly, just for a moment. "I have been waiting to be whatever help I can in your quest for Elizabeth Pringle."

Martha suppressed the desire to laugh at the grandiose tone, and realising just in time that he wasn't joking, she thanked him for contacting her. "I seem to think of more questions every day," she went on, "but first, coffee, or do Buddhists not drink it? I'm sorry, I know this may sound ridiculous, but you're the first one I've ever met."

Saul smiled, transforming his face into a concertina of creases. "Listen, if I thought you'd installed an espresso machine in Elizabeth's kitchen, I'd be in seventh heaven, I tell you."

"So to speak," laughed Martha, enjoying the rhythm of the flirtatious banter. "I can do better than Nescafé, at least."

"Please bring it on, the stronger the better."

Beneath his maroon robes Saul wore a white tee shirt, which stood out against his tanned arms. The lines around his eyes had paler crevices forged by the sun and the wind. He had a long aquiline nose and his right ear was pierced with a small gold ring. Catriona had been right. He had a sexual magnetism, a monk who exuded an aura, not of benign gentleness, but rather of an unnerving energy and disconcerting directness.

"Do you mind if I smoke?" he said, taking out a small battered metal tin embossed with flowers, before she had the chance to reply.

"Not at all, go ahead."

He opened the lid and removed a pack of cigarette papers and some pungent rolling tobacco. "Would you care for one yourself?"

Martha shook her head and watched, mesmerised, as he deftly filled the paper and worked it gently until, as if by magic, a perfect cylinder appeared between his thin bony fingers. "I haven't seen that done in a long time," she said, laughing.

"It's like a ritual — the tin, the tobacco — I can't do away with the habit. It's a weakness, I guess." He lit the cigarette. "One amongst many."

Martha breathed in the sweet aroma. "I'm just a party smoker, really."

"Well, just give me the word," he said looking at her, his eyes dancing.

Martha didn't know whether he was meaning a cigarette, or a party.

They sat in the garden, and after their first sip of black coffee from Elizabeth's old stove-top coffee pot, and just as Martha was working up to her first question, Saul took command. "I have a proposition. Come over to Holy Isle." He took a draw on his cigarette and continued, looking straight ahead to the bay. "You should see it just as she loved it, in all its early summer glory." He turned his gaze to her. "We spent a lot of time there together just talking . . . and not talking." He took one long final drag. "I think it would help you to understand her. That's what you want, isn't it?"

Martha lowered her eyes as she detected a trace of belligerence in his words, and automatically matched his tone. "Were you shocked when she left the house to my mother?"

"Not at all," he said more softly, as he stubbed out his roll up in the flowerpot beside him. "She had her reasons, and I for one respected her judgement. She was a very intuitive person, and spiritual, too, though she told me she'd gotten more and more cranky about organised religion over the years. In fact we crossed swords a few times."

"Over what?"

"Lots of stuff. For one thing, reincarnation was never going to fly with her." He chuckled at some remembered remark.

"And does it fly with you?" Martha retorted.

Saul narrowed his eyes. "I'm open to everything."

Martha sensed the challenge but she wasn't going to rise to the bait, and instead replied sweetly, "That's good."

He stood up and pulled his robes around himself. "You ready to go?"

"What, you mean right now?"

"Why not? It's a beautiful day. Have you somewhere else you have to be?"

Martha, a little taken aback, shook her head. "No, I suppose not."

As they walked to the pier, Martha half running to keep up with Saul's long loping stride, he stopped and turned to her. "One thing I'm sure you'd like to know. Elizabeth sometimes reminisced about a lovely summer that was so warm that she worked every day in her garden. She said that she watched a young woman pushing a big dark blue pram past the wall most days, backwards and forwards along Shore Road, and listened to the soft sound of her talking to her little girl, and the baby would burble and laugh, as if they were having a funny conversation. She said it was like music, carried to her on the wind." He paused. "It was you, wasn't it, in the pram?"

Martha stood, round eyed, absorbing what Saul was saying. For the first time she saw the scene. Her heart hammered as it came to her that she and Elizabeth Pringle had existed in the same space. She was overwhelmed by the realisation that she and Elizabeth had breathed the same warm summer air, heard the same sounds, perhaps watched the dancing dipping flight of the same butterfly. The little rosy-cheeked girl and the silent solitary woman had been on different sides of the same old stone wall. Did they look at each other at exactly the same moment, sending an invisible thread spinning between them? Was Elizabeth somewhere deep in Martha's memory?

She heard Saul speak again as if from a great distance. "I think that Elizabeth had made the decision to leave your mother the house a long while back, that summer, even."

With an enormous mental effort Martha pulled herself back thirty-one years into the present.

"But she never mentioned it?" she said, gripping onto each solid word, struggling with the sensation that she might slip back into that summer at any moment.

Saul shook his head. "Not once."

"Don't you think that's a bit strange?"

"Only to people used to making other people's business their own."

Martha bit her lip. First Niall, now Saul, and neither of them knew her at all.

Indignant, she was about to ask Saul if he was criticising her, but before she could, he changed the subject. "Listen to that," he said, and approaching the end of the jetty she heard the tinkling sounds of the metal clips on the rigging on the boats at anchor, which were bobbing gently in the breeze. "I always associate that sound with the start of the journey over to Holy Isle. It was also the soundtrack of my childhood."

Martha looked at him quizzically. "Isn't this a strange place for you to be living?"

Saul laughed, throwing his head back in amusement. "What you mean is 'how did a forty-three-year-old New York Jew turn into a Buddhist and wash up in a spartan cell on a Scottish island, especially when he has a weakness for cigarettes, malt whisky, and other people's company?' "

Martha wondered if what he really meant was "the company of women" but instead she asked, "Well, how *did* you come to be here? I don't presume anything, I'm just interested. It's dangerous to make snap judgements, don't you think?" She was faintly irritated with herself as she registered how prim and self-righteous her words sounded.

Saul laughed again. "Well, Miss Martha, ain't that the truth."

She made for the little commercial Holy Island cabin cruiser tied up at the red sandstone pier, its brightly coloured pennants, strung from the mast to the stern, fluttering in the breeze.

Saul put his hand on her arm. "That's for the paying public." He nodded further up the pier. "This is *our* luxury liner." He pointed to the little skiff lying low in the water. It was the same one she'd seen heading for the shore that first day.

Saul climbed down the iron rungs sunk into the wall of the jetty and onto the boat. He steadied it for Martha to follow, and took her hand to guide her to where she was to sit, on a brightly patterned Indian mat covering a little bench, her back to the prow. Saul sat at the stern and rowed out of the harbour, before standing up and pushing his robes well out of the way of the outboard motor. Then he yanked on the engine and settled back down, his hand on the tiller, and his eyes on Martha. Moments later they were chugging across the water at a gentle pace.

She turned to look ahead. The long whitewashed two-storey house and the magnificent tall lighthouse changed from distant shimmering shapes into solid buildings as they drew near Holy Isle.

What neither of them saw were Niall and Catriona, standing on the grass by the shore across from the Glenburn Hotel, turn at the familiar sound of the little engine, from surveying the hotel's roof, to watching the skiff's progress across the bay.

Martha sat back round to face Saul when she heard his voice raised a little above the sound of the engine. "You asked why I came here."

"I just wondered. I would have thought it might have been more tempting to be a Buddhist somewhere, well, more conducive, like California?"

"Ha, you make it sound like a lifestyle thing. It's not about the weather or the beaches, but on one level you're right. I suppose you could say it was the call of the wild."

He told her he had been living in the Meatpacking District before it became gentrified, when there were no exclusive members' clubs, no glass-fronted hotels, their roof-top pools filled with overfed loafer-shod frat boys and the wealthy from Wall Street. There were just thousands of meat workers, their faces haunted by tiredness, grafting day after day in the long nineteenth-century meat sheds, shouldering thousands of hulking carcasses into lorries to satisfy the voracious appetites of America.

"Did you work there?"

He had Martha's full attention.

"No. Their work was almost done even before I got up. I just heard the huge refrigerated trucks pull away from the bays and rumble over the cobbles to wherever they were headed. No, not me. I managed some bands, scribbled lyrics and wrote poetry. Sometimes I performed it, often right next to my apartment in a twenty-four-hour diner called Florent. But the two French guys who owned it have shut up shop now. They didn't like the area any more either, with its ten million dollar lofts and armies of stick people. Anyways, the thin people all thought I must be good, although my poems were nothing special, and I acquired a reputation I certainly didn't deserve. As Elizabeth would say, 'I had a bit of a hit for myself.' "

158

Saul smiled. He was, he said, a latter day beat poet manqué, blagging his way into glamorous parties and hoovering up enough Bolivian marching powder to feed the country's street children for a year. Not that he paid for any of it, he said.

He ran his hand across his face, wiping away sea spray. "I'm sure you can imagine the whole sordid scene."

"So what happened? How did it all end?"

He laughed. "I can feel your sympathy wafting towards me. "It didn't really. There was no *Pulp Fiction* moment if that's what you're thinking. I just woke up in someone's marble bathroom one morning, bleeding so heavily from my nose that I thought I must have inadvertently shot it off. It was all rather pathetic, if you really want to know."

"So you were saved by Buddhism?"

Saul gave her a look, and sighed. "Actually I realised I was just lost in a crowd."

He told her that he'd read an article about Holy Isle which made it sound like Paradise, "if you'll forgive the overused metaphor," and just packed up and left.

"What friends, family, everything? You didn't think you'd be more lonely here?"

He shook his head slowly. "It hasn't worked out that way. There were no family ties to speak of. My parents had survived the Holocaust only to be killed by premature old age, I guess — that and smoking. My big sister married a farmer from Iowa and has done more than her fair share to keep the planet populated; she hasn't really got time for much else."

"And the everything?"

Saul shrugged his shoulders. "Nothing to tell, really. Just a series of failed relationships. It was a pretty easy decision, so I cashed in and sold my loft to some x-ray thin starlet, for a killing."

She raised her eyebrows, and he smiled. "Hey, I know, not very zen of me. Anyway, enough. I'm boring myself, so I'm sure going to be boring you."

The truth was, she was intrigued by Saul but, she was relieved to realise, not smitten. As he took her arm to help her out of the skiff she thought it might be fun to tumble into bed with him, but she wouldn't fall in love. With Niall, though? She just couldn't fathom her feelings.

As they walked up from the shore of Holy Isle together, Martha took in the gaudy, naively painted statues and tall lanterns lining their route. They stood to the side to let a group of Soay sheep cross their path, followed by a procession of waddling ducks and ducklings, all of which studiously ignored Saul and Martha.

"It amazed me to learn about all the holy men who've come here," said Saul.

"Are you including Richard Gere?"

Saul didn't dignify her sarcasm with a reply. "We're hoping the Dalai Lama will spend his seventy-fifth birthday here, but he's a popular man."

Saul indicated the path along the shoreline towards the south end lighthouse. "Shall we walk?" They fell into an easy stroll. "Elizabeth was fascinated by the idea of Retreat, and she was curious *and* a little horrified when I explained that nuns withdraw to an enclave at the headland along here," he said, pointing towards the lighthouse. "A group of ten women began a four-year retreat last fall."

"Do they live in silence?"

Saul told her that they could talk to each other or to their spiritual teacher, their Master, if they wished. They had books, and the garden to tend and enjoy, and peace for deep meditation, he said, but Elizabeth, for some reason, was visibly uneasy at the thought of their confinement.

"And yet she had made her house pretty much her own form of retreat."

"Yeah, that's the way it seemed to me when I met her."

They reached a small turning off the path, no wider than a goat track and lined with ferns. "In fact, I want to show you something," Saul said as he plunged into the tall foliage. "Fifteen centuries ago St Molio, St Columba's disciple, lived up here as a hermit." Martha followed him the short distance to an open mouthed cave, no wider than a rowing boat set on its side. "Elizabeth told me she would often shelter in here when it rained, looking out over the water to the fields at King's Cross."

Martha crouched down, as Elizabeth had done, and suddenly she was back on the beach at King's Cross, paddling with Susie in their matching candy-striped Oshkosh dungarees while Anna lay on the travelling rug, resting on one elbow, watching the two of them run in and out of the water in their jelly shoes, shrieking and laughing as the waves lapped over their rolled up trousers. Their father, as always, tended the frying pan on the Primus stove, shielding the flame with their old striped windbreak. Martha closed her eyes; she could almost smell the sausages and catch the echo of Anna's voice: "John, I'm sure they're burning." Then her father's patient reply: "Anna, darling, you always say that. Leave this to me." He looked over to his girls. "Your mummy's the queen of the kitchen, but I'm the king of the sausage sizzle."

She wondered why it was that Arran had always had a special pull for her, and not for Susie. Perhaps her sister's memories of family life when their father had been its centrifugal force, were too painful. She thought how careless she had been, never to ask Susie if that was why she used to excuse herself from Martha and Anna's weekend trips.

"Martha?" Saul touched her arm. "You're miles away."

She refocused reluctantly. "I was remembering an idyllic summer's day over there, on the beach, with my family, many years ago."

"Perhaps Elizabeth was watching."

"What?" She was startled. "What do you mean?"

"Maybe she was here," he said. "Hey, I don't mean to spook you."

But she wasn't spooked. She just stored away the thought.

Saul ran his fingers over some runic inscriptions carved into the overhanging stone. "Elizabeth told me that St Molio had left these marks. She said, 'You know, Saul, I think the village thinks of me as a hermit, but it's just that I have nothing left to say to most people.' Then she smiled at me and said, 'Perhaps I should scratch something meaningful on the coal bunker.' "

"Ha," laughed Martha. "I'll have a look when I get back."

They stepped out of the cave and made their way back down to the path.

"If Elizabeth was so solitary there must have been something very special about you and Niall that brought her out of herself."

"I think she made an exception for us. We were the late arrivals in her life. Niall's passion for gardening reawakened hers, and I, well, I think she and I nurtured each other's spiritual side, if that doesn't sound too arrogant of me." He paused and smiled at her. "Though I'm sure you would tell me if it did."

Martha flushed. "No, it doesn't at all." Then she remembered the photograph. "But she wasn't always alone. I found a photograph of her with two children, Esme and Peter. She looked like she knew them well. Did she ever talk about them?"

Saul shook his head. "No, but she did say more than once that she had been very fulfilled by her vocation. Perhaps the children were her pupils."

"The photo seems to be more intimate than that," Martha said pensively.

They were interrupted by the faint sound of murmuring voices coming towards them, and from around the hillside appeared two women, walking closely, their heads together. They stopped, surprise evident on their faces.

Saul gave them a short bow. "Martha, please meet Sister Indra, head of the *Sangha*, that's the Sanskrit word for our monastic community, and one of our newest nuns, Sister Sara."

Martha stepped forward to shake hands with the two shaven-headed nuns, who were wearing the same long saffron and maroon robes as Saul. Sara, the younger of the two, who had a teardrop shaped tattoo on the back of her left hand and a small ruby nose piercing, shook her hand warmly.

Sister Indra ignored Martha's outstretched hand and put her own hands together and bowed in greeting, a thin smile hardly altering her cool stare. "Welcome to Holy Isle. Saul has told us a little of your . . . what shall I say . . . good fortune."

Martha bristled, was everyone passing judgement on her? But before she could think of a suitably tart reply, Sara broke in. "How do you like living in Lamlash?"

"I've been coming here ever since I was a child," she said, in a voice edged with irritation.

"That much we already know," Sister Indra said dryly, "but living here is rather different."

Sara made another stab at conversation. "I teach a yoga class on Thursdays in the long barn beyond the Post Office. You would be very welcome."

"Thanks, perhaps when I get settled."

"Catriona says Sara is a good and wise teacher," Saul chipped in.

Martha noticed Sister Indra's eyes narrow almost imperceptibly, and at that moment the conversation finally faltered.

Saul bowed to both nuns and led Martha on towards the lighthouse.

"Did I detect a certainly chilliness in the Mother Superior?" asked Martha.

"There you go again, ever alert to the angle," Saul said in a sardonic voice.

Martha persisted. "Do Buddhists have relationships?"

"If you are asking whether I have carnal knowledge of Sister Indra, the answer is no."

"I wasn't actually, but OK," said Martha, sensing she was pushing her luck, "interrogation over."

Just then she caught a glint of light off glass. "What's that?" she asked, pointing upwards to a group of buildings almost camouflaged by the profusion of bright yellow whins and a line of tall saplings like willowy sentinels.

"They're for the 'hideaways' as the locals call them," answered Saul. "Our retreat huts. Some inhabitants are monks, others are visitors in need of a period of silence and introspection." Saul grinned. "'Hideaways' is a good name for them, isn't it? I have only ever been on retreat for three days, and only once in the three years that I have been here."

"Perhaps you're not cut out to be a monk."

"Perhaps not. I certainly couldn't cope with only my own shadow for company, but my teachers are patient. I repeat every day, *We do not receive wisdom, we must discover it for ourselves after a journey through the wilderness, which no one can make for us, which no one can spare us. For our wisdom is the point of view from which we come, at last, to regard the world.'*

Saul told her that Elizabeth liked him to recite the words to her, and she would say, "I wonder how long it will be before I ever find the wisdom to regard the world!"

They had recited poems by Longfellow and Christina Rossetti to one another, and she talked about the solace that she found in poetry. She told him that when she taught her pupils a poem, however short, she thought of it as giving them a small gift they could keep in a little pocket in their lives.

"That is a lovely thing to say."

"She was remarkable. To the outside world she was restrained, a woman of few words, but as we got to know each other she became more free and more expressive."

Saul stopped and looked over towards Holmlea. "She taught me, '*Does the road wind uphill all the way? Yes, to the very end. Will the day's journey take the whole long day? From morn to night my friend.'* "

The words reverberated around Martha's head and as she looked over to Holmlea, she thought of Anna. "There's no other way, is there?"

Saul turned to face her, his eyes sad. "No, there isn't, we all just keep going. That's what Elizabeth said, too."

They sat in the long shadow of the afternoon near the lighthouse, but not so close as to disturb the nuns behind the walls. Saul took out a flask and two plastic beakers from his satchel. He poured the first cup and passed it to Martha.

"Homemade lemonade with a little mint. It's one of our specialities. Sláinte."

"Sláinte." She took a sip. "Mmm, lovely, I bet this would taste great with gin."

"Gin and lemonade? Not a drink I ever tried," he said, sceptically.

"There's an Ayrshire gin that goes with anything; perhaps I'll get Catriona a bottle."

"I don't think she's one for spirits. Wine's more her thing."

Martha raised her eyebrows. "Maybe you're right. You know her better than I do, I'm sure."

"Ah, a question disguised as a statement? Another trick of the trade?"

"No, no, it's not," protested Martha.

Saul got up and put on his dark, square sunglasses. "I'm sure if Catriona wants to tell you, she will. Drink up and I'll ferry you home."

ELIZABETH

Robert was a great one for surprises, and gifts. On the last day of term in the June after we were engaged he met me at the school gates in the pony and trap with a glorious bunch of sweet peas. Concealed in the centre was an illustrated edition of *A Child's Garden of Verses*. He said he did such things because he loved to see the delight on my face. On another occasion that summer he fashioned a swinging garden seat from an oak that had fallen at the Whitehouse, complete with a striped awning, and set it on our lawn in the middle of the night for Mother and me to find in the morning. Even she could not hide her pleasure at such a gift, as he pushed her to and fro in the sunshine. That he thought of her made me love him even more.

But that autumn Robert surpassed himself. On the last Saturday of September he collected me early in the morning, before eight o'clock, when there was a trace of crispness in the air and the sun was yet to burn off the haar. We had made a plan to tour our favourite places on the island, to see the autumn colours. Mother had taken a great deal of trouble over our picnic, with homemade meat loaf, chutney and freshly baked bread.

She had wrapped plates in linen napkins and made a flask of Russian tea. We were to make our first stop at Glen Rosa where the plantation of larch made a golden pattern against the green spruce, and the vivid burnt red hues of the sycamores stood out on the hillside. But when we arrived at the Glen Rosa turn, rather than swinging to the track on the right-hand side, Robert urged the pony on, and soon we were sending up the curlews as we trotted up and down the hills of the String Road. When I asked Robert why he had changed our plans, he simply smiled and said mysteriously, "We're on our way to a rendezvous," and he kept checking his watch. Less than an hour later we were in sight of the sea and the sun was warming our faces.

It was just as we reached Shedock that I became aware of the low monotonous drone of an engine in the distance. "Look up!" Robert said excitedly. I tilted my face to the sky, squinting at the bright blowsy clouds, hanging on to my forest-green felt hat with one hand.

Coming towards us from the Mull of Kintyre was the little plane that plied between Campbeltown and Glasgow. The noise roared louder and louder until finally it swooped down lower and lower, so low the air quivered and our clothes flapped, and then suddenly it was down, bumping across the field for a moment before it juddered to a halt. All the while I held on to the metal bar with my free hand, as Robert tried to keep the pony from bolting in fright at the crashing din. Once he had steadied her, he put on the brake, jumped down and handed the reins to one of the village boys with instructions to take the trap back to the farm. It was only then that it dawned on me that we weren't there just to see the spectacle of the plane landing and taking off again. I was going to fly in it!

I looked at Robert incredulously. He took off his cap and swept it low in front of me. "Your carriage awaits, ma'am." Then he put out his arms to lift me down.

I am not a nervous person, but the thought of hanging in the air in that contraption made me feel quite faint, and I remember I had to suppress a wave of nausea. Nowadays, of course, people treat flying much as they would getting on and off a bus, but that Saturday was the first and only time in my life that I have stepped into a plane.

I glanced up at the cockpit and a vivacious looking girl a few years younger than me smiled and waved. Her name was Winnie Drinkwater and she became a legend, her name known all over the globe. I was to learn that a month after her seventeenth birthday she had become the youngest woman in the world to fly solo.

She jumped down the steps to meet us, in her navy-blue serge flying suit, a tight leather belt accentuating her tiny waist, and a pair of black shiny lace up boots. She had an extravagant mop of curly blue-black hair that flopped over her dancing eyes.

"Hello," she said, shaking my hand. "It's a wonderful day for flying . . . and for surprises."

A nervous laugh stalled in my throat. "I can't quite believe it. Am I really going to be up in the clouds?"

Robert laughed. "You'd better believe it! So high up, all the people on the ground below will look like scurrying ants."

170

I gripped the ropes on either side of the steps and ducked as I entered the tiny fuselage. At first I could not see properly. It was as if I were inside a metal cocoon; I had never been in such an enclosed space. There were just four rows, with one seat on each side, and as soon as I sat down I grasped Robert's hand tightly across the aisle, oblivious of the other passengers already on board. For the first time in my life I was engaged in something that was completely beyond my control. My heart was thudding so hard I thought it would burst out of my chest as our pilot guided the little twin-engine plane skittering over hummocks of grass and clumps of cowslips, all the way to the far end of the field. Then she turned it round deftly and put the engine at full throttle until the roar was deafening. She called out to us, "Hang on to your hats," and then suddenly we shot forward and up into the sky as if we'd been fired from a caterpault.

Seconds later we were soaring over the hills, past the farms dotted below. It was so thrilling, so exhilarating, that there was no room for fear as the little plane dropped a few feet and rose again, taking my stomach with it. I wanted to shout out, "Look at me look at me." Far below us, the steamer at Brodick pier belched sooty smoke, heralding its departure, and coal boats and pleasure cruisers patterned Brodick Bay. As we crossed the gleaming waters of the Firth of Clyde I looked north up Loch Long to the mountains beyond.

I held onto Robert's hand the whole way, careless of the glances of the two other passengers, a farmer from Kintyre and a physician from Glasgow, who told us

171

airily that for them this was a regular journey. Our excitement must have been infectious, because soon they began pointing out landmarks, the ruins of Portencross Castle at West Kilbride and the round crenellated folly on the hill above Lochwinnoch.

We had been in the air for less than thirty minutes when Winnie called to us that we were about to land at Renfrew airfield, and seconds later we glided softly to a halt, the whirring blades turning ever more slowly, as if exhausted by the effort of carrying us to the mainland. As they rotated for one last time, a mechanic came forward dragging two blocks on ropes, which he wedged under the wheels of the plane. Winnie unstrapped herself from her seat to open the door, and then she waited for her four passengers at the foot of the steps. I don't know what came over me, but I was so giddy with excitement that I hugged her, almost a perfect stranger, goodbye.

Robert had planned the day meticulously. A taxi was waiting at the airfield to take us to Paisley railway station, where we joined the throng of people dressed in their finery for a day out in Glasgow. Many of them were the young women who toiled in the textile factories, working the hundreds of looms, weaving fine paisley-pattern shawls. Mother had an exquisite one that was left to her by her grandmother, a square suffused with fifteen different jewel-like colours woven into the thousands of droplet shapes that covered the surface. When she draped it over her shoulders it made her look even more beautiful.

The platform was a sea of hats and printed dresses, which the girls had sewn in the modern style with a simple collar and a dropped waist, and the men, laughing and flirting with them, were all smoking, and now and then one would check his pocket watch, or hit his friend on the arm with a rolled up newspaper. And when the train came, everyone rushed on board chattering excitedly, Robert and I included, caught up in the fun of it all.

When we arrived under the cavernous glass roof of Central Station, a small dark cloud cast a fleeting flittering shadow over the promise of the day. All around us were the ritual dances of greetings and farewells, waves and hugs, tears and handshakes. Robert turned to me suddenly and pulled me to him, and all the noise fell away as he spoke urgently, the words catching in his throat. "I couldn't bear to leave you even for a month, a week, a day, Elizabeth. Never." As he clutched me I realised he was shaking. "Never." There was a fear in his eyes.

I tried to make light of it, laughing. "I'm like a sticky willow. Nothing could prise us apart!" But the only way I could banish his words was to store them as one might put a piece of marble in a deep pocket, to be taken out later and turned over and examined for tiny fissures.

He kissed me, right there, on the station concourse, in a long passionate embrace that took my breath away, and it was only when a little boy wolf-whistled beside us that we stepped apart, like dancers when the music stops. Robert just grinned at me and pulled me to his side, put my arm through his, and guided me out onto the street.

He had made a reservation at the newest tea room in the city, the Gordon. He would not have chosen the smoking room but for the fact that he had read that the new owner, James Craig, was intent on filling the walls with new Scottish art.

At first I was dazzled by the light streaming through the tall windows and the rich burnish of the new mahogany panelling, but as we settled into our seats my eye was drawn to a painting of a tawny calf standing in the dappled light beneath a tree, its inkpot-black eyes staring at us in curiosity. Beside that canvas was another, a bowl of open-faced roses, their petals of different pinks, and so vibrant that I imagined I could smell their scent through the acrid fumes of cigarettes and pungent pipes.

When we moved to Holmlea, Mother and Mary planted a profusion of rose bushes, and at the end of each summer when the heads started to droop, Mother and I filled Kilner jars with petals of every colour: yellow, crimson, peach, white and deep pink. We pressed them down until the glass was full to the brim and then poured in water to the top, screwed the lids on tightly and placed the jars on window ledges to infuse in the light, for weeks. Then, once we'd strained the petals, Mother would sprinkle rosewater in the linen before she ironed it. I do it still.

"How amazing!" exclaimed Robert suddenly, and pointed over my shoulder at a large oil painting. The inscription on the frame read, "Auchindrain, Arran".

The sun was shown low in the sky, and the chalky white gable end of the farmhouse glowed yellow beside the shore. In the grass between the house and the water, the artist had painted a young woman in a long skirt, a bright blue striped apron tied about her waist. Her hair was scraped back into a bun and she was holding a basket against one hip; all around her were sheets laid out on the grass to dry. She looked across the fence directly at the artist, strong and secure in her own domain.

"Imagine that," Robert said quietly, his eyes shining, "Auchindrain, so many years ago. It is quite something to think that soon we will be there as man and wife in our own home, and it will be you standing there on our land."

I tasted coffee for the first time that day, rich black nectar served to us in a fine china cup by a slip of a girl in a perfectly pressed black and white uniform who spoke with a Highland accent. She was no more than fifteen, probably far from home. I wondered how long she would stay in the sooty noisy city, perhaps in some lonely lodging, before she decided she wanted more and booked a passage from the Broomielaw to New York or somewhere further, following family or friends. After she had attended to us she fell back to her place in a line of waitresses along the wall, standing expressionless until the next customer beckoned.

Robert took a cigarette from the yellow and red Gold Flake packet he kept in his jacket pocket, and tapped each end down on the box. I liked the way he looked when he smoked, casually blowing the plume up into the glass cupola above.

Although Mother and Mary enjoyed cigarettes together, I have never smoked. It was something that reinforced their companionship, and so I do not think of it as a solitary occupation. There was just one time, last summer, when I was curious to try one of the little cigarettes that Saul kept in his leather satchel and which had an altogether more pungent aroma.

"Really, Elizabeth? I don't want you to feel woozy. And I don't imagine you have ever broken the law in your life, and marijuana is technically illegal. Though I don't hold much with that."

"What are they going to do with me at my age, Saul? Lock me up in Brodick Police Station? It's time I had a little adventure, don't you think, and it doesn't appear to have done you much harm."

He laughed at that, shaking his head as if indulging a child. "OK, on your own head be it, but I think you'd better sit down first."

He opened up a pair of deckchairs and when we were both settled he passed me the thin cigarette. I grasped it between my fingers and Saul grimaced at me.

"Elizabeth, relax, you're squeezing the life out of it."

I rearranged it a little between my second and third finger and put it to my lips. I inhaled too deeply and immediately felt the smoke hit the back of my throat. I coughed until my eyes watered, but I put it back to my lips and inhaled more softly. I remember Saul saying, "Hey, Elizabeth, it's meant for sharing."

I felt a little lightheaded and loose limbed, and my mouth seemed to move quite differently to the words I was speaking, but I sank down further, safe in my deckchair, drinking a pot of tea and eating my way through a tin of shortbread. It tasted even more delicious than usual. I say that modestly, but it was strange because it was my usual recipe. Saul read from a poetry book he took from his satchel, and I listened very intently as he recited one Elizabeth Bishop poem in particular, which I often tell to myself now when I sit in the pale evening light by my sitting room window.

> But secretly, while the grandmother
> busies herself about the stove,
> the little moons fall down like tears
> from between the pages of the almanac
> into the flower bed the child
> has carefully placed in the front of the house.

That was the only time I smoked marijuana with Saul, but that night, alone of any, I slept from the moment I lay down until I heard the scratching and scraping of two seagulls on the slates on the roof above my bed, squabbling over their morning scraps.

Mother had known all along about Robert's plans for that day, and I wanted it to be special for her, too. So he and I walked to Daly's department store, which shimmered with huge crystal chandeliers, and glass cabinets of exquisite perfume bottles.

177

In the haberdashery department I asked to see a pair of their finest tan leather gloves. I had quite an array to choose from but I settled on the softest Nappa leather ones. I thought they would soothe her hands and that, in spite of herself, she would be pleased to wear them to church, placing them on the ledge of her pew beside her old Bible, which was inscribed with the names of my grandparents and their parents before them.

The woman behind the counter complimented me on my choice and wrapped the gloves in tissue and placed them in a pink and white spotted box, which she tied with a velvet ribbon. "I wish you luck wearing them," she said, as she handed over the package.

"Oh no, they're not for me," I said, "They are a present for my mother."

"Well then, you are a lovely daughter," she replied, smiling at us as we turned to walk away.

Robert looked at his watch. There was to be another surprise. "We have to hurry," he said, propelling me along crowded pavements to the La Scala cinema. On either side of the entrance hung identical posters of Gary Cooper in army uniform, and Helen Hayes dressed as a nurse. *A Farewell to Arms* was my introduction to the horrors of the First World War, the war that had claimed my father. I'm ashamed to say that what struck me most, as we sat in the plush scarlet velvet seats, our heads close and Robert's arm around my shoulder in the manner of all the young couples there, was the resemblance between Gary Cooper and Robert, not the tragedy unfolding on the screen in front of me. When, in later years, at a time of sadness, I read

Hemingway's great novel, the film seemed sentimental and slight by comparison.

That day, though, I was young and besotted and I teased Robert mercilessly that I had had yet another surprise because now I had a film star for a fiancé. Robert laughed ruefully as we sat huddled on the top deck of the ferry ploughing its way home through the waves, rain beating on the umbrella we held close over our heads, and whispered in my ear, "I'd like to see Gary Cooper wrestling a Blackface ram to the ground."

MARTHA

"Just look at it! It's so dull nowadays. When I used to dye it with henna, it was fluorescent orange when the sun shone on it."

Martha caught Anna's animated girlish tone, and then Bea's throaty laugh. "Ha, maybe we could make it a little wild again. We could buy henna powder, and then I could wrap your hair up in pieces of cloth, the old way."

Martha lay on the bed across from the open window in her old room, listening to the two women in the garden below, tuning in to their easy conversation. It was almost too painful to hear, the fleeting appearance of the mother she adored, the vibrant heart of the family, quick witted, sometimes goofy, the party giver, the picnic maker, the constant parent. She squeezed her eyes shut, waiting for the reappearance of new Anna to spoil it all.

Martha and Bea had collected her mother from Kingswood the night before. The introductions had been uneventful, Anna nodding as if she'd known all along that Bea was arriving. She merely got into the car, said, "It's time we were all home" and leant over from the passenger seat and kissed Martha on the cheek.

Martha had shown Bea to Susie's room, a temporary measure until she could fix up Anna's study, so not worth mentioning to her sister, she thought. But the anticipation of the inevitable conversation to come had assumed overwhelmingly stressful proportions as Martha rehearsed all the explosions that she was sure would detonate on the line from Copenhagen. She knew all along that she would eventually take the coward's way out. The night before, at midnight, a whisky on her bedside table, she had composed an email that read like a catalogue of necessary information. But she finished it with the words, "I'm lying here gazing at a photograph of both of us with Mum when we came to visit you. She looks so happy. And Susie, I just want to say that I am sorry I ignored your advice about Andrew, but I'm probably too late saying it. I am looking forward to you coming home soon. And going to Arran, too. Do you remember the house Mum and Dad used to rent on Shore Road towards Clauchlands, much further along than Holmlea? It was called Seabank. Arran was part of our childhood. Love Martha xoxo"

She took a sip of Bruichladdich and read over the email, staring finally at the last two words, dashed off automatically. She pressed Send and stared at the screen for a moment. Did they love each other?

She ran through a Rolodex of memories, searching for something that would be sure-fire guaranteed proof, the gold standard of sisterly love. A moment about which she could say, "That's it. That's the one. That's how I know we love each other." But there was no such perfect memory. Instead she felt the crushing weight of one long buried night.

First, she remembered the sounds, the noise of children shouting and laughing, their voices rising and falling in the bright light. Guy Fawkes was always a big event in The Oval. John Morrison decorated the garden with fairy lights and lanterns on long extension flexes while inside, the house was aglow with candlelight. The mothers stood in the warmth drinking wine and gossiping beside tables laden with their dishes of chilli and lasagne, macaroni cheese, trifle and competing fruit-and-cream-laden pavlovas. The children ate toffee apples and fizzy drinks and tore around the garden in a kaleidoscope of anoraks, stripy scarves and hats and brightly patterned wellington boots. Every so often they paused to glance impatiently at the fathers, all hunkered down in the little pleasure garden across from the garden gate, where they were setting the firework display by the light of their torches, sending beams of light to and fro.

"Why can't they hurry up?" asked one of Martha's schoolfriends, imitating her own mother's insistent voice.

"My dad's setting up a mega rocket," another one announced proudly.

At that year's party, as usual, Susie was Martha's burden, younger by three years but as far as ten-year-old Martha was concerned, a baby, endlessly trailing at her side with duffle coat hood up, nose dripping disgustingly and big blue saucer eyes permanently locked on her sister.

She grabbed Martha's arm. "I want to play, too," she whined, "you're being horrible and I'm going to tell Mummy on you."

Martha kept her back turned, intent on her Primary Six friends who were all trying to light sparklers with a cigarette lighter. "Shut up, Susie, and leave me alone or I'll lock you in the shed," Martha snarled, and pulled her arm from Susie's grasp. The other girls burst out laughing and Susie, humiliated yet again, began to wail.

"Shut up. Shut up, you freak," shouted Martha, who was trying to concentrate on igniting her sparkler. It caught fire with a crackle, and in an instant she wheeled round and waved the spitting silver wand backwards and forwards, inches from her sister's eyes.

Susie screamed and clutched her face. "Stop it, stop it, you're burning my eyes!" she yelled, terrified, and immediately, as if a switch had been thrown, Martha's friends' laughter turned to screaming too, and in the commotion, their father appeared suddenly, scattering all the children, and scooped up Susie. "I can't see anything. I can't see anything, Daddy," she sobbed. "Martha put her sparkler into my eyes."

Silence. Children stopped chattering. Fathers stood up from planting their rows of fireworks and looked on in silence. Mothers broke off conversations and guiltily rushed outside to see if it was their child who was hurt. Everyone looked at Martha.

"Right, my girl," said Anna, "upstairs." And she marched her older daughter past the sea of frowning

183

faces, into the house and upstairs to her room. "How could you do such a thing, Martha? I'm ashamed of you."

Martha's cheeks were scarlet and tears started to stream down them. "Have I made Susie blind?" she said in a small voice.

"No, she's not blind, but Rhona's dad is looking at her now to see if the sparks have hurt her face. You will stay right here. You will not come out of your bedroom again tonight. Do you understand? How could you do that to your sister, Martha?"

"I want to see Susie. Please, Mum, please," Martha wailed, but Anna was already on her way out the door, and when she closed it without replying, Martha crumpled to the floor, her whole world collapsing. She must be a bad person, she thought, and in her anguish she believed that neither her mother nor her father, and definitely not Susie, would love her any more.

She lay listening to the murmur of voices below. What could they be saying?

"What a terrible thing to do to her sister."

"She was showing off to her friends."

"I've told Rhona not to play with her anymore."

"What a nasty girl."

When the fireworks began, Martha stayed facing the wall, her duvet pulled tightly around her. Every so often the bedroom lit up with explosions of colour from whizzing Catherine wheels, and then the rat-a-tat of the rockets followed. She listened to the excited whoops and claps, the drama all but forgotten by the crowd, and, eventually, drained by it all, she fell into an exhausted sleep.

As the early light filtered through the curtains she was faintly aware of the click of her bedroom door, and then she felt a rush of cold air as Susie lifted back the duvet and climbed in beside her and put a hot hand on her cheek. Martha began to cry. "I am so sorry, Susie, I'm so sorry." Susie patted her sister's forehead over and over again. "It's OK, I'm not blinded. Daddy said you didn't mean it. You missed all the fireworks, Martha. That's a shame." The two girls fell asleep again, Martha with her arm around Susie, her face buried into her sister's matted morning hair.

Now, more than twenty years later, Martha lay in the same bed. As her mind picked up the memory of that awful night again, her relationship with Susie still seemed as childish.

She looked at her watch: 10.00 a.m., an hour later in Copenhagen. Soon Susie would ring to begin her interrogation. She needed coffee. She raised herself up out of the old soft mattress and rummaged in her wardrobe for her frayed towelling dressing gown and ancient slippers.

Downstairs, she went to the open front door and saw Anna and Bea sitting together on the garden bench, a cafetière of coffee on the low wicker table in front of them and two of Anna's favourite mugs in their hands. The crack of the gravel announced her approach. "Morning, Martha. Come and meet Bea. She's come to stay with me for a while."

"Yes, Mum," Martha stooped to kiss Anna on the forehead, "we came over from Arran yesterday and picked you up from the hospital. It looks as though you've made a new friend already."

"I've got lots of friends," Anna said petulantly. "What are you saying? That I have no friends?"

Bea stood up quietly, put the mugs back on the tray and disappeared inside. Martha sat in her place. "I was just meaning that Bea is a new friend, and it looks like you are getting on well."

Anna turned to her, fear in her eyes. "I looked at a photograph of you this morning, but I couldn't remember who you were. I'm losing it, Martha, aren't I?"

"It's OK, Mum," Martha said gently, "the doctors say some days will be better than others, and you seem to be having a good day today."

"Yes, but how long before I don't know the good days from the bad ones?"

Martha put her arm round Anna and her mother laid her head on her daughter's shoulder. "All I see when I close my eyes is a black tunnel. There's no door at the other end, and I know that eventually the dark will cover me, and I won't be able to scream for help because I won't be able to breathe, because I won't remember *how* to breathe."

Martha took Anna's hand; it was all she could do not to cry. "Mum, it won't be like that. I'm sure it won't be," she said firmly, banishing doubt from her voice. She looked over to the house and glimpsed Bea, standing a little back from the window, observing them.

She waved at Martha and smiled. "Let's go inside, Mum. I need coffee."

Anna sat down in her usual armchair in the sitting room, staring at the television screen. Martha couldn't tell from her expression whether the reporter's urgent tone and the images of shell-shocked children staring back at her from the remains of a bombed out Afghan village, meant anything to her. She withdrew, closing the door gently, and joined Bea in the kitchen, where she was looking through a pile of books on dementia.

"Gosh, that's a lot of homework."

"I found them in the study." Bea looked up at her sympathetically. "Your mum has underlined passages."

Martha sat down heavily. "I didn't even know they were there."

"I think she has been trying to prepare herself, no?"

Martha nodded. "And the irony is that then you forget you were preparing," she stopped, "or maybe not. In the garden a moment ago she was visualising her fears. I felt so useless."

Bea put her hand on Martha's. "She knows why I am here. She understands. When she reached the bottom of the stairs this morning she gripped onto the banister. She didn't know what to do next, but then she told me she wanted to show me the Orchid House in the Botanical Gardens. She said she used to take you and your sister when you were the same height as the orchid trays, but you didn't like it because the air felt 'all soapy'."

"That's true! I'd forgotten all about that. I still don't like orchid houses. I always feel the orchids are about to attack."

At that moment the phone rang, and Bea, noting Martha tense, lifted the wicker basket and signalled that she was going shopping.

"Well, Martha, it was great to wake up to that email. All cut and dried. Jesus, I don't know where to begin."

"Wherever you want, Susie. I'll explain it."

"Look, I haven't got long now. I'm about to have an interview for a space in a new design studio."

"Let's talk later, then," Martha said in a clipped voice.

"No way. You drop two bombshells. The house in Lamlash and this Polish woman. What's her name, Beatrice Starkey?"

"It's Starecki."

"Whatever. We know nothing about her."

Martha tightened her grip on the receiver. "I wouldn't have arranged it," she said pointedly, "if I thought it was a bad idea."

"But did you check her credentials?"

"I met her and I thought she was kind and caring, and someone who Mum would take to."

"Oh, I am sure you did, because *you* can't be with her because of your little house adventure. But the woman's not qualified."

"Not qualified in what, Susie? She's a trained nurse."

"But how can you be sure she's not robbing us or something?"

Martha was speechless. Anger rippled through her like molten iron.

"Martha . . . are you there?"

"What the hell do you mean, Susie? If that's what's worrying you, not whether Mum is actually safe and calm and content, then you'd better get right over here now and sod your interview," Martha hissed quietly, for fear Anna might hear.

"For god's sake don't be so hysterical, Martha. I'm only saying."

"Only saying what? That I'd leave my mother with someone I didn't trust?" Martha paused, her voice quavering. "Actually, Susie, why on earth am I justifying myself to you? You always do this. Is there anything else you wanted to say before you have to rush off?"

Susie didn't reply.

"Well, is there?"

Then Susie spoke, her voice verging on the contrite. "No, not really. Look, I'll try to get home soon."

Martha heard the catch in her voice, and gave way. "That'd be good, Susie. We'd both love to see you. And good luck with the studio."

"Bye, Martha. I miss you both."

The line clicked dead and Martha put her head in her hands. What was the expression? She thought for a moment. Yup, they were two people separated by a common language.

She had an overwhelming urge for strong coffee, and, had there been one to hand, a cigarette. She microwaved the last of the brew in the cafetière and

189

took a long medicinal drink of the scalding black coffee.

When Bea returned, Martha was still sitting at the table, somewhat despondent, leafing absently through a copy of *Elle Decor*. She put her basket of fresh vegetables and a still warm sourdough loaf on the table, and pointing to the magazine, cleared her throat and said shyly, "I was thinking, if you need a carpenter, I can recommend a very fine one. His name is Tomas, Tomas Starecki."

Martha looked up at her and smiled. "Thank you, Bea. If you say so, he must be good."

ELIZABETH

On Hogmanay, the year we were betrothed, Robert and I set off with the pony and trap to visit Robert's distant relative at Auchindrain Farm. We were both excited at the prospect of looking over what would be our home after the wedding. We wrapped ourselves in layers of woollens under our oilskin coats. Mother had warmed two bricks and wrapped them in cloths to put on our laps, and as we trotted along the coast we shouted to each other above the sound of the waves on the wintry sea as they pounded against the outcrops of red sandstone.

Old Angus Stewart was to move to his sister's croft in the springtime, and by then Robert would have started at the farm, learning to work with the beasts, taking care of the milking and the slaughtering. It would be quite different to the farm at Balnacraivie, where the Stewarts had, from year to year, almost a thousand head of sheep.

We talked about our plans for a new venture at Auchindrain. I would make cheese. I had heard about a short course at Auchincruive Agricultural College by Ayr.

"It will certainly be a very strange honeymoon," Robert said, teasing me, "but at least we'll be in a cottage in the grounds." It would give the farm a new lease of life and it meant that my husband and I would work as a team. It felt very modern, and although I would no longer, as a married woman, be a teacher, we would be making a better life for ourselves together.

I had prepared a basket for Mr Stewart with a jar of Mother's apple relish, some freshly baked bread, and bramble cordial. I also put a few stems of Christmas roses together in damp tissue.

As we approached the farmhouse, we could see Angus Stewart standing in the doorway, smoking his pipe. Before we could dismount, he came forward to meet us, a tall gaunt man with sunken eyes and a yellowing pallor. His pipe was clenched firmly between his teeth and one hand was hooked in the pocket of his overalls, which were buttoned up over his collarless shirt; a flat cap sat low over his forehead.

"You've not heard then?" was the extent of his gruff greeting.

"Hello, Angus, heard what?" Robert's voice was calm.

"I sent word just yesterday with the postman."

Robert helped me down from the trap. "Is there something wrong?"

"My sister's boy is coming back from Canada."

Neither Robert nor I registered what was happening to us. We stared at him blankly, but my heart was racing.

"We had people there, but he couldn't make a go of cutting timber. It wasn't for him, more's the pity," Angus Stewart paused and pulled on his pipe, "and by rights Auchindrain should go to him."

Robert was speechless. I looked round at him to see his face contorted by disbelief and anger.

"But it was a promise made to Father five years since! You made that promise."

"Aye, but the boy is closer kin." Angus Stewart looked at me steadily, as if ignoring Robert. "I am sorry for it, but there's nothing to be done."

Robert was rigid, every muscle tense, as he absorbed the enormity of the blow. I took his arm, frightened that he might lose himself, but he shook me off. It was the first time I had seen him so furious, and so anguished, and so powerless.

"But we are to live here after we are married." His voice was threatening.

"Aye well, Robert, that cannot be. It is final. There is no more to be said." The timbre of the old man's voice echoed the cruel finality of his words.

I remember I was so stunned that in an almost involuntary gesture born of a long instilled politeness, I proffered Angus Stewart the basket. But in a flash, Robert had grabbed it from me. "This was a gift to wish you a guid new year, but you'll have a better one than I will." He threw the basket to the ground. The jar smashed into a sticky glassy mess and the flowers were strewn over the moss and stones in front of us, but Angus Stewart did not move a muscle. Then Robert lifted me onto the trap.

I had not said a word throughout, and even though we had had a terrible shocking blow, I would have said goodbye, for he was my elder. But the humiliation and desperation had so transformed Robert's handsome young face that I looked away from Angus Stewart, and we left Auchindrain in silence.

We turned the pony and trap and made for the road. Robert gripped the reins, his mouth set hard. "The old bastard. I swear he enjoyed that. He's destroyed everything for us," Robert shouted into the wind, and then he let out a furious animal cry of anger, so loud I thought it might travel back to Angus Stewart's ears.

I tried to order my thoughts, to be the practical one. I took his arm, said what use was it to dwell on the actions of a thrawn old man who was doing right by his nephew? Wouldn't he have felt compelled to do the same? But it was too soon for a rational conversation. I put my face into the wind and closed my eyes, for now it was Mother who consumed my thoughts, and once again I cursed her decision to sell Benkiln. That was where Robert and I should have lived; that was where I would have raised my children.

Robert sank into a dark brooding silence on the journey home to Lamlash, and as the winter light quickly faded, our only guide was the icy white moon reflecting on the water. I glanced at his face, which was now suffused with fear. "I have nothing to offer you, Elizabeth, no home, no income."

"We will think of something," I broke in quickly, in case he might say he was not fit to marry me, words that when spoken might hang in the air, souring it even more.

"There is nothing on Arran for me, Elizabeth, nothing. I want to be my own man. I want to work on my own land and be a husband that provides for his family."

"But Robert, it is too soon to give up hope of a farm. We will need to look harder, ask everyone we know."

"There is no farm to be had. You know that." Robert raised his voice.

"Perhaps we'll have to go to the mainland, then, and look in Ayrshire," I heard myself saying plaintively, shaken by Robert's vehement tone. In truth I had no desire to go to the mainland, but I did not want to sound fainthearted.

"Or further afield," he whispered, but I closed my ears and my mind to any thought of living anywhere where Arran was out of my sight.

I pressed my arm through his and we rode on in silence, lost in uncharted territory. As we approached Homelea I saw the familiar glow of the oil lamp beckoning us, and was calmed by the certainty of that at least. I knew that however much I resented the sale of Benkiln, Mother, perhaps in silent acknowledgement, would respond to our plight.

"We should tell Mother straightaway," I said. "She is very practical and she might be able to help."

I felt Robert stiffen a little. "I don't want to appear a failure to her," he said.

But in fact it was she who fired Robert's imagination. She changed everything.

★　★　★

195

The loss of Auchindrain hung over us like a heavy dark cloud. I put my love for Robert at the very centre of my life; but although I knew he adored me, for he told me often enough, I had moments when my fear for our future together crushed the breath from me. There was no certainty now, no enjoyment in daydreams, only awkward conversations. When I tentatively broached the possibility of our staying with Mother at Holmlea, he looked at me incredulously and said in a cold voice, "That might be an answer for other men, but not for me."

I must have looked crestfallen because he scooped me up then and buried his face in my neck and said, his voice cracking a little, "I'm sorry, Elizabeth. No matter what, we will be wed. But we will be together in our own home, and our own bed."

Secretly, I despaired. It was a difficult time. There were precious few jobs and farmers thought it a better calculation to weather poor prices than to up sticks, so there were no leases to be had in the whole of Ayrshire, or on Kintyre, for that matter.

At the end of January, when Mother and I were sitting together in the evening, her needle rhythmically working over a hem of a skirt, and I planning a lesson on *Treasure Island*, she put down her work and said, out of the blue, "I have written to Walter and Jessie McMillan."

I must have looked at her incomprehendingly. She hadn't talked about her aunt and uncle for years. They had emigrated, long before I was born, to a sheep station in Western Australia that they named Kilbride.

When I was little they had sent Mother a hand drawn map of the territory. I remember we laid out the drawing alongside the atlas on the damask cover of the dining table, and using my grandmother's magnifying glass, we pinpointed the station, beside the Murchison River and more than four hundred miles north of Perth. I can say that so precisely because the atlas, with the map marking the page, is in the bookcase still.

"I met cousin Isa from Catacol at the bank in Brodick last week. She said Jessie and Walter have thirty thousand Merino sheep and are prospering, but they are elderly, and of course they have no issue. Apparently they want to retire and hand over the station to a member of the family, so why not to Robert and you?"

I could not believe what I was hearing. Fury rose in me as if my chest had burst into flames. Not only had Mother acted independently of me without a second thought, she hadn't considered, or cared, whether I would have wanted to go to the other side of the world. Worse, she knew I would not.

"You don't mean for Robert and me to go to . . . Australia?" My voice was shaking. "I could never go that far away and leave you, or Arran. This is my home," I shouted, "and you said nothing to me about this, *nothing*."

"Control yourself, Elizabeth," she replied sharply, "you have to think about what is best for Robert. This is not just about you."

"Have you talked to him behind my back?"

"Please do not take that tone. Of course not. It would not do to get his hopes up. No, when I receive a reply from Walter and Jessie, that will be the time to talk to Robert."

"What if I were to ask you not to talk to him about it, ever?"

"Why, Elizabeth, I did not think you would be that selfish!"

"Please don't talk about selfish. You sold the farm without thinking about me."

There, it was out in the open, but Mother would give me no quarter.

"Because it was a decision for me, and me alone."

"But how do you know he would want to go?" I said, faltering, accepting defeat, because we both knew the answer to that question.

"Elizabeth," she sighed, and spoke more gently, "there is nothing for him here, and he is an ambitious young man. This would be an opportunity to make a new life, a different kind of life. If the McMillans say yes, you must grab it, for both your sakes."

In truth I was shattered, as much at my mother's willingness, desire, even, to see me go as the idea of being so very far from home. Though it was a well trodden path. Almost everyone on Arran had relatives in Australia or New Zealand or Canada. There was even one family who had recently left for South America.

I did not know whether to tell Robert. It would make it all the more real, and there would only be more disappointment if the McMillans turned down the idea.

And once the idea had taken root, if it were not Kilbride then he would find some other sheep station in that vast country.

I could not keep Mother's plan from him, but before I told him, I had made a plan of my own.

I had heard that Mr McGillvray, who owned the garage and petrol pump in Whiting Bay, was thinking of retiring. It was obvious to me that soon there would be more and more cars on the roads on Arran, judging by the increasing number of Rileys and Fords that arrived in the summer, loaded with holidaymakers and luggage. Perhaps I should have asked Robert before I approached Mr McGillvray but, I reasoned, if I was too late and he had already sold his business, what would be the point in telling Robert?

When I visited the garage I was very discreet, and asked Mr McGillvray to keep my enquiry confidential. He told me that two or three people had expressed an interest in the business but nobody had yet made an offer. What was more, he told me that there was a little cottage on the hill behind the garage that was included in the sale. To me it seemed too good an opportunity to miss. I had my savings, which would make a substantial deposit, and I reckoned the bank would agree to loan on a promising business. My mind raced ahead, adding a shop to the garage, perhaps beehives and chickens in the garden, but I wanted to pick my moment to talk to Robert about it.

He had bought tickets for a fiddle recital and dance at Brodick Hall that Saturday. It was a bitter cold night when we boarded the bus at Lamlash with all the others going to the dance. There was much singing and a great air of merriment, and I remember that Robert turned to me and told me that he was so proud to be my beau. He had to shout above the revelry and just as he spoke there was a break in the singing and everyone heard his declaration. There were hurrahs and the bus fell into clapping. We were both too happy to be embarrassed, and my heart soared because I had grown unused to seeing Robert so youthful and carefree.

When the bus reached Brodick we all tumbled out towards the beckoning noise and smoke, but I took Robert's arm and steered him beyond the hall, towards the golf course. "But Elizabeth, we'll freeze," he protested.

"I don't care. Please, Robert," I pleaded. I had worked out my strategy carefully. "I have important news."

We walked on the soft grass along the first fairway. I told him about my visit to Mr McGillvray's garage, careful to make it clear that I had said nothing about Robert's circumstances.

Immediately, he halted and yanked his arm from mine almost violently. "You spoke to him without talking to me first, Elizabeth?" His voice was barely controlled.

"Yes, but only because it might have been sold already and I didn't want to get your hopes up."

"What on earth made you think I would want to run a garage?" Anger glittered in his eyes. "I know nothing about cars. I don't care about cars. And now you've

200

humiliated me. Going about touting for work for me."
He laughed bitterly. "Now I look a fool."

But I did not stop. "But you could learn about cars,
Robert. It would mean that we could stay here."

"Be clear, Elizabeth, if that is the only thing on offer
then I don't *want* to stay here." He marched off, back
towards the hall, so that I had to run after him to catch
up.

"I'm sorry, Robert," I said, with tears pricking my
eyes in regret and frustration, because I knew that I had
only succeeded in making the prospect of Australia
more attractive to him. There was no point in keeping
Mother's endeavours from him now, so I asked him if
we could walk along to the Douglas Hotel to sit for a
while.

My mouth was dry. We ordered a pot of tea, but
although the hot liquid fortified me a little, when I put
the cup down it rattled on the saucer. I knew what his
reaction would be to the news about Kilbride, and once
I had sketched out Mother's plan, his eyes shone with
excitement, all ill humour gone, forgotten.

"Elizabeth, this is a God-given chance for us. It's
amazing. We were meant to have a different kind of
life."

He was too caught up in it all to care whether I
wanted that different kind of life. And then, in front of
all the others taking tea, he came round to my chair
and lifted me up, whirling me around, my feet flying. I
laughed in spite of myself and then I struggled, a little
embarrassed by the commotion, and implored him to
put me down.

I looked him straight in the face. "Robert, could you really leave all this? Leave your family behind?"

"All what, Elizabeth? We can't live on scraps of this and that, a day on the hay, a month's shepherding. That is not what I want. With you by my side I could go anywhere."

"But what about me," I said in a small voice, "what about what I might want?"

I watched him clench his jaw and saw, for the second time that night, a flash of anger.

"You know, sometimes I think your mother cares about my future, our future, more than you do."

When we finally walked along to the hall, Robert's words reverberated in my head. "I could go anywhere." The evening passed in a haze. Perhaps people thought me stand-offish and rude, but my mood was low. I had managed to persuade Robert not to talk about Australia to anyone for fear of another disappointment, but I am sure it took all his willpower, because from the moment I told him about Kilbride, he thought, and spoke of little else.

In the weeks that followed we both waited anxiously for the postman; I hoping that the McMillans would say no and Robert willing the opposite, for in his dreams we were already in Western Australia and the sheep station was his.

Mary was the only person in whom I could confide and who understood the competing claims on my heart. On one side there was Robert, the person who made me feel more cherished than I ever had before, and on the other the island itself, which was my anchor, the centre of my life, my home — and not just Holmlea, and Holy Isle, and Glenashdale Falls; I even felt the castle was home.

Sometimes, when I was small, as young as eight, Mother and I spent the night with Mary when she was staying at Brodick Castle. I learned the provenance of every piece of furniture and ornamentation, the ormolu mirrors and Aubusson carpets; but what impressed me most as a child, was the electric lights. The castle was the only place on the island to have electricity then, powered by a small hydro plant with water provided by Claddach. I was so unused to seeing the entirety of a room after nightfall that I was enchanted by the decorated plasterwork on the ceiling and the cornices bathed in bright light, as I lay on my back in the tall mahogany bed with barley sugar posts at its four corners.

After that I could never understand why Mary preferred the Whitehouse, where there were only oil lamps that hissed and wavered and sent a bitter smell into the air. She used to say, "It's a blessing I have a modern house like this to escape to when a sou'wester blows through every crevice in the castle." The Whitehouse was her haven, with its elegant Edwardian proportions, fireplaces inlaid with Delft tiles patterned with peacock feathers in blue and green, and the carved mantelpieces, each adorned with copper inlay. She and Mother spent evenings in the big comfortable drawing room, sewing and playing cards, while I lay contentedly on the feather sofa reading about Miss Havisham and her cobweb-covered bride cake.

So when Mary had offered us the Whitehouse for the wedding tea I had been happy beyond measure, and I remember that so fierce was my embrace, I almost winded her. She and I made plans to decorate the short walk from the kirk to the house with jars filled with late summer roses from the castle, and to collect bags of petals in the days just before the marriage, to be strewn along the path before us as Robert and I arrived.

But now that the prospect loomed that we might depart for Australia days after the wedding, my chatter became a little too bright, too brittle, until one day Mary clasped my hand and held onto it tightly and said, "Elizabeth, I beg of you, do not take against your mother for this."

In truth, I could not reconcile Mother's love for me and this act, as I saw it, of betrayal.

"My heart is so heavy. How can it be that the two people I love most in the world are making me so unhappy? And I know I am being selfish, but I can't help it. It is the rest of my life, and I feel as if I have no control at all over what happens to me."

"We have to make choices, Elizabeth, and when they are hard choices, the right decision is not always immediately a happy one."

"But I feel no excitement at the prospect of living on the other side of the world. How can Mother want me to go? I can't understand it. This is my home."

"You can make a home there, and a future. That is what Izzy is thinking about, my dear."

"But this is my home. If I close my eyes I can see every twist and turn on the String Road. If I conjure up

204

the roses in our garden I can smell their scent. Holy Isle is my constant companion. I want to live here with Robert, nowhere else."

I felt my heart straining when Mother and I were together during those weeks, but tried hard not to show it. I would steal a glance at her, or spy on her unawares, making an inventory of her, committing to memory the shape of her eye in profile, her hair softening into grey and held up in a bun, and the way her hands would move to her face to fix back tendrils. I studied every vein and line on her hands, the furrows on her brow and the way her still slender neck sloped down to her strong angular shoulders. If I close my eyes now I can see her as I saw her the day the news came from Australia, standing, her back to me, a still silhouette at the dining room window, the letter gripped in her hand, her arm rigid by her side.

Now my pen is shaking, and I fear my writing will be illegible if I do not stop for a moment. Saul warned me that my memories would rain blows on my heart. I will walk in the garden for a while. Niall is not here to distract me. He is on the other side of the world. Sometimes, when I look at him he reminds me of Robert, his determination, his pride, even his stubbornness; straight arrows, both.

I feel better for having stepped outside. The primulas on the edge of the border that runs to the gate are all in bloom, creating splashes of colour, yellow, purple and red, perhaps a little too gaudy, and behind them the tall black tulips with their dense petals look very dramatic against the stone wall. It was Niall's idea to plant black parrot tulips, and in great number. When he arrived with five-dozen bulbs I called him a scatter-cash. "Trust me, Elizabeth, you want instant impact," he said. I wasn't so sure, but in truth they make quite a display, and they must like it in my garden because they have thrived, despite the wind and the salt in the sea air.

My little friend hopped in and out of the border just now, like a tiny red bouncing ball, matching my pace as I walked towards the gate, as if to say, "Excuse me, remember the garden is as much mine as it is yours." He is the same robin who has made his home in the laurel tree for the past five years. Sometimes he flies onto the window ledge and serenades me if I am standing at the kitchen sink. Other times, if I am reading on the garden bench, he will sit on the arm by my elbow and wait for a present of cake crumbs. He is a solitary soul. I say "he" because that's how I think of him, but perhaps it is a female robin, a sister looking out for me. Whichever it is, I feel cheered by the beautiful bird cocking its little head towards me as if to say, "Elizabeth, push on. Push on."

The McMillans' proposition was straightforward. We would have our own house on the sheep station and Robert would work alongside Walter for three years, on a salary, and a generous one at that. Jessie would teach me the accounts. If after that time all was well, they would retire to Perth and Kilbride would be ours, on the condition we paid them a monthly stipend until the death of both husband and wife.

Robert was elated. "We'd be fools not to go! We'll never get another offer like this. Elizabeth, think of it, we'll be running our own sheep station."

I had no choice. I had nothing with which I could make a counter offer, and besides, to Robert it was a wonderful adventure, the chance for him to prove himself on a bigger canvas. If another opportunity had arisen, even the position of manager of the Home Farm at the Castle, it would never have been enough for him now that he had Australia in his sights and Kilbride in his grasp.

I looked down at my hands, clasped in my lap so tightly they were mottled bright red, not wishing to catch his eye for fear of crying, and whispered, "I don't think I have the words to describe how hard it will be for me to leave." But as soon as I had spoken, I could not stop myself and tears came in single rivers, and fell on my hands, and the more I tried to hold them back, the more they came.

Only Mary knew the depths of my anguish, as a diviner senses water.

Saul once said to me that the world is divided into people who "transmit" and those who "receive". In fact he used all manner of strange expressions, but when I think about Mary she certainly had the latter personality. It was she who bore the weight of the emotional distance between Mother and me after the decision was made. Without her, we could not have endured it. I know that it was hard for Mother, but only because she told Mary that the enormity of what she had set in motion had only struck her when she realised that she might never see me again.

So it was left to Mary to rekindle our excitement about the wedding, and her good humour was infectious. It was she who insisted that rather than have a shop-bought dress from Copelands in Glasgow, we should order the palest ivory Chinese silk for the gown and the finest lace from Morton's Lace Mills in Darvel to overlay it, and to complement Mother's veil. I sketched a drop-waisted ankle length gown with three-quarter length sleeves and sent the drawing and a note of my measurements to Mary's pattern maker in Paisley. Back came the detailed paper pattern, and Mother and I cut the fabric on the dining room table before setting to work at the treadle sewing machine, which we dragged to the dining room window.

I remember that my bouquet was the subject of much deliberation. Mary fretted that the gardens at the castle favoured flowers and plants that bloomed in spring and summer, apart from the late flowering roses, and I was to be married in September. Mother decided that it would be both pretty and unusual to hold fuschia stems, heavy with their vibrant bells. She said it would give the posy a Japanese look, like a Hornel painting.

Mother was very interested in art, and when she travelled to Glasgow she often visited the gallery of Aitkin and Dott to see some modern paintings. So when "Bunty", as Cadell was known, came to stay that spring at the Whitehouse as Mary's guest, Mother and I joined them for dinner.

Francis Boileau Cadell was well known by the early 1930s, though previously in his career he had been criticised for being "all colour and no form," a view with which Mother had always disagreed. He had come to Arran to fulfil a commission from Caledonian MacBrayne to paint their fleet of passenger boats. Mother was especially pleased to be asked to dinner with him, and they immediately hit it off. He was an irrepressible character with a friendly face and a pipe clamped between his teeth, dressed in a kilt with tweeds and a tam o'shanter perched on his head at a comical angle. I had never seen a man making a fuss of Mother before, and it brought out a girlishness in her that I had never witnessed before. Before the night was over he had asked if he might sketch her. Mother immediately declined, now embarrassed by the attention, protesting that my wedding dress was her priority.

"Nonsense, Izzy," insisted Mary, "you will wear your eyes out if you sew from morning till night. You must let Bunty sketch you. He can't paint funnels all the time."

And so it was. The next afternoon, after sewing from first light, Mother disappeared upstairs and returned in her fine midnight-blue cashmere, a faint dab of rouge on her cheeks — or perhaps the pretty rose glow was simply her excitement — and then she set off for the Whitehouse.

When she returned I asked what they had talked about all afternoon, while she sat for him on the window seat in the upstairs drawing room.

"Oh, art, and this and that. The war, what he did in France," she replied, and wouldn't be drawn further. She had shut me out once again. I had been so happy to see her the centre of someone's attention, but she would not allow me to be privy to one of the more interesting conversations of her life.

Over the years, when I look back on the few days they spent in each other's company, I have been ashamed of my harsh judgement, for I am sure that the bond they made was born out of the war. Cadell had served with the Argyll and Sutherland Highlanders and was wounded in France. It was Mother's only opportunity to ask questions she could never have asked of anyone else. When I look at the ink and watercolour portrait, I imagine their conversation, Mother's pent up questions, her looking into the middle distance as Bunty described the villages, the Cypress trees, the endless flat vistas and huge skies, the trenches and the rations, the smoking and the boredom and the fear, and going over the top, and the repeated deafening rat-a-tat-tat of the covering machine-gun fire as they ran forward.

MARTHA

Martha opened the door of the Glenburn, a handsome apothecary bottle of gin in one hand, and called out Catriona's name to an echoing silence. As she passed the open door of the residents' lounge, she saw her stretched out, asleep on the sofa. The cascade of strawberry blonde hair around her face gave her the appearance of a reclining pre-Raphaelite; there were papers scattered on the floor beside her.

Martha was about to turn and tiptoe on upstairs to her room when Catriona woke with a start and, realising Martha was studying her, she put her hands to her face, but not before Martha had noticed her bleary eyes.

"Catriona, are you OK? You look exhausted."

"I'm fine," she whispered, her voice barely audible, "I didn't sleep well last night. I came in here to go over the accounts, but I must have drifted off."

"It's awful when sleep won't come," Martha said sympathetically. "All that 'dark night of the soul' stuff. Want me to leave you?"

Catriona shook her head and raised herself onto her elbows. "No, I'll be fine in a minute."

Martha was surprised at the change in Catriona in the couple of days she had been away, her air of fragility. "I'll make you a cup of tea. Or," she held up the bottle, "even better, a gin and tonic."

Catriona blinked at her and smiled wanly. "You know, I think I'll go for the tea."

"Ha! So Saul was right. He said wine was your thing."

"But right now, Earl Grey's my tipple of choice."

Martha sensed a shift in Catriona's mood.

"We saw you out on the boat."

"We?"

"Niall and I." Martha felt heat flood through her body. "Was he helpful?" Catriona asked tentatively.

"Yes," replied Martha carefully, "he was. I'm beginning to see that Elizabeth Pringle drew strength from them both, Saul and Niall."

"They're both good for that. I should know," sighed Catriona, leaving her words hanging in the air.

"You're not the only one who makes mistakes," she said as Martha returned with their tea.

"Want to talk about it?" enquired Martha gently.

"Actually, yes. I've had no one here I *could* talk to." She laughed. "It would be like taking an advert in the *Arran Banner*."

Martha sat on the edge of the sofa listening intently while Catriona told her about the young architect who'd been recommended to her for the hotel renovation, six months earlier. Guy had been very talented, with lots of good ideas, and she'd been flattered when he started to pay her as much attention as the project, but she hadn't counted on Niall's hostility. "It was bewildering," explained Catriona, "I would ask him why Guy irked him so much and he would just shrug. "I don't trust him," he would say. "Call it intuition."

The more he criticised, the more she pursued the relationship. "I railed against Niall the same way an adolescent battles against a parent. It was the only time since Mum and Dad died that we have ever clashed. And when Guy began to spend more time here, I tried to tell Niall it was because of his great attention to detail, though of course, it wasn't. He just wanted sex, nothing more, and nothing less, like beer on tap. And Niall was right, I was infatuated."

Catriona described how she would try to resist him and he would simply become sarcastic, mocking her design ideas and claiming she knew nothing about aesthetics. Instead of standing up to him, she became insecure. One day he arrived and immediately started to berate her for choosing "middlebrow wallpaper". It was such a ridiculous criticism, she said, that she had burst out laughing, and Guy had responded in a fury, his scarlet, sneering face thrust into hers as he hurled insults at her.

At this moment Catriona had noticed Saul passing, pausing a little at the crescendo of invective. They had recently met, the only two passengers on the bus from Brodick to Lamlash one afternoon, and he had been at his most entertaining. Before the journey was over he had offered to bring her one of his cookery books — treasured possessions from his old life. But when he arrived the next afternoon he had also brought mackerel from friends at the harbour, he said, and had asked if he could prepare a meal for her.

"Wait a minute," interjected Martha, "sorry to be pedantic, but I thought Buddhists ate neither fish nor fowl, nor beasts of the field?"

Catriona laughed. "Well spotted. There are one or two kinks in Saul's faith, to say the least, and besides he was 'offshore'!"

She resumed her story. "He came back to check on me, the day he overheard the quarrel. Guy had gone but I was still shaky and I was so relieved to see him. I didn't have to tell him anything. He knew. We sat and drank a bottle of wine at the kitchen table and he calmed me down. 'Look at you Catriona,' he said, 'you don't deserve to be abused. You should be cherished.'

"When he left, he put his hands on either side of my face and told me that day or night, if I needed him, I was just to call the Long House, and he would come straight away."

Martha realised that she had seen Guy for herself. It must have been on one of her first days on Arran. They had been walking towards Paterson's store from opposite directions. He was tall and classically handsome with a mop of brown hair. He wore a tight zipped up Belstaff jacket, drainpipe jeans and brown suede brogues, and his head was down as he charged ahead of her into the shop, but she saw him glance at her through his oversize black spectacle frames.

"Can I have my order?" he said gracelessly, ignoring Billy Paterson as he took the bundle from him and sifted through it. "Where's *Blueprint*?"

"I don't think you asked me for that," replied Billy evenly.

Guy, still not meeting the shopkeeper's eye, a sharp breath through closed teeth, said "I think you'll find I definitely did."

Billy Paterson took his pencil from behind his ear and slowly and deliberately traced his way through each page of the order book while Guy drummed his fingers on the counter.

"No, there's nothing here I'm afraid."

"Oh, for fuck's sake." He grabbed his magazines and charged out of the shop.

Billy looked at Martha, raised his eyebrows, and in a feat of extraordinary dexterity, winked at the same time. "It's incomers like him that give incomers a bad name." He smiled. "I'm exempting you from that category, of course."

"Thank you, I'm honoured," Martha said, laughing.

It was only now that it dawned on her who he reminded her of. She turned to Catriona. "I realise I've seen Guy, in the paper shop, and you know what? It's extraordinary but he looked like Andrew. He had the same sense of entitlement, he *behaved* just like Andrew."

Catriona grinned. "It's good to know I'm not the only one who falls for these types."

She and Saul had started to spend more time together. He told her about his old life. She spoke for

215

the first time, to someone other than Niall, about her parents. He told her about two women he'd slept with on the island, "with no expectation on either side of anything more than comfort and company." But that was not what he wanted now. Catriona took him to her special place where she went to be alone with her thoughts, away from paint and invoices and the open, empty reservation book . . . if she was honest, away even from her brother. They drove around the coast to Machrie and walked up onto the moor over the sphagnum moss and springy heather, through the soft ethereal mist until, amidst the cairns and hut circles built six thousand years ago, into the protective embrace of three bronze age stones, red sandstone pillars, the tallest eighteen feet high, which faced each other like three wise ancients talking about grave matters of state. Catriona told Saul that archaeological studies had shown they had been placed on the moor in the best position to be seen from as wide an area as possible. "Stand in the centre," she said, "and feel the power of the stones as they tower over you, and you'll yearn to understand who put them there, and why, and who touched them, who knew they were almost home when they saw them in the far distance." Catriona and Saul stood close together, surrounded by the giant sentinels, and looked beyond the Mull of Kintyre to the Paps of Jura. She said she found it hard, as an archaeologist, to accept the inability to solve every prehistorical puzzle. He told her that the first time he had seen her outside the hotel, painting the new signs, concentrating hard, her hair falling around her beautiful face, he was enchanted, and now she had mesmerised him. Catriona blushed, as she related Saul's words.

"And Guy?" asked Martha.

"He came back two weeks later to check the last of the work, strolled in as if nothing had happened, expecting me to be as pliant as ever. I asked him to leave straightaway and he launched a particularly vicious volley of abuse, not realising that Niall was working in the garden. He came barrelling through the door and pinned Guy against the wall, threatening to kill him if he talked to me like that again. If I hadn't started screaming at them to stop, one of them, and it would have been Guy, would have been badly hurt."

She shook her head. "Niall behaved like a man possessed, but you know, when I think about it, that is exactly how I would have expected him to react. He has always been protective to a fault, and he meets fire with fire."

That night Catriona had locked the heavy storm doors at her brother's behest but long after dark she heard a knock. When she had asked who was outside, Saul replied, "Something told me you needed me to come back from Holy Isle."

"Don't you think that's strange, Martha?"

Martha looked out at the scudding clouds, and squeezed Catriona's hand. "Do you feel up to a walk to the house? It's another lovely afternoon, and I'd like you to come with me."

As they strolled along Shore Road, Martha stopped and turned to Catriona. "If I hadn't met you I'm not so sure I'd have stayed."

Catriona gave her a sideways glance. "Oh, there might have been other reasons to stay."

"Oh yeah," Martha replied sardonically, a blush spreading across her face, "and I bet that would have gone well."

When they arrived at Holmea she showed Catriona the sketches Niall had made for the kitchen. "He's good, isn't he?"

"Yes, he's good at lots of things, my brother." She glanced back at the sketches. "I could ask a builder I know, Johnny Wilson, about the job."

She wandered down the hallway towards the half open door of the sitting room. Pushing against it she said, "I would never tire of looking at these tapestries. They could last me a lifetime."

Her eyes rested on a profusion of greenery in an embroidery worked on fine linen. A majestic oak was so perfectly stitched it appeared to be growing out of the canvas, its new leaves unfurled and glossy green, in perfect satin stitch. The tree was the centre of attention and around its steadying roots animals congregated, as if in a scene from *Snow White*. There were rabbits, red squirrels, stoats and field mice, beside them owls and finches, and visible through the blades of grass, iridescent blue-black beetles, delicate spiders and ladybirds whose red wings, spotted with tiny black dots, were fanned in readiness for flight. Every moment spent studying the tree was rewarded by a new detail, a bat hanging contentedly on an outer branch, a speckled thrush atop a nest tucked deep in a strong fork, an adder curled up between two roots.

Catriona traced her fingers over the canvas. "What a labour of love," she exclaimed, "I have never seen anything like it."

Martha stood back from the wall. "Do you see the fairies hidden in the foliage?"

"*More* fairies?" said Catriona as she peered at the tiny figures clothed in tawny tunics, their eyes two single elongated emerald green stitches and their wings, streamers of silver thread. "Were you ever in the Brownies?"

Martha shook her head. "Mum was a bit of a hippy. She thought it was a sinister paramilitary organisation."

"Well, I was a loyal wood sprite, and I think these are sprites. Oaks are their favourite trees, *if* you're a believer." She peered at the embroidery. "Elizabeth Pringle must have had some affinity with the netherworld. Or maybe she was just a little batty."

The linen canvas was set in a beautifully grained oak frame painted with oak leaves. At the top, in the centre, was the word "Quercus" and at the bottom was painted, "Oak of the Sun".

Martha walked around the room. "I have the feeling that I am looking at a giant puzzle. When I put the tapestries away while the work's being done, I must try to remember exactly where each one is hung."

"But where will you stay?"

Martha paused for a minute. She had thought to stay at Homelea, but Catriona jumped in. "Stay with me; I'd love that. I mean as *my* guest, not an hotel guest."

"Really? Thank you, I would love to . . ."

"But?"

Martha took a beat. "If it's all right with you, I'll come and go between the two. I want to get a feel for the house, and I don't want to get in your way."

Catriona looked at her incomprehendingly.

"When Saul's around, I mean."

"Don't worry. Sometimes he stays, other times he's on Holy Isle."

"Does Sister Indra know?"

Catriona nodded. "And so does Niall, but I wouldn't talk to him too much about it. He and Saul circle each other a bit."

Martha looked surprised. "I don't imagine I'll be engaging Niall in conversation about anything any time soon."

"Really? He told me he was going to cook dinner for you."

ELIZABETH

In the spring and early summer, much of my time was taken up with my pupils. I remember so well the girls begging me to bring a piece of silk and a square of the Darvel lace to the classroom. They had shyly asked if I would draw a picture of my wedding dress, if they promised, they said very solemnly, to keep it a secret. "It is so bonnie, Miss," said little Jane Johnstone when I showed the girls a sketch, "you will look like a fairy princess."

"Hardly, Jane," I laughed, "but I'm sure I will *feel* like a princess just for the day."

"Will there be a scramble?" asked another.

"Of course there will be a scramble, and there might be a silver sixpence among the farthings."

They all clapped and said they would come to the church and throw petals and rice.

In the lengthening evenings I sewed a going away dress, and Mother and I marked out a silver-grey fitted coat with a lambskin collar from the Copeland's catalogue.

It is all so vivid to me, and the longer I live, the more I can revisit some moments of pure happiness, without sorrow clouding my eyes. But now I am so very conscious that the sand is draining fast into the glass below, and I cannot afford to dwell on that time. I have to reach the end before it is too late. Saul does his best to keep me on an even keel. "Elizabeth," he says, "you will live until your story has ended."

Robert made all of our travelling arrangements, and busied himself with all manner of books about Australia, and travelling to Auchincruive Agricultural College to hear lectures by a Scottish farmer who had returned from New South Wales. Robert had great plans to introduce different breeds of sheep at Kilbride, and told me he had the farmer from Australia worn out with his questions. He worked so hard during those months, hiring himself out to farms around the island when he was not needed at Balnacraivie, saving every penny he could, so that often we only saw each other on a Sunday, when we would cycle for miles.

I wanted to commit every inch of the island to memory. I imagined myself lying in bed on the sheep station under a vast black sky, miles from anywhere, listening to strange night time noises like the kookaburra of the round song we sang in class, picturing Goatfell rising above Brodick Castle in the sunshine and then in the gloaming, that beautiful special time, Mother drawing the curtains and setting out her playing cards for a game of patience.

But I tried to banish these thoughts, for they filled me with dread. Try as I might, I could not rid myself of the notion that Robert was so taken up with his adventure, so buoyed by all the envious words from other young men on the island, that it came to matter less and less to him that I was only going because I loved him and wanted to be his wife. That was what it sounded like to me when he said he would not look back for a moment. He was simply impatient to be away. He would remember Arran he said, by the shepherd's crook he had whittled from an old oak that had been felled to ease a bend on the road up the brae from Lamlash. That would be enough for him, he said.

During the evenings that Mother and I spent sewing my wedding dress, I started to notice her cough, though she behaved as if she was unaware of it. It came from deep in her chest, a repeated rasping noise. Once, when she found it hard to catch her breath, I jumped up and rushed to help her and I was sure I noticed a little blood on the handkerchief she quickly put in the sleeve of her cardigan. "For goodness' sake, Elizabeth, sit down. It's nothing. Don't make a fuss." She would not hear of a visit to the doctor, however much I begged. "It is only a tickle. Why ever would I spend money on the doctor, just to tell me as much?"

But in the mornings, when, as usual, she rose before I did, I lay and listened to her in the bathroom, and I was sure that what I heard, a sharp cough quickly stifled, was Mother burying her face in a towel to keep her discomfort from me.

She spent very little money on herself but she allowed herself what she called, somewhat in jest, "my great extravagance". She and a number of other women from "The Rural" had joined Lamlash Golf Club three years earlier, as soon as it was decreed that lady members would be welcome, a privilege for which she paid one pound and five shillings a year. I remember the sum only because it was a bone of contention that the men paid just five shillings more, but could vote in matters to do with the club, unlike the lady members. Mother played golf with three others, on the first Friday in the month. "The Lamlash hacking and yacking club" she used to call the foursome, and she looked forward to it come rain or shine.

I have had to will myself to remember the day. It was 15 August 1933. The morning began bright and blustery and at noon, before she left to walk to the golf course, we hung washing out together, enjoying flinging the billowing sheets over the line, trying to peg them as they flew into our faces and screwing up our eyes against their blinding whiteness.

She had only been gone an hour when heavy spots of rain plopped onto the ground and, within minutes, a deluge consumed Lamlash, a downpour so heavy that Holy Isle was lost behind a grey curtain of water that descended from the sky into the sea.

I took an umbrella and raced to the golf course to find her, running so fast I had to press my hand to my side to try to stop the pain of a stitch. I sped down the steep road that crosses the course, all the while calling out for her, until finally I spotted the group huddled under a tree, their summer clothes drenched and clinging to their bodies like a cumbersome second skin they could not shed, and their hair, usually so neat and groomed, like a dark slick of oil covering their skulls. As I neared, I could see that they were laughing and smoking, and waving at me as if I was the comical sight racing towards them through the downpour with my umbrella flying. But when I reached them, I could see the relief on Mother's face, and that despite her protestations, she was glad I had come for her. When I propelled her back to Holmlea as quickly as I could, and helped her out of her clothes, something hitherto unimaginable, and ran her a bath with lavender salts, she turned to face me as I helped her in, and said, her voice breaking, "You are the most thoughtful girl in the world."

But neither the warm bath, nor the thick steam that rose from it, could soothe her laboured breathing. I filled the stone bottle with boiling water and wrapped it carefully in a soft wool cover and put it beside her in bed, tucking an extra eiderdown around her, but she shivered and coughed through the night until I could bear it no longer and without telling her I was going, ran for the doctor. Dr Ellery brought me back in his car straightaway, and as soon as he saw Mother, even before he sounded her chest, I knew from his voice that she was gravely ill.

"Mrs Pringle," he said gently, holding her hand, "Elizabeth and I are going to help you into the car. We'll get you to hospital where we can look after you for a wee while, just till your cough eases and your chest clears."

I think that in her delirium everything was shrouded in fog, his words distant muffled noises, because she made no reply, no objection.

225

Much later the next day, as I sat in her hospital room, my chair by the bed, my head near hers on the pillow, I felt the faint pressure of her hand as she stroked my hair, just for a moment. I looked at her but her eyes, the lids pale with tiny purple veins at her lashes, remained closed as she forced herself to breathe, short shallow breaths.

In the afternoon the nurses sat her up gently to administer an inhalation and to wash her back with warm cloths, but she was so weak I could see that she was desperate to sink back down again.

I had sent word for Mary and Robert to come quickly, and when Mary arrived first, Dr Ellery bade us both sit down in the bare white-tiled office he used at the hospital. "This is quite irregular, Your Grace, as you are not family, but I know how close you are to Mrs Pringle, and I fear Elizabeth will very soon need your support."

Mary reached for my hand, but I could not move, paralysed by the confirmation of what I already knew but did not want to believe.

"Elizabeth, in the past few months, has your mother been short of breath or complaining of a pain in her chest or her back?" Dr Ellery enquired.

I thought I detected a note of reproach and I stammered that she had been coughing a lot. He sighed. "I'm afraid that I am quite sure your mother has pneumonia, and combined with an already weakened chest, and perhaps cancer of the lung, she has little with which to fight." When I immediately said that although the school term had started I would stay at home to nurse her, Dr Ellery shook his head and said more kindly, "No, she must rest here, where we can look after her."

Mary put her arms around me and I collapsed against her. At that moment Robert arrived and she passed me to him, asking Dr Ellery if she could sit with Mother for a while.

All I could think about was keeping Mother alive. I asked Robert to cycle straightaway to the butcher for a piece of steak, and I ran home to prepare beef tea. I put the steak into a stone jar, filled it with water and tied greaseproof paper tightly over the top before I set it to simmer in a pan of water for an hour. Then I packed Mother's prettiest linen nightdress, her silver-backed hairbrush and the lambswool socks she had knitted for me the Christmas before. I strained the beef tea into a flask and ran back up the hill to the hospital.

Mary was still with Mother, sitting close, soothing her brow with a damp muslin and talking quietly to her all the while, to try to banish the fear that must have been in her heart.

"How has she been?" I whispered, and as I spoke she opened her eyes and looked up at me. "I have brought you a flask of beef tea. Do you remember you used to make it for me when I was little?" She smiled faintly and beckoned to me. "I'd like some very much, Elizabeth," her whisper turning into a racking cough.

Mary helped her lift her head and shoulders a little from the pillow while I fed her, blowing gently on the liquid first, lest it hurt her lips, and although it was a great effort, she managed to swallow two or three spoonfuls before lying back down heavily. She felt for my hand. "That tasted good, Elizabeth. You remembered the pepper."

That night, alone with her in the little bare room, with its worn linoleum floor and scent of carbolic soap, I sang the "Skye Boat Song" to her and described the day all those years ago when our little rowing boat bobbed and danced in the waves of Lamlash Bay. I talked of much more besides, the day we absentmindedly put salt rather than sugar in the preserving pan with our raspberries, or the Sunday afternoons when she read *Treasure Island* to me. I reminded her of the time when I had closed the classroom door on a Friday afternoon, leaving tadpoles in an old Belfast sink, and when the children arrived on Monday they, and I, were astonished to see little frogs hopping around the classroom. She laughed at that, but then I had to help her catch her breath, and as she put her handkerchief to her mouth, I noticed the spots of blood again.

I sorely wanted to tell her I knew the source of the unhappiness that had lodged in her heart for so long, but I feared I would only hasten her death. I just willed her to live, and I would have gladly transferred my strength to her had it been possible.

Dr Ellery came in to administer morphine just before midnight, and she breathed a little easier, but in the morning when I could see that she was weaker still, I lay down beside her, gently raising her head in the crook of my arm. She looked at me and I saw that her eyes were wide with fear. I wanted to crush her to me, to bind her tightly to me, but I feared I would break her

228

into pieces. I longed to hold her forever, but with each hard-fought breath I knew she was slipping from me.

In my head I was screaming, "Don't go, don't go," but I told her that I had loved her, always, always, always, and not to be afraid.

A nurse glided into the room silently and stood by me, her hand resting on my shoulder, and moments later, with only the smallest of untroubled sighs escaping from her softly parted lips, my mother died. I put my head down on the bed and remained there until at last the nurse separated us, and with her arm around me, guided me out of the room to a seat near the window. She gave me hot sweet tea, and I stared out at Holy Isle without seeing anything at all.

For many years I locked those memories away. That day was too painful to revisit, but now I have written of it, I have a little peace, for today at least. Saul says that we bury our pain so deeply that sometimes we can never find it, but it keeps hurting us nonetheless.

Mary and Robert were the two pillars on which I leaned during the days that followed. It was they who made the preparations for the funeral, and when the day came they entered the kirk on either side of me. I almost fainted when I saw the sea of people, every pew filled, and I had to hold tight to Robert when I heard the swelling soaring heartfelt sound of more than two hundred voices singing Mother's favourite hymn, Hymn 21. When I heard the words, "Frail as summer's flower we flourish, Blows the wind and it is gone," my tears finally came, but they were bitter tears and, far from feeling comfort in the Lord, that day I lost what faith I had.

I stood at the door of the kirk, as if in a dream, with Robert and the minister by my side as the mourners filed past, the men clutching their rough woollen caps, the women in their dark Sunday hats, quietly paying their respects. I stood straight, my eyes dry, helping them past, smiling at each familiar face and at people I had never seen before. Some simply took my hand, others made remembrances and I thanked them. Then I watched as the men lifted the coffin onto the cart, which was draped in black cloth, and Robert took the reins to guide the horse slowly to the cemetery with the men following on foot, their heads bowed. In those days it was very rare for women to go the graveside, and in truth I did not want to see, or hear, the earth falling hard on the coffin after it was lowered into the lair.

Mary took my arm and we walked together to the Whitehouse. In the drawing room she poured two glasses of pale whisky from a crystal decanter. I had never tasted the spirit before. It caught my throat and then softened and left a warm rich taste in my mouth.

"This will do us both good," Mary said as we sat on either side of the fire. "Izzy and I sometimes sat just like this, in the afternoon, sewing and nursing our whiskies . . ."

Her voice trailed off and when I looked at her I realised she was shaking, all composure gone, tears falling down her cheeks unchecked. The strength she had summoned for my sake since Mother died had ebbed away and finally, she gave way to her grief. Now it was my turn to be the comforter. We sat peacefully together, sometimes silent and at other times recalling something of Mother, each from our own deep store of memories.

Since the day I had found Mother on the golf course I had given scant thought to the wedding, but now, sitting with Mary, I came to a sudden decision. "We sail to Australia in less than six weeks. I can't be married here. How could I see all those people again? And not in that church."

Mary's eyes widened in astonishment. "But Elizabeth, are you seriously saying you won't get married in the kirk? There's no no other way. And you know it's what Izzy would have wanted."

"I can't do it," I said, "I can't."

Mary took my hand. "I can't imagine how dreadful this is for you, but soon you are going to begin a new chapter of your life."

"But I love my life here." Then it came to me as clear and piercing as the sound of a crystal bell. "And Robert doesn't love me enough to stay."

"Look at me, child," Mary replied gravely, returning my steady gaze. "Do you love him enough to go, Elizabeth? Only you can decide that."

At that moment the air froze, and I could hear the beat of my heart booming so loudly and frantically I expected Mary to hear it too. I nodded my head slowly, as if in a trance. Then I heard her say, "Well then, you will have to be wed."

I willed myself back into the drawing room. "I have heard that a ship's captain can perform marriage ceremonies. We can be wed when we leave Greenock."

Mary looked shocked. "I have heard that too, but what will Robert have to say about this? And besides, is it entirely legal?"

"It will be as legal as it needs to be."

"And Robert?"

"He will not care. We will be on our way; that is what will matter to him. Yes, that is what we will do."

Mary was deep in thought but all she said was, "You are more like your mother than you know."

She asked me to stay at the Whitehouse until we sailed but I could not bear to be away from home for a single night before I had to close the doors for the last time. Mother's death had thrown everything off kilter. I could not even think of selling Holmlea, or renting it out. I harboured a dream that we would return to it in three years' time for a sojourn before we took over Kilbride for good.

When I broached the subject with Robert of cancelling the wedding and being married on the ship, it was just as I thought it would be. "Elizabeth, it is a decision for you, my darling. I will marry you on land or on sea. I don't care about the church," he smiled conspiratorially, "and it will make our going even more of an adventure."

And so to the people Mother had issued wedding invitations, Mary wrote a note asking them instead to a farewell lunch at the Whitehouse the day we were to take the steamer to Greenock.

In the weeks that followed, she and I spent many hours together. For a wedding gift she gave us a set of the finest leather luggage: a wooden-framed trunk tooled with Robert's initials, and for me, three cases with the letters EMS. Together she and I packed for the unknown, and on the very top, wrapped in tissue paper, I put Mother's finest woollens and her favourite summer dress, a yellow and cream check in lawn cotton. The house would be looked after and aired now and then by one of Mary's estate workers. I gave her Cadell's painting of Mother for safekeeping. "How wonderful," she exclaimed, "I can have a word with Izzy every day."

The new plans were made. Robert had arranged that we would be wed as soon as the captain had navigated the ship from Greenock out into open water. He worried over me now, and sometimes I would catch him glancing at me when I was making a mental note of everything familiar that I was about to lose. As the day of our departure loomed closer, my dread of it grew ever greater.

I will have to stop writing now. My eyes ache and in truth I feel overwhelmed by it all sometimes. I wish Niall were here to entertain me for an hour or two with talk about the new hybrid roses at the castle, or to share some scurrilous gossip about the younger gardeners. I am the only person to whom he confides such tittle-tattle. He takes his position very seriously and worries about the welfare of his staff. To the outside world I imagine he is a bit of a closed book but here he is different, and I like it that I had his confidence.

"Elizabeth," he once said to me, laughing, "I can let off steam with you because I know it will never escape up the chimney."

Will I ever see him again? If I close my eyes I can see him pushing the big heavy roller down to the seaside wall and back, as if it were as light as a carpet sweeper, not travelling quite as straight as I'd like, but well enough. He insisted that I sit down. "Elizabeth I *want* to do this for you. It gives me pleasure," and then he laughed. "OK, if you really want to, you can supervise me."

Last night I poured a whisky from the special bottle Niall brought me from the distillery at Lochranza as a farewell present before his trip, and I slept a little better. If I am to get to the end of it all I have to keep writing, because all the whisky on Arran will not be enough to fortify me for much longer.

The day before we were due to sail, I went to the cemetery as I had done each day since the funeral. I took some snowdrop corms, Mother's favourites, honey-scented, with snowy white petals marked by two beautiful jewel-like green spots. I knelt beside the grave to dig in the little bulbs near the headstone, and at that moment I was filled with panic. My head swam and my breath came in gasps as if I were near to drowning. I put my hands on the headstone to steady myself, but the stone felt soft and clammy and the blood in my head was like the sound of a great torrent of water tumbling out of control, for it was at that exact moment, as I put my trowel into the earth, that I realised I could not leave. I could not leave her. I imagined her still with me, by my side and in the air above me; I imagined that some invisible tendrils of her hair were holding onto me, and no matter that I loved Robert deeply, that he was the only man I wanted, I would not go with him.

I ran from the graveyard and hurried along the shore to the Whitehouse and asked if Mary's driver could take a message to Robert to meet me at the Falls. Then I took the bus to Whiting Bay and started up through the woods, tears blinding me as I careered along the path, my mood frenzied as I relived all the times we'd spoken endearments and made protestations of love in this very place. I reached the tree that become the repository of our dreams, and traced my hand across all our carvings, pressing my fingers hard into the grooves and spirals, and then I stretched up my arms and with both my hands, I covered our two names, and stood waiting there, my cheek against the ragged musty bark, for Robert's footfall.

As he came towards me his face was solemn and sadness surrounded him. He knew without my saying. He put his finger to my lips and I clutched him, feeling his solidity, breathing in his brackish scent. He had tears in his eyes. "I can't do this without you, Elizabeth. You are the strong one. I don't think you know it, but you are." His voice cracked. "And you are my true love."

"And you are mine but I can't leave, it is all too soon. I am so sorry, Robert."

He sat down on the grass and buried his head in his arms. "Then I must stay and wait until you're ready."

"No, you must go on. You've made all your plans for Kilbride. I will follow you, but please, I cannot go now."

He looked at me, fear in his eyes. "But how can I be sure that you will come?" There was no reproach in his voice.

I took his face in my hands and kissed his eyes and tasted his warm salty tears, and then I kissed his mouth and pushed him gently back on the soft moss, and unbuttoned his shirt. He put his hand on mine to stop me, but I took it and kissed his calloused palm and then placed his hand on my breast. "Please, Robert," I said. I had no fear, and an excitement rose in me at the certainty of what I was doing. I wanted to give him the only thing that was mine to give, and when he entered me slowly he kept his eyes on mine and although I felt a sharp stab of pain, it gave way to a feeling of ecstasy, that I had proved to him that I loved him. We stayed in the woods until the sun went down, our pale bodies entwined on the carpet of moss and grass, holding on to each other, feeling how we fitted together, committing our lovemaking to memory.

When our guests gathered at the Whitehouse the next day, we stood hand in hand, and Robert told the farewell party that we had decided that it was too soon after my mother's death for me to travel, and that he would go on ahead to Kilbride. When we all walked to the pier the steamer was already there, its funnels blowing smoke hard, as if it were showing its impatience to be away.

Robert was at his finest that day, and putting his arm around me he asked the throng all to look after me because I was the person most precious to him in the world. As the ship's whistle sounded, he pressed his hand in mine and I felt a smooth cool oval, like a stone, except it was a silver locket. He whispered to me to open it when he was gone and in it I would find a lock of his hair, and then he kissed my forehead very gently.

It was only when he stepped onto the gangway that I truly understood that he was leaving. It could have been the very bridge to the other side of the world. I felt Mary slip her hand into my free one, and I squeezed it hard in an effort to control myself. My heart racing, I waved farewell as people all around shouted out, "safe passage!" "fair winds" "good luck, Robert."

As the steamer headed out towards the Firth of Clyde, Robert stood at the stern, waving. Then his hand dropped to his side and my tall handsome betrothed became a forlorn figure, immobile, staring back at me, until the boat taking him the first short sailing to Greenock on his long journey to Australia, disappeared from view.

MARTHA

Martha walked a little way up the hill on the road out of Lamlash and turned right onto the rough track that dipped down steeply before it cut across the golf course and then, rising again, ended half a mile beyond, at the cemetery. When she reached the top she could see that there were two separate graveyards, a recent addition and an older smaller one. The original was set within low stone walls on which were mounted simple wrought iron railings, rusted brown with age and weather. The tall gates were shut, tied together with a pink string, so visitors entered by an old swing gate. Martha pushed it forward, stepped into the space, and let the gate fall back again with a clatter, sending a family of rooks up from the trees beyond the graveyard walls, cawing in protest at the disturbance.

There were gravestones of all sizes, a few ornately carved but most were simple slabs of grey stone, and almost all of them were patterned with blooms of the palest lichen, which spread over the letters and words as if protecting them from the elements. Martha could still make out all the names of the dead, many of them buried one upon the other in ancient family lairs, reunited after years apart.

Dark green moss grew in the crevices where the headstones met the bright grass. Some headstones, perhaps feeling abandoned, had finally given up and fallen over, always, Martha noted, with the inscriptions looking skywards. Fairy foxglove had threaded itself through the graveyard walls, intermingled with outcrops of ferns.

Then she caught sight of a splash of colour, the pink and purple bells of a small fuchsia bush, and as she walked towards it she saw that it had been planted beside a recently dug grave. Above the rich brown earth was an old headstone from which the lichen had been scrubbed to reveal the inscription.

"Here lies Isabel Pringle who died 15 August 1933, aged 46, beloved wife of James Allan Pringle who died 30 November 1918 in France, aged 29."

Underneath were the newly carved words, "Elizabeth Mary Pringle, their daughter, is now at peace, reunited at last with her family on 30 January 2006."

Martha stood transfixed. Not only had Isabel Pringle been a young widow, Elizabeth had also been bereaved young by the early death of her own mother.

Everything was still, save for the gentle buzz of bees gathering pollen from the heather on the hillside.

"Hello, Martha."

She wheeled round and saw Saul walking slowly up to the gate.

"Saul, you gave me a fright. I didn't expect to see you."

"And I didn't expect to see you, either. I've always been alone here." There was something faintly proprietorial in his tone that suggested he wasn't all that happy to find her beside Elizabeth's grave.

"I wanted to pay my respects, and I suppose try to feel closer to her."

"Well, she's here all right. In the air and the trees and on the ground where we walk." He stood on the other side of the grave. "It's a beautiful old headstone, isn't it?"

Martha nodded. "I had no idea she was alone for such a long time. I mean, I don't know that, but it looks that way."

Saul said nothing so she persisted. "Did she talk about it?"

"Sometimes," he looked up at her, "but never in a self-pitying way."

"Why did she never marry her sweetheart?"

Saul looked at her interestedly, his eyes suddenly fixed on her. "How do you know she had one?"

"The carvings on a tree that Catriona and Niall showed me, initials."

He just smiled and shook his head slowly. "She wasn't one for revealing secrets. We had different kinds of conversations. It was more that she was wise about the nature of solitude, choices made, that kind of thing. But then she also taught me that it was good for the soul to be nurtured by another human being."

"You miss her a lot, don't you?"

"I feel her near when I come here and that helps, but yes, more than I could ever have imagined."

"I think Niall feels the same way."

Saul looked at her intently. "I don't doubt it, not at all." He paused, and Martha coloured, embarrassed that he might think she was making out that she was the keeper of Niall's secrets. "I was sorry he wasn't here for the funeral."

He pulled his robes around him and looked down at the grave. "She wanted to be buried in a reed coffin and be placed with her mother. That was her only wish, well, that and no church service, only a simple graveside ceremony."

Martha felt tears prick her eyes and Saul carried on quietly. "She was buried on a crisp cold day when the sky was like a huge blue canopy with not a single cloud. Some of the older people in the village came, and some of the volunteers and gardeners from the castle. I read "The Lake Isle of Innisfree". She knew it by heart, but she told me that she liked to open Yeats' poems and read them before she fell asleep at night." Saul smiled sadly at her. "And I shall have some peace there, for peace comes dropping slow."

Martha suddenly saw his face differently. He seemed older, more careworn, his eyes, usually such a brilliant grey blue, were opaque and tired, his shoulders hunched. "Are you OK?" she enquired tentatively.

He straightened up a little, and shrugged. "Hey, it goes with the territory. I'm a Buddhist for Christsakes. We thrive on inner turmoil. It's nothing that Elizabeth's presence and some quiet meditation won't help."

"I think that's my cue to go," smiled Martha.

"Not on my account," said Saul and paused before he went on, "but before you do go I've got something that might help you get to know Elizabeth."

Martha looked at him keenly.

"She was very generous. She made three bequests before she died. Each one was worth twenty-five thousand pounds. One to the Holy Isle community, for tree planting, another for the gardens at Brodick Castle, the last to the War Graves Commission. She only told me because we had talked about how the community has been struggling to find money to plant some rare species of trees."

"Thank you for telling me." Martha smiled, storing away the information. "There's such a lot that I will never know. I think of it as a gift, so, really, thank you."

Saul smiled. "You would have liked her a lot."

Martha left Saul sitting in the graveyard and headed back to Holmlea to begin packing away the books, and the pictures, the tapestries and myriad pieces of china for safekeeping. They had come to assume the same importance as her own belongings and already in her mind she was putting them together, imagining how her books would look, intermingled with Elizabeth's, how she would always use Elizabeth's china and her beautifully pressed linen.

She was deep in thought as she walked along Shore Road towards the house, so much so that it was only when she reached the front door that she saw a bunch of red roses on the mat with a note rammed into the middle of the flowers. Her legs almost buckled, and feeling the bile rise in her throat, she put her hand over her mouth. She should have written that letter telling him to keep away.

She looked around quickly, just to make sure Andrew was not lurking somewhere, and then she took the flowers into the kitchen and put them in the sink.

The note looked like it had been scrawled in a hurry.

"Tracked you down to say goodbye but I had to get the afternoon boat back. I'm going south on the sleeper tonight. Left the flowers with your gardener. He had put a pot of hydrangeas on the doorstep, but he took them with him. Just as well I brought the roses. Cheers, Andrew."

Martha stood, rigid with fury, her fists clenched so tightly that her nails almost punctured her palms, and when she closed her eyes, what she saw was not only surprise on Niall's face when he spotted Andrew sauntering up the path, but his incredulity, and disdain.

She looked at her watch. She had an hour before she was due to take the last ferry to the mainland. She looked at the old tea chest she had found in the garden shed. She had planned to pack away the beautiful china tea set she had discovered in the sideboard in the dining room, the delicate gold-rimmed pink and white banded cups and saucers in perfect condition. She had turned a translucent cup round in her hand, marvelling at such craftsmanship, and wondered if it was Isabel Pringle's wedding china.

But now, instead, she carried the tea chest to the bookcase and filled it with all of Elizabeth's gardening books, sheaves of magazine cuttings about different soils and pests and irrigation, her closely written plant notebooks and folded over seed packets. Then she put the box at the front door. She would give it to Catriona to pass on when she got back.

As she packed her bag for Glasgow she heard the soft plop of rain hitting the windows, and then, harder more insistent drumming as the squall transformed into a torrential downpour. The weather was closing in fast and she remembered Catriona remarking that the new captain played by the rules. He wouldn't risk sailing in atrocious weather, and when he did sail, he waited for no one.

Martha reached the long straight in the road down to Brodick and felt a sudden thud in her chest as, through the rain-spattered screen, she made out Niall's Land Rover coming in the other direction. As he drew nearer, she braked a little and raised her hand from the wheel to wave, but the car sped past her, Niall's eyes firmly focused on the road ahead.

By the time Martha reached the ferry the Beetle's windscreen wipers were fighting a losing battle. She gripped the steering wheel, just about able to make out the men in hard hats and fluorescent waterproofs waving her along the causeway and into the huge yawning hull. The boat strained against the heavy braided ropes holding it fast to the pier, battling the ferocious swell.

She climbed the steep stairs from the car deck, calculating that, if it was going to be a dreadful crossing, she'd be less likely to feel sick if she was in the open air. She sat outside, her back firmly against the seat, feet hooked under the wooden slatted bench in front of her, her oilskin coat belted tightly, as the ferry reared and rolled in a pitched battle with the Firth of Clyde. Overhead, terns swooped back and forth across the stern until one would stop dead, hanging in the air, calibrating the wind, and then as quickly fall away to let another take its place. Martha kept her hat low over her face in a futile attempt to escape the spikes of driving rain.

ELIZABETH

I thought about Saul last night, and wondered whether I'm drawn to him because when I hear his voice, its cadences remind me of another, someone I'll come to soon enough in this accounting of my life.

"You know, Elizabeth," he said in his New York drawl, "it's not a million miles from nihilism and hedonism to Buddhism, but it sure makes you feel a lot more alive in the world, and that the world itself is more alive. Or maybe it's just because I think there's some kind of purpose to it all now."

Could it be that I am part of his purpose? He has never pressed me to reveal my stories and my feelings, but rather, in his quiet reassuring presence, I feel myself unlocking a little more each day.

After Robert left, Mary was insistent that I return to work quickly. Otherwise, she said, I would have too much time on my hands. And besides, "It will be the best way to show people that you are your mother's daughter."

I had given up my position at Shiskine Primary School at the end of the summer term and a new teacher from the mainland had taken my place, but there was an opening at the school in Lamlash when Mr Fulton had to step up in preparation for the retirement of the headmaster. It was a big class, and in addition to my teaching role, I had to be at the pier every morning, ready for the arrival of the four children from Holy Isle. At the end of the school day I would supervise their safe return, walking them back to the little boat that took them home. I suppose I immersed myself in the school, filling a void that was as deep and dark as the black pools up Glen Rosa.

Sometimes, when the sky was heavy with rain and the wind moaned, the little ones looked frightened as the boatman lifted them down to sit side by side on the boat's narrow benches, and there were days when my heart was in my mouth as they set off home in the gloaming. I would put my field glasses to my eyes and watch as they were tossed about in the foaming waves, their little heads hardly visible above the sides of the boat, until they reached Holy Isle jetty.

But it was a curious thing that, in the safety and warmth of the classroom, the children loved to frighten themselves with poems about the sea; they would beg me for some verses of "The Ancient Mariner." "The ship drove fast, loud roared the blast, And southward aye we fled." They would squeal with delight and on occasion I would have to shush them when Mr Fulton's silhouette cast a shadow on the thick wavy glass in the classroom door. More than once that autumn they had to sleep in the beds of their Lamlash school friends when the bay was transformed into a mass of treacherous racing water.

My class was filled with the most enchanting of children, the girls in their white pinafores, their hair tied back with a long ribbon, intelligent expectant faces eager for learning, and the boys, their hair close cropped, concentrating, scratching on their slates, sending a shiver up my spine. They nourished me as the days became shorter and the light a thin watery grey, so that the lamps had to be lit in the classroom from the moment the bell sounded for the start of lessons.

At Christmas the school was closed for just a single day, and although I had invitations to lunch from both Mary and Mr and Mrs Fulton, I had no heart for conversation and knew I would be poor company.

I rose early and made my way to the cemetery. I brushed some papery brown leaves from Mother's grave and read from a little green leather-bound anthology of poetry she had given me the previous Christmas. It was inscribed, "To my dear daughter Elizabeth, from your loving Mother." I opened the book where the red ribbon marker divided the pages, at a poem by Emily Brontë.

Though earth and man were gone,
And suns and universes ceased to be,
And Thou wert left alone,
Every existence would exist in Thee.

In the graveyard I did not feel so alone. I liked the company of the headstones, the sound of the wind. On Sundays, when others were in church, I spent an hour or so there, even in inclement weather.

On Christmas Eve I had received a telegram from Robert.

"Arrived safely in Fremantle. Setting off for Kilbride. Happy New Year when it comes. All my love Robert."

I kept it in my pocket and I stood by the wall of the graveyard and read it over and over. Already his departure seemed so distant, the picture of another life that was not mine.

When I visited Mary at the Whitehouse at New Year I showed her the telegram. I remember that she did not enquire about my plans, but when I said to her that I was no nearer going than I was in September, she put her arms around me, looking anxiously into my eyes, and said she thought I would feel stronger in the spring. Spring was an optimistic time, she said, a time of new beginnings. Meantime, she suggested that I help her with her charity work. January was always a hard month, she said.

And so on Saturdays we travelled the island together. Although one of the estate workers often drove her, when we were together she took the wheel of the big car with the polished wood running board and huge silver headlamps that I used to play in. I sat beside her, perusing her list of places to be visited and trying to suppress my car sickness as we juddered up rutted tracks and bounced and splashed across stony burns in spate, delivering food parcels to isolated crofts and elderly tenants. We made fine companions, she and I.

I remember how upset I was when, driving the coast from Lochranza to Corrie, she announced that she had to leave for London the next day. She'd had word that her sister was sick, and she might be gone for a few weeks. She must have registered my apprehension because she quickly said, "You could take the train and visit for a few days. It might prepare you for going away."

I only heard the last sentence. I looked out of the window and she faltered a little. "You *are* still going, aren't you?"

My mouth was dry and my head ached and I could not find any words. She took my hand. "Elizabeth, are you sick?"

I shook my head and told her that I was sure she was right, that in spring I would feel a lot brighter.

Although I put on a brave face when we said goodbye, I was devastated to see her go, my emotions uncontrollable, out of all proportion to an absence of no more than two months. I withdrew into myself; the children were my only salve. The world around me seemed muted, muffled. Even Mother's rose tapestry, the one she drew on the canvas with the vase in front of her and then stitched into glorious corals and pinks, lost its vivid colour and seemed a shadowy, gloomy thing.

I would sit, listening to the rhythmic tick of the clock, mesmerised, hours passing in a blankness. When I opened a book, even a favourite one, there was no pleasure on the page, only grey gauze before my eyes. It became a herculean task to open the door and walk along to collect the children from the pier, and I hurried back home at the end of the school day. Finally I realised I would have to rest a while from the classroom, that the children were unnaturally quiet, giving me furtive worried glances. It was as if I were submerged, barely hanging on to my sanity, living in a nether-world from which I couldn't escape, and it was in this drowning state, locked inside Holmlea, that I took my fountain pen in my hand and somehow, words appeared on the page in front of me.

Dear Robert,

This letter is so very hard for me to write and I know it will break your heart, as mine is also shattered.

You must know that I will always love you. I did not trick you, or lie to you. I think that deep down, after Mother's death, you doubted that I would go with you. Do you remember when, after the funeral, you asked me if I did truly want to go to Australia and be your wife? You must believe me, that when I said I did, that I believed my place was by your side, I was speaking the truth. But I know now that will never be possible. I have failed you.

My dearest Robert, I owe it to you to tell you this quickly; I must break off our engagement in order for you to be free. I only hope that in releasing you, you will find someone worthy to be your wife and helpmate, and that you will be able to take over Kilbride, as we planned, and you will prosper.

I have let you down, and very much more than that, and I am truly sorry for it. The memories of everything we shared, and what passed between us at The Falls, will remain with me forever. You will always be in my thoughts.

Please forgive me.

Elizabeth

I left the house and walked to the Post Office in a daze, and when I passed the envelope to Mr McNeish, he winked. "That lad'll be pining for you, Miss Pringle. I hear the sheep station's in the middle of nowhere. Ah well, the post takes that long, you might be there afore the letter."

I took a deep breath but I said nothing, and he stammered, "I'm sorry, Miss Pringle, I spoke out of turn." To relieve him of his embarrassment I summoned the words to opine that the postal service had a lot to cope with, what with all the mail going from Arran to relatives who'd left for far off places. I had spoken more words to Mr McNeish than I had to anyone for more than a week.

Then I gave one of the telegram boys a penny and asked him to take a note to the Whitehouse that I had written to Mary, to await her return. And then, as I walked back along towards Shore Road, I looked in the window of Mr Kerr's grocery store, to make sure there were no customers, and went in to buy some flour and butter and eggs.

Mother had nursed him when he returned from the war with one arm blown off by a German hand grenade. He said that she had been the most patient, kind-hearted person he had ever known. She altered his

252

jackets for him, unravelled his two sweaters and knitted them again neatly, and was always on hand to strike a match for him. There was precious little employment after the war, and none for Matt Kerr, so the people in Lamlash put together to buy him a horse and cart for delivering heavy groceries, and he always brought Mother something special. He worked hard and prospered and along with a big win on a horse, he had enough to build a general store. Every year he gave fifty pounds to the library. He was the kind of man I imagined my father to have been.

That day he looked at me and said, "You are as pretty as your mother, but you are looking a wee bit peaky," and he slipped a little parcel of tablet into the paper bag along with my groceries.

I returned home and went to bed. I drifted in and out of consciousness, the days merging into night, until after almost a week of listlessness, the fog began to clear and I felt a little stronger. I pulled back the curtains and the sun no longer burned into my eyes, and my body no longer ached. I left the house and walked slowly along to Clauchlands Point, listening to the seabirds whirling and calling out along the shoreline.

The next morning I was awakened by an insistent knocking on the storm doors. When I opened them Mary was standing on the step, a worried look on her face, and at the sight of her my heart lurched with relief, and we embraced, tears running down my face. We sat together in the warmth of the sunshine at the window in the drawing room, and bit by bit I pieced together a picture for her of the half life I had been living, the trance-like state in which I had spent the days and nights.

She listened to me quietly, and then chastising herself for her absence, she said, "I should have seen the signs, Elizabeth. I shouldn't have left you. You are so very precious to me. You *will* be well again. I will make sure of it."

She told me that I had done a brave and selfless thing in setting Robert free. Then she glanced at my left hand. "Why are you still wearing your engagement ring?"

"I just do not have the strength for people's questions," I replied.

"You must take it off, Elizabeth. If you do, people will notice but they won't ask you questions. They might talk about it to each other, but that you can always ignore."

Saul took me across to Holy Isle today, supposedly to show me how the rock whitebeam saplings were progressing, but I knew he thought it might be my last time there, and I silently thanked him. We walked more closely than usual and his hand was often on my elbow, until I said, almost sharply, that I wasn't in the habit of stumbling. But I glimpsed myself on the path ahead of us; I knew that I could count my steps on this earth, and leaned in a little towards him. "You have been a gift to me, Saul," I said. He stopped and took my hand, "No Elizabeth, I'm the lucky one. I know what it is now to be close to someone, and have you to thank for that."

We walked on, sending a pair of peewits flustered and flapping up in the air from their nest hidden in the long grass, and I sensed that Saul had something he wanted to tell me. Perhaps he thought this might be the last walk that we would take together. I stopped. "What is it, Saul?" He turned and looked at me, a little taken aback. I smiled. "I can see that your soul is restless."

He closed his eyes for a moment and then he told me that something had changed, and that I had had a hand in it. He no longer wanted a solitary life.

"Elizabeth," he said, hesitating a little, "you and I have never talked about this, but I have known some women here, fleetingly, but now I've found someone —" he broke off and threw his arms out in front of him. "Look at me, I am a forty-five-year-old man, standing before you and I'm scared. How ridiculous is that?"

At that moment the years fell away and I could feel sadness flooding through my body; but if I could help him, if I could say one thing that would steer him towards happiness, then I might atone a little, an infinitesimal amount, for my own failure.

I smiled at him. "I know, better than most people, that you have to grasp the chance with both hands. You must let her in, Saul . . . allow yourself to be loved."

He put his face up to the sky. "Imagine if I hadn't come here, if I'd stayed in New York. I torture myself thinking about it. If I hadn't made this journey, what would have happened to me? Maybe I was destined to come here, to meet you, and her."

I waited for him to tell me who she was and I must have looked at him quizzically, because he burst out

255

laughing, as if all his pent up emotion had suddenly been released. "Elizabeth, you are so well bred. I don't think I've ever met anyone as polite, and restrained. Her name is Catriona. She's Niall's sister."

The moment he said her name, I had a vision of her kneeling over a flower bed in the garden of the hotel, her long red hair held up loosely in a band, much of it escaping, falling round her strong shoulders. I had passed one day and she had looked up and waved shyly. There was something about her easy manner that reminded me of Anna Morrison, the young woman who had pushed her little girl in her pram along Shore Road all those years ago, and who had wanted to buy Holmlea. I had thought of her often, and about the unconditional love of a child, love in its purest form, uncomplicated by the warp and weft of life.

"I have seen her working outside the hotel," I said. "So beautiful, and vivacious. If she has even just a single one of Niall's qualities, she'll be blessed. And so will you."

The air was alive with the intensity of his feeling. I could almost touch it. Suddenly I was back in another life. "A long time ago I once knew great passion, Saul. It was such a terrifying exhilarating feeling." If he was surprised at my sudden revelation, he didn't show it. I took his strong smooth hand in my two old papery blemished ones and held it tight. "You are going to make your life here, I know you are, and it will be a happy one." I knew it because I could see it.

When I wrote to Robert breaking off our engagement, I believed that I would never know

256

another man, never be held, never be cherished, but I was wrong. I did not seek him out; he caught me unawares. It is something of his fervour that I see burning in Saul. But I am getting ahead of my story.

Slowly, and with Mary's gentle encouragement, I regained something of my old self. She had been right; people never asked me about Robert, or expressed surprise that I was still living at Holmlea. I resumed teaching, and the school was the centre of my life.

The children in my class knew all about ships. The Firth of Clyde was the gateway to the world and the waters off Arran teemed with every kind of vessel, from the grandest liners to coal ships and steamers, Navy frigates, magnificent ocean-going yachts, fishing boats and skiffs, but there was nothing so thrilling as the prospect of the sailing of the *Queen Mary*.

I made her our class project and the children wrote politely to John Brown and Company at Clydebank requesting information about the new liner. When packages of drawings and diagrams arrived along with copies of the draughtsmen's measurements for the hull and the stern and the cross sections, we pinned them up on friezes on the classroom wall. We painted and cut out pennants and the flags of John Brown, and Cunard and White Star, and the Red Ensign, all of which we hung on string from one side of the classroom to the other. It was almost unimaginable to us that the biggest object in the world was being built on the Clyde and that we would see it before it commanded the waves.

In the autumn of 1935, Jeannie and John Forrest were taken by their parents to visit John Brown's and

257

returned to tell of the three huge funnels, the forward funnel the tallest, the last almost eight feet shorter. Jeannie said she had had to cover her ears, such was the noise of the riveters and welders at work, and the hammers of the hundreds of carpenters fitting the miles of planks on the decks and the luxury lounges. The children took the percussion instruments out of the big wicker box in the corner of the classroom, the timpani, the xylophone, the triangle, the tambourine and the drum, and we tried to create the cacophony of sounds we imagined echoing around Clydebank from dawn to dusk as the men hurried to complete the ship for the spring.

On 15 April 1936, the *Queen Mary* sailed for Arran. It was a beautiful ice clear day, and the whole school headed to Clauchlands Point. The children were beside themselves with excitement, and were awestruck when they heard her three whistles blowing from ten miles away, heralding her arrival. Small aircraft roared overhead, glinting in the sunshine, circling over the great ship as she sailed forth, tipping their wings at us as they flew back and forth from ship to shore like frenzied flies. All manner of craft, decked in bunting, blew their own tinny whistles as they sailed out to greet her, taking care to keep clear of the wash, and soon we saw the vast black hull and the smoke billowing from the forward funnel, which was painted the bright orange of the Cunard Line.

Boys and girls alike were jumping up and down waving hats and flags, and then, overawed by her sheer size as one thousand feet of ship seemed to bear down on us, they were suddenly silent, transfixed and open-mouthed. Soon we could see craftsmen, engineers, officers and seamen dotted over all the decks, waving to us, proud men who had created this magnificent object of beauty and power.

First she made steaming tests in the Irish Sea, and then on the Saturday, at six o'clock in the morning when the air was so cold you could see your breath, it seemed as if the whole island had gathered on the shore to watch her begin her speed trials. I have never witnessed anything like the thrilling intoxicating sight of the *Queen Mary* that day. The excitement and tension were palpable as she started to run the measured mile, each run approximately four minutes long. She needed ten minutes to get up to speed and ten minutes to slow down and when she sounded her whistles at the start of the mile, the men on the shore studied their pocket watches and the children started their own count, their shouts becoming louder and louder until she blew her whistles again to stop the clock. At her fastest that day she recorded almost thirty-three knots.

By three o'clock that afternoon she had made fourteen runs, and like a great graceful sea creature she came forward, between Clauchlands and the tip of Holy Isle, as if to salute us. Then she sounded three long farewell blasts, and from the decks the crew threw thousands of coloured streamers as she turned to make for Southampton and from there on across the Atlantic to New York.

We stood on the Point watching the magnificent liner until she was a tiny speck in the distance, and all the crafts in attendance had turned for home, their oil lamps bobbing up and down, throwing motes of light dancing across the water. We witnessed history that day. Twenty-five years later, John Forrest, who had stood beside me on the rocks, sailed for New York on the *Queen Mary* as the new Chief Engineer. He wrote me a letter from the engine room, on Cunard embossed paper.

> Dear Miss Pringle,
>   I am here because of you. You inspired us with your enthusiasm for the greatest ship the world has ever seen, and sitting here in the vast engine room, with the noise of the great pistons pounding, I remember that wonderful day when the *Queen Mary* came to Arran. I was bewitched. You set me on my future path, and for that I am eternally grateful. The child who has you for a teacher is blessed indeed. I hope this letter finds you in good health.
>   Yours sincerely,
>   John Eason Forrest

I came to think of teaching as my calling. It may sound boastful but I will allow myself to be so, because I think I was an exceptional teacher and I am being truthful when I say that in my long, long life, it is the only thing of which I am proud.

MARTHA

Martha drove into Glasgow still entertaining wild imaginings of the encounter between Niall and Andrew, the worst of which involved Andrew grabbing Niall's rake from the Land Rover and stabbing it into his face, blinding him with the lethal prongs, but as she swung the car into The Oval, and through the garden gates, the dazzling scene illuminated by her headlights instantly trumped her fantasies.

Two big terracotta pots filled with blue hydrangeas flanked the front door, a border of forget-me-nots threaded through with the egg yellow of limnanthes ran under both front windows, lattices at each corner supported a profusion of deep pink sweet peas, and finally, at right angles to the house, two rows of sunflowers, staked with canes, stood to attention facing each other. It was as if her childhood home were in the middle of a giant acid trip. The sheer gaudy brilliance of the transformation made Martha laugh out loud.

She put her key in the door and called out to Anna and Bea.

"Hello, hello," answered Bea excitedly, "we're in the kitchen."

Martha pushed open the door to find the two women engrossed in a game of Uno. Anna, cigarette in hand, was frowning intently at her cards and, when she looked up, she didn't seem to register her elder daughter.

"Anna," Bea said quickly, "you've been looking forward to Martha coming so, so much, and look at the beautiful red roses she has brought!"

"By the looks of the garden, you hardly need these," said Martha, grinning, as she leaned in to Anna and gave her a kiss on the cheek. "It's great to see you, Mum."

Anna looked over at Bea and then hugged her daughter. "Chanel N°5 . . . Martha always wears that, don't you, darling?"

"Ha! Anna is very good with smells, *dzieki bogu*," Bea said, clasping her hands together as if in prayer.

Martha looked at them both, bemused.

"*Dzieki bogu* means 'thank God'," said Bea, and added somewhat redundantly, "in Polish. Yesterday I thanked Him a lot. I put bacon on the grill for our lunch and then I went outside to help Anna with the planting. Well . . ." Bea put her hand to her forehead, "of course I forgot all about it. I must be getting old, no?"

Martha gulped, and looked nervously at Anna, who just smiled, enjoying the story.

"Your mother said to me in a very calm voice, 'I can smell bacon burning somewhere.' Well, I was on my feet in a moment, but it was awful, flames were coming up from the foil under the bacon. It was lucky you had a little fire extinguisher. I am terrible. I am meant to be the one who remembers, and I could have burned the house down."

"But you didn't, Bea, it's OK, really." Martha was as keen to get off the subject as she was to be reassuring. "How have you been, Mum, apart from sensing trouble?" She intertwined her fingers with Anna's. "You've done amazing things in the garden."

"You like it, eh?" interjected Bea, looking pleased. "Ruby helped us. We took a list to the shop and she said that anything Anna wanted, Anna would get, and all flowering already. Isn't that lovely? Even big sunflowers. Your neighbours in The Oval have all said it's wonderful, haven't they, Anna?"

She stood up from the table, taking the gentle silence as her cue to leave. "I will say goodnight to you now. The taxi is coming early and I have to pack my new things. I got the boys their own copy of *Harry Potter and the Half-Blood Prince*. Do you know, Roman sent me a postcard with the strange words," now she spoke with slow exaggeration, " 'splinter-filled buttocks and bulging piles, signed Guthrie Lochin.' " She looked pleased with herself for remembering it all. "I knew from the Arran postmark it was him. Hah! I had to ask the postman what was the meaning of the word, "piles". Hah! They think they can embarrass their granny. I'll show them what embarrassing is when I get off that ferry."

As Bea made to go she glanced at Anna, who was studying the Uno cards again with a look of intense concentration, and she beckoned Martha out of the room and into her makeshift bedroom in the study.

"Don't worry too much, my dear. Anna is happy, really. We go out wandering together and sometimes we stop and have a seat in the play park. Anna likes that. I don't know, but maybe it reminds her of when you and your sister were little. Of course, sometimes she is watching the children and she is far away in another place. But she's not unhappy."

She put her hand on Martha's arm. "Do you know what I think?" Bea went on without waiting for Martha's reply. "Anna needs to feel safe, that is the most important thing in the world for her because sometimes the world frightens her, but don't worry, I keep her safe."

"I know you do, Bea, and I am really grateful to you." Martha paused. "I'm sorry, I never asked; is the money enough?"

Bea put her hands up in front of her and said emphatically, "Yes, yes, please; it is all good."

Martha looked around the study. She had planned to take advantage of Bea's short trip to Arran to make more space for her belongings, and besides, she knew that Susie, when she arrived, would not be happy that Bea had been camping out in her room. "I'm sorry you haven't even had a room of your own. I'll sort everything out while you're in Lamlash, I promise."

Bea shrugged her shoulders. "What does it matter? I only go there to sleep, other times we are so busy!"

Martha remembered the blaze of colour outside. "The garden must have taken you days to do."

"It was good for us both. We worked together on our hands and knees. In one of her books I read that when someone has dementia, and the hours and days don't mean anything, the seasons still make sense, and so I am trying, as fast as I can, to make every season in the garden. When I come back we will plant daffodil and crocus bulbs for next spring. We have planned it together . . . that's good, no?"

Tears sprang to Martha's eyes and she hugged Bea, comforted by her reassuring solidity.

There was no sign of Anna when Martha returned to the kitchen and for a moment she panicked that her mother might have been listening to their conversation, but nor was she in the sitting room. She went upstairs and, looking into her bedroom, she saw Anna sitting on her old bed, stroking the brightly clashing squares of the knitted woollen blanket that had lain there on top of the duvet since she'd had been little.

The angle of Anna's head, her slender fingers moving rhythmically across the blanket, took Martha aback. She looked little different to the woman who had sat with her in the very same place, days after her husband had died. "Martha my darling girl," she had said, "listen to me. You don't have to be strong for Susie, that's my job, and you have to cry sometime, too." Susie had lain in an exhausted sleep beside her, her tear-stained face buried in their father's favourite old sweater. And Anna had been true to her word. Her strength had been immense, exhaustive, fierce, as she spun a protective web around the three of them.

"Hello, Mum," she said softly, so as not to startle her, but Anna carried on stroking the blanket, as if undisturbed. "I still love my bedroom you know. Do you remember when you split the bunk beds and I used to curl up where you are now, and listen to all the noise and laughter downstairs when you and Dad had your friends round? It made me feel very safe."

Martha sat down on the bed beside her. "Mum, it's my turn to make you feel safe, it's my job now. Bea or I will always be here, that's a promise, and tomorrow Susie will be here too and then the three of us will be together again."

Anna kept tracing her fingers over the wool, looking down at the cover, until suddenly, she started to weep uncontrollably, silent tears at first and then racking sobs that spoke of secret terrors and hopelessness. Martha gathered her up, the smell of her achingly familiar, and Anna clung to her, shaking. They sat together, holding each other, illuminated only when the moon escaped briefly from behind the heavy clouds until at last, Anna, calmer, put her hand on Martha's cheek. "Thank you, darling. Sometimes I can't find any words, I don't know what they mean anymore, they're all jumbled up. I'm tired now. I want to go to bed."

Martha helped her mother up and put her arm round her as they walked along the landing to her bedroom. Anna let Martha help her out of her clothes and into an old floral high-necked nightdress she had had since she was married. Martha folded back the duvet, and once Anna was settled, she pulled the cover

266

up carefully, tucking the edges into the mattress, and bent down to kiss her.

Martha poured herself a large Macallan from the drinks cupboard and sat down at the kitchen table, glad of the soothing quiet that had enveloped the house. She turned on her laptop and, sifting through all the random junk, she found a new email from Catriona.

Hello Martha,
    Hope everything at home is better and Bea and your Mum are fast becoming friends. I've given Niall your mobile number. Hope that's OK!?
    Catriona xoxo

Martha began to type.

Hi Catriona,
    Bea makes Florence Nightingale look like a slouch. I cannot tell you how much of a relief it is to have her here. You are a star. No problem about giving Niall my number.

Her hands hovered over the keyboard as she contemplated asking why he wanted it, but then she ended the email with a kiss, remembering that needy was not an attractive look.
    Before she went to bed she looked in on Anna. Her mother was lying on her back, sleeping peacefully with one arm thrown up behind her head, as vulnerable as a

child. As Martha studied her, she saw Susie reflected in Anna's features, more than she had ever realised before, the strong arched eyebrows and long lashes, the upward curve of her lower lip.

Martha was more anxious than excited at the prospect of Susie's arrival. There was no single moment in their history that Martha could point to and say — that's where it all went wrong. Over the years she and Susie had simply engaged in low-level sniping, a perceived slight here, an observation taken as criticism, and occasionally a hail of arrow-sharp words let fly in both directions. There had been a bad year when Susie, at seventeen, had disappeared into a vortex of vodka and weed-fuelled binges, staying out all night, skipping school and getting screwed. Martha tried to shield Anna from her younger daughter's excesses. It was she who cleaned up the sick and went to the chemist, lying through her teeth to procure the morning-after pill for her, and it was she who got her back on track for her final school year, all the while shuttling backwards and forwards to lectures in Edinburgh. Later, when Susie was safely enrolled at art school she hugged Martha, just once, and thanked her in dramatic fashion for "saving her from disaster," but mostly Susie seemed to feel a toxic mix of embarrassment and resentment at being, as she saw it, beholden to her older sister. And even when Martha praised her for an elegant design, or a beautiful combination of colours, or the sumptuous texture of a new fabric, Susie somehow heard a false note.

And so it was when Susie finally arrived the next afternoon from Copenhagen after a delayed flight, exhausted and a little the worse for wear. She dropped her battered leather suitcase in the hall, kicked off her high-heeled boots noisily, and planted a kiss on Martha's cheek.

"Hello big sister, everything under control?"

Martha took in Susie's perfect outfit, the straight tight jeans and the expensive striped silk sweater, which hung beautifully over her slim toned frame.

"We're all fine, it's lovely to see you. You look great," she added.

"Where's Mum?"

"She's having a nap."

"Shame, I was looking forward to seeing her sitting in her chair at the kitchen table."

"She gets tired easily. She was looking forward to you arriving this morning."

Susie made a face. "The plane was delayed, Martha. It happens. I don't control the skies."

"Hey, come on," Martha said soothingly. "I wasn't making anything of it. Why don't I make you a coffee?"

"Is there any wine in the fridge? The journey was pretty gruesome, actually. I could do with a pick me up."

"Of course, if you want some. I'll open a bottle."

"Do I detect a bat squeak of disapproval, a little *tut*?"

Martha ran the back of her hand over her brow. "Please, Susie. I'm just so glad you're home. I really don't care if you have a drink. I'll pour you a glass and let's just talk. I was going to clear some of the stuff in the study to give Bea some space of her own, so why don't we go in there?"

Susie sat on the daybed sipping her wine, while Martha emptied a tall cupboard to make way for Bea's clothes. She enthused about Bea and Anna's routines, trying as best she could to paint a picture of a happy house in quiet harmony. "Half the time I don't think Mum acknowledges Bea's presence, but she obviously feels comfortable about it. I mean, she's not agitated with Bea. I don't think so anyway."

Martha noticed, with growing irritation, that Susie had started flicking through books and magazine cuttings before she dropped them into cardboard boxes, studying them as if they were of monumental importance. Martha tried to keep her temper in check, but when she knocked over a picture frame and smashed the glass to smithereens, she exploded. "For fuck sake, when did I get to be so fucking clumsy."

Susie looked at her in astonishment, her eyes wide. "Hey, Martha, calm down, it's only a photograph."

Martha muttered that she was fine, but as she crouched down to pick up the jagged shards of glass, her head was pulsing, as if a hammer were trying to crack through her forehead from the inside.

She looked at the photograph lying on the floor. It must have been behind the school photo of an angelic looking Susie in her white shirt and tie. It was a black and white photo of her mother and father, their noses pressed together in profile, looking like a Mamas and Papas album cover. Anna wore a floppy hat, her dad's hair was long around his face, John Lennon glasses glinting. She turned the picture over and read the inscription aloud. "'Balnacraivie Farm, summer 1970.' Any idea where this is?"

Susie looked at the photo and shook her head. "It means nothing to me. Dad looks handsome though, doesn't he? You could ask Mum." Martha looked doubtful. "Why are you making that face?" Susie shot at her. "Just try her. Is she *really* that bad?"

Martha ignored her and fetched a dustpan and brush from the kitchen to sweep up the sharp shards of glass.

Susie watched her for a while and then said quietly, "Well, is she? Tell me."

Martha didn't know where to begin, how to convey Anna's erratic behaviour, the vacant looks, her quicksilver moods, her sudden lucidity.

She was about to reply when the door opened and Anna, dressed in an old embroidered cowboy shirt Martha recognised as her dad's, looked around the room. "Where's Bea?" she said, a hint of panic in her voice.

"She'll be back soon, Mum. She's visiting her grandchildren in Lamlash for a couple of days. Look, Susie's just arrived."

Susie smiled up at her eagerly and rose to greet her, but Anna frowned and looked around the room, her eyes darting from place to place. "Where are *my* grandchildren?"

Martha glanced at Susie's shocked face, and then approaching their mother, spoke softly. "Mum, you don't have any grandchildren yet. Susie and I don't have any children. Look, Susie's here. She just got in from Copenhagen."

Anna refocused her eyes on her younger daughter and said in a puzzled distant voice, "Susie? Where have you been? I've been looking everywhere for you, darling."

Susie rushed to Anna and put her arms around her, her face a mixture of relief and vindication. "I've been in Copenhagen, that's where I live now, you must remember that. Oh Mum, it's so good to see you. And I can smell Rive Gauche," she said as if it meant everything. "Some things just never change, do they?"

"Have you come to take me swimming?"

Susie looked at Martha, who mouthed "yes." Encouraged, she replied, "Yes, just like you used to take us when we were little, and we tried to swing on the high rings. Do you remember, they hung over the pool, from one end to the other?"

Anna sifted through a jumble of memories. "And I used to doggie paddle along in the water in case you fell in."

"Yes! You did. That's what mothers are for," said Susie, choking up.

The outing to the old Victorian swimming pool began well, the sisters linking arms with Anna, Susie chattering excitedly about her new design studio in Copenhagen; but Martha noticed her mother's puppet-like smile, the vacant glassy eyes.

They reached the pavement edge. They waited for some cars to pass by, and then Anna froze between them.

"Come on, Mum," coaxed Susie, "the road's clear." But Anna shrank back, unable to step forward, looking down at her feet. "I don't know what to do," she said in a frightened voice.

"It's only one step, Mum," said Martha gently, "c'mon, just move one foot forward a little."

Anna stared down at the kerbstones, as the seconds ticked past as slow as minutes, until finally she stepped gingerly onto the road, and then her terror was forgotten in an instant.

It was exactly as Bea had described a week earlier. Was the pavement edge a recurring trauma for Anna, or a brand new fear each time? Martha had no way of knowing, no manual to tell her that A leads to B.

She saw the consternation on Susie's chalk white face and threw her a reassuring look as if to say *it's over, stay calm*.

When they reached the pool Anna removed her clothes, folded them mechanically and pulled on her old red halterneck swimsuit. The girls bobbed along on either side of her as she swam up and down the length of the pool on her back, moving through the water with long confident strokes, her upturned face now tranquil. Then she looked from side to side and, laughing, said, "Come on you two, get swimming, I'm not a baby, you know. I've been doing this for years!" and with a quick flick of her wrist she splashed them both and sped on, leaving Martha so elated she was almost lightheaded, while Susie grinned across at her as she wiped the spray from her face.

As they strolled home in the warm sunshine, Susie described her life in Copenhagen, not noticing that Anna seemed to be a million miles away. Martha listened quietly; her sister's enthusiasm for the quirky restaurants and the wild Danish coastline, the rolling haar and huge skies was infectious. She wanted to celebrate, to mark that moment of utter clarity in the pool.

As they approached The Oval she broke off, and made for Ruby's Flowers where she found the florist engulfed in an avalanche of blooms newly arrived from Holland. The heady scent of freesias filled the shop. Martha picked up a huge bunch for Anna, and for Susie, a pretty silvered-glass candle vase.

"Anna is one of my favourite customers, Martha, and now Bea, too. They brighten my day," said Ruby, a broad smile on her face as she wrapped the gifts. "I wish there were more people like them."

When Martha opened the front door she could hear the crackly strains of Jefferson Airplane's "Volunteers of America" on the stereo, one of the old albums her mother had taken to playing recently, but of Anna herself, there was no sign. When she opened the kitchen door Susie was sitting at the table, staring ahead, her eyes red-rimmed and her hands shaking.

"OK, what happened?" said Martha, in a quiet resigned voice as she put an arm round her sister.

"It's so awful, Martha; I can't believe it. She filled the kettle with milk and flicked on the switch before I even knew what was happening."

"And what did you do?" said Martha accusingly, "you didn't shout at her — did you?"

"Yes, Martha," said Susie, pushing Martha's arm away, "I fucking shouted at her. All right? I shouted at her to stop, and she got a terrible fright and now she's in her room lying face down on her bed and she won't speak to me."

"Look, Susie," said Martha, yielding a little, "it takes a while to get used to all this; you never really know what's going to happen next. It's always going to be like this and you just have to roll with it."

"Well, I don't know if I can 'roll with it'. It's as if she's trying to upset us."

Martha raised her eyebrows, about to protest, but Susie went on in a plaintive voice, "I know, I know. That's crap, but it's so hard."

Martha looked at her sister's tear-stained, frightened face. Now, finally, she might understand that Anna was never going to get better. For that alone, the visit had been worth it. She handed Susie the package from Ruby's. "I hope you like it. It's a present for your new studio."

Susie unwrapped the paper carefully and, lifting out the vase, looked at Martha in surprise. "Did you know this is by Karen Karlsson?"

"No, is it? Is it OK?" Martha stammered, thinking, shit, something's coming.

Susie shook her head and laughed sarcastically. "You don't remember, do you?"

Martha tensed. "Remind me."

"She was the one who accused me of copying a pattern of hers. In Copenhagen? Anyway, my drawings were dated and logged and she had to apologise." Susie glared at her sister. "Remember? No, of course you don't, even though it could have killed my career stone dead before it got off the ground. You don't even remember that I called you, stressed out of my head."

Martha winced, finally recalling the night she talked an hysterical Susie down. "I'm sorry, Susie, on both counts. I should have remembered, and I shouldn't have bought you it. That was rubbish of me."

"It doesn't matter," Susie sighed, "thank you anyway; it's a nice piece."

The row hovered in the air, not quite over, and then Martha risked reigniting it.

"I'd like to talk about Arran, Susie. The house is as much yours as it is mine. I want you to be involved."

Susie looked at her incredulously. "Come on, try to be honest, Martha. If that was really the case, wouldn't you have asked me about it before you took it on?" She went on without waiting for a reply, her speech well rehearsed. "No, I've been thinking about it; Arran was yours and mum's thing. After we were little I never went on one of your weekends. Maybe I wasn't invited." Martha made to protest, but Susie held up her hand. "I'll be happy to visit sometime but it really isn't anything to do with me." She started to tidy up the table, scrunching the packaging from the Karlsson vase tightly between her hands. "In fact, I should have said, I have to take the first plane back tomorrow to see a new client about a commission." She avoided Martha's eye. "Sorry, but they can only manage a lunchtime meeting."

Martha didn't know whether to be furious with Susie or to congratulate her. She hesitated for a moment, then put her hands square on the table in front of her. "That's wonderful, but it means you won't meet Bea."

Susie puckered her lips. "Well, you've already made that decision, too, so I don't need to meet her, do I? Anyway, if mum's happy, I'm happy."

Martha felt a fierce heat spread through her chest. If she'd had any doubts that their mother was her concern alone, Susie had just banished them. But she had no appetite for another fight and, trying to keep her voice light, she said, "OK. If you're going to the airport early you'd better get a good night's sleep. I'll pour you a malt for bed."

Susie's departure the next morning was met with indifference by Anna, who was totally absorbed in arranging the freesias, slowly, one by one, in a tall old crackle glaze pot. "I'll phone you from Copenhagen, Mum. I'll tell you whether I have a big new client or not." Susie kissed her mother and gave her a brief hug. "Wish me luck."

Martha thought she was hearing things. She grabbed Susie's case and led the way out to the waiting taxi, hissing over her shoulder, "Why did you say you would call her? You know she gets confused by the phone, Susie."

"Why not?" Susie replied, her eyes narrowing, as the sisters turned towards each other like two rearing rattlesnakes. "How the fuck else am I going to talk to her?"

Martha spoke slowly and deliberately. "All I'm saying is, it's sometimes stressful for her."

"Don't patronise me, Martha," Susie yelled, "I'm not stupid, though it's pretty obvious that *you* think I am."

The taxi driver ducked below the dashboard and started to fiddle with something under his steering wheel.

"Susie, this is real," Martha pleaded. "Mum's going to get worse and we haven't even talked about it properly, and now you're off back to Copenhagen."

"Oh, so fucking off back to Arran doesn't count? Get over yourself, Martha. That's it. I'm off."

She banged the door of the cab shut, causing the now scarlet-faced driver to wince, and sat back in her seat staring straight ahead, her pixie features contorted into an angry glare. Martha stood on the hard gravel, watching her sister retreat, listening to the taxi engine grow fainter, waiting for her heartbeat to slow down.

She returned to the kitchen where Anna was sitting looking out of the window at the blue tits pecking at the feeders Bea had hung from the branches of the apple tree like Christmas decorations. She put her arms round her mother and laid her chin on her shoulder.

"That's Susie away safely, Mum. Cup of tea?"

"That would be lovely, darling," Anna said, turning round and smiling up at her daughter innocently.

Could it be an act, Martha wondered? Was she aware that her daughters had been fighting about her? Martha wanted to scream with frustration at this tricky illness that toyed with Anna, the goblin thief that robbed her mother of herself and which was always skulking around causing mayhem.

She poured Anna her favourite Lapsang Souchong tea and watched as she sat sipping it slowly, mesmerised by the birds fluttering and chirruping around the coconut halves and peanut holders.

Martha heard the beep beep of an incoming text. "Hello, Martha. When will you be back? I have a pot of hydrangeas for you. Roses probably dead by now. Niall"

She felt a thrill of excitement as she stared at the message. She read it over several times until her equilibrium returned, and she was calm enough to reply. "Back tomorrow on the last boat. Thank you — I love hydrangeas. Would you like to bring them tomorrow night? Martha." Then she thought, to hell with it, and added an "x".

ELIZABETH

We all knew war was coming. The island had never been so busy; sometimes it was hard to see the water in the bay for all the ships at anchor. Everyone was employed in one endeavour or another in support of the war effort. Marcus Stephen and his twin brother Michael took turns at the helm of the Gate Ship all through the war, letting vessels come and go through one of the two booms that were swung across the Bay from each end of Holy Isle, to deter enemy submarines. If we were in any doubt about the possibility of an attack, the sinking of the *Athenia*, which had just left Glasgow for Montreal, by a U-boat off Rockall on the very day Neville Chamberlain announced we were at war, shocked us into the reality of what lay ahead.

The rain lashed that day, and the wind howled around the island. I waited at the end of the long pier, ready to welcome hundreds of children and their teachers from Clydebank and the Glasgow parishes of Ruchill and Govan, in the hope that we could keep them safe from the German bombs. For many of them it was their first time out of the city, never mind on a boat at sea. We greeted them as they made their way uncertainly down the gangway of the *Davaar*, a steamer I had always loved to watch coming into Lamlash, low and sleek in the water, its single funnel tall amongst the masts. Never had it ferried such a cargo as this.

I studied the bewildered faces as they scanned their surroundings, trying to make sense of this strange place, their bags slung across their bodies, a few of them clutching rag dolls or rough hewn little wooden toys. They were so very young to be away from home, and I don't imagine that on that first day many of them understood what war was or why they had had to leave their parents.

Some returned to Clydcbank after a few months, too homesick to stay, and perished in the Clydebank Blitz. That was when we actually heard the horror of the war, the dreadful onslaught of the bombs, a thousand raining down on shipyards and houses over two black nights. I sat in the dark listening to the muffled rumble of the explosions thirty miles away, and knew that by the time it was over, many of the Clydebank children in my classroom whom I had come to know and care for, would have lost siblings, parents and grandparents.

But on that first day of the war, on the third of September almost two years earlier, we settled every child with a family in the village, their teachers too, and tried to make them feel as welcome and secure as we could.

Then the commandos arrived, five hundred of them. They'd walked more than one hundred miles, all the way from Galashiels to the Ayrshire coast, so their march from the ferry at Brodick, the three miles to

Lamlash, must have seemed like an afternoon stroll. They too were billeted from one end of the village to the other.

Sometimes they disappeared into the hills for days, and we would hear the rat-a-tat of their guns from high in the hills. On other days we watched as one by one they ran off Lamlash pier, splashing into the water with their full kits on their backs, whooping as they went. Or we would spy them in the distance as they made one assault after another from amphibious craft onto Clauchlands Point, at all times of the day and in the dead of night.

Yet the Germans knew they were on the island. People talked about the broadcast by the traitor, Lord Haw-Haw. They had listened to their wirelesses in astonishment, stunned to hear him say, "We didn't get them in Galashiels but we'll get them in the Duke of Montrose's Rose Gardens." But they never did.

The commandos transformed the village. There was much excited talk that the actor David Niven was amongst their number, but I never saw him, nor I think did anyone else. Perhaps it was his handiwork that you can still see on the stone on the front facade of the kirk, a neat row of indentations left behind when one commando shot the weathervane off the top of the steeple one Sunday evening after returning from drinking in Whiting Bay, by all accounts a late summer rhododendron stuck into his Glengarry alongside his black hackle.

It was the strangest of times. We were in the midst of war but the island had never been so lively. Mr

McKelvie who had a joinery business at the pier spent the whole war making wooden targets, which were mounted on iron triangles and towed out into the Firth of Clyde for bombing practice. He must have made hundreds of them, for planes swooped and attacked most days, as the crews made ready for raids over Germany.

Local musicians had never been in such demand. There were dances, musical evenings and plays held every week in the village hall. In one of the public houses, two beer taps ran continuously into a big zinc bath, such was the soldiers' thirst, but we begrudged them nothing.

Some days, I sat in the garden and watched the spectacle of little Swordfish planes practising landing and taking off from the giant floating airstrip in the bay, which was nicknamed the Lily Pad. From a distance the planes looked as if they were dancing on and off the surface of the sea, like dragonflies touching down momentarily before quickly flitting off again, lest they get trapped in the weight of the water.

Once, I took some of the teachers from Clydebank over to Holy Isle. We walked up Mullach Beag and watched the merchant ships and frigates plough out to sea to certain danger while, in the other sea lane in the Firth of Clyde, returning boats raced past them, bound for home and desperately hoping for safety.

The women I knew during those years were friendly enough, and I enjoyed their company, but when they talked of their fears for their brothers or boyfriends or husbands in the fighting, I mostly stayed silent. I remember that one teacher, Margaret was her name, asked me if I had a beau, and caught off guard, I replied that many years ago I had been unable to follow the man to whom I was betrothed to Australia. I must have looked troubled because she apologised for asking. "I'm sorry, my mouth ran away with me," she said, all a fluster. Perhaps I should have confided in her more but I was not one for spilling out stories.

It was to Mary that I turned when I felt hollow and sick at heart. Even as the years passed, Robert was always somewhere in my thoughts, and now I feared for him. Australia had entered the war alongside Britain and I longed to know whether he had enlisted, but I had long forfeited the right to ask questions.

Six months after I had written to tell him I could not follow him to Australia, I had received a short letter back.

Dear Elizabeth,
    You have broken my heart, and I am at a loss to understand you. I am not going to return to plead with you, even if I could find the money to make the journey, for I fear it would be of no use. Besides, your aunt and uncle have been very good to me and are keeping to our arrangement, and they are so very frail I could not leave them, or Kilbride, at this time. They have put their faith and trust in me. I wish you could do the same. I am bereft, but I must take this as your final word. I cannot imagine loving another woman as I have loved you.
    Yours aye, Robert

At night when I pulled the heavy black blinds, I was wracked with the not knowing.

That Christmas, Mary held a carol service at Brodick Castle. She invited some of the islanders and the soldiers and sailors, many of them Canadian and a few Americans, who were stationed on the island. As I walked into the drawing room after the singing, carrying a tray of mulled wine and whisky and green ginger, standing in front of me were Angus, Robert's oldest brother, and his wife, Ellen. I had not seen them for more than seven years. I was so taken aback I stopped dead, gripping the handles of the silver tray, the glasses shifting dangerously.

"Elizabeth, it is so good to see you. You look well," said Ellen kindly, and then she very gently took the tray from me and set it down on the grand piano. I was at a loss for words, memories of Robert and I sitting at her kitchen table, her welcoming manner, her fondness for me, came flooding back.

Now she came to my rescue. "I hear you are a wonderful teacher. I have my spies and they tell me you treat the evacuees as if they were your own."

"We all do our best for them. They're so far from home, I couldn't imagine . . ." I stammered and flushed when I realised what I'd said.

I looked at Angus, gathering all my strength. "How is Robert? Is he safe?"

"He's safe, yes, and he's doing everything he can to feed and clothe the Anzac forces," he said, in a matter-of-fact voice.

His words took a moment to sink in, and Ellen touched my arm. "Robert tried to enlist, even though he was too old, but the government was more interested in his farming skills. He's done so well. Kilbride is one of the biggest sheep stations in Western Australia now."

I could not hold back my tears. "Oh, I am so glad he is not in the fighting," I whispered.

"Elizabeth, it has been a long time since he left. Please don't blame yourself for what happened." Ellen smiled at me imploringly. "And he *is* happy now. He's married to a Scottish girl, Laura Scott. She's from a fruit-farming family in the Clyde Valley, and now they have orchards too at Kilbride. He is doing well, Elizabeth. I promise you."

I felt faint. He was married, but of course he was. It was only in my selfish imaginings that he had remained alone.

Mary must have been watching from the far side of the room where she was talking to one of the gamekeepers, because she swiftly wove her way through her guests, and, taking me gently by the elbow, asked the Stewarts to excuse me. She wanted me to meet some of the soldiers, she said.

I spilled everything out as she steered me into her sitting room and she held me tightly as I cried for everything that I had lost. The dam I had built, stone by stone, since Robert sailed, cracked, and it was only with Mary's patient help that I slowly repaired it. She always made a place for me in her life, in between the estate, her plant study, her tenants, her family, who were now themselves scattered to the four winds. "Izzy's girl is my girl, too," she would say when we gardened together, threading trellises with fronds of passionflowers, or pulling weeds from the lily pond.

I am growing so very tired now. It feels like only yesterday that I helped Saul plant some rock whitebeams, such is the long span of my life, and now I can hardly hold my pen. Everything is quickening. I am not scared of death, but I must find the strength to get to the end.

When the 11th Commando sailed in the New Year on two ships, in time to join a convoy heading round the Cape, their leaving was made worse by the dark wintry weather, which turned the sea into a mass of cold grey steel. Hundreds of people gathered to see them go, and the commandos stood to attention on the deck, proudly wearing the Black Hackle. We, and they, knew that they had been training for the toughest of battles. We had watched them transform from gangly, high-spirited young men into a disciplined fighting force, and we were all proud of them. When we heard, that summer, that so many of them had fought and died in the Battle of Litani River, a sadness descended on Lamlash. They were ours, and now they were dead.

I often thought of them, killed so far from home. Increasingly I came to detest all the bustle and activity on the island when, for so many, life had stopped. The sight of holidaymakers picnicking on the beach, cavorting in and out of the sea while the warships were moored in front of them, became unbearable, unseemly even. It was made worse by the fact that Arran was dealing with its own unexpected disasters; men were killed here, far from their own families. Their remains are still on the island, some of them still lost, others, in war graves.

And yet, I too became part of that strange dichotomy. In the midst of war came an unsettling happiness. I look back on it now as if I were observing someone else's life through a steamed up window, the words and gestures mesmeric, almost indecipherable, and certainly not made by the woman I became after it all had ended.

Death shadows life, stalking its every move, but since the war, there is a single sound that I hear as an intimation of imminent disaster. To this day, when the distant drone of an engine disturbs the night sky, nausea and panic rise within me. It is a noise I still fear, as I feared it then, when the skies above Arran were filled with planes. We were on the path of the North Atlantic route bringing aircraft from Canada and America to the base at nearby Prestwick airfield, and hence to battle. Who could have foreseen that the magnificent peaks of Goatfell, and her jagged, ragged crags, would be transformed into a death trap for so many — airmen, gunners, engineers, bombers — that the hills themselves became a threat to life? Military planes were caught in bad weather, or low cloud. One even snagged on a wire fence on top of a stone wall, erected to keep the sheep from leaping to freedom. It was a cruel obstacle course, a warped game of the war.

The first crash was on 10 August 1941, when twenty-two passengers and crew took off from Prestwick for Gander in eastern Canada, and the pilot, climbing through low dense cloud, could not clear Mullach Buidhe, north of Goatfell.

The whole island grieved for the dead, all of whom but one were laid to rest on Arran. Those who searched the hills for bodies would never see their own lives in the same way again. They were all driven by a single purpose: to bring the men back from amongst the stones and the heather where they had fallen, and give them peace.

On the Sunday after the first crash, I went to the kirk to honour the dead. I sat on the cool oak pew where Mother had worshipped every Sunday of her life, her hands holding her gloves on her lap, her eyes focused on the arched window beyond the pulpit. After the service I walked back to the Whitehouse with Mary and told her that I planned to approach the Home Guard, to ask to be allowed to join in the mountain searches should another plane come down. I reasoned that I was as fit as any and I knew the hills, the gullies and the crags better than most. Death was something I had faced, I said. I remember she put her arm around me. "But Elizabeth," she said, "could you cope with the horror of it?"

"You know I can," I replied evenly, "and we owe it to them. Did I not learn that watching you and Mother tending men who were disfigured and scarred? They were prepared to sacrifice their lives. You never flinched at their injuries, at their ravings, did you? You never doubted that you had to do something."

I was acquainted with some of the men in the Home Guard; fishermen, farmers, shepherds, the bank manager, but I was the first woman to ask to take part in the searches. There were no rules governing such a request; no one objected, or, it seemed, even gave it a second thought.

I would lie awake at night, listening to the thrumming of aircraft overhead, willing them a little higher in the sky, my heart thudding when an engine roared louder and I thought I could feel its vibrations shaking the very walls of the house. After America entered the war, thousands of aircraft followed the same route, and it was only a few months after the first crash that there was a second collision with Goatfell. This time it was a US military aircraft, flying from an airfield on the east coast of America to the US Air Force Base at Prestwick.

At dawn I woke to an insistent knocking on the storm doors and minutes later I was huddled on the back of a covered lorry with the other volunteers, sheltering from the soaking driving sleet beneath the flapping tarpaulin. We studied maps by torchlight and listened to instructions about where the search would begin, and how many airmen were missing, though we knew that rescue was a forlorn hope.

That early morning we moved up the glen to the crags where snow was lying, some of the men carrying rolled up stretchers on their backs, which from a distance looked like medieval weapons. We were spread across the hill, climbing steadily, scarves wrapped around our faces against the weather, our eyes scanning the terrain ahead in expectation of the worst, but we found nothing that day. It was only when we moved to the Sleeping Warrior the next morning that we found the plane and the airmen and, silently and methodically, we all worked together, the men's caps off, our faces grim and blank, looking for identification, making notes, and sending up flares.

In the classroom the children spoke about the crashes, giving each other what details were passed around the island, or repeating overheard fragments of conversation — whether it was a Bristol Beaufort or a Liberator, a Flying Fortress or a Lockheed Lodestar, how many engines it had, whether it was carrying torpedoes. Their fascination was natural, not disrespectful or callous, and when they asked me questions about what I saw on the hills, their hills, I tempered my replies only to spare them certain details, and to omit the facts that were to remain secret.

In the summer of 1943 we were called out the morning after an unexpected storm the previous night had claimed a US bomber on the south-east ridge of Beinn Tarsuinn. As we walked in bright sunlight, up Glen Rosa, past foxgloves and adders tongue and honeysuckle, accompanied only by the sounds of bees and the cries of a lapwing, intent on what lay ahead of us, I heard a voice at my shoulder. "It's a terrible thing to have to look for death in the middle of such beauty."

I was startled by the rich mellifluous American accent and, turning round, I found myself looking up at a handsome, tall, auburn-haired man, his hazel-green eyes framed by dark eyebrows. He was dressed in his US Air Force uniform, his shirtsleeves rolled up, and he put his hand out towards me. "Sam Delaney, pleased to meet you, Miss." His grip was firm and cool, and lingered a moment.

I introduced myself and he smiled. "I was surprised to see a woman in the search party. But it sure is a pleasant one," he added quickly.

"And I'm surprised that an American officer has joined us," I replied, blushing in spite of myself.

"May I walk with you?" he asked, and I had the uncomfortable sensation of experiencing both a sudden thrill, and a shudder of distaste. This wasn't a summer hike. In truth, though, we had spoken few words but I was already captivated. My heart racing, I nodded. "If we speak quietly. It's not really the place for conversation."

"I don't think it will do any harm," he said, his eyes smiling, "and it might make the day a little easier, don't you think?"

"I'm sorry," I stammered, "that sounded like a reprimand. I didn't mean to be rude, I just don't want to be disrespectful to the dead."

"No offence taken, not at all."

He told me that he was a major in Air Transport Command at Prestwick, too old to fight. He was a commercial airline pilot and had accepted a commission to organise the flights on the North Atlantic Route. He had requested to come to the hills to help.

"After all," he said, "these are American airmen, and I have a duty to them and their families."

We walked on together, and he remarked on my tall shepherd's crook.

"It's good for pushing aside the foliage. It's very deep at this time of year." I paused, trying to find the right words. "When we're searching for—"

He broke in. "It takes someone special to do this, you know, to climb up here in all weathers knowing what lies ahead. I salute you."

"Please don't," I replied quickly. "In the awful scheme of things, it's nothing."

Sam Delaney unnerved me. His easy warm manner and the quiet strength he exuded were intoxicating. We all stopped to slake our thirst and I poured him a cup of lemonade from my flask, and as I passed it to him, his fingers brushed against mine.

He took a sip. "This is delicious, thank you, but won't you have a cup?"

When I said I would have some after he finished, he protested and insisted that we share. We passed the cup back and forth shyly, each transaction more intimate than the one before, until as he put his head back to drain the last few drops, I thought I might faint. He gave me his hand and helped me up from the heather, and I shuddered at the sheer force of the attraction between us. With Robert I had felt an innocent tender love, but this was heady and shocking, as if I had been swept up inside a tornado. I had never before felt the thrilling, frightening, desire to possess another human being and to be possessed.

When we reached the ridge I forced myself to move apart from him as we explored the rocks and gullies for wreckage, but even then I felt drawn back into his orbit. It was sacrilegious even to entertain such thoughts when we were engaged in such a sombre task, but all that day I yearned to be near to him, to feel the heat of his body beside mine.

As I write these words I have reawakened long buried emotions, language which is so unfamiliar that I have the sensation that I am writing automatically, my pen hurrying across the page. It is revealing my younger self to me, the person I was, for a while, more than sixty years ago. I do not know whether I am surprised or not.

The search that day was fruitless and we returned to Brodick, all of us despondent, haunted by the now familiar failure.

Sam caught up with me as we walked back to the lorry and suddenly whispered to me urgently, "Elizabeth, can I see you home?"

I shook my head, fearful of what might happen once we were behind closed doors. But he persisted, and finally I said I would meet him at Ayr railway station the following Saturday at noon.

He did not rejoin the search, for which I was grateful, and I spent three long hot and tiring days on the hills with the others from dawn to dusk, until finally we discovered the fuselage wedged into a deep gully. We all stood on top of the hill, our eyes closed and heads bowed, as one of our number read a prayer. Then we marked out the area with flags for the soldiers to retrieve the wreckage and bring the airmen down off the ridge to be buried on the island or sent home to be near their loved ones.

As we descended Glen Rosa I picked some wild flowers and, early the next morning before I left for Ayr, I walked to the graveyard and set them in a jar of water by Mother's headstone. I lay a while on the grass outside the cemetery, carefully smoothing down my lightweight summer suit, apprehensive and confused about the day ahead.

As the train approached Ayr station I was consumed with nerves and had to plait my fingers together in my lap to stop my hands shaking. I thought I saw the other passengers looking at me furtively as if, somehow, the purpose of my journey was written all over my face. When we slowed at the platform I glimpsed Sam looking anxiously into the carriages as they passed, until he saw me and broke into a broad smile, swinging his jacket over his shoulder and tipping his soft brown fedora at me.

When the train stopped he opened the carriage door and helped me down. My heart beating wildly, I shook his hand. He smiled and bent forward, his lips brushing my cheek. "I thought you might not come," he said, his voice urgent, "and I would never have seen you again." He cupped his hand around my elbow as we walked along past busy bright shops, for all the world like any courting couple. In truth we were two strangers, hardly speaking, in a place neither of us knew, in the midst of a war, each of us suddenly unnerved by the desire that had driven us to this impetuous, awkward assignation. I longed to kiss him, but there was an invisible barrier that I did not have the language to remove.

He had made a reservation in a restaurant in the High Street, but as we neared it I glanced round at him, and I thought I saw doubt in his eyes. We came to a little covered wynd and I asked him if we could stop there for a moment. Stepping into the cool darkness, I felt calmer, and I stood back and looked up at his expectant face. "If you have made a mistake, if this is too hard, please tell me," I implored him, "and we will part now and I will go straight home to Arran."

He immediately moved towards me and, putting his arm around my waist, kissed me, tenderly at first and then with a ferocity that stole the breath from me. I kissed him back, fitting my body to his. My boldness felt reckless and exhilarating. I had become another Elizabeth Pringle, and I hardly knew her.

We sat on a semicircular banquette in the restaurant, our backs resting against the plush velvet upholstery, the pristine white tablecloth and gleaming cutlery and crystal in front of us. A piano played softly in the far corner of the room.

Sam leaned towards me, an uneasy look passing across his face, and before he could speak I put a finger to his lips. "I know," I said quietly, "and I want nothing from you that is not yours to give. And soon you will return home, and I know that, too."

He lived in Chicago, in the suburb where he had grown up, in the avenue where Hemingway was born, with the childhood sweetheart whom he had married, and who had borne him twin boys who were now eight years old.

I responded with my own thumbnail sketch of my life, and in the telling it seemed threadbare and unremarkable; even the few sentences I spoke about Robert sounded perfunctory and mean, whereas I was enthralled by his stories of Michigan Avenue, and the lake that looked like the sea, and the mobsters that ruled the city during Prohibition. He listened as I described the farm that was no longer ours and told him about the father I lost, and the children whose thirst for knowledge I wondered at every day. It was queer trying to paint a picture of my life, for I had never explained who I was to another person, nor had I worried about what they would think of me. And only as I was reaching for and arranging the words, describing Mother's strength and her stoicism and her compassion, did I realise how much I wanted him to understand the life I came from.

He told me about the base at Prestwick, where hundreds of young fighter pilots from Nebraska, or Ohio, or Maine, most of whom had never before been outside their state, prepared themselves for missions over France and Germany. He marvelled at their acuity and their ability to get into the cockpit day after day, when they had witnessed friends with whom the bonds had been forged so swiftly and intensely, shot down in a brutal sudden end. Often it was he, older, but with the respect shown by one pilot to another, who talked to them about their worst days in battle and sometimes, their best.

We sat, our heads close together, mapping each other's face as we talked, oblivious of the time and the comings and goings around us, until we became aware that the piano had fallen silent and the murmur of voices had faded to nothing. I looked around at the empty restaurant, a single waiter lingering, watching us, and realised that I would have to hurry to the station if I were going to make the train to the boat.

Sam took my hand in his and lifted it to his lips. "I want to hold you, Elizabeth. I want to bury my face in your hair and kiss the nape of your beautiful neck." In that moment I learned about the power of desire, and the invisible barrier between us was broken.

As we arrived at the station I reached forward to him, our bodies meeting perfectly. I whispered that I would come back the following Saturday, and I would not return to Arran until the Sunday. He kissed me then, and I had never been so conscious of the contours of my limbs, the weight of every bone, the softness of my skin electrified by his touch. I felt as if I was levitating, each of my senses heightened.

On the boat that night I stood, my face to the wind, amazed at how strong and alive I felt. For the first time in my life, I was going to yield to pure passion for its own sake, selfishly, without a promise, and with the promise of nothing.

Mary and I had a rendezvous the next day at the Whitehouse. I had planned a project for the children returning for the autumn term, for which I had asked them to collect broken china from the shore during the

298

summer holiday. Thousands of pieces lay scattered on beaches all over the island, from long-ago sunken ships and the plates and cups and saucers dumped at the old cowp on the hill near Lamlash and washed down to the water line. There were beautiful patterns and colours, china of every kind: Bells, Doulton, even Royal Copenhagen. We were going to glue the fragments in patterns on terracotta pots and fill them with spring bulbs. I had been inspired by a book I found in Mary's library on the Spanish-Catalan architect, Antoni Gaudí, who reassembled broken tiles into beautiful patterns. I remember Mary looked especially handsome that day, in a geranium-red twinset and circular black and white checked cotton skirt, but I noticed she was thinner, and slightly stooped.

As we strolled down to the beach to look for a last few pieces, she put her hand on my arm gently and turned to study me. "Elizabeth, you seem different today, quite radiant in fact." She laughed. "If I am not mistaken, you look, well, you have an aura — that's perhaps the way I should put it."

I was taken aback and looked away from her steady gaze. Was it really so obvious?

I stammered that I had met someone who had joined one of the search parties, and her eyes widened. She looked at me eagerly. "Ah, is it someone I know?"

My heart sank. I could never, and would never, lie to Mary. I would never forfeit my anchor, my weather vane, the only person I had who was family in all but blood. I shook my head. "He's an American, an officer."

I waited for her questions as one might stand before a knife thrower, but none was forthcoming. Instead she took my hands in hers and looking at me steadily, her face kindly, she said, "Be careful, Elizabeth, a grand passion is a wonderful thing, and Lord knows you deserve it. But you gave up everything — everything — to stay here. He must not break your heart."

How much I loved her then, for her unswerving faith in me, and her wisdom. I smiled at her, colouring a little. "He nourishes me, Mary, he makes me feel more alive than I have done for many years, but please don't worry, my heart is not his to break."

We worked our way along the beach together, bent over like the women I often watched picking sea coal, exclaiming excitedly to each other when we found a delicately painted piece, or two pieces of the same pattern, until we had filled our bags. Then we sat together looking over to Holy Isle, enjoying the wafer-thin cucumber sandwiches and shortbread that Mary's cook had prepared. We drank Darjeeling tea from a silver flask, and Mary told me that she and my mother had once taken the very same picnic up the Ross Road to the lone tree on the hill, and had looked down on our old farm.

"I thought Mother never went back," I said in surprise.

"Only that one time," answered Mary quietly, "a year to the day that she heard that your father had died."

"What did she say?" I asked tentatively.

Mary hesitated. "Do you really want to know?"

I nodded my head slowly.

"She said, 'I will tell you, Mary, James has cheated Elizabeth and me of our happiness. Arran is truer, and more dependable than he was.' "

I felt my stomach tighten the way a Livingstone daisy closes when the light disappears.

I woke soon after dawn on Saturday with the sun spilling through the curtains, casting a soft glow over my bedroom, and I felt the warm breeze steal in through my open window. I had thrown off the covers in the night and I lay on my back for a while with my eyes closed, listening to the birds excitedly calling to each other, as if they were anticipating the day ahead.

I drew a bath, dropping in some lily-of-the-valley perfume of Mother's and afterwards I dressed slowly, luxuriating in the feeling on my skin of the pretty peach silk slip, edged with lace, which I had retrieved from the back of my dressing table drawer where it had lain, wrapped in tissue paper, since the day I unpacked my trousseau. Then I put on a pale green and yellow lawn cotton summer dress with a low collar, and tied with a thin belt. My legs were bare and I wore the only high-heeled sandals I possessed. I brushed my hair from my face, sprayed it with cologne and put a little Vaseline on my lips. I packed a small valise, and before I left the house, I picked a pair of cotton gloves from the drawer in the hall table. Then I untied Mother's rose gold wedding ring from the velvet ribbon in the bureau and slipped it into my purse.

Sam was waiting for me at Ayr outside the railway station, standing beside a borrowed dark blue Alvis sports car. He came towards me, delight on his tanned face, pulled me to him and kissed me, his arms on my back pressing so tightly that I felt the heat of his body spread through mine. I kissed him on his neck and whispered to him that I had missed him my every waking moment.

We roared along Ayr's tree-lined roads and on to the coast, laughing at the sheer pleasure of being side by side, the wind flying through our hair, his firm hand holding down the skirt of my dress. We arrived at the beach at Dunure, where he spread a tartan rug on the sand and opened a wicker basket in which he had put some cheese and a bottle of French white wine, but I had taken only a sip before he leaned across and gently pushed me back on the rug, moving his hand to the nape of my neck, and with his lips parted, he kissed my throat, pressing the same spot with the tip of his tongue. I felt my body relax, and he took a drink from his glass and passed the wine between my lips, catching the drops that spilled from my mouth with his soft thumb, while he kissed me tenderly and the scent of the lemony wine rose between us. He caressed me until I begged him to stop and wordlessly we walked back towards the car, his arm around my waist, firmly holding me to him as we stumbled through the warm sand.

Sam turned the car into the Abbots Park Hotel, a handsome Edwardian sandstone building set back from the road in lush green grounds. I removed my glove and slipped on Mother's wedding ring. When he came round to help me from the car he put his face to my hair and whispered, "The furious storm through me careering, I passionately trembling." We walked into the hotel, his arm around me protectively, and he signed the register, Mr and Mrs W. Whitman. Propriety honoured, the receptionist gave us the key to a suite.

We surely were not the first wartime lovers to have ascended the stairs of Abbots Park, dizzy at the promise of what lay ahead. As soon as we were inside the door we fell upon each other and covered each other's face and neck in a frenzy of kisses. I stood, my back straight against the wall, as he pulled the bow of my sash apart and undid the buttons that ran down the front of my dress one by one, until it fell open. Pulling off his shirt, he put his face to the edge of my slip and cupping my breasts in his hands he pressed his tongue between them licking beads of perspiration from my skin. I arched my body against him and taking his hand I guided it down over my navel and placed it between my legs, my hand on top of his, holding it there, gasping as his fingers circled me softly. He said my name over and over as he lifted me up, my legs curled around him, and laid me down beneath him on the high bed. I had never imagined that I was capable of wanton behaviour, but it was as if a dam within me had burst and we made love that day and night like two people starved, slowly suffused with more and more pleasure, exploring and devouring every inch of each other, so as not to miss one single possibility of passion. It was as if I were drinking in life itself.

★ ★ ★

In the morning we lay entangled among the sheets and pillows, and he propped his head on one arm and looked down at me, smiling sadly.

"I have never been with another woman before," he said quietly, and I replied, "and I am sure you never will be again." I knew I was right.

Was I immoral? I look back on that short intense month in the knowledge that what we did was wrong, but I truly believed that no harm would come to him or his family because of it.

MARTHA

Martha put a bottle of Sancerre in the old fridge as soon as she arrived back at Holmlea, switched on a few of Elizabeth's lamps, their parchment shades creating a lovely glow, and placed a couple of hastily bought candles in the kitchen and sitting room to fill the house with the scent of oranges.

She looked at herself in the mottled silvered mirror in the hall, rushed upstairs to yank off her sweater in favour of a scooped neck red top, pulled her hair back loosely into a clasp, and put a pair of pretty gold hoops in her ears. She was just dabbing a little Chanel N°5 on her wrists when there was a knock at the door, and she opened it to find Niall, all but obscured by a profusion of blue hydrangeas.

"Hello, Martha," he said a little gruffly, "a housewarming present, for the garden."

Martha laughed. "I don't think they'd get through the door anyway. They're beautiful, Niall, thank you." She was pleased by the sound of his name on her lips. When he placed the pot outside the door and joined her in the hall, he seemed to fill up the space.

He looked around at the soft lighting and put his nose to the air. "Expecting someone? Sorry, I'll be off."

Martha aghast, stuttered, "No, actually, just you." How dare he make fun of her? "I was only being hospitable, don't worry I wasn't going to throw myself at your feet."

Niall's eyes creased and he broke into a sly grin. "Evidence would suggest I'm not your type."

Stung, Martha was about to tell him not to flatter himself when they were startled by the sound of laughter outside the house. "Well," she said, "saved by the bell. Or rather, your sister, and, if I'm not mistaken, your favourite Buddhist."

Niall looked a little crestfallen, but she grimaced at him, opening her eyes wide. "Perfect timing, couldn't have been better." She flung open the front door and watched them as they strolled up the garden, arm in arm, their heads tilted towards each other.

Catriona called out, waving a bottle, "We were taking in the night air and we thought you might like to share a glass of wine." As they stepped into the hall she was clearly startled to see Niall leaning casually on the door frame of the kitchen. "I hope we're not interrupting anything," she said, glancing at Martha.

"Nothing at all," Martha said hastily. "Niall just brought over the hydrangeas he'd been keeping for me."

"I saw them, lovely!" said Catriona. "Hey," she looked from Niall to Saul, "have you two ever been in Elizabeth's house together before?"

Both men shook their heads. "Saul, good to see you," said Niall, with a warmth that surprised Martha.

"You too, man, especially here. It feels good. I think Elizabeth will be smiling."

Martha looked Saul over. Gone were the saffron robes; now he looked every bit the New York poet, his lithe frame in a grey tee shirt, faded black jeans, and a pair of battered baseball boots. "Off duty?" she said jokily.

"Clothes do not always maketh the man," Saul shot back, laughing, "to paraphrase something Mark Twain *didn't* say!"

He noticed the cardboard boxes of books and the wooden crates in which Martha was preparing to stack all the pictures and tapestries. A look of curiosity crossed his face.

"Please, sift through them," said Martha encouragingly, "maybe there'll be something you'd like to keep."

She went over to the boxes, bent down and trailed her hand along the richly decorated spines. "I'm fascinated by what Elizabeth read. There's everything here from Charles Kingsley to Laura Ingalls Wilder, and look at this beautiful edition of *The Count of Monte Cristo*." Martha held up a book bound with soft crimson suede.

Saul went down on his knees and began searching for something, picking books up one by one and setting them carefully on the rug. "Here it is. This is it!" he exclaimed. He carefully picked up a book with a brown leather spine and a water-damaged parchment cover on which was pasted a diamond shaped printed paper, edged with flowers.

An Essay
of the
Nature and Actions
of the
Subterranean
(and for the most part)
INVISIBLE PEOPLE
Heretofore going under the name of
Elves, Faunes and Fairies
Or the lyke
Among the
Low country Scots
&tc &tc &tc

He turned the slender book slowly in his hands. "Elizabeth told me about this one day. It was written in the seventeenth century by a Church of Scotland minister who communed with fairies. Not something you could say about many ministers, eh? He lived in a town called Aberfoyle and died in mysterious circumstances."

"Maybe he was taken by the fairies," laughed Martha.

He handed the book to Niall, who studied the pages. "It doesn't look much like a seventeenth-century book to me."

"It's not. It's a rare copy made almost two hundred years later. Elizabeth told me she was given it by another Church of Scotland minister."

"Communing with fairies doesn't sound like any of the Sunday School stories we were taught," said Catriona.

"Come and look at something." Saul beckoned them over to the wall, where he was peering closely at a tapestry. "There's an inscription here I want you all to see." His eyes focused on one tiny part of the canvas for a few moments. "I've found it. It's incredible, look at this." He pointed to a tree trunk on which were sewn some tiny letters in silver thread. He read quietly, "Then a spirit passed before my face; the hair of my flesh stood up: It stood still, but I could not discern the form thereof: an image was before mine eyes."

"What is it?" asked Martha.

"It's from the Old Testament. Job, chapter four, verses fifteen and sixteen," said Saul. "Elizabeth quoted it to me. She thought there might me something she called, 'middle nature between man and angel.'"

Niall shook his head. "I just can't imagine her talking like that." Then he went on quickly, "but I don't doubt you, Saul, not at all."

"Perhaps the tapestries were her way of bearing witness," Martha said quietly.

Saul nodded. "Elizabeth was fascinated by the possibility that Reverend Kirk was convinced of this netherworld, that he had been there, and he seemed to be able to reconcile it with his Christian faith."

He searched a little further into the book, and then he read aloud again. "They live much longer than we, yet die at last, or at least vanish from that state. Tis ane of their tenets that nothing perisheth but (as the Sun and the Year) everything goes in a circle, lesser or greater, and is renewed and refreshed in its revolutions."

Niall shook his head slowly. "I had no idea that she had these beliefs. Though when I think about it, sometimes she did speak in a spiritual kind of way about nature when we were gardening together."

Saul smiled, and said, in an unconvincingly nonchalant voice, "Did it ever occur to you that she thought of you and me, in some way, as her guardian angels?"

Niall looked sceptical. "Too far, Saul. You don't really believe that, do you?"

Saul shrugged. "Not literally, but I do think she believed that she had met us for some purpose."

"Woah . . ." interjected Catriona, "this is getting just a little bit weird."

Saul kissed her affectionately on the cheek. "Sorry, I didn't mean to freak you out, but Niall's right, she *was* spiritual. Otherworldly, even, sometimes." He took a long sip of his wine and looked round at them all, pausing to stroke Catriona's arm. Then he took a deep breath. "At the end of the book there's a chapter on second sight added by someone else, and it made a big impact on her. In the weeks before her death she saw something strange, and then she remembered the chapter and read it to me."

Catriona took the book and, turning to the end, she found a page marked with a dried bay leaf. "Listen to this. 'Natives of St Kilda have a particular kind of second sight which is always a fore-runner of their impending end. Some months before they sicken, they are haunted by an apparition, resembling themselves in all respects as to their person, features, or clothing. The image walks with them in the fields in broad daylight and if they are employed in Delving, Harrowing, Seed-sowing, or any other occupation, they are at the same time mimicked by this ghostly visitant.' "

The four sat without speaking for a moment before Catriona broke the silence. "She thought she had a sort of shadow . . . now, don't you think that's spooky?"

Martha chipped in. "Look, I know I'm the only one who never knew her, but perhaps it was just that she was very elderly. Maybe her mind was going. I don't mean to be disrespectful, but—"

"She was sharp as a tack when I left for the field trip," Niall broke in quickly, staring straight ahead, avoiding Martha's eye.

"And at the end, too," said Saul, thoughtful for a moment.

They sat a while, drinking, and the women listened as Niall and Saul shared stories about Elizabeth Pringle. Martha caught Catriona's contented expression as she sat between her brother and her lover, witnessing the rapprochement.

Niall recalled Elizabeth's delight when he had brought her a huge box of nasturtium seedlings, and her initial disbelief when he told her that people often put them in salads. "I was sure she would know, but she thought I was teasing her, testing her. That summer she was so tickled by the idea, she put them in everything, from scrambled eggs to fairy cakes."

311

"Ha! I can raise you on that score," said Saul, laughing. "She asked for a joint one day, well, she called it my 'funny-smelling cigarettes.' I warned her she might feel a little strange, light-headed perhaps, but there was no putting her off, no sirree. She took to puffing like a pro, and boy, did she inhale! After a few minutes she started sighing and giggling, and then she said, 'My heavens, I feel a little skittish,' and lay down on her back on the grass, staring up at the sky and telling me the clouds were made of cotton wool. Man, I thought she might never get up."

"Maybe she was seeing fairies up there," laughed Catriona.

Niall looked at his watch and pushed his seat back. "Well, it's almost the witching hour." He looked across the table to Martha, his face apologetic. "I have to go. I need to be up extra early for a team meeting at seven."

Catriona caught the glance and put her hand on Saul's arm. "We'll walk ahead, Martha. Just lock up when you get in."

Martha carried the glasses to the sink, holding them tightly by their stems, nervous suddenly at being left alone with Niall. Why had he not gone with the others? She jumped when he suddenly spoke.

"I'm sorry if I was sarcastic. It was rude of me. Sorry."

Martha shrugged, and lied. "I didn't really notice it. I've a lot going on just now so I'm a bit preoccupied. Maybe I should be the one apologising, for being snippy."

"Anything I can help with?"

She turned round. "I'm not sure you'll really want to hear the kind of stuff I mean."

"Try me," he said, putting his hands on the back of a chair, staring directly at her, his face so damned handsome it almost knocked her off balance.

"Well, I'll try to make this brief . . ." And then the words tumbled out like cascading ping-pong balls. "OK, I think you already know that mum is in a sort of no man's land, also I'm really struggling with my younger sister, I suppose we just don't speak the same language and she's kicking against me. And you — believe me this is *very* minor in comparison — appear to be judging me for my crap decisions when it comes to past boyfriends . . . That's it, really. No, wait, there's more. If I'm honest, I'm not sure you think I should even be here."

She looked at him, tirade over, her face burning, appalled to realise she was near to tears.

Niall's face was impassive. He pulled the chair out and sat down again. "Maybe we should have another glass of wine."

Shaking a little, and immediately regretting her outburst, Martha opened the fridge, reached for the Sancerre and brought two fresh glasses to the table.

Niall opened the bottle, and said gently, "Where do you want to begin?"

Martha couldn't fathom what was going on. But then she was used to her antennae malfunctioning. What the hell, she thought.

She explained that Susie's hostility was in part because she thought Martha was judging her for making bad, selfish choices.

"Do you? I mean, do you judge her?"

"She's in denial about Mum for sure, and she certainly resents me."

"I have a younger sister too, remember?"

Martha leaned forward and put her arms on the table. "Catriona's wonderful, though."

"Yes, she is; but that doesn't mean it hasn't been hard. I put myself in loco parentis, and she certainly kicked against that."

"But you're so close."

"Now, yes, but I had to learn to back off." He looked at her sympathetically. "Maybe you should do the same. Really back off. Let her deal with your mum in her own way. You'll just have to take the strain for a while longer. You're not her parent."

Martha took a long sip of wine and felt her tears welling up. This time there was no holding them back. "Well, you're seeing me at my pathetic worst. Self-pity's not very attractive, is it?"

Niall reached over to the dresser and picked up an embroidered tea towel. When he passed it to her she buried her face in it and then she thought she heard him say quietly, "That's funny, because I think you are really very attractive." Martha kept her face clamped to the damp linen. She must have misheard. "Martha, are you OK?" She finally dropped the towel and saw his embarrassed face.

"Look, I'm sorry. I shouldn't have said anything about the guy with the roses."

"Andrew," said Martha, flatly, her heart banging about in her chest. "Well, that was a big mistake from the start. Mortifying really."

She was still fixed on Niall's words, "you are really very attractive", as he stood up quickly and said, "Better be going. Let me drop you at the Glenburn."

Now Martha was completely confused. Hadn't they been talking about their families a moment ago? Had he really said what she thought he'd said? She must have drunk too much wine.

Smarting from her own foolishness, she said in a clipped voice, "Only if it's not too much trouble."

As she was about to lock up, she went back inside and heaved the tea chest into her arms. "For you, Elizabeth's gardening books and all her notes," she said as she handed the box to him heavily.

"Thank you," he said. "I'm looking forward to going through them and reading all her annotations. She was brilliant at that. She always had good insights."

They drove in silence along Shore Road. Here we are again, thought Martha, side by side in his Land Rover, stuck for words.

At the Glenburn Niall left the engine running and jumped out of his seat to help Martha as she started to climb down onto the metal running board. Her stomach flipped as he laid his hand on the small of her back, but just as he began to pull her towards him, they were startled by a big barn owl, flapping low across their path, so close that they both felt the cool whoosh of air from its wings on their faces. Martha cried out in surprise, and Niall steadied her. "I wonder if it's an omen," he joked.

Martha looked at him askance. "Please don't say that. You sound like Saul."

"But it could be a good omen. I'll check." He laughed, kissed her swiftly on the cheek and jumped back into the driver's seat. "Sweet dreams," he said, and put his foot to the floor.

When Martha opened the door of the Glenburn, the hotel was in darkness. Holding onto the smooth banister she picked her way up the stairs gingerly, counting the steps, trying to remember which of the stairs creaked the loudest. She felt a little unsteady, more from the lingering rush of Niall's firm hand pressing on her back than the wine.

She picked up her mobile. Miraculously there was a signal, so she squinted at the tiny screen and tapped the keys. "Thanks for advice about Susie. Would like to make you dinner but kitchen not really up to it yet. Maybe I could buy you a fish supper? Mx"

She thought enviously of Saul and Catriona, cocooned together. Saul stayed more often now. She wondered what Sister Indra made of his increasing attachment to Catriona, and his breezy brand of Buddhism. She lay with the curtains open, watching the now familiar mesmerising glow of the lighthouse light waxing and waning.

She was almost asleep when her phone beeped on the bedside table. "Fish and chips not necessary. My kitchen in working order. You come to me. Tomorrow night? Niall x"

Martha replied immediately with a simple x.

ELIZABETH

I can count the days and nights I spent with Sam Delaney on fewer than the fingers of my two hands, but the memory of their intensity stayed with me for years, until, as everything does, his face faded into the deep chasm of my past.

I am finding that the monumental effort I am making to remember myself as I was then disturbs and unsettles me. It makes me doubt. Should I have searched out another man with whom I could have shared such passion? I had squandered one chance and taken hold of the second, although I knew he could never be mine. Perhaps I thought that I didn't deserve a third.

The image of young Anna Morrison, cooing to her daughter as they passed Holmlea, comes to me more often now, and I wonder what kind of mother I would have made. I like to imagine I would have been more like her and less like my own, but then I am my mother's daughter, and in other circumstances perhaps she too would have been more carefree, more adoring, more like Anna Morrison.

★   ★   ★

During those precious days and nights together, Sam and I made Abbots Park our base, each time in the same bedroom, our enclosed febrile place, a secret netherworld. When I stepped through the door I lost all inhibitions. I had no code for how I behaved, no boundaries; I just wanted to drink him up. I revelled in his pleasure in my body. I feasted my eyes on his nakedness, his supple limbs, the muscles in his back, the birthmark at the base of his spine.

When we ventured outside, in the old sports car, I held myself differently, conscious of my body beneath my clothes, the swell of my breasts and the little mound of my stomach, my skin alive to thc slightest touch. We explored the Ayrshire countryside, picnicking on the coast looking out to the great granite rock of Ailsa Craig, and strolling by the River Doon near Alloway Kirk. We found the famous Electric Brae at Croy Bay and felt our stomachs churn as we drove slowly downwards, but felt the road rising beneath us.

We exchanged fragments of our lives but Sam was careful never to venture any stories about his home life, and it was territory on which I would not trespass. I made myself promise that, though I tortured myself with imagining.

Of course there came the day, as I knew it would, when he told me he was returning to that life. His mission at Prestwick was over. We had driven to a little loch near the village of Straiton where, without mournful silences or any dolorous preamble, for which I was grateful, he told me that he was returning to Chicago the next week. We would not see each other

319

again. Suddenly I felt exhausted, drained of all the emotion I had expended thinking about this day. I even felt a strange relief in the certainty of it. He kissed me for a long time, tenderly, and buried his head in my neck, as if this was our goodbye, two lives splintered as quickly as they had fused.

He held my hand as he drove the narrow roads through the hills to Ayr. I noticed a copse of trees in the centre of a field, and I squeezed his hand and asked him to stop the car. Like two sleepwalkers we crossed the lush green grass and entered the cool shade of the tall Scots pines. We watched each other as we undressed, capturing every detail, remembering each movement, tears blurring our eyes, and in that hour we gave each other a small part of ourselves that was a farewell gift.

MARTHA

On the spur of the moment, Martha decided to get ready for her dinner with Niall, at Holmlea. She gathered up her bottles and creams into a bag and an hour later she was running a bath in the cast iron enamel tub, pouring in a decadent amount of Chanel N°5 bath oil and praying that the ancient immersion heater would not give out. She wiped the steam from the old mirror above the basin and, studying her face, she realised with a start that something was different. Her eyes were clearer, her skin less lined under her rather neglected eyebrows, her sometimes grey pallor had a healthier glow, and her lips had lost their tight strained appearance, which the trademark slash of kabuki-red lipstick she had worn in Edinburgh had only served to emphasise.

She lit a scented candle and put it on the metal rack that lay across the bath. As she lay soaking in the soothing heat, she looked down at her body, thinking how long it had been since anyone but her had seen it, and even longer since anyone had appreciated it. By the time her relationship with Andrew was in its death throes, he wouldn't have noticed if she had turned into H. Rider Haggard's shrivelled Ayesha.

She banished thoughts of him lest he contaminate the evening ahead, and instead imagined Niall's hands exploring her body. She lay, languidly trailing her open fingers through the perfumed water until the bath cooled and rain began to batter down on the skylight. She dried herself with one of Elizabeth's rough bath towels, hardened by age, and then smoothed a shimmering body lotion over her skin.

If Martha's old life had dictated a rack of designer labels, on Arran the only discernible fashion trend seemed to be jeans, fleeces and hiking boots, but she had brought her favourite jersey wrap dress in a pretty blue and cream print, and a blue camisole. She fished a dark blue lace bra and matching briefs threaded with satin ribbon out from her bag, and dressed quickly. She pulled a pair of fishermen's socks over her bare legs, then her wellington boots, and ran downstairs, stuffing a pair of flat gold pumps into one pocket of her parka, and a bottle of Alberino into the other.

At the hallway mirror she applied a little eye shadow, a couple of coats of mascara, and dabbed on some coral-coloured lip gloss. Martha paused for a moment, her heart beating louder than a brass band. "For the love of god, please don't screw this up," she said to herself.

She took Elizabeth's ancient bike from the shed and cycled, head down against the warm summer downpour, towards the heart of the village. She turned the corner at the Sheep's Head tavern and pushed the bike up the hill as the street lights flickered on and transformed the sheeting rain into a curtain of glass beads. When she reached the top of the road, apart from the beckoning rectangle of warm light from Niall's house, she was surrounded by the gloaming.

Martha settled her bike by the door, catching the strains of Little Feat and the accompanying clatter of kitchen pans, and knocked. Nothing happened, so she banged harder, pulling her parka down over her forehead, until finally Niall opened the door. He grinned at her. "You dressed for dinner." Before she could say anything, he put his hands to her wet face and kissed her softly on the mouth.

Martha's heart was thudding so hard she was sure he would feel the vibration. She took a step back, fished the wine out of her pocket and handed it to him and he watched her pull off her coat, then her boots and socks.

"I'm sorry, I should have come for you. You look like some strange creature that's just emerged from the sea," he said, laughing.

"Can I straighten myself out?" she asked, suddenly perturbed.

Niall showed her the way to the bathroom, and she looked in the mirror, aghast. Something resembling a panda stared back at her. Her face, framed by wet straggled hair, was patterned with black streaks and patches of sooty purple eye shadow. She tried to wipe it off with dampened lavatory paper, but only succeeded in rubbing her cheeks into a mottled pink that read for some kind of skin disease.

When she returned, barefoot, to the living room, Niall was standing at the kitchen island ready to hand her a glass of wine. "All gone?"

"Very funny," she said. "I think it might be semipermanent."

When he smiled she was caught off guard again by how attractive he looked in his open-necked checked shirt with sleeves rolled up to reveal his tanned downy arms, slim jeans and bare feet. Then she worried for a moment that she might be fixating on his eyes, the way they appraised her with such a steady, almost amused gaze.

She turned away, composing herself, and looked around the room. The walls were painted a brilliant white, Persian rugs were spread on the polished oak floor and a big luxurious purple velvet sofa addressed a long low leather one, encased in polished steel. It was flanked by oversize glass lamps that cast a warm light. Below a long clerestory window she was surprised to see a series of prints, each one a profusion of brightly coloured birds, composed of cut out coloured pieces from clothing catalogues. "Where did you get the Fred Tomasellis?"

"You sound surprised."

"I have one, too. I've never met anyone else who even knows who he is."

"I bought them from a gallery in New York, when I stopped off on my way back from a hiking holiday in the Sequoias."

Martha would have liked to ask with whom, but checked herself. Then she turned round and stepped back, dazzled by the canvas filling the wall in front of her. Its saturated colours lent the image of Holy Isle an intense blue glow under a brick red sky. The sea was a deeper blue. Only a distant lone seagull taking flight from a telegraph pole distracted the eye.

"Craigie Aitchison. My God, you have an original Craigie Aitchison," Martha said admiringly. "How wonderful."

Niall came and stood close to her. "Isn't it? People say if you keep a painting in the same place for long, you stop noticing it, it loses its power to move you. Well, not this one.

"It belonged to my parents, so it was part of my childhood, but until I came to work in Brodick, I'd never been to Arran." Niall paused for a moment. "And now I look at both the painting and Holy Isle every day. Isn't that something?"

He told Martha that the only time Elizabeth had come to visit his "big glass box," as she called it, she had sat for a long time gazing at the Aitchison. She had met him, once, almost forty years earlier, she said, when he came to Arran to scatter his mother's ashes, and he had told her he was absolutely mesmerised by Holy Isle. Niall smiled. "Of course Elizabeth loved that, a kindred spirit. But then she said a strange thing. She said, 'I'm not surprised that you have a Craigie Aitchison, Niall.' I took it as a compliment."

"Perhaps she was making connections. I'm increasingly getting the sense she liked to do that."

Martha walked over to the curtain wall that looked out over the roofs of the houses below to the blackness beyond, broken only by a scattering of bobbing masthead lights on the boats in the bay, and the sensuous sweep of the lighthouse light. Her head was full of her surroundings, each painting, rug and lamp rendering Niall even more attractive than before.

She turned and looked to the back of the room, where he was collecting everything for dinner around him. "This is such a great space, and you've made it really lovely."

He flushed a little. "I wanted it to feel as if the house had grown out of the woods. You can see what I mean in the bedroom, but it's best to see that in daylight when there's bird life on the branches."

He stopped, and clicked his fingers. "The owl. Ha! I looked it up the internet, and there are a lot of omens to chose from: good fortune, or a sign that an unmarried girl is about to lose her virginity."

They both laughed, just a little nervously, and Martha swiftly raised her glass, "to the architect, the cook and the soothsayer." She looked at the food laid out on the counter, fish, lamb fillet in a marinade and Arran cheese, her favourite things, but what she wanted was for him to sweep it all aside and take her, right there, on the counter.

She wandered over to the window again and looked out into the darkness. This time she switched focus and saw Niall in the reflection, looking up from the counter at her, studying her.

He seared the scallops, pressing them gently into the burning butter, and then placed them on plates alongside some wild rocket and pomegranate seeds, and carried them to a small pedestal table set with tall candles in modern silver candlesticks. "I moved the table from the window so we wouldn't be free entertainment for the village."

"Is that what happens when you have someone to dinner?"

"I don't know. You're my first dinner guest."

"I'm honoured," said Martha, dipping her head to one side. "Mmm, these are so good." He smiled with pleasure at the compliment, and poured them both some more wine.

"Oh, I asked Ronnie, at the castle, about the photo. He had a vague recollection that she was friendly with a minister and his children in the 1950s. Said he remembered seeing them having afternoon tea at the Kingsley Hotel in Brodick when he worked there. Apparently the minister came to the island with one of the seaside missions and then stayed on for a while at a church in Brodick."

Martha listened intently. "Thank you, it's something at least."

"He also said that his sister, who lives up Cemetery Road, often saw Elizabeth there until quite recently, not inside the graveyard but sitting on the hillock next to the cemetery wall, always in the same place, on a raised flat stone, sitting perfectly still. I had no idea she went there. She never spoke about it, not to me at least."

Martha decided not to mention her conversation with Saul at the graveyard.

She put down her knife and fork and looked straight at Niall. "I don't want you to think that I'm obsessed with Elizabeth; it's not as if she consumes all my waking hours, but . . ." She stopped.

"Go on, please. Say anything you want," said Niall.

"I can't shake the powerful feeling that she's leading me somewhere. Why else would she not have had the house cleared out when she went into the nursing home?"

"I don't know," replied Niall evenly, "but there's nothing wrong with searching for clues. When someone leaves you their house, you want to know why. And, by the way, I *don't* think you're obsessed."

She relaxed, her prepared speech over, and took a sip of wine. Niall flicked on some music. "Buffalo Springfield. God, it's a long time since I heard them. They were Dad's favourite." She started to feel that the world was a more forgiving place. "You calm me down," she blurted out.

He gazed at her until she looked away. "I like your conversation," he said. "I like the way your face is a little flushed. I like the shape of your lips. I like you being here."

He got up from his chair and leaned over her. Martha raised her face to his and kissed him gently at first, and then she felt a rush of pure passion and as he put his hand round the back of her neck, threading his fingers through her hair, she pulled herself up to him. They stumbled over to the velvet sofa, all thought of dinner abandoned, and rained kisses on each other until Martha, warmed by the wine and suffused with the heady sensation of desire, raised herself up from the sofa and unwrapped her dress.

★ ★ ★

The high-pitched whine of a coffee grinder finally jolted Martha into consciousness and she emerged from under the white linen duvet and looked directly at a panorama of trees, almost blinded by the shards of sunlight that shot like lasers through the branches. For a short panicky moment she had no idea where she was, and then the glass window in front of her swam into focus, and her eyes followed a pair of chaffinches flittering and flirting round a rowan tree.

Niall opened the door, holding two cups of coffee. "It's a lovely way to wake up, isn't it?"

Martha laughed. "Watching the woods, or in your bed?"

He sat down on the side of the bed, pushed her tousled hair back from her face gently and whispered in her ear, "Both."

Martha took his hand and kissed it, and closed her eyes for a moment as she rewound her way through the evening before. "I have no idea what time it is," she said languorously, stretching her arms above her over the mess of soft pillows.

"It's half past eight," answered Niall, leaning forward to kiss the hollow of her underarm, "and I have to be going, or else the rhododendrons will turn into triffids."

"What? Oh, shit. Mr Wilson the builder is coming at nine, with his architect."

Niall took a bathrobe down from the hook on the door and wrapped it around her as she jumped up from the low bed. "You'll be great sport for the curtain twitchers this morning, cycling along in your sexy dress."

She gave him a withering look. "Just what I need, a reputation."

Niall slipped his hands inside her robe and cupped her breasts. "Yes, you do." He kissed her tenderly, moving his tongue over hers. "You look even more alluring in the morning light, if that's possible."

She showered and dressed quickly, and as she was leaving the room, she noticed the small table by the window on which a profusion of pink cactus flowers almost obscured a photograph. A young couple stood in front of a red sandstone house, the little boy holding his mother's hand and the younger girl laughing in her father's arms were unmistakably Niall and Catriona. She wondered if last night they both had deliberately not talked about their families for fear that still raw, complicated emotions might have broken the spell. Or perhaps they were just mad for each other.

She pedalled furiously past the harbour and along Shore Road, looking neither right nor left, and as she saw the house ahead of her in the distance, her heart sank as she made out two figures leaning on the wall beside a blue van, following her progress as intently as if they were watching the Tour de France. She slowed to a less frantic pace and as she approached, the more portly of the two called out, "Fine morning for it!" Mr Wilson touched his cap in greeting and hooked his hands back into his overalls. She gave him a wan smile.

She parked her bike inside the gate and Mr Wilson introduced her to Douglas Gordon, a friendly faced middle-aged architect in jeans and a battered corduroy jacket whose pockets bulged with notebooks. He shook her hand firmly and she detected a faintly apologetic air, as if he were slightly embarrassed by his colleague.

Fishing the front door key out of the deep pocket of her parka, she prayed there was no mail on the mat, and then she remembered that the post didn't arrive until the afternoon. Thank God for island life.

Martha made them all coffee, and using Niall's sketches and a pile of magazine cuttings, she explained to the two men how she wanted to transform the kitchen and dining room into a large open space. They listened patiently as she said that of course she realised they would have to replumb and rewire, put in central heating and lay a new floor, but, to save money, she said, fearful they would think her a scattercash, she would decorate upstairs herself.

"Ah, well then," said Mr Wilson with an amused look on his face, "that will make all the difference." He raised his bushy grey eyebrows, which matched the hairs protruding horizontally from his ears, and glancing at the silent Douglas Gordon, said, "And how long would you like this to take, lass?"

"Aren't you supposed to tell me that?" she replied, pointedly directing her question to the architect. "But 'as quickly as you can,' is the answer."

Well, what do you think, Douglas? We can get the building permission from your cousin in the council." He made great show of seemingly totting it all up in his head. "Right now, if we leave the small matter of the roof till the spring, and I use my crack team, *and* we forego our day of rest, just for you, we'll do it in three weeks."

"Really? In three weeks?" Martha sounded sceptical. "That would be a miracle!"

"No miracles," he replied, "but God did send me the next best thing, a Polish foreman."

She showed them to the door and as he was about to step outside, Mr Wilson stopped and looked at her inquisitively. "I never knew Miss Pringle to say hello to. My wife was wondering, were you related?"

It was Martha's turn to be amused. "No relation at all."

The builder looked at her expectantly.

"It's a complicated story."

He leaned in towards.

"I'll tell you about it over a whisky in my new kitchen when it's all finished," laughed Martha, "a large one."

Mr Wilson looked crestfallen. "I'll hold you to that, Miss Morrison, indeed I will," he said, pulling on his old tweed cap, and tugging it down for good measure.

Martha set to work, emptying the kitchen cupboards of what bits and pieces there were. There was a mish mash of old crockery, mostly Mason's Ironstone, and another painted china tea set, blue and pink anenomes on a stippled green background, marked with the initials EMP on the underside. She carefully wrapped it all in tissue paper and sealed it in a wooden box. Then she took the cookery books from the shelf, *The Glasgow Cookery Book, Mrs Beetons's Book of Household Management, Rowallan Creamery Guide to Cheesemaking*, and a number of notebooks full of handwritten recipes.

She noticed a little book lying on its side at the back of the shelf, titled *All About Arran*. She looked inside at the publication date, June 1933, and then she turned the page and found both sides crammed with a sea of names in childish handwriting. She could just make out the words in the middle, "To Miss Pringle from all her pupils in Shiskine School."

Martha flicked through the headings, "Arran in History", "Rambling and Scrambling", and when she came to the chapter on "Flowers and Plants", she found a folded note tucked tightly into the spine. She put the book on the table and carefully pulled out the paper, but as she studied it, she started to lose her balance. She held onto the edge of the table and focused on the page again. There was no mistaking the handwriting. It was a letter from her mother to Elizabeth Pringle.

Dear Miss Pringle,
    Please forgive me if you think I am pestering you. After I put my letter though your door yesterday it occurred to me that I should tell you that I do have a family connection here. My grandmother's favourite cousin is Ellen Stewart from Balnacraivie Farm near Shiskine. Perhaps you know her? I spent many happy holidays there when I was a child. Anyway, please don't worry, I won't put any more notes through your door.
    Best wishes, Anna Morrison

PS. Your lupins are fabulous!

Martha stared at the letter, amazed. Anna had never mentioned Ellen Stewart. She tried to remember where she had seen the name of the farm before, and then it came to her. Balnacraivie was written on the back of the photograph inside the frame that she had dropped and smashed on the floor of the study at her mother's house. As she re-read Anna's words, it dawned on her. It was most likely that she had distant relatives on the island.

In an instinctive, reflex action she lifted the phone to dial home to talk to Anna, before the sickening realisation that she'd so readily admonished Susie for the very same thing. She heard the screams of the seagulls fighting furiously over food scavenged from the bins, and the unmistakable *cack cack* of an incoming heron scattering them before he slowly flapped down to steal the spoils.

Martha sat down and buried her head in her hands as the image came to her of Anna, looking at her own letter, understanding nothing.

ELIZABETH

The night that I saw Sam Delaney for the last time I walked the three miles from the ferry to Lamlash, firm ground beneath my feet. It was as if I were returning for the first time since I had met him that day on the hillside. I wondered if I had embarked on a kind of madness, and now, all passion spent, I was safely home again.

I sought out Mary the next day, and I worked beside her in the garden, my physical presence a reassurance for both of us that I had survived the storm, perhaps even been strengthened by it, and was back on dry land again. As she took off her gardening gloves to wipe her brow she turned her head from the glare of the sun and observed me for a moment, and gave me a smile that told me that she loved me, and did not judge me, and that she understood.

Three days later, at dawn, I was awakened by the sound of urgent banging on the storm doors. I jumped out of bed, disorientated for a moment, and then with a sickening feeling I realised what the knock presaged. I pulled on the pile of clothes I kept at the ready, but I could not lace my boots properly, my hands were shaking so much. As I climbed unsteadily onto the back of the lorry, the rescue leader passed on what scant details he had. A US Air Force plane with seventeen people on board had lost contact over the Mull of Kintyre. No one knew whether it had downed on Arran, or on the mainland, or in the sea.

It was all I could do not to cry out. I squeezed my eyes closed, oblivious to the others, and counted back the days frantically, trying to remember when Sam said he was flying home, but I was too agitated and nauseous to think straight. I put my hands over my mouth and swallowed hard to keep the sickness down, and as we roared towards Glen Rosa, I tried to block out all thoughts of finding him on the hillside, and concentrated instead on the sound of the engine, the gears changing, the jolt of the accelerator. After that day there would be seventeen more families, bereft, cheated of their loved ones.

There were more than a hundred of us on the hills that morning, moving fast, scrambling over the crags, often on our hands and knees, sometimes lending a helping hand over a gully, sheepdogs racing back and forth, a small twin-engine plane above our heads scanning from the sky. Then someone arrived with more news from Brodick. The airplane we were searching for was a Lockheed Lodestar, which had been due to land at Prestwick at eleven o'clock the night before.

I made for a small hillock out of sight of the others and, falling down on my knees, my stomach convulsed and I retched until I could be sick no more. I put my

336

head against the cool rough granite, at first only consumed with relief, and then I was flooded with cold shame as I realised I was rejoicing when somewhere, perhaps over the next ridge, there was carnage. I vowed to stay on the hills until the very end.

We searched for four days and found nothing. I could hardly walk I was so exhausted, but I would have gone back for a fifth day had the main search not been called off. We gave up reluctantly, with only smaller search parties returning to the hills over the next weeks. We had failed, and this time, more than any of the others, I found it hard to hide my distress.

One day in class, one of the younger girls, Elspeth Birnie, asked innocently, "But Miss, why have you stopped looking? The plane must be there. You can't leave them all out in the wind and rain on Goatfell."

I turned away from the class, but not before Elspeth had noticed my eyes filling with tears, and staring at me in horror, she squealed, "I'm sorry, Miss. I'm sorry. I shouldn't have said anything." Her anguished sobs echoed round the class as thirty frightened faces looked at me for reassurance. I regained my composure, and said gently, so as not to scare them further, "Elspeth please don't cry. You have every right to ask. I am sad that we haven't found the plane. We try our best, because we want to bring some peace to their families, but sometimes we fail." I had put a map up on the wall marked with the North Atlantic route, and we had talked in class about the planes that flew north to Greenland, crossing the Atlantic where the ocean was at its narrowest.

337

But Elspeth was right. The plane was there. It was discovered in the November of that year, by a hill walker, on the east face of Caisteal Abhail, the second highest point on Arran. As it had turned to make its final approach to Prestwick it had come in too low and had struck the crag in full flight, with such force that the wreckage was spread over a quarter of a mile. Every single one of us returned to the hill, along with members of the US military, to do what we could to gather up the dead.

After the war, the families of the men killed on the mountains came here, and come still, and I have always hoped that they have found some solace in the beauty of the place. I have tried to tend the graves for them. I do not like to think of the dead, alone, so far from home.

MARTHA

Martha lay looking at the soft indentation next to her on the bed, lazily remembering the night before when Niall had arrived at the hotel late, and had come upstairs with two large glasses of malt. They had clinked glasses and he had told her about the little wooden Japanese-inspired bridge that he had designed for the estate and which he had put in place that day with two of his team. It had been a long hard day he said, but a fine one. She loved this about him, his skill, his creativity, his easy physicality.

They lay like spoons as he kissed her shoulder blades, her body a creamy white in the moonlight. He traced his hand down to the rise of her buttocks and rested it there, with the softest of pressure, until she couldn't wait any longer. She turned to face him, breathing in the scent of pine wood, teasing his smiling mouth open with her fingers, before she moved her hand down beneath the sheets.

It was late before they finally slept, and now Martha reluctantly hauled herself out of bed, catching sight of a jar of sweet peas on the floor just inside the door, a note tucked amongst the petals.

"Don't leave for Glasgow before I see you. I have something to tell you, Cx"

She showered and dressed quickly and called out to Catriona as she ran down the stairs, but the only sound emanating from the kitchen was the muffled strains of competing, hectoring voices on Radio Four. She glanced out of the glass front door, and was surprised to see Catriona and Saul in an intense, and very public, embrace on the grass across the road from the hotel. Saul took both Catriona's hands to his face and kissed them, and then he walked away, a definite spring in his long loping step.

Martha tapped on the windowpane and Catriona waved and ran across the road towards the hotel.

"I want to show you something," she said excitedly as she took Martha's hand and led her into the kitchen, quickly silencing the cockfight on the radio. She took a flimsy shiny piece of paper from her pocket and passed it to Martha.

"Oh my god," Martha looked at her in astonishment, "I think this is something wonderful." She squinted at the grainy picture, turning it around, baffled. "But I can't really work out exactly what I'm looking at."

"You are looking at a six-week scan of twins who look exactly like a pair of tiny cashew nuts."

"*Two babies*," exclaimed Martha as she hugged Catriona, "how amazing. Show me properly."

Catriona explained the ultrasound photograph, and at last Martha could just make out two tiny shapes suspended in what looked like a blizzard. "I can't quite believe it," she told Martha. "It was only a fortnight ago that you found me on the sofa. I thought I was just a bit peeky but two days ago I started feeling sick as a dog, so I did a pregnancy test, but that didn't tell me anything about *twins*! I've just had the scan. It could be two boys, two girls, one of each. I don't care what they are."

Martha trod carefully. "And what about Saul? Was he surprised?"

Catriona lifted a strand of hair from her face and put it behind her ear. It struck Martha how ethereal and radiant she looked. "No, he had wanted us to be careless. And of course," she said, smiling, "that was incredibly exhilarating. He was very definite about wanting us to have children, quickly. I really think it was something to do with Elizabeth's death."

"Maybe, but could it not just be that he's in love with you? It's obvious, Catriona, at least it is to me."

"Is it? I knew I was in love with him when I asked him to come with me to see the standing stones. I would never have taken him there otherwise, they're my special place. In fact they're a sort of vindication of who I am. When we were there he told me that meeting Elizabeth Pringle had changed him. She had awakened his capacity for love. Amazing, really."

"What about Holy Isle?"

Catriona smiled. "He'll always be a Buddhist, and Holy Isle will still be his spiritual home. When I told Saul I was pregnant he went over to talk to Sister Indra and I couldn't quite believe it but she said to him, 'Compassion is the very heart and soul of awakening.'"

"Interesting," said Martha, thinking back to her last conversation with the Buddhist nun. "I have definitely misjudged her."

"To be honest, he has tried her patience."

Martha thought for a moment. "Wait a minute, how stupid am I. Should Saul be celibate?"

Catriona nodded, laughing. "He's been in the Community for three years now, and I think he probably broke the first of Lord Buddha's training rules within six months. It was important for him to tell her and anyway he *had* to talk to her. I'll be the size of a house soon."

Catriona explained that Saul would come out of the *Vinaya*, the rules by which the Community lived, and would be a lay member rather than a monk, though he would still donate the royalties from his lyrics.

Martha looked at Catriona, her eyes wide. "I didn't know . . . Is that a big deal?"

"Seems to be. It keeps them in mung beans, anyway."

"And Niall, have you told him?"

"Yes. We had a cup of tea together just before he left this morning. He was very calm about it; he seemed taken with the idea that we're growing a family again."

As Martha wrapped the blue crackle glaze vase she had bought from the potter at Shiskine for Anna's birthday, she pondered Catriona's news. It was extraordinary how light it made her feel, joyous even. It was the same sensation she had when she looked across to Holy Isle, or when Goatfell's misty cap blew away, leaving the peak clear in the sky. In the eight short weeks she had stayed on the island, she felt less brittle, more optimistic. Although she had always thought of herself as utterly rational, she also believed that it was no accident that she was here, and that in the hazy unmapped distance this was where she would remain.

She arrived back in Glasgow laden with presents. As well as the vase she had brought a tall white orchid and some of Catriona's homemade shortbread. Opening the front door, she heard a wave of laughter coming from the kitchen. As she walked through the hall she stopped to listen, suddenly incredulous. Susie was back home, unannounced and unbidden. Home, less than a fortnight after she had flown off in a fury.

She pushed the kitchen door back and her sister, beaming, rushed over to her, her arms out. "Martha, how lovely you look," she said effusively, before hugging her.

Martha responded warily to Susie's squeeze, taken aback. Once upon a time, Anna had said almost these exact words. Her mother, too, was smiling at her brightly, but her eyes betrayed her confusion, and Bea simply raised her eyebrows as if to say, I don't really know what's going on either.

"Bea's made a delicious looking birthday cake for Mum," Susie said pointing at the beautifully decorated cake, the top covered in blue and purple flowers fashioned from royal icing. Martha looked from the cake to Bea, to Susie. "Bea's wonderful! When I arrived last night we introduced ourselves properly, didn't we Bea? I'm sorry, Martha," she rushed on, genuine regret in her voice, "I should have let you know I was coming."

Martha resisted the temptation to ask what had brought Susie hurrying home for fear of detonating an explosion. Instead they sat drinking tea, the atmosphere a little unreal, Martha exchanging stories with Bea about Arran while Susie listened, and Anna sat quiet and still.

After a while, Martha opened her notebook and took out Anna's second letter to Elizabeth Pringle. "Mum, could you have a look at this?" she asked as she unfolded it and put it into Anna's hands.

Anna studied it for a long time, and when Susie looked quizzically at Martha, she indicated to her to be patient.

After what seemed an age, Anna looked up at the three waiting women. "Well, isn't this something. We got engaged at Balnacraivie. Ellen Stewart was a lovely woman. I recall the meal she made for us. It was a steak pie and tipsy cake, and someone arrived with a fiddle, I don't know who it was, and we danced in the farmyard."

Martha sat, her mouth agape, while Susie read over the letter. "Mum," she said, "fancy you remembering that. You never told us. We should go there sometime."

Martha seized her chance. "Mum, do you know why you wrote the letter?"

Anna shook her head slowly.

"But do you remember, when we were little we used to have summer holidays in a house along Shore Road, called Seabank?"

Anna just kept shaking her head, and then her mood shifted and, agitated, she began banging her hands on the table. "I'm sorry, I'm sorry, I'm sorry," she wailed, and she began to make heart-rending sounds as if she were keening.

Martha put her hands firmly over her mother's. "Shhh, Mum, It doesn't matter, really it doesn't. We'll just go to Balnacraivie, as Susie says, one day soon."

Later that night Martha and Susie sat down at a table overlooking the old stableyard in the Ubiquitous Chip. It was Martha's suggestion that they discuss nothing until they were alone together, and the Chip was the place for family summits. It was the Morrisons' favourite restaurant, where Anna and John had celebrated their wedding. It was a once-a-year treat when the girls were little and then later, when it was just the three of them, Anna had taken them there when each had graduated.

Now Martha spoke carefully. "It was a shock to see you, Susie, but a lovely one. Did something go wrong in Copenhagen, though?"

"No, Copenhagen is all fine, but I wasn't."

Martha listened as her sister told her what had led to her sudden return. Susie had been cycling along a busy street in Copenhagen when she heard a loud, angry commotion, cyclists yelling, repeatedly pressing their tinny bicycle bells, and dissonant protesting car horns. She stopped and looked back, and standing stock still in the middle of the road was a man, perhaps in his sixties, dressed in a smart shirt, but in his pyjama bottoms, his feet bare, tears streaming down his cheeks. Susie threw her bike to the ground and ran back along the road, dodging the traffic, calling out to people to get out of her way. When she reached the man she took his arm to get his attention.

"I will never forget the look in his eyes, Martha," said Susie, trembling as she spoke, "it was a terrible mixture of terror and bewilderment, and desperation, too. I don't think he knew how he got there, or where he was. I started to guide him to the pavement, and he didn't resist me. People were just standing around gawping at him. It was awful, awful. I asked him his name and he opened his mouth to reply and then he stopped and shook his head. He looked, well, sort of ashamed. It broke my heart, Martha. So I called the police and they came for him with their siren screaming and their blue light flashing, and then people stared at him even more."

Susie began to cry, wiping the tears as they ran down her face. "I could not stop thinking about Mum, and what happened to her at Kelvingrove Gallery. I looked at this helpless man, who had suddenly been stripped of his dignity, and I knew, in that instant, that I *had* to come home. I had to come home, Martha, because we don't know how long we've got Mum, or how long she'll even know us."

She pressed her fingers into her eyes to stop the tears, and as Martha looked at her the memory came to her of the little girl she had frightened that long ago fireworks night.

"Hey, Susie, it's OK," Martha said softly, regret welling up inside her. "You're home in time because there will be good days yet. I know there will be."

But Martha's words sounded like platitudes, as unconvincing to her own ears as they must have been to Susie's.

She sniffed away her tears and breathed deeply. "You should be proud of me, Martha, I'm already set up. Alistair and Paul have given me some studio space at Timorous Beasties."

Martha was impressed. "I didn't know you knew them!"

"You never asked," Susie said flatly. "I met them when they lectured at St Martin's and we stayed in touch. And that's not all," she said, perking up. "I don't mean to boast, but do you remember that client meeting I had to race back to Copenhagen for?"

Martha leaned in expectantly.

"I got the commission. It's for a new china pattern for Crate and Barrel and it comes with an advance, a big one, so I'm going to buy a flat here."

Martha clasped Susie's hands in hers. "We need champagne!"

"Oh, and one more thing,"

"Something else?"

"Congratulations on finding Bea. Mum adores her."

Martha and Susie walked home, arm in arm, a little unsteadily, and as Martha scraped her key around the lock, Anna opened the front door, holding the crackle glaze vase.

"Thank you for this, Martha, it's lovely, it really is," she said, and without another word, turned to go upstairs.

The girls looked at each other, united in surprise, and then called out goodnight to her, but there was no reply as she disappeared to her room without a backward glance.

Bea was sitting at the kitchen table, a box of children's paperback books in front of her. Susie pulled the bottle of champagne out from her handbag and poured them all a glass. Bea told them that Anna had brought a big box down from the cupboard in the little room at the top of the stairs and had rummaged through it.

"She knew exactly what she was looking for," said Bea, sipping her glass of champagne. "I think she was trying to bring a memory to the surface and catch hold of it." Triumphantly, Anna had pointed out Susie's childish handwriting scrawled across the cover of a Mallory Towers story, and Martha's equally young hand on the flyleaf of a well thumbed copy of *Little Women*. Anna had sat tracing her fingers across the pages, and then she had said, with great conviction, "I think I'll give the girls a bed time story tonight. John's not here, so I'll be the story teller."

When Susie heard this she let out a little cry, and Martha's head started to swim. A vivid image of Anna had come to her. She was sitting on Martha's bed consoling her after reading the page in *Little Women* in which Beth puts down her sewing needle, realising she is near death. Martha had been terrified, making Anna promise she would never die, nor Daddy, nor Susie.

Martha left the kitchen and stood in front of the hall mirror. She brought her face into focus, searching once again for the indelible imprint of her mother's features, the curve of the high cheekbone, the indentation between her eyebrows, the bow of her lips. She closed her eyes, searching for an image of the mother Anna once was. Dismayed, behind her eyelids she could only see light and shade. She checked herself and straightened up. If she could not cope, then how would she be able to stop Anna falling into the abyss?

ELIZABETH

In the years that followed the war Arran became a quieter place, except in summer. In July and August, holidaymakers filled all the houses whose owners had decamped to little back houses built for the purpose, or they booked boarding houses, or pitched tents on farms, or stayed from one year to the next in handsome hotels built in the Edwardian era. The beaches were patterned with gaily striped windbreakers and tartan travelling rugs, and every child making sandcastles appeared to be sporting two towels sewn together with openings at the neck and for the arms.

During those two noisy busy months, I kept to my garden. There was always plenty to do. I had crops of raspberries and gooseberries to pick, and peas and leeks and lettuces to tend to in the patch at the back. I lost myself in a book for hours, sitting in my deckchair, the same one that is in the shed yet, my head shaded by Mother's wide-brimmed straw hat.

One of my favourite books was *Sunset Song*, which made quite an impact when it was published. I would like to have met someone like Chris Guthrie. She was a straight arrow, and she had such hard times to bear. If I had a heroine, it was her. I thought of her when unwanted thoughts crowded in, moments when I yearned to know how Robert was faring, when I had the bitter-sweet notion that he was happy and content. At other times I would read Robert Louis Stevenson's short story, "Thrawn Janet" and wonder whether I might come to resemble her in my old age, crooked, solitary, perhaps even a little frightening.

I used to order books from Alexander's store in Brodick, and I looked forward to the arrival of my packages very much. In the new age of the paperback, hardback books were my only real indulgence, apart from a good bottle of malt whisky. Alexander's also sold every kind of toy imaginable and, in the 1950s, the shelves were stacked with all sorts of games, boxes of snakes and ladders, jigsaws and Airfix kits for rainy days, of which there were many, Matchbox cars, wooden skittles, brightly coloured spinning tops, packets of scraps, and of course buckets and spades galore.

I had cycled over from Lamlash, on an exceptionally hot July day, to collect a copy of *Lord of the Flies*. I had read that EM Forster had chosen it as his book of the year the previous Christmas, and I was curious and intrigued to read William Golding's portrayal of his castaways. I had often observed my pupils' behaviour to one another, as they marked out the leaders and followers, the weak and the strong.

As I was waiting at the counter while Mr Alexander rummaged in the dark recess of the shop to find my package, I overheard an argument behind some shelves.

"But I saw it first."

"Why would *you* want it?"

"Why shouldn't I have it?"

"Because you're a boy, stupid."

"I can have it if I want it."

"I'll tell Daddy."

I put my head round the aisle and saw a little tow-haired boy sitting on the floor clutching a box containing a wide-eyed doll, his sister standing over him menacingly, attempting to prise the box from his fingers while he bit his lip, trying not to cry. When they noticed me they fell silent, the boy's beautiful blue eyes brimful of tears, and his hot face, flaming red.

It was not in my nature to interfere, but he looked so very unhappy. "Can't you each have a doll?" I said.

The girl looked shocked. "But he's a *boy*."

"Is that not allowed?" I replied, smiling.

"Peter was supposed to buy a car with his holiday money," the girl said firmly.

"But I don't want a car. I want a doll," replied Peter, his voice quavering.

I looked around the shop. "Where are your mummy and daddy?"

The girl replied, "Daddy's at the Mission on the beach," and then more quietly, "Mummy's dead."

"I am sorry to hear that," I said, wishing I had been gentler, more circumspect. "Does your daddy know where you are?"

They both shook their heads sheepishly.

352

"My name is Elizabeth Pringle," I said. "Perhaps I should take you back to the beach. Your daddy might be worried about you."

"He's too busy with the seaside service," replied Peter in a small, deflated voice.

I asked the girl for her name. "It's Esme," she said, shyly.

"That's a very pretty name." I put out my hand. "Pleased to meet you both."

As we crossed the road I could make out the familiar refrain of the Seaside Mission song.

> Come and see the Master,
> He alone is true,
> He will pardon sinners,
> He'll even pardon you.

It had always been a mystery to me why ministers would encourage children to believe they were sinners. I hoped that the young congregation would be too engrossed in fashioning pews out of sand and decorating them with shells to notice that they were being branded with sin. But more bewildering to me was the fact that their parents, busy sunning themselves, or reading or gossiping together, didn't appear to care.

The man I took to be Peter and Esme's father was in the middle of telling a group of children about the Mission's plans for the next day's activities, and as we came into his line of sight, he looked at us quizzically over the heads of his young flock. As soon as he had given the blessing, he hurried over, and ignoring me, took hold of Esme's arm a little roughly. "Where have you been? I told you not to leave the beach."

"We went to the shop with our holiday money," said Peter in a squeaky voice, shrinking from his father.

"Esme, I told you to look after your brother. I'm working, I can't watch you all the time."

Now I interjected, remarking that they had been quite safe in Alexanders, and also very entertaining, discussing what they might buy.

Peter shot me an anxious look and I smiled at him reassuringly.

Their father, a small slightly rotund figure, looked at me for the first time. "I am so sorry. How rude of me. I am Alistair Smart and these, as you've gathered, are my children."

I shook his hand. "Elizabeth Pringle. I live in Lamlash."

"Well, I must thank you for bringing the children back. Can we buy you a cup of tea for your trouble?"

I looked at Esme and Peter's eager faces, and in truth, I thought it would be pleasant to have some company.

"Thank you, it will fortify me for my cycle ride back up the hill."

"You cycle? The children are keen for me to rent bikes for them, but the Mission takes up a lot of my time."

"But we're *so bored* on the beach," said Esme plaintively.

"That's enough, Esme. Miss Pringle will think you are very spoiled."

I thought, how quickly one notices the absence of a wedding ring.

We sat under a parasol in the garden of the Kingsley Hotel, the children delighted by their tall glasses of Cremola Foam, into which the waitress had dropped a scoop of vanilla ice cream. The Reverend Smart explained that he had taken advantage of a month's leave of absence from his parish in Aberfoyle to run the summer mission. He had thought it would be a change for them all after the recent death of his wife.

"The children told me," I said. "I was sorry to hear about your loss."

He sighed. "It is the will of God."

"Then he is not very merciful," I said immediately, before I apologised for speaking out of turn.

"Please don't apologise," he said sadly. "Sometimes it's hard not to think that myself."

We watched Esme and Peter play croquet and I remarked that he had charming children. He laughed. "Do you think so? They are not always so obliging, I can assure you."

"What children are," I replied. "I have thirty in my class."

"Then you must be enjoying the peace."

"To tell you the truth, I miss them." And then, without thinking, I suddenly blurted out, "I would be very happy to look after Esme and Peter. We could cycle together; I could show them the island."

"Would you really?" he said, rather too quickly. "Wouldn't it be an imposition? I'm afraid my remuneration from the mission . . ."

I stopped him, embarrassed. "Please, I don't want to be paid. It would be a pleasure for me."

He called the children over and told them the news — he did not ask them whether the idea appealed to them. Esme was wide eyed. "Really? You would look after us?"

"And take us exploring?" chimed in Peter as he jumped up and down on the spot. He looked uncertainly at his father, who mouthed back at him, "say thank you."

"Thank you, Miss Pringle."

I laughed, and told them they would have to call me Elizabeth, or else I'd think I was in the classroom.

The next day I collected Peter and Esme from the dank dark little bungalow on Ormidale Road that the Reverend Smart had rented for the month. I had made egg sandwiches and sliced some tea loaf, and I made Mother's lemonade recipe and fitted the packages and bottles into my bicycle basket. They were ready with their rented bikes and Esme told me that the man at the bicycle hut had had to raise her seat, because she was ten, and almost five feet tall. Then it was Peter's turn. "I'm eight and a half," he said proudly.

I'd planned a trip to Blackwaterfoot, but I had not taken into account that although I cycled most days, the children did not, and soon the joys of freewheeling down into the valleys were far outweighed by the effort it took to push their bikes up the hills, as the road rose and dipped towards our destination. At first they were too polite to complain but eventually Peter, exhausted, asked if we could turn back.

"But look!" I said enthusiastically, "I can see the sea." He was fading fast, though, so I put his bike in a ditch by a larch tree and covered it with ferns. "Come on, Peter, I'll give you a backy the rest of the way there," I said, but he was whip smart and knew quite well that would not solve our problem.

"But how will we get home?" he wailed.

"I have a plan."

Esme looked doubtful.

I told them that the post bus left Blackwaterfoot for Brodick at four o'clock, and I knew for sure that Mr Menzies the postman would take us, and the bikes if there were room. The children cheered up, and Esme and I pedalled down to the shore, while Peter wrapped his arms around my waist. I felt his hot little cheek pressing into my back.

After our picnic at the swing park, I asked them to stay put while I went to the Post Office but when I walked back towards where I'd left them, I could see neither child. I thought my heart was going to explode with fright, but when I ran to the grass I spied them, fast asleep on their backs behind a little hillock, arms and legs splayed out, their angelic faces turned up to the sun.

I sat down beside them and let them sleep for a while, shading their faces with my body, watching the gentle rise and fall of their chests and the involuntary movements they made in slumber, pursing their lips to expel a breath like a soft purr, and occasionally rubbing an itch on their noses.

The ride home on the post bus was the highlight of that first outing and over the next few days we swam in the rock pools that dotted the sides of Glen Rosa, and took the bus to Lochranza and played hide and seek in the castle on the shore. We even went round the little island of Pladda on the Waverly paddle steamer. With each passing day I got to know the children better. I learned that Esme loved paper scraps, particularly flowers, and Peter liked me to read aloud to him as we lay in the sunshine. He would pretend he was Dicken from *The Secret Garden*. "Mummy used to read to us at bedtime and she didn't mind if I cuddled one of Esme's dolls, not like Daddy."

I noticed Esme giving him a sharp look. "I think every child should have a doll or a teddy to cuddle," I said gently.

"See, Esme," said Peter triumphantly, "and Elizabeth is a teacher!"

Esme relaxed. Then, out of the blue she asked, "Is your mother still alive?"

When I replied that my mother had died more than twenty years earlier, she asked me shyly if I still missed her, and I became conscious of Peter studying me intently.

"I think about her almost every day. I have so many memories, and they are very precious," I added.

Tears started to roll down Esme's face, and she sobbed, "Mummy used to brush my hair for a hundred strokes every morning."

I took her hand, and then I asked Peter what he thought of when he remembered his Mummy. "She made pancakes for breakfast and she smelled nice."

One morning, as we were getting ready to go out and the Reverend Smart was about to leave for the Mission, the weather turned in an instant from glorious sunshine to hailstones as big as golf balls and we all had no option but to shelter for the morning in the dreich little house. The children and I set up the card table by the window and began a jigsaw while their father sat with his books. I remember it was a rather twee picture of a thatched cottage, with enough thatch to make my head hurt as we searched for pieces.

Esme noticed the cover of one of the books by his elbow. "Daddy, tell Elizabeth about the fairies. Please," she added quickly.

He put up his hand in protest. "Esme, enough. Miss Pringle won't be interested."

I came to her rescue. "Why don't *you* tell me about it, Esme."

Delighted to have been given the responsibility, she began, "Daddy found a book in the manse that was written by a minister in Aberfoyle four hundred years ago."

"But this book was printed in 1815," Peter added in an important voice.

Esme went on, "His name was the Reverend Robert Kirk, and he believed there was a fairy kingdom, and he visited it and he saw what they ate, and he wrote all about it in this book, and all his 'S's are 'F's, which makes it a bit hard to read."

Alistair Smart passed the slim volume to me. "It's a strange old book, but it seems that the Reverend Kirk had no trouble reconciling Presbyterianism with some sort of fantastical netherworld, which he claims is populated by fairy families, and beings called Siths, some of which are our other selves." He paused. "Some kind of fantasy with which he entertained himself, but deeply felt."

Peter brought the book over to me and I looked at the words on the bookplate on the frontispiece. "An Essay on the Nature and Actions of Subterranean Invisible People, Elves, Faunes, and Fairies and the Lyke."

"You're very welcome to read it," Alistair Smart offered, "but it's an oddity, that's for sure."

That night I did not sleep at all. It took only a short time to read about the minister's fantastical world, but I returned to one chapter again and again, for although I am a rational person, and at that time had little thought of a spirit world, it gripped my imagination. I felt as if I had unlocked the door to another reality. Reverend Kirk described a place called a Faerie Hill, or a "howe," a mound beside a graveyard, dedicated to receiving souls until their bodies arise, and they are joined again.

The children were eager to find out what I'd made of the Reverend Kirk's book. Mindful of their father's views, I said as truthfully as I could that perhaps the minister had a wonderful imagination, and that maybe he had seen something, a glimpse of a bird stretching its wings, or a bat hanging in the shelter of a tree, or leaves fluttering back and forth whispering to each other on the wind, which he took for fairy people, and out of that single moment he had been able to weave a magical story.

"Hmm," said Esme, furrowing her brows. "Daddy wants us to believe in God when there is no proof that he exists, and he doesn't want us to believe in fairies when there is no proof that they *don't* exist."

I burst out laughing and gave her a hug. "Esme, you would make an excellent philosopher."

I had become very fond of the children and it was clear that during those few weeks they had become attached to me. As the time loomed for their departure, I was conscious of them keeping closer to me, each of us making excuses to stay longer at the end of the day. I tried to cheer them up with the promise of one last adventure, and arranged for the ferryman to make a special trip for us to Holy Isle. We were looking for buried treasure, just like Jim Hawkins. I bought wooden swords and eye patches from Alexanders and made old scarves into bandanas. Dressed in our costumes, we climbed to the top of Mullach Beag, and with an old brass spyglass of my father's we searched Lamlash Bay for pirates. We cooked sausages on what was probably a dangerously old Primus stove I found in the outhouse and ate far too much toffee. I hid two cotton drawstring pouches filled with pennies between the rocks, and Esme and Peter whooped and hollered as they searched them out, jingling the treasure in their hands on the bus home to Brodick, the three of us squeezed onto a seat for two, their heads bobbing on my shoulders as they slept. I promised I would wave them off at the pier the next day, and I knew it would take me all my strength not to weep.

That night, as I was sketching a picture on a canvas for a new tapestry, thinking about the colour of thread I would use, I was startled by the door bell, so unused was I to it being rung. When I opened the door and found Alistair Smart on the doorstep, I was sure something had happened to one of the children.

"No, no, they are both fine," he said nervily, stepping briskly, unasked, into the hall. "I asked Mrs Murchie, who rented me the house, to watch them for a while."

I showed him into the sitting room and offered him a whisky, which he politely declined, but I nonetheless poured one for myself. We sat, the atmosphere awkward, perhaps because I had an inkling of the reason for his visit. I did not have long to wait for his speech.

"Miss Pringle, or may I call you Elizabeth, as Esme and Peter do?" he asked, and went on without waiting for my reply. "The children have grown very fond of you and I know they are going to miss you very much." He stopped and cleared his throat a little. "I'm sorry, I'm not sure how to put this. I know that we do not really know each other, but I admire you very much, and we are both on our own."

I made to speak, to stop him before he went any further to the embarrassment of us both, but ignoring the look of consternation on my face, he ploughed on.

"The parish of Aberfoyle is mine for as long as I wish it, and the manse is a fine house."

I could wait no longer. I was not prepared to go along with a proposal more at home in a Jane Austen novel. "Stop, please," I said, raising my hand, palm towards him. "I don't want you to say anything else, if you are suggesting what I think you are suggesting."

He fiddled with his clerical collar. "I'm sorry for blurting it out like this, but would you consider . . . You would be very welcome in our family."

"To look after your children," my voice was quiet and controlled, "that's what you mean, isn't it?"

He turned even redder and I could see beads of perspiration forming on his forehead as he nodded. "I am asking you to consider marrying me."

I kept my temper in check so as not to wound. "Mr Smart, I know you are thinking of your children, but you have misunderstood me, I think. I will miss Peter and Esme, of course I will, but I could never marry for that reason, and I'm afraid I could not imagine there would be any other reason."

He sprang to his feet so fast he almost lost his balance. "I'm so sorry, I shouldn't have presumed. It was very selfish of me."

"It's all right. No harm has been done. It must be very difficult for you, but I am not the answer . . ." I paused. "I was going to say 'answer to your problems' but that would be wrong. Your children are bright and loving and a credit to you, and your late wife."

He smiled wanly and replied, "What you really mean to say is that I should tend to my own flock rather better than I do."

"It's you who is saying that, Mr Smart, not me."

He asked if I would still be at the harbour the next morning to say goodbye to the children. I nodded. "Of course, I would never break a promise."

After he had gone I went into the kitchen and poured a glass of water, and as I raised the glass to my lips I realised I was trembling, and I felt a wave of nausea. I sat down to steady myself, and then I picked up my bicycle lamp and cycled to the Whitehouse, grateful for the cool night air on my face. As I pedalled up the drive I heard Mary playing her favourite Mozart piano concerto, number twenty-one, her fingers light on the keys as she felt the music. I knew her eyes would be closed as they had always been when she played the piece for Mother.

I was shown into the drawing room, and straightaway she sensed something was wrong, but it was only when I described what had happened that I realised how intruded upon I felt. I also began to doubt myself. Had I inadvertently given Alistair Smart hope through my easy affectionate relationship with Esme and Peter?

"Don't be so hard on yourself," Mary chided, "you were simply giving these children some much needed attention, and some fun." She took a long draw of her cigarette. "Elizabeth, you have to stop doubting yourself."

But there was something else. "Mary, I lied to him. When he asked me if I would be there to say goodbye in the morning, I said *of course*, that I would never break a promise. But that's not true, is it?"

She held me away from her and pushed a strand of hair from my eyes as she had done so many times when

I was a child. "That was a long time ago. You have to let this go or it will cripple you."

We talked late into the night. Mary loved to talk about Mother, and I loved to listen. She had told me many times about Mr Cadell's infatuation with her, although as Mary would say, "he was a confirmed bachelor," and how Mother was flattered in spite of herself, how she blossomed during that summer. "You are so like her, you know," Mary said fondly, "and I see it more as you grow older, your high forehead, the way you carry yourself, the way you smile."

As we sat together in the lamplight, I noticed that Mary seemed less strong, almost a shadow of herself, and sometimes she would put a slender lined hand to her temple and press, as if trying to banish a pain. Then panic washed over me, and a selfish thought in its wake: that I would lose her soon, and then I would be truly alone.

I am finding it harder and harder to write now, and my breath is a little short. I sit here in my tweed skirt and cardigan and sturdy shoes that I can hardly lace up any more, something which distresses me, and I am invisible to most people. I saw myself in front of me yesterday and I know that life is pulling away from me, but I cannot let go yet, not until I have finished.

Saul will come soon and urge me on with his gentle words. I am sure now that I will not see Niall again, not in this life at least, and so I close my eyes and conjure up his face, and I can feel myself smiling.

★ ★ ★

The next day when I walked to the bus stop to wait for the bus to Brodick, I felt iron heavy, as if I were trying to pull against an unseen weight. At the pier I searched for the children amidst the chaos of departing holidaymakers; parents, children, grandparents and barking dogs, all mixed up in a jumble of luggage and golf clubs and rolled up windbreakers, but it was Esme and Peter who found me. The three of us hugged and clung to each other, exchanging endearments and whispering our farewells while their father stood a little apart, keeping his distance. I had brought the Reverend Kirk's book with me, but Alistair Smart said he had no need of it. "Keep it," he insisted, a regretful sheepish look on his face, "as a memento of your time with the children. They will certainly never forget you."

How quickly they were gone and I was almost alone again. I turned once more to Mary. I always refused to see her as anything but a tall strong oak under which I could shelter. But now her gaunt appearance, her rasping breath, the cough that followed her laugh, haunted me. I could see she was slipping away, her body making its preparations, and I was terrified of losing her. Mary, Duchess of Montrose, had helped me grow into the person I became. And from the moment she had shown me how to plant a sapling in the new woodland she had designed when I was a ten-year-old slip of a girl, she was a kind and patient teacher.

I sit here, a tapestry of a deep pink rhododendron on the wall beside me, sketched by Mary and sewn by me, and as I look at its rich silk petals, evenings in her private sitting room at Brodick Castle come to me.

366

When Mother and I visited, Mary would often have prepared a large marquetry tray on which she had placed a white damask napkin. Then, from a wooden garden box lined with moss, she would carefully lift eight rhododendron flower heads, naming each one slowly and precisely as she laid them on the napkin before placing a name card beside each of the blooms. She delighted in introducing new varieties, sometimes the fruits of new expeditions, and so no two games were ever the same. Some had spectacular names, the griesonianum, for example, with its showy red long-tipped flowers and pretty white attendants, or the vibrant yellow trumpets of the apiensc, and the dense creaminess of the beautiful roza stevenson.

I had to study the tray for five minutes, counted out by the ornate porcelain clock on the mantelpiece, while she repeated the names, then she covered the tray with another damask cloth before she deftly fished out the name cards, and then, time gone, with a great flourish she lifted the cloth off once more and I had ten minutes to try to write down the names of the eight flowers. Rhododendron cerasinum was my favourite then, and Mary made sure it was always on the tray. Later she gave me a gift of my own cerasinum and I still look out for the day every year when the huge, deep cerise frilly-edged bells first unfurl and reveal their dazzling white centres.

I close my eyes and I can still see her in her garden at the Whitehouse, hunched over a flower bed on her kneeling mat, deep in thought, her black and white spaniel lying beside her, inspecting her work.

I could not imagine the day when she would no longer roam the island that she loved so much, and so when she spoke of what would happen to the castle after she was gone, I would try to shush her. She would retort, "Come, Elizabeth, Lord knows I don't want to live forever. No family, at least not this one, can afford to look after all this." She gestured up to the top of Goatfell. "So, I must be practical if the estate isn't to become a wilderness."

She died in her seventy-third year, but to me she still had the essence of the beauty that De Lázló captured in the portrait he painted of her when she was just twenty-eight, which hangs in the drawing room of the castle still.

An estate worker, his hands wringing his cap, his head bowed, brought me the news. At her funeral I hid myself at the back of the kirk and when suddenly there was a great swell of singing not only from the congregation, but the crowd outside, "Oh love that will not let me go . . ." I rushed out of the church in Brodick, my heart racing, gulping for air, and once I was back in Lamlash, I made my way to the empty garden at the Whitehouse. I sat on her favourite seat and breathed her in from the scent of the grass, the damp earth, the pungent aroma of artemesia and lemon thyme.

It was the beginning of my slow withdrawal, not so dissimilar to the retreats that Saul described, except that the walls were of my own making. I continued to play a small part in the outside world, to whom I was a spinster teacher, who helped when help was needed, who had polite encounters with neighbours, who rarely went to church. Someone of whom people would make the odd inquiry about a certain plant, or ask for a suggestion for a colourful shrub for a west-facing garden.

Saul said he found it hard to reconcile my agile mind with my lack of interest in the bigger world. He was amazed that wars and assassinations and disasters seemingly passed me by. Of course, they did not, but I disliked the speculation and sensation of uninformed conversation, so I read the newspapers, but kept my counsel and, excepting for one new departure I was, for the most part, alone.

As Mary had wished, the castle was passed to the Treasury, and thence on to the National Trust, and so within two years of her death it was to be opened to the public, and for that, volunteers were required. I needed no prompting and indeed I was the very first to volunteer. No one more than I, beyond the family and the estate staff, knew the castle more intimately. I had taught for as long as I could, but Mary had left me a bequest in her will, and as I lived frugally, I had no need of my meagre salary. I knew that she would be happy that I was there, tending the rooms where Mother, she and I once sat together.

I took particular responsibility for the china room, where I catalogued and cleaned the exquisite porcelain, pieces of early Meissen, and Limoges, and Wedgwood. I used to spin out my tasks, such was the pleasure in holding the cups, admiring their luminescence and delicacy, and turning them in the light of the long narrow window, the better to catch every detail of the skilled brush of the china painter.

Then I would take my place in the drawing room as "part of the furniture," quietly observing the visitors, answering questions if asked, enjoying people's evident delight in the reception rooms and the hitherto private areas. Often, lulled by the soft ticking of the rococo clock, I would drift with my memories, and be startled by a parent shouting a warning, as their child was about to pull the silver worm from the mouth of the goose nestling atop the Chinese porcelain soup tureen, or dart under the rope barrier, aiming straight for the gilded, yellow silk love seat.

I made my way to the castle one day during the week, every weekend, and holidays besides, to help in the gardens as well as the house. It always lifted my spirits, and after I encountered Niall, I looked forward to my visits with renewed eagerness. We always had something to teach each other. I made notes about my observations for the days I would see him, and he would have tales of a new hybrid, or a special bequest that allowed for a drainage scheme, or a footbridge over one of the burns.

He was away on his travels that fateful day when I fell on the road in Lamlash, and made a decision that I should give up the castle before I became a burden. On that day, unbeknown to me, I was about to embark on another journey, mapping out my past as the future quickly began to fade in front of me.

MARTHA

Martha drove from the ferry straight to the Brodick Bar to meet Niall for lunch. Little stabs of excitement pricked her skin at the anticipation of conversation peppered with the flirtation that comes from the memory and promise of a shared bed. She was eager to tell him about Anna's recollections of Balnacraivie, and to share her thoughts about Susie's sudden return.

She spied him straightaway in the corner of the restaurant, intent on a sheaf of papers spread out on the table in front of him. She called out his name as she approached and he broke into a broad smile, and to the enjoyment of the mainly retired lunchtime diners, stood up, leaned over to her, and kissed her tenderly on the lips.

Just as she was about to tell him about Susie's epiphany, he took her hand. "Martha, I've had some news. Something I want to talk to you about."

She scanned his face for clues, looking for calamity. "Is it serious?" she asked uncertainly, her mouth suddenly as dry as parchment paper.

Niall laughed. "Hey, what's wrong? Don't worry."

She relaxed into her seat a little.

"I've been invited to go to New Zealand at the end of the year to deliver a lecture. Actually, it's not any old lecture. It's called the Banks Memorial Lecture."

"It sounds very grand," she said, in a lighter voice.

He explained that it was in honour of Sir Joseph Banks, who was the botanist on Captain Cook's first voyage to New Zealand, and that the horticulturalists there, "some of the finest in the world", had asked him to talk about the landscape and parkland at Brodick Castle.

"That's amazing, it must be a great honour. You'll go, won't you?"

"It depends." He took a deep breath, and looked at her evenly. "I want you to come with me. We could make a trip of it. Stay for a month, travel, stop off on the way."

Martha was too stunned to speak. A thousand thoughts careered around her head.

"Imagine, a week in Hong Kong, or Beijing perhaps." He stopped, reading her mind. "Come on, Martha. There's Bea now."

She shook her head, possibilities emerging, complications knocking them down. But the prospect of their being alone together so far away held no fears for her. That, she thought, is the litmus test of my feelings.

"Actually, there's not *only* Bea now. That's what I wanted to tell you. Susie's come home, and it seems to be for good."

"That's fantastic. Even better."

"Aren't you forgetting the house?"

"It's more than a hundred years old, Martha. It'll still be standing when you get back."

"And I've only been here a few weeks."

"We wouldn't be going until November; that's more than three months away."

"What about Catriona?"

"Saul's here, and we'll be back well before the twins are born."

She leaned towards him and whispered, "Is there anything you haven't got covered? How would you deal with my guilt, for example?" It had flashed through Martha's mind that a month in New Zealand would count as one selfish act after another. "I'll need to ask Susie, and Bea."

"Of course." Niall grinned at her.

She looked round and spotted the elderly couple at the next table, eyes trained on their food, listening furtively, as anxious as Niall for her answer. She burst out laughing. "It does sound amazing." The elderly couple smiled their affirmation.

"I'll take that as a yes," Niall said as he lent across the table and, threading his fingers through her hair, pulled her to him for a chaste kiss on the cheek. "One thing's for sure, Elizabeth would have been very excited. Before I left for Malaysia she read up on it much more than me. I think she exhausted the man who runs the mobile library." Martha watched his face cloud over. "I still can't believe I wasn't here with her when she died." He hesitated for a moment. "This may sound strange, but I feel the loss of her just as acutely as the death of my parents."

Martha remarked gently that she liked it when he talked about his relationship with Elizabeth. It helped her get to know them both.

"I'd talk without stopping for breath if only it would bring her back."

ELIZABETH

I woke in the middle of the night last night, from a
dream so vivid I thought that my father must surely be
sitting by my bed. In my vision he was there, his
military cap set firm on his head, his moustache neatly
cut, and the skin under his blue-grey eyes, unlined. He
was wearing his army uniform, the khaki serge tunic
closed to the neck, the brass buttons gleaming, his
leather belt held together with a metal clasp, and he
was sitting in Mother's dressing table chair, at my
shoulder, holding my hand in his. He was exactly as he
appeared in the photograph he had sent from France,
the blood coursing through his veins, alive in the world.

I watched his mouth moving slowly, his lips moist as
they formed the words, his voice low and lilting.

> I have but to be by thee, and thy hand
> Will never let mine go, nor heart withstand
> The beating of my heart to reach its place.

And then I heard myself cry out, the sound of it
echoing around my head as I opened my eyes in the
darkness, searching for him. I imagined I might see him

as one sees the imprint of a negative photograph, but there was only the solid emptiness of the night. My heart beat faster as I realised that I had heard the words my father had spoken long long ago, when I was a child.

I switched on my bedside light and went down the stairs, holding onto the banister tightly. It upsets me greatly that I am unsteady now when I used to be so strong. I pulled the blue leather-covered book of Robert Browning's poems from the bookcase in the hall, and as I opened it, a papery rose fell to the ground. I looked through the pages and found the powdery pink imprint on the page of the poem, "Any Wife to Any Husband", and when I saw it, the image of my mother came to me, in her chair in the sitting room, the Christmas before she died, the volume of poetry open in her lap. It was her voice I remembered reading the lines, but I do not remember a rose marking the page that day.

When shall I look for thee and feel thee gone?
When cry for the old comfort and find none?
Never, I know! Thy soul is in thy face.

MARTHA

Martha felt a little skittish as she drove to Holmlea, her hands vibrating gently on the steering wheel, a small ball of excitement in her stomach. This wasn't the same recklessness that had caused her so much grief before, she thought. She knew in her gut that Niall, she could trust with her life.

When she opened the front door she almost collided with Mr Gibson, who was standing gesticulating and shouting to his workmen who seemed to fill up the downstairs space, their raucous banter competing with not one but two radios, each blaring music on different stations, while hammers banged to a different beat. A huge steel beam was already in place above a gaping hole between the kitchen and the dining room, and long wires hung everywhere like stunned worms.

One of the men came out of the kitchen wiping his hands on his overalls, and then shook her hand. "I'm Tomas, Bea's son."

Martha smiled warmly, recognising the same broad open face. "Of course you are. It's lovely to meet you—"

Just then Mr Gibson broke in. "This was on the doorstep for you. I nearly stepped on it when I arrived this morning." He handed her a slim padded package and waited expectantly for her to open it. A disappointed look crossed his face when Martha thanked him and carried it, intact, upstairs.

The cardboard was stamped "Fragile" and on the cream label on the back was printed "The Ingleby Gallery." She opened the parcel carefully and her heart flipped as she lifted out a print of a slender grey earless dog standing on a rich coral-red ground. Martha recognised the Craigie Aitchison work immediately, one of a series he made featuring his favourite dogs, Bedlington terriers. It was one of her favourites, and signed by the artist. She stared, puzzled, and then fished out a printed card from the package. "I remember Mum gave you an Aitchison, now you have two. I'll come and help you hang it. Love, Susie."

She sat the picture in the light of the window and gazed at it. It was as if the colour was vibrating on the canvas, and the Bedlington was about to prance towards her new owner.

Eventually, the workmen pulled the plugs out of the radios and shouted their goodbyes to one another, and she could almost hear the house sigh with relief as it fell silent. Martha rewrapped the Aitchison and put it at the back of the wardrobe alongside the Cadell, and then she used the old curtains as dustsheets and draped them over the bedroom furniture. Now that a month in New Zealand was even just a possibility, she had a lot to do before the autumn.

She walked around both bedrooms, wondering whether to start stripping the walls, but there was something enchanting or even modern about the children's wallpaper, and the floral pattern in the other room would look lovely, she thought, with dark painted wood.

She would tackle the bathroom instead. Martha loved the shape of the room, the embrace of its slanted eaves, and she had resolved to keep the old claw foot bath, but the dull lilac art deco wallpaper and the green linoleum would have to go. Now, with the evening light filtering through the skylight, was as good a time as any to start.

She retrieved a scraper from a pile of the workmen's tools, picked up an unused dustsheet and filled a bucket with soapy water. She worked steadily, sponging a section of the wall at a time, then ripping away the wet strips of the stylised wavy design, moving from one side of the bathroom to the next until finally she came to the wall sloping down from the skylight. She felt an ache in her right shoulder and the light was fading, but she was so engrossed in the challenge, she pushed on with the help of the single electric strip above the sink on the opposite wall.

Martha knelt down to begin clearing away the lower area under the eaves that ran straight to the floor, and as she scraped upwards from the skirting board, she felt the flat edge of her pallet knife slip into a gap in the plaster, and saw that the wallpaper had obscured a little door into the eaves. She sat back on her heels,

379

uncertain what to do next, an uneasy feeling spreading across her chest.

The facings had been removed so that the door was flush with the wall, and the edges had been sealed with Polyfilla and glossed over. Martha worked away to remove the wallpaper until she finally revealed the whole of the door. Only then did she see the keyhole.

She paused and wiped a strand of hair away from her face, blinking, trying to suppress her jittery feelings. She thought of calling Niall, after all she was planning to do that later when he finished work, but she decided her nerviness was bordering on pathetic, so she worked her fingernails into the edges of the door, trying to lever it open at different points around the three sides, but it wouldn't budge.

It was then that it dawned on her. Of course, it was locked, but she knew where the key was. She went downstairs to the bureau, dropped down the lid, and from the little drawer in the middle she removed the velvet ribbon on which were tied Elizabeth's engagement ring, the wedding band, and the two keys, one bigger and more crudely fashioned than the other.

Before she climbed back up the stairs she switched on the landing light, as much to try to banish her anxiety with brightness, as to illuminate the locked door.

She knelt down again and put the bigger of the two keys into the keyhole. It turned easily with a gentle click, and Martha, startled, pulled her hand away, her mind racing. Was this Elizabeth's doing, or perhaps an earlier owner? She stared at the door, running through a list of the belongings that people stowed beneath the eaves — money, jewellery, old papers tied with ribbons, strongboxes, army uniforms, cartons of books, love letters, pictures, photographs, toys.

She stood up, her reassuring litany complete, and went down to the cupboard under the stairs to rummage for a torch. She found a rusty one on the shelf, and miraculously, when she squeezed the rubber button, it still worked. She returned to the bathroom and gently prised open the now unlocked door. Tentatively, she peered into the dark dense void and, switching on the torch, she slowly swept the beam around the space.

At first she could see nothing, but then the light caught the outline of an object. She yanked her arm back, casting the eaves into darkness once again, and concentrated on trying to slow her breathing and her heart rate with long steady inhalations and exhalations. Nothing moved, but then how could anything move? The door had been sealed for years.

She extended her arm slowly, shining the torch once again into the gaping door frame, and concentrated the beam on the distant shape. Now she could see clearly that it was a brown leather suitcase, with two brass catches and a lock in the middle, and on the top she could just make out under a light film of dust, a set of initials. She leaned into the space on her hands and knees and gently pulled the almost weightless suitcase along the floor and out to rest on the dustsheet amongst the scraps of wallpaper. Now she was intrigued.

Martha wiped away the stoor to reveal the initials EMS. For a moment she was perplexed, and then she remembered the initials on the engagement ring that hung on the velvet ribbon in front of her. It came to her, that this suitcase had been made for a trousseau.

She took the key back out of the lock and turned the smaller key on the velvet ribbon between her fingers. She had no doubt that it would fit the suitcase, but she wondered whether she should stop now, if she had any business prying into Elizabeth Pringle's past. But then, Elizabeth might have forgotten the suitcase was there, and if not, it was like the Cadell; hers to find. She left Homelea to Anna, and that meant everything in it.

Martha sat motionless, staring at the leather suitcase, readying herself to open it, but when she tried to insert the little key into the lock it was as if her fingers had pins and needles. They itched and tickled, and she had to pause a moment and shake her hands steady again. Then she turned the key and slowly flicked back both catches and as she lifted the lid, she saw cream silk fabric in deep folds, which seemed to fill the suitcase. Then she noticed an edge of lace beneath one crease and as she pulled the silk aside she jolted back on her heels, her hands pressed to her mouth, trying to make sense of the scene before her. Nestling in the middle of the case, surrounded by the soft material, was a little cocoon-shaped bundle of ivory lace, wrapped up tightly. One end rested on a tiny embroidered muslin bag full of lavender, and a silver chain attached to a locket was threaded through the lace in a perfect heart shape.

Martha let out a cry and backed away from the open suitcase, for what she was looking at, she was sure, was not a child's doll, a plaything, but a baby, and as she stared, the image of the tiny shroud imprinted itself on her mind. Her heart was racing as she scrambled, half tumbling half running, to the bottom of the stairs and out into the cold evening air, where she sank into the garden seat, her eyes blurred with tears.

Her thoughts came in a rush. She had to find Niall. Her phone and her car keys were in her bag in the hall, but however irrational it was, she didn't want to go back into the house alone. Instead she grabbed the bicycle from the side of the house and pedalled hard along Shore Road in the twilight, praying that Niall was at home. When she saw the bright light shining from the big window above her she almost fainted, and she yelled out his name as she banged her hand insistently on the door.

Niall opened the door and looked at her tearstained face in surprise, but before he could say anything, Martha put her arms around him, and holding fast to him sobbed, "I've found Elizabeth Pringle's secret, Niall, it's terrible. I think I've found her baby."

He held her away from him, uncomprehending.

"It was in a suitcase under the eaves. It's all wrapped up in something."

Niall looked at her, horrified. "What . . . Are you sure? Are you sure it's a baby?"

Martha nodded her head. "It can't be anything else." She looked at him unsteadily. "It's so sad, Niall. I wonder how long it's been there." And then she searched his face. "Perhaps something really awful happened."

Niall guided her gently to the sofa and poured her a whisky. "Drink this," he said, as he tried to fathom what she had just told him, "while I try to get hold of Saul."

A few minutes later he returned and sat down beside her, and put his arms around her firmly. "Martha, listen to me, Saul and I are going along to the house and Catriona is going to come here to be with you."

"No," she said, and then she repeated more emphatically, "No, I'm coming back with you, Niall. There might be a letter, or something else I missed."

As she calmed down, Martha thought of Elizabeth Pringle wanting her there. She had been meant to find the baby, she was sure of it. "I have to be there, Niall," she whispered. "It's where I'm going to live, so I need to go back."

Niall gave up the battle. "Well," he replied, "one thing is for sure, Catriona is not coming with us."

When Saul and Catriona arrived a few minutes later, both ashen-faced, they sat together on the sofa, her hand over his, while Martha, composed now, recounted how she had discovered the suitcase. Saul, fighting to keep himself together, finally put his head in his hands.

"Did you know, Saul?" asked Niall, his tone more resigned than accusing.

Saul looked up, tears in his eyes. "I knew there was something, something that had troubled her most of her life, but it was not for me to ask." He faltered, and Niall broke in, bewildered, "I had no idea, no sense of it at all. None."

Martha put her hand on Niall's arm. "We need to go. I don't want to wait any longer."

They drove the short distance to Shore Road in silence, each one fearful of what lay ahead, and when they reached the house, Niall turned to Martha and took her hand. "Do you want to stay downstairs for a minute until Saul and I have seen . . ." His voice, barely audible tailed off. "Until we've seen whatever it is we'll see."

"No, we should go upstairs together."

They entered the house and closed the door behind them, and Martha put on all the lights. As the two men reached the top of the stairs she could see they were both struggling to keep control.

Niall entered the bathroom first, and Saul followed, his head bowed. Then they crouched down together beside the suitcase. "Oh, Elizabeth. Elizabeth," Saul intoned, rocking a little back and forth, while Niall simply stared in disbelief.

The suitcase was laid out like a tiny silk-lined coffin, the little cocoon of lace no more than twenty-five centimetres long.

"Her name was May."

Both men, startled, looked up at Martha.

Niall, his moist eyes questioning, said, "But how do you know it's a girl?"

Saul suddenly understood. "It's the tapestry isn't it?"

Martha nodded slowly, her eyes filling with tears. "It's the month that's embroidered along the bottom of the picture, but it's also her name. I'm sure it is."

Saul sat back on his heels and closed his eyes, his hands together in prayer.

"What should we do now?" Martha whispered.

Niall closed the lid gently. "I don't think we should unwrap the lace because it's possible that it's preserved the baby."

Martha uttered a little cry. "Oh no, I didn't even think of unwrapping it. But, could it really? It's so long ago."

Niall put his arm around her and said in a strangulated voice, "Martha, listen to me. We don't know how she died, if she was stillborn or . . ." He stopped, darting a look at Saul. "Or if something else happened."

Saul looked up at Niall in dismay, a shadow crossing his face. "You really think that Elizabeth could have killed her own baby?"

"No, Saul, I don't. I really don't."

"Poor Elizabeth. Whatever happened, she had to bear it all her life. She had to live with the weight of that sadness," said Saul quietly.

"We'll have to let the police know, and there will be a postmortem, I suppose. I'll call Andrew James at the station. I'm sure he'll know what to do," said Niall.

He lifted the suitcase gently and carried it to the sitting room where he placed it on a low table. Then he pulled the curtains and they locked up the house.

That night Martha lay on her side in bed looking out at the silvery reflection of the moon on the water, Niall holding her close, his chest against her back. Since she arrived in Lamlash she had been trying to gather fragments of Elizabeth Pringle's life, to understand her even a little, and now she realised the only thing she knew was that every breath Elizabeth took, every thought, every action, had been governed by the birth and death of her daughter.

"I was meant to find the baby, wasn't I?" she said suddenly, "but did anyone else know?"

Niall kissed her hair. "Sshh. I don't know, Martha. We can start looking through the house again tomorrow. There may be other clues."

"Who would have thought Elizabeth Pringle had a secret life," said Sergeant James when Niall called him soon after six the next morning. "We used to talk about her sometimes. She taught my great-uncle and took him to watch the *Queen Mary's* speed trials when he was a wee boy. You know he became a director of John Brown's engineering?"

Niall listened to his friend patiently. "I'm sure there are a lot of people with fond memories of her, Andy, so can we try to keep this quiet?"

It was agreed that Niall would retrieve the suitcase from Holmlea before Mr Wilson and his men arrived, and that it would be kept safe in a small room at the police station in Brodick until a forensic pathologist was available to examine it.

"I'm going to call Professor Sue Black straight away. She's the best in the business, and if she's not busy digging up bodies in some former warzone, I can ask her to come quickly."

"How do you know her?" Niall asked.

"I went with her to Pristina to the mass grave. She was something else, amazing to watch, so dedicated, and tough as nails."

"I didn't know you went to Kosovo."

"Ah well, Niall," he laughed grimly, "Elizabeth Pringle's not the only one on Arran with secrets."

Martha and Catriona walked arm in arm together to Holmlea in the morning sunshine. The road glistened from a passing squall, and a bright rainbow created a halo in the distance behind Holy Isle. "Look," said Catriona, gesturing to the sky over Mullach Beag, "maybe it's a hopeful sign from Saul."

The visit was at Catriona's insistence. Saul had returned to Holy Isle and she had tentatively asked Martha if she minded going to the house. It held no terrors for her now, she said, and besides, she needed fresh air to counter the waves of nausea that persisted, most often in the heat of the hotel kitchen.

The two women sat on the garden seat, the atonal sounds of the building work like a modernist symphony at their backs. "Perhaps that's why Elizabeth Pringle stayed here her whole life," mused Catriona, "because May was here."

Martha stared out at the water. "How did she bear it? Maybe she thought she was protecting the baby, and if you think about it, they were together when Elizabeth was alive, and now they are together in death."

Catriona shivered and Martha said quickly, "I'm sorry. Let's not talk about this." Then she added emphatically, "You mustn't get upset."

But they couldn't drag their thoughts away from the baby. They sat a while staring out at the sparkling water, each working away silently, teasing out fragments of what they knew about Elizabeth Pringle.

Martha finally shifted in her seat and, in an unnaturally bright voice, asked Catriona if Niall had said anything about the trip to New Zealand.

"There's nothing like swapping one beautiful wet mountainous island for another," said Catriona, with a wry smile.

Sergeant James had caught Professor Black at her desk in Glasgow and she volunteered to come straightaway. She was eager to see how intact the baby was. Sorry, she had said, to sound gruesome. She'd seen cases like this before, babies left in the rafters of an attic, or under the eaves, or even inside old chimneys, lying on wide ledges.

Andy James collected her from the afternoon boat and brought her to the police station where Martha and Niall were already waiting. Catriona telephoned the Long House to send word to Saul to hurry back from Holy Isle.

Professor Black was a vivacious woman with a warm and direct manner. A tumble of red hair was held back from her freckled face with two clasps, and her vivid green eyes rested on them one by one as she shook their hands, her grip reassuring and firm.

"Andy said you'd like to be present, and that's fine," Professor Black said in a matter-of-fact voice, "but just to warn you, even though it appears that we are dealing with a death that happened a long time ago, it can still be distressing when I uncover the corpse." She looked at Martha's ashen face and said gently, "Are you absolutely sure you want to watch?"

Martha nodded, pursing her lips. "Will you be able to tell us how the baby died?"

"Only if there's a ligature, say, or if the skull is smashed."

Now it was Niall's turn to baulk, his face chalk-white.

"It's up to you," she said, looking directly at him, "but I will say, for what it's worth, it will be fascinating." Niall collected himself and nodded towards her.

"OK, Andy," she said, "let's get started. I'll be photographing everything, for the record."

At that moment Saul knocked gently on the open door and walked in silently.

Professor Black, noting his robes, smiled. "Your faith will be a comfort, no matter what you see in the room." She explained to the others, "Forgive me if you know this, but for Buddhists the passage to the next life will have happened a long time ago." Saul responded with a short bow, the strain showing on his face.

They entered the small whitewashed room, lit only from above by a large metal skylight, and unadorned except for an office table on which lay the closed suitcase and an anglepoise lamp. Sgt James closed the door gently behind them. They watched as the forensic pathologist went through the same ritual she had performed thousands of times before. First she pulled on her cotton overalls and piled her hair into an elasticated plastic cap. Before she put a mask over her mouth, she handed everyone haircovers and masks, and asked them to stand back from the table. Then she switched on the lamp and unfurled a roll of green cotton to reveal pockets of gleaming instruments. Beside them she laid a white sterile mat, which she had shaken out of a plastic cover, and her camera.

The silence was so loud it filled the whole room. It was as if they were hermetically sealed in time and space from the world beyond. Professor Black pulled on her surgical gloves, teasing and flexing her fingers into every last spacc. She looked around the group, her steady serious eyes an even more brilliant green against the white of her mask. There was a sharp click as she flicked back the catches and opened the lid of the suitcase.

Saul hummed softly for a few moments, his eyes closed. Sue Black glanced up, acknowledging the sound, but, her focus undisturbed, she gently lifted the lace parcel onto the mat. Taking her scissors, she carcfully and deftly began to cut through the layers of lace that were wound round the baby.

"Right," she said quietly, not raising her eyes from the table, "I'm going to talk you through this."

Martha felt Niall tense beside her as they watched Professor Black make the final cut into the lace. Then, picking up her tweezers, she gently folded the fabric back, and they could just make out a tiny, fragile skeleton. It was almost pink in tone, its legs and arms crossed as if it were still in the womb, the skull smooth

391

and each of the vertebrae intact. Although the ribs and backbone and skull were clear of skin, it appeared as if there were pieces of dusty paper attached to the legs and the feet.

Martha put her hand to her mouth to trap a cry, to stop a sound before it threatened Sue Black's concentration.

The pathologist put her hands down on the table beside her, hardly moving, giving the others time to get over their shock and take in what they were seeing but not understanding. For her, it was different; the signs, the experience, the judgement — it was all almost automatic, but nonetheless she was always moved, and she always made sure she reserved as much compassion for the living, as the dead.

"The first thing to say," began Sue Black, in her quiet authoritative voice, "is that I can't tell if it is a boy or a girl."

Martha was about to interject, but thought better of it.

"You'll notice that there is no smell at all. That suggests to me that the baby was wrapped up very soon after death, which meant that it was essentially sterile, and hence easier to mummify."

She looked around at them. "Look at this, please."

Martha put her hand on Saul's trembling arm, coaxing him to move forward.

"The bones have been held in place by cartilage and muscle, and on this skeleton, we're lucky enough still to have some skin." She pointed with her tweezers. "Do

392

you see this? It looks rather like lacework on paper, like a thin doily. That's skin. Look, it's on the feet, too."

Niall swapped his weight from one leg to the other and drew his hand across his brow, putting his finger in the corner of his eye for a moment.

Sue Black took out a ruler and measured the long bones, the femur first and then the tibia. "This was a small baby, perhaps thirty centimetres long." She paused, straightening up for a moment before resuming her hunched position. "Which suggests to me that it was not full term. And now for the difficult part. My job isn't to determine the cause of death, but in fact I can't see anything to suggest any trauma. There's no damage to bones, none of them lies at a strange angle. I can't be absolutely sure the baby wasn't suffocated, but I seriously doubt it. I don't think there was any violence inflicted here."

Niall and Saul both sank back, taking in Sue Black's verdict, each man now visibly distressed.

She looked at them both over her mask. "I am so sorry, it can be overwhelming. Andy said you both knew the woman who hid the baby. This must be a shock for you." She looked around the group like a kindly mother, surveying their drained white faces. "Why don't you go outside while I take my photographs, and Andy and I fill in the record?"

They walked out to the reception area, removing their masks as they went, moving slowly as if in a daze. Niall had his arm round Martha, Saul followed behind, his head bowed, and when Sue Black joined them a few moments later, few words had passed between them.

"I'm afraid I can't be sure when the baby died, but it was obviously a long time ago," she said. "I'm no expert on fashion but it looks like a wedding dress, which suggests that the lace wrapped around the corpse might have been a veil."

"The baby was a girl," Martha said suddenly.

"How do you know?" asked Sergeant James.

"Elizabeth Pringle left clues in her needlework."

He looked at her closely. "So, do you know what happened?"

"No, but it must be something to do with her wedding. Her engagement ring is on the velvet cord along with the keys."

Sue Black shook her head. "It's heartbreaking, but sadly this is not a unique story."

She explained that women sometimes gave birth after concealed pregnancies and with no money or support, or to avoid the shame, they did the only thing they thought they could, and smothered the baby. "But," she added quickly, "I'm not saying that happened here."

Saul turned and looked out of the window, his hands resting on the window ledge.

"I have a theory that Beatrix Potter wrote about the tragedy of all this in the story of Samuel Whiskers," said Professor Black. "Do you know it?"

Niall looked startled. "Elizabeth had that book. Remember, Martha?"

"So you know the story? The rats kidnap a kitten, wrap it up in dough and hide it." She paused. "But it's just a theory."

Saul cleared his throat. "When can we bury her?" he said, in a voice that carried the weight of all their anguish.

"Soon," said the policeman, "but she's been waiting a long time, a couple more days won't make much difference." He looked at their shocked faces, Sue Black's included. "Sorry, that wasn't meant to be as callous as it sounded."

They each thanked the pathologist. "I was happy to come," she replied, "and I'm glad you're all here. Often this is a solitary task and there's no one connected to the body. No one who cares, either. At least you can give her a burial, beside her mother."

The three of them returned to the Glenburn and found Catriona on her hands and knees scrubbing the floor. "I had to keep busy," she said, when Niall protested and helped her up, "otherwise I'd just cry. What happened?"

"Elizabeth had wrapped her up so carefully. She'd swaddled her the way you would to settle her, to make her feel secure," said Martha quietly. "That somehow made it less stressful for me." She darted a worried look at Catriona. "I don't know how much to say."

Catriona jumped in. "I'm fine, really I am. So, it doesn't look like Elizabeth killed her?"

"I would never have set foot in Holmlea again," said Martha, shivering a little. "There must be houses where exactly that has happened, and people don't realise it. How horrible."

At that moment the door opened and Saul appeared, carrying a small cardboard box. It struck Martha, that, for the first time, he looked all of his forty-five years. His face was hollow and his shoulders bowed, and his eyes looked raw and red-rimmed. Silently, he set the package down on the table in front of them. They all looked at him, bemused, but he kept his eyes firmly on the box.

"Elizabeth gave me this for safekeeping. It's her memoir. She said that I would know when it was time to open it." He looked up at the others with a haunted expression. "This is the time."

Niall stared at him, incredulous. "You don't think you should have mentioned this before?"

Catriona winced. "Niall, please, come on. Let Saul explain."

"I haven't spoken about it because I didn't know what it was that was troubling her. When she thought death was nearing she seemed to become more agitated. I was so worried about her. I thought there must be some kind of secret."

He turned to Niall. "Believe me, Niall, if you'd been here I would have talked to you. But I thought perhaps, if she wrote it down, it might help her, bring her some kind of peace." He took Catriona's hand. "I only told Catriona about it after you found the suitcase."

"But what if I hadn't? Found the suitcase, I mean, or come to Arran even. What would you have done then, Saul?" It was Martha's turn to sound reproachful.

"Look," said Saul, "I don't know, and that's the truth. Maybe I'd have given you the memoir anyway, once I was sure you were going to stay." He leant heavily on the table and said, his voice agitated, "Look, Martha, Niall. I knew nothing about this."

"All right, all right, Saul, it's OK," Niall said, now conciliatory. "Have you read it?"

Saul shook his head slowly, his voice faltering. "It's just as she left it. I haven't opened the box."

"Well, here goes." Niall opened the cardboard flaps and removed an oak box, decorated with delicate mother-of-pearl flowers. There was a little key in the lock. Niall turned it and lifted the lid. A dark blue, hardcover, speckle-edged notebook lay inside, on top of a number of letters tied together and a sepia photograph of a man in army uniform. Niall took the notebook out, and, looking steadily at Martha, passed it to her. "You take it," he said softly.

When she opened it, she saw written on the first page, "Elizabeth Mary Pringle, 1911–2006."

"Look at that," exclaimed Martha, "she was sure of her death."

Saul clasped his hands tightly together on the table, and Catriona put her hand on his.

Martha looked round at the others. "One of us has to read this, at least the part of it that matters, right now. What should we do?"

Finally Saul said he would try to find it.

As he pored over the densely written pages, Niall left the table and stood looking out of the window to the rose garden at the side of the hotel, his hands thrust into his trouser pockets. Catriona made a pot of tea, and served it in her mother's old Minton cups and saucers, china she'd never used before. It was somehow fitting. But Martha sat motionless, imagining Elizabeth at Holmlea, gardening, sitting with her tapestries, her poetry books. Were they a salve? Did she think about May every day?

At last, Saul looked up from the notebook that held the secrets of Elizabeth Pringle's life, tears at the corners of his eyes. "I've found it, but I can't read it out loud. You need to read it for yourselves."

He scraped back his chair and got up heavily, and weeping quietly, he left the room.

ELIZABETH

There can be no more waiting, no more hours when I grip this pen in my aching hand and hold it over the page in cold dread, unable to make a mark on the paper. I have come late to this chapter of my story, and my heart is as heavy as a stone. I can put it off no longer for my eyes are failing me and I feel my strength ebbing with the speed of a rip tide. Everything is out of kilter now, but I must return to the turn of the year after Robert had sailed for Australia.

It is true that I was plunged into a terrible darkness. It was as if I were being dragged down into a whirlpool, my body bound by heavy chains, being sucked into a vortex as powerful as Corryvreckan, and when I opened my mouth to scream for help, the sea rushed into my lungs and I was drowning, my mouth full of salty gritty water. In my delirium I could not tell day from night, but I could see Robert standing in the distance in the half light, like a statue in the middle of an empty landscape, and then suddenly he disintegrated into rubble. I saw the same horrifying scene over and over again. It was in this state that I wrote the letter. I knew then that I would not follow him.

After that I slowly came back to life, walking a little towards Clauchlands Point, talking to no one, my head down. I ate simply, nourishing my body with eggs and cheese and what fruit I had bottled in the store cupboard, and finally one day I put my face up to the chilly sunshine and my head began to clear. I was ready to return to the classroom, but not as the person I had been before.

As the winter eased up a little and the first delicate snowdrops pushed their way through the ground by the garden wall, I decided to pick a small bunch for my desk in school. As I bent down with my scissors, I felt dizzy and a sharp pain pierced my stomach. I clutched the rough stone dyke to steady myself until the agony eased a little, and then I pulled myself up and walked slowly to the house. I lay down in front of the fire on Mother's tapestry cushions, and once I had slowed my breathing, I suddenly became aware of another sensation, of a fluttering movement in my stomach, like a butterfly trapped in a velvet bag, beating her wings against the soft fabric with all her might, and then falling back, exhausted.

I moaned; now I was terrified. Had I ignored the signs, the twinges in my stomach, the unusual tenderness of my breasts, the faint nausea in the mornings? I counted the days. It was the middle of February. I was twenty weeks' pregnant, and fear flooded through me like molten iron. There was no one I could tell, not even Mary, for I was too ashamed. There was no one who could help me. I could not even send a telegram to Robert, for then the world would know, and in any case he would be powerless to do anything for me.

I went upstairs, holding on to the banister for dear life, pulled off my clothes in the bedroom, and putting my hands on either side of my stomach, I felt the little soft mound that could not be smoothed away. My heart was beating so fast I thought I might faint and my mind jumped wildly from one thought to another. The letter I had written to Robert would not have reached him yet, and now everything had changed. We were going to have a child. He was going to be a father and we would be a family, a family. It was such an enormous overwhelming moment. But even so, I knew I couldn't ask him to come back. I would have to go to him, and break with Arran for good. But I couldn't travel to Australia in my condition, all alone. I knew not a soul in Glasgow. Were there places I could go in the city, to stay, until the baby was born, and then I could make my way to Kilbride and Robert? I lay down exhausted, and immediately fell into a dreamless sleep.

When I awoke it was already morning, and I still felt wretched. I took my bank book from the bureau drawer, along with the details of Mother's estate, the shares that were now mine, and the cash box she had kept at the back of the bureau. There was money enough for all my needs, and more.

The room started to move in front of me and I lay down on the rug until the nausea passed. I had to face up to what I had done. I was not yet twenty, with child, unmarried and alone. I had shamed my family. And yet the thought of holding my baby in my arms obliterated all else, for just a moment.

I carried on at school, disguising my rounded stomach with long cardigans buttoned over my skirts. I was lucky that it was the fashion then, and it was safe to say that no one would ever have imagined that Elizabeth Pringle would be pregnant.

I looked in the telephone directory, surreptitiously, in Brodick Library, and found a gynaecologist on Berkeley Street in Glasgow. I wrote to make an appointment for the local holiday the next week and received confirmation by the return post.

On the following Monday I took two hundred guineas out of my savings account and set off for Glasgow. I thought I would be embarrassed when the doctor examined me, but Mr McCann could not have been kinder or more courteous. He told me his family always took a house on Shore Road for the six weeks of summer. "Do you know the one?" he asked. "It has a long sloping garden, round the corner towards Clauchlands Point. Ferguslea, it's called."

I told him distractedly that I did, and then, when I asked him if I could be sure of his discretion, he looked quite offended. That was when I decided to tell him about my predicament. He smiled at me in a kindly way, and he told me where I could find the ticketing office to buy a second-class passage for Australia for when the baby was born. Then he gave me the address of a nearby hotel where I could stay for three or so weeks before it was due.

"I will deliver your baby safely, Miss Pringle," he said, "and we'll be ready. First babies rarely come early." That is what he said. That is what he said to me that day. I will never forget it. His voice has come to me unbidden down the years, when I am kneeling in the garden, or listening to the chatter of families on the beach: "first babies rarely come early."

I should have telegraphed Robert then, when I was in Glasgow. Why did I not? I knew the letter I had sent would take many weeks to reach Kilbride, and I thought I would wait until I had left the island for good.

My hands are shaking now, and my head is pulsing, and tears are coming to my dry aching eyes. I have, for a very long time, thought that I had none left to cry. Will I feel "unburdened" as Saul would have it, when this is all written down in front of me, my testimony? He is a gentle soul. He has not inquired, and I could not say the words out loud. But is it really possible to hold onto a secret for more than seventy years and then to be released from it, and from living itself, as light as air, like a bird on the wing?

On April the thirtieth I woke in the ink-black night, gripped by a shuddering pain that left me clawing for air. It was as if my body were trapped in a vice that was being tightened, gleefully, by an unseen hand, inflicting agony turn by turn. Even the moon was hiding, cowering in fear, and I remember only the slow flash of Stevenson's Lighthouse, blinking its warning to everyone lest they sail too close to the rocks.

I was shaking and writhing with terror so that it took me all my concentration to light the lamp without setting fire to the house. I ripped off my nightdress, and when I looked down at my stomach it had become hard and shiny and distended. My breath was coming too quickly, and I was powerless to slow it, but I knew it was all happening too soon, and fear closed over me like an avalanche.

I dragged myself to the bathroom on my hands and knees, but no matter which way I turned, I could find no relief from the searing pain, and I started to pant and whimper and cower like a wounded animal. Even if I had had the strength to crawl down to the front door to cry for help, who on earth would have been there to hear me?

I gripped the side of the bath and lay with my head on the cold enamel rim, as the contractions roared in like giant roiling waves. It was then that I thought I might die, and I can still hear myself bellowing, screaming for my mother. I was desperate for water and I grabbed at the sea sponge on the bath tray, and ran the cold tap through it. I clamped my teeth onto it and sucked as hard as I could.

Then I felt the rush of warm water between my legs and knew I was near to giving birth. Somehow I pulled towels down from the cupboard and, as I was on my hands and knees spreading them around me on the floor, I suddenly felt an overwhelming urge to push, an impulse so momentous, so primal, that I could not have stopped even if I had tried. I pushed so hard I felt as if my body might explode. I gritted my teeth, every fibre of my being tense, and then I managed to grip the bath again and raise myself up on my knees. I squeezed my eyes shut and at that moment I saw Mother's face before me, gazing directly at me, and I kept looking at her, as from somewhere deep inside me came a fierce howl, and then another one, and then the baby moved down and I was sure I was being cleaved in two.

I lurched forward and she slipped out of me, all bloody and wet onto the floor. Suddenly I heard her cry out, little quivering mewling sounds, her fists waving in front of her tiny downy face. She was calling to me. It was the only sound I heard her make and I can hear it still. But before I could hold her to me, the room began to spin and I fell sideways and was sick on the floor, and in that instant I lost consciousness. I could not help my daughter. I could not help her to live, and I could not save her. I must stop for a moment, but only a moment, because I cannot last on this earth much longer. I do not want to.

I have taken a glass of whisky to fortify myself. The liquid burns my throat, but I want to feel the sensation of pain, even now.

I do not know how long I lay unconscious, but when I opened my eyes, the lamp was out, and in the dawn light I could see my daughter lying close to me on the crumpled bloody towels. My beautiful perfect girl, no breath of life escaping from her, her skin translucent and an ethereal blue, and when I lifted her into my arms she was ice cold. She was so light, so fragile, her balled fists no bigger than the top of my thumb, and her eyes were shut as if she had looked around at the cold grey world, and the only thing in it her pathetic inert mother, and had decided that she did not want to see it any more. She had been alive, but I had made her suffer, abandoning her to her fate in a cold unknown place.

I have always wondered whether she scented me, sensed me close, saw me, hated me. I have tortured myself in so many ways, but worst of all, did I lose consciousness because I was lacking the fierce protective instinct of a mother for her child? Was there an infinitesimal part of me that did not want her enough?

I lay huddled with her, bereft, sobbing for the daughter I would never know, never sing to, never look at with fierce joyous love.

I have lived with her death all my life, and with the knowledge that had I told Mary, confided in her, trusted her, as I should have, then my daughter would be alive, and Robert and she and I would have been a family. But I failed her.

My only child was born and died on the first day of May. I put my silk wedding dress in my smallest suitcase and spread Mother's veil on the soft eiderdown on my bed, and then I bathed my daughter gently, wiping my tears from her cold skin. I laid her on the fine lace, and then I wrapped her carefully, swaddling her little body tightly. I set her down amongst the folds of silk as if I were settling her for sleep, repeating her name, May Pringle Stewart, until at last I closed the lid of the case, and placed her under the eaves so that she would be with me always.

In the days that followed, I hardly left the house. I left a note for the postman under the stone at the door to pass to the headmaster to say I was poorly and would not be at school for a little while. Several times I gently pulled the suitcase out from under the eaves, thinking that I would hold her again, but each time I put my hands on the brass clasps, I stopped, unable to open the case. It was her resting place now.

When Mary knocked on my door on 10 May, I stood in the shadows by the kitchen until I recognised her through the etched glass door, and as soon as I opened it and saw her shocked face, I broke down, my legs failing me. It was no wonder she immediately grasped me and led me into the sitting room.

In the long hours of darkness I had come to the decision that I would confess to her, and her alone. She listened quietly, my hand in hers, as I relived that day at the Falls, for it was important that she knew that it was I who wanted to lie with Robert, that it was a gift I gave to him. But when I tried to talk about my daughter's death, words failed me, and it was she who blurted out words, blaming herself for leaving me, for failing to see the signs that I was pregnant, even if I myself did not. I had never seen my mother's friend, usually so composed and tender-hearted, so distressed, and in that moment, it was I who comforted her.

She begged me to tell her where May was buried, but I shook my head, adamant that it was better that she didn't know, except to say that she was safe, and no one but Mary would ever know. "Not Robert?" she asked imploringly, "are you sure, Elizabeth. Doesn't he have a right to know?"

I shook my head. "And torture him all over again? How could I do that to him?"

From that day, Mary made no judgement on me. She was there at my shoulder steadying me when I walked back into the school, and how I needed her, for when I returned to my class I saw my daughter in each of the children I taught, when I saw their eyes light up in delight at a story, or at learning a new poem, or opening the door of the dark cupboard in the classroom and looking in wonderment at the stem of a hyacinth emerging from the bulb. My dearest friend Mary understood that the children were my salvation, and when she died, she took my secret to her grave.

I know where May's soul is resting, waiting. I sit on the small mound of grass beyond the cemetery, knowing her spirit is close by. When Anna Morrison, or perhaps another, reads my story, my wish is that May's body and soul be reunited, and be buried with me, her mother, and with Isabel Pringle, her grandmother.

MARTHA

Martha drove over the String Road towards Blackwaterfoot, the roof of the Volkswagen down, feeling the warm breeze on her face as the road rose to meet the huge azure sky. There were red deer grazing high up, the points of their antlers standing out on the purple ridge, like sculptures.

It had been almost a week since she dragged the suitcase out from under the eaves, and the image of the perfect shroud still threatened to knock her off balance when she least expected it. Now, though, the grim discovery was slowly giving way to something almost indescribable. As she read and re-read Elizabeth's memoir, Martha sensed she was beside her, hearing her breathing softly, sharing her joy as a little girl, the sea spray on her face, her father's moustached face thrown back in laughter. She saw Elizabeth and Robert shouting to each other over Glenashdale Falls, shy and chaste, young people in a long-lost world. Most of all, Martha was humbled by Elizabeth's stoicism, her acceptance of solitude, the way she kept the faith with her daughter until the very end.

Each day that Martha read the pages of Elizabeth's handwriting, she learned something more from her, and with each chapter she felt herself more drawn to her. She walked in Elizabeth's steps, searching for the plants and flowers that she had marked in her gardening journals, which Niall had brought back to Holmlea. She sat by the burn near Shiskine School where Elizabeth used to eat the lunch made so lovingly by her mother, and she studied Cadell's portrait trying to fathom the hurt Isabel had unknowingly, surely unknowingly, caused her only child. She wandered through the Castle gardens searching out the snowbell tree where first Elizabeth encountered Niall, and then on up through Glen Rosa where she sat for a while on Torr Breac.

At Holmlea she sensed Elizabeth's presence, peaceful now, watching the house taking on its new shape. She hoped she would be happy that she had kept the brass bed, and the wallpaper with the children playing that she had chosen when she herself was a child, and that the place where Martha had decided to hang her two Craigie Aitchison prints would meet with her approval.

Saul had assuaged his grief by quietly making the preparations for a simple graveside dedication, to take place the following day. He had chosen poetry, selected a Holy Isle rock whitebeam to plant in the woods beside the cemetery, and arranged for the engraving on the headstone.

Niall spent long hours fashioning a beautiful casket from a larch that had recently been felled at the castle.

410

Now May lay inside, wrapped in a jewel-coloured paisley-patterned woollen shawl that Martha had found in Elizabeth's dressing table drawer.

As she reached the top of the String Road, the sea ahead of her shimmered. In the silver haze, she could just make out the Mull of Kintyre and in the far distance, the faint outline of the Paps of Jura. She turned left up a single-track road, which climbed into the hills above the coast, until she came to a neat white-painted sign for Balnacraivie Farm. She pulled onto the farm track, which was lined by a high copper beech hedge, and soon she arrived at a handsome stone farmhouse, covered in Virginia creeper.

She stopped the car in the farmyard and was greeted by a chorus of barking. Three collie dogs suddenly appeared, racing round the Beetle, encircling it as if it were a huge metal sheep they had been waiting their whole lives to herd. Then she heard a series of sharp shrill whistles, and instantly the dogs scattered and disappeared into three kennels, which sat in a line at the back of the yard.

She turned to see who possessed such an ear-splitting command and a tall sallow-skinned man in his fifties, dressed in faded blue farm overalls, strode towards her from the byre. His thick wavy hair was falling over his broad handsome face and his hands were casually thrust into his pockets. "Hello, can I help you?" he asked in a deep lilting voice, his eyes twinkling.

"I'm Martha Morrison, from Holmlea in Lamlash."

411

He shook her hand firmly, and laughed. "From Lamlash? You're a long way from home. Robert Stewart, pleased to meet you."

Martha froze.

"Is something wrong?" he asked. "You look like you've seen a ghost."

"I'm sorry," Martha said, reddening. "It's just that you are very familiar to me."

He looked at her quizzically. "But I don't think we've ever met?"

"No, but there is a connection."

"Well, then," he broke in, "come inside for a coffee and tell me about it."

Robert Stewart poured her a cup of steaming hot coffee from a silver vacuum jug and offered her a scone from the wire rack on the big oak kitchen table. She watched politely as he put a knife and a plate down and pushed the butter dish towards her, but before she took a bite, Martha took Elizabeth's memoir out of her bag and laid it in front of him. "I'd like you to read this. It concerns your family, and in a very distant way, my family, too. Our great-grandmothers were first cousins." He stared at her in surprise, and she went on, "But mostly it concerns your great-uncle Robert."

Now she had his full attention. "After whom I was named," he said.

"And I think you must look like him, too," Martha replied. She put her hand on the book. "This was written by Elizabeth Pringle, the woman he was engaged to before he left for Australia."

Something registered. "She wouldn't follow him, or so the story went."

"But there's more, and it's in here." She paused. "There was a baby."

Robert Stewart looked shocked. "A baby? Are you sure? What, born here on Arran?"

"Yes," she said, pushing the book towards him. "I'll leave you to read it for yourself."

"We'll be having a big scandal then," he said in a gruff low voice.

Martha shook her head and smiled sadly. "No, actually, when you read it . . . I don't know, but I think you'll just think it's heartbreaking."

That evening, as the sun cast its last rays through the forest, Martha, Niall, Saul and Catriona walked up to Glenashdale Falls, along the path cushioned with soft pine needles, through the dense undergrowth, fireflies and Painted Ladies fluttering before them as if they were leading a procession. They had the woods to themselves, and when they reached the tree where Elizabeth and Robert had carved their initials, they stopped, and for a moment they stood in silence, listening to the falling water. Then Niall took out an old penknife and carefully and solemnly carved the letters MPS beside those of her parents, while the others looked on. And as they slowly retraced their steps they sensed the trees leaning in towards them as they passed, the forest now complete.

★ ★ ★

The next morning they gathered by Elizabeth's grave. The headstone now had a second newly carved inscription. "Here lies May, daughter of Elizabeth Mary Pringle and Robert Stewart, who was born and died on 1 May 1934."

As Saul was about to speak, a car drew up nearby and they all watched as Robert Stewart and his wife came towards them, Elizabeth's memoir in his hand.

Martha smiled and made way for them at the graveside.

"This is in memory of May, Elizabeth, and Isabel Pringle," began Saul.

> She walks in beauty, like the night
> Of cloudless climes and starry skies;
> And all that's best of dark and bright
> Meet in her aspect and her eyes;
> Thus mellow'd to that tender light
> Which heaven to gaudy day denies.
>
> One shade the more, one ray the less,
> Had half impaired the nameless grace
> Which waves in every raven tress,
> Or soflty lightens o'er her face;
> Where thoughts serenely sweet express,
> How pure, how dear their dwelling-place.
>
> And on that cheek, and o'er that brow,
> So soft, so clam, yet eloquent,
> The smiles that win, the tints that glow,
> But tell of days in goodness spent,

A mind at peace with all below,
A heart whose love is innocent!

Niall knelt down and placed the casket in the grave,
and each of them sprinkled some earth over it, making
a gentle pitter patter sound, before he carefully covered
the hollow with spadefuls of the rich brown soil. Then
Martha and Catriona each put a jar of roses on the
grave and Niall took a small trowel from his pocket and
cut through the grass on each side of the headstone and
planted tiny handfuls of vivid forget-me-nots, pressing
their roots gently into the ground.

They left the graveyard through the rusty old gate,
which creaked and clanged as they pushed it backwards
and forwards. One by one they stepped out onto the
hill in front of the cemetery wall and stood looking over
Lamlash Bay towards the purple and brown patterned
hillside of Mullach Beag, the fresh breeze sending the
clouds scudding across the sky.

"It's an Arran day, all right," said Niall, as he put his
arm around Martha to walk back down to the shore.

The next fortnight passed in a frenzy of activity at
Holmlea, as Mr Gibson and his men put the finishing
touches to the new kitchen that stretched from the back
to the front of the house. Catriona had painted the old
dresser a dark blue, and together she and Martha
mixed Elizabeth's crockery with her, filling the shelves
with an even greater mismatch of flowers and stripes
and polka dots.

The carpenter had built a bookcase along the back wall of the living room, and Martha put her novels side by side with Elizabeth's books. Sometimes there were duplicates; a first edition of Mary Webb's *Precious Bane* sat next to the tattered Virago paperback, which Anna had passed on to Martha when she was a teenager.

With Niall's help she hung the Craigie Aitchison prints and the Fred Tomaselli pictures on the brilliant white walls in the open-plan kitchen, but she waited until she was alone to unwrap Elizabeth's tapestries and pictures. As she lifted them out of the box, one by one, her heart beat faster, until she finally found the canvas she was looking for.

She sat it against the wall where the light was best and, kneeling down, studied the fairies entwined with the dark green ivy, the garlands of nemophilias, and the name of Elizabeth's daughter embroidered into the stem of a bluebell. It was only when she looked closely at the word "May" that she noticed two tiny speckles of darker green on the stem, one on each side of the word. She peered more closely and there, in the finest of threads, were the letters E and R.

She sat back on her heels, staring at the tapestry. At that moment, in the silence, she felt Elizabeth's presence as never before. It was as Saul had said. She was in the air, in the tapestries, in her books, in her story.

Martha hung the tapestry above the fireplace, and on the mantelpiece she put the marquetry box that held

James Pringle's letters and Elizabeth's engagement ring.

Martha had set her writing table at the window, and on it she had put a new jar of sea glass, collected from the beach across the road. It made a colourful paperweight, Niall's drawings for the renovations beneath it. She sat at the table and looked over to Holy Isle. It was like a great benign sea creature filling the horizon. She had always imagined it protecting Elizabeth Pringle from the open sea, but now she wondered if Elizabeth had been hiding behind Holy Isle, sheltering from the world.

Martha stood at Brodick pier watching the ferry cut through the waves, its bridge a dazzling white. It always surprised her how quickly the boat approached, as if she were running for port, excited to be back again. Martha loved to watch as the captain reversed towards the pier, easing her in expertly, sending the brackish oily water churning and foaming. She waited at the barrier, scanning the bobbing heads of the passengers clattering down the gangway, until she caught sight of Bea, her arm hooked through Anna's, traipsing along at an angle, and Susie close behind, trying to manoeuvre a bolt of cloth under one arm and a suitcase in the other.

Martha ran forward, waving excitedly, and she heard Susie call out, "Mum, look, Martha's over there." Anna simply gazed around her at the noisy chaotic crowd, but Bea tried to wave back with her free arm, to which was attached a small overnight bag.

Martha rushed up to her and relieved her of it, and gave Anna a kiss. "You're finally here, Mum. I'm so happy, and it's such a lovely day, I've put the roof down."

Anna stood smiling at her daughter, saying slowly, "Martha, it's you, it's you!" She hugged her back.

Susie said gently, "Mum, we're back on Arran! I haven't been here for years but Martha's staying here and we're going to see the house where she's living."

Anna swung round violently, shouting at her younger daughter, "I don't want to go. I won't go."

"Why not, Anna?" asked Bea gently. "We talked about the house and how lovely it would be to come to Arran and see it."

Martha noticed how clearly and patiently Bea spoke.

"I don't want to go. I want to stay in my own house," Anna wailed petulantly.

"Of course, Mum," coaxed Martha. "This is just a visit. Then you will go home to Glasgow. Meanwhile, Bea's looking forward to seeing her grandchildren."

"I don't want to go, I don't want to go." Anna's now terrified voice rose to a crescendo, and Martha saw every head turn sharply towards her, a sea of narrowed accusing eyes, and as quickly look away again.

"Mum, it's OK," said Susie, "we won't go to Martha's if you don't want to. Would you like a cup of tea instead?"

Anna looked hopefully at her younger daughter. "Can we have it now, Susie?"

"Of course," she replied. "I know a lovely place, over the hill from here, right on the shore."

418

They drove to Lamlash and pulled into the drive. "It's great, Martha," whispered Susie appreciatively, as her older sister disappeared inside the house to fetch the tea things.

Anna stepped gingerly out of the car and stood looking out to the bay, shading her eyes against the glare of the sun. No one spoke, but Bea and Susie watched as she walked down to the wall that bordered the road, moving her lips almost imperceptibly, singing the "Skye Boat Song" quietly to herself over and over, the lullaby that used to settle her daughters so long ago.

Martha reappeared from the house, a tea tray in her arms, and watched the scene before her. Bea went to Anna and guided her towards two deckchairs, where Susie was laying out a tartan rug. Susie whispered to Martha, "Genius, getting Tunnock's teacakes. Just genius."

Anna and Bea sat side by side sipping their tea, the girls resting on the rug in front of them. Anna leaned down and picked up a teacake, carefully removing the round chocolate-covered biscuit from the shiny wrapper. She ate slowly, as if she were thinking about every mouthful, and then they all looked at her surreptitiously as she scrunched the red and silver foil into a little ball, and turned it round between her fingers, concentrating on it as if nothing else in the world mattered.

"When you were both little, you loved Tunnock's teacakes. I used to hold onto these wrappers until we had a pile of them. Do you remember? Then we used to roll them up tight into little balls. Do you remember?"

she said again, insistently. Martha and Susie shot each other a look of surprise. "And I helped you thread them into necklaces. I kept a big roll of red twine and a darning needle in a jar on the mantelpiece." Anna kept her eyes fixed on the glittering ball. "Maybe they're still there."

Susie looked over to Martha again and saw tears running down her face and onto her skirt. She inched across the rug towards her sister and gently wiped her face. "It's all right, Martha, it's all right," she said.

"Yes, Martha, it's all right, it's all right," echoed Anna.

Martha put her head on her mother's lap, and Anna began to stroke her hair, her thumb and forefinger gently smoothing her daughter's brow. The only sound was the distant chirrup of the sandpipers running forwards and backwards along the shore in search of insects.

ELIZABETH

When I put down my pen today I will have no need to write again. I have decided to leave Holmlea for a small nursing home where I will die very soon. I have no desire to live amongst strangers at this late stage. Surely it is time now? It is only the writing of this story that has kept me alive, and although it has taken every ounce of my strength, it has brought me the chance of some peace at the end of my life. I have so much gratitude for Saul. He gave me the strength to put one word after the next, in the hope that I could atone for May's death and have her near me always.

I never thought that I would see Robert again, but I was wrong. It was a beautiful August day, an Arran day that had arrived with rain riding on the wind, battering at my windows, waking me early. I remember it well, because I had planned to run the roller over the grass, and now every blade would be heavy with water even if the squall passed. But I have always loved the rain, the surprising refreshing touch of it when I turn my face heavenward, my eyes closed, and the trace of sea salt it leaves on my lips, or the sight of it sweeping in, like a shroud being pulled across the bay.

That day the wind blew the rain westwards to the Mull of Kintyre, leaving the air crystal clear and the sky cloudless. I decided I would cycle along to Murchies to collect some provisions and, as I parked my bike outside the store, I saw a tall man in tweed trousers and a waistcoat coming towards me, a brown felt fedora set at an angle across his forehead. I knew immediately that it was Robert. I could tell it was him from his gait and the shape of his jaw, the way he swung his arms close by his side.

I could not move, my heart was beating so fast, and I felt giddy. I wasn't prepared for the sight of him, much less to talk to him, but I had no escape.

He looked at me, astonished, and quickly removed his hat. His thick hair still fell a little over his brow but it was peppery white now. I could see that his eyes were the same bright blue, his weather-beaten face was lined, but as handsome as when I used to close my eyes and imagine him.

He smiled as he put out his hand, staring at me, and his voice, inflected with an Australian twang, trembled a little. "Elizabeth. Elizabeth, is it really you?" he said, gazing at me as if he could see into my soul.

He kept my hand in his, and I just stood, speechless. What would I say? What pleasantry could I utter? It would fall like dust from my lips. How could I sweep away thirty-seven years?

It took me so long to form the simple, almost mechanical sounding words, "Hello, Robert, it's wonderful to see you . . ." but before I could even try to think what I might say next, I heard someone calling. "Granddad, granddad, wait up!" I looked past Robert's shoulder to see a tall boy running along the road towards us.

Robert's eyes betrayed his agitation, but he turned to greet his grandson warmly. "Greg, come and meet Elizabeth Pringle, someone I knew a long time ago."

The boy looked at me eagerly. "G'day, ma'am. Pleased to make your acquaintance."

I remember he shook my hand vigorously, but I was so startled by his appearance. "You look just like your grandfather did when he was little more than your age," I blurted out, my voice catching a little.

"Well, I'm fifteen now and Granddad came to Australia when he wasn't much older, isn't that right Granddad?"

"A few years, Greg," Robert said, darting a look at me.

Greg jumped in. "You could clear something up for me, if you don't mind. Granddad says he was a good athlete at school. Do you know if he's just bluffing?"

"If he says he was, then it must be true." I smiled nervously, desperate for the encounter to be over.

Robert looked at me the way he used to do when we were betrothed. There was no mistaking it, and I blushed in spite of myself.

"Greg is my only grandson. His grandmother died not long after our son was born."

"I'm sorry," I said, my voice barely a whisper, "I didn't know."

"Thank you. It was a long time ago."

423

"It must be good to be back at Balnacraivie," I said, regretting it immediately, as a dark flicker crossed his face. Then he looked at me sadly, as if lost in the past for a moment, before he collected himself. "I promised Greg I'd bring him over to Edinburgh for the Commonwealth Games. He's a great swimmer himself."

I looked at the boy, so young and hopeful, on the brink of his life, and I was tongue-tied, in turmoil. I looked beseechingly at Robert and he must have sensed my panic, for he placed a hand on Greg's shoulder and said they had better be on their way.

The boy said goodbye and started to wander on, and as he did, Robert reached for my hand and said quietly, "You are as beautiful as I remember you that day at the Falls. I have never forgotten you, Elizabeth. I want you to know that I bear you no ill will, now or before. I only wish you well."

I wonder if he had thought about those words, planned them for years. Should I have run after him, grabbed him, told him everything? What could have come of it? If I had unburdened myself, what then? It would only have caused him pain.

My hand is shaking and the rhythm of my heart is uncertain. I am entrusting these pages to Saul. If Anna Morrison does not reply to my letter, I have made provision that my house, and everything in it, should be bequeathed to the Holy Isle Community. I am ready now. My time on earth is over.

Elizabeth Mary Pringle

Acknowledgments

First I would like to thank my literary agent Felicity Bryan who has the patience of Job and gently cajoled me along, Joanna Scott Kerr for her invaluable suggestions, Liz Laird for her incisive notes, my editor Lisa Highton for her wise words and unfailing good humour, Helen Coyle whose copy editing was more than even that and Federico Andornino at Two Roads for taking such good care of my book, and me.

Thanks too to Stuart Gough and his colleagues at the Arran Heritage Museum for answering query after query, to Gavin Fulton for pointing me in a couple of directions, and to the forensic anthropologist par excellence, Professor Sue Black for her guidance.

To my early readers, Lesley Lockhart, Tanya Hudson, Bridget McCann, Fiona MacInnes, Sarah Lynch, Janice McKnight, Claire Stevens, Jean Carwood-Edwards and Lorna Murray who reported on my drafts at key stages, I owe you for your wonderful friendship.

Thank you too to Caitlin and James Clements who encouraged me when I was flagging, and a special thanks to Alan Clements for his faith in me and unfailing support every step of the way.

The Legacy of Elizabeth Pringle has as its background the history of the Island of Arran, but it is entirely a work of fiction.

ISIS publish a wide range of books in large print, from fiction to biography. Any suggestions for books you would like to see in large print or audio are always welcome. Please send to the Editorial Department at:

ISIS Publishing Limited
7 Centremead
Osney Mead
Oxford OX2 0ES

A full list of titles is available free of charge from:

Ulverscroft Large Print Books Limited

(UK)
The Green
Bradgate Road, Anstey
Leicester LE7 7FU
Tel: (0116) 236 4325

(Australia)
P.O. Box 314
St Leonards
NSW 1590
Tel: (02) 9436 2622

(USA)
P.O. Box 1230
West Seneca
N.Y. 14224-1230
Tel: (716) 674 4270

(Canada)
P.O. Box 80038
Burlington
Ontario L7L 6B1
Tel: (905) 637 8734

(New Zealand)
P.O. Box 456
Feilding
Tel: (06) 323 6828

Details of ISIS complete and unabridged audio books are also available from these offices. Alternatively, contact your local library for details of their collection of ISIS large print and unabridged audio books.